KAIJU KIRIBATI
Kaiju Deadfall 2

JE GURLEY

KAIJU KIRIBATI

Republic of Kiribati (pronounced Kir-ih-bahs)

An island republic of Micronesia in the South Pacific consisting of the Gilbert Islands, the Line Islands, and the Phoenix Group, a total of 33 islands.
Capital: Tarawa
Population: 105,000, half of which reside on Tarawa
Language: English, Gilbertese

1

Friday, Dec. 15, 2018 5:30 p.m. GILT   Tarawa, Republic of Kiribati

A fine mist of sea spray, smelling of salt and primordial life, splashed Lilokwa Batra's face as he balanced on the prow of his *proa,* the outrigger canoe he had crafted with his own deeply lined, calloused hands. The day was warm with little wind, and the water was cool and refreshing on his skin. He let it run down his dark, weathered face and licked the salty brine from his upper lip. He could see the sandy reef twenty feet beneath the keel of the thirty-foot long outrigger through the crystal clear, teal water, but just ahead beyond the northeast tip of Naa, the northernmost island of the Tarawa atoll, the water changed to the dark blue hue of the deep ocean.

His sharp, dark brown eyes probed the depths of the water ahead of him for signs of *te takaba,* delicious snapper. He had line and weights for tuna or trevally, but today he wasn't fishing for money. He wanted snapper or even *te mon,* soldier fish, for his family and friends.

Saturday was his daughter's birthday and there would be many people at his home on Buariki to help celebrate her thirteenth year. He planned to surprise her with the *riwuit* he had secretly labored on for weeks in his friend's work shed so she wouldn't see it. Smaller than his thirty-foot *tipnol poa,* even smaller than a fifteen-foot *kor-kor,* the *riwuit* racing proa would teach her the fundamentals of handling the larger outrigger canoes and provide hours of fun for her and her friends. He hoped she liked it.

Sometimes he worried for his daughter's cultural education. Though it was the capital of the Republic of Kiribati, Tarawa was just a tiny speck of coral in the Southern Pacific amid a hundred other islands, home to less than 50,000 people. Perhaps it was time to take her to Australia to see a real city. He had visited Papua New Guinea as a child, and the image of the tall buildings and the throngs of people in Port

Moresby lingered with him until this day. She would enjoy seeing the Sydney Opera House. She loved music.

"A little more to port," he called out to his short, stout friend, Teto Remengesau, at the rudder. He shifted his weight to his right when the proa's outrigger *ama* lifted from the water as Teto moved the rudder sharply.

Lilokwa was proud of his proa. He had built it himself, using the bones of other proas crushed by the local reefs and abandoned on the beach. His *vaka*, the main hull, was rugged and sturdy with a slight upward tilt at the prow to cut the water more cleanly while turning. An ironwood foil beneath the shorter ama provided greater stability when turning. The outrigger connected to the main hull with two *akas* he had cut himself from the lumber from a machine crate he had salvaged on the dock in South Tarawa. The white oak was solid and strong, twisting just enough to handle the biggest waves. His curved, crab-claw polytarp sail was blue and white, visible for miles, and caught the slightest breeze to propel the proa like a flying fish across the water's surface.

Lilokwa pointed to the shallows of a reef just ahead of them. "I see a school of fish. Lower the sail."

Teto smiled, flashing a gold tooth. "*Teraka* is kind to us today."

Lilokwa nodded. "The god of fishermen wishes my daughter to be happy."

Lilokwa did not believe in the old gods; he barely believed in the One God, but Teto did and agreeing saved arguing. As Teto reefed the sail, the proa slowed until it barely sliced the water. Beneath the surface, two large snapper swam lazily around a small rock protruding from the sandy bottom. Lilokwa eyed the spear gun lying in the bottom of the boat, but with it, he would get only one fish. Since he needed both and the water was less than five feet deep, he decided to use his net instead. He gathered the weighted woven nylon strands in his hands, waiting until he was directly over the snapper before tossing it, careful to keep his shadow or the shadow of the proa from spooking the fish. He held onto the lanyard as the net settled over the fish, looping it around his wrist, and then yanked it sharply to draw the edges of the net together. The trapped fish fought valiantly, like Titans of the sea, wrenching the net back and forth beneath the water, but he held on tightly.

"Got them!" he yelled.

As he pulled the net up, he noticed the reflection of the sky on the surface of the water growing brighter until it washed out the patches of clouds smeared across the sky. He had noticed the alto cumulus clouds when they had set sail because of their fish-scale appearance. He had thought them a good omen for fishing. At first, he thought a cloud had passed in front of the sun, dimming it briefly, but the brightness came from the east, and the sun was now low on the western horizon. He stopped what he was doing and turned to Teto. Teto stared slack jawed at a bright object crossing the sky from the northeast to the southwest.

"Is it a jet?" Lilokwa asked, shading his eyes for a better view. His heart sank thinking of the hundreds of people aboard a burning airplane crashing into the ocean.

Teto shook his head. "I don't think so, Lilo. It's too big." After a long pause, he added, "I think it's coming this way."

Lilokwa detected the growing edge of panic in the normally imperturbable Teto's voice. His own heart beat faster at the vista of the strange object growing larger by the second. A red-orange halo formed in the clouds around the object. It looked as if aimed directly at his small canoe. Whatever the object was, he did not like it.

"Take us back to shore," he said, now as alarmed as his friend.

"I bet it's another of those alien pods," Teto said, as he raised the sail and pointed the proa south to Buariki. He dipped his paddle in the water and urged the proa to greater speed with strokes of his powerful arms.

Lilokwa recalled the three alien *Kaiju* monsters that had almost destroyed America four months earlier. One of those had landed in the ocean off the coast of San Francisco, he remembered with a sinking feeling. Was the same hell descending on them? The glowing object pierced the halo like a bull's eye and ripped through a bank of clouds, leaving a swirling contrail in its wake. Now, the object was larger than a summer eve's full moon and so bright he could not look directly at it.

"Hurry, Teto!" he yelled, urging him to paddle faster. He eyed the small 25-horsepower gasoline engine on the stern of the canoe, but it could push the boat no faster than under sail with a good breeze and Teto's paddle.

With a roar so loud that it vibrated the surface of the water, the object shot overhead less than two thousand feet above them. The thunder of its passing deafened him. The gust of air filling the vacuum the speeding object left behind threatened to rip away the sail. The air sizzled from its heat, scorching his upturned face and his hands. Seconds later, the flaming object struck the ocean near Maiana Atoll, twenty-seven miles south of Tarawa. The superheated object struck with a force one hundred times greater than the first fifteen-megaton hydrogen bomb, codenamed *Castle Bravo*, exploded on nearby Bikini Atoll in 1954. The object's fireball punched straight through the water into the bedrock below. A cloud of steam billowed skyward, followed by a darker plume of molten limestone and pulverized basalt.

Lilokwa held his breath, but at first, nothing happened. Then, just over a minute later, his canoe shuddered as it danced on the surface of the water. The impact sent tremors racing outward through the dense earth, lifting the burden of water above it. Schools of reef fish, confused by the disturbance, leaped from the water as if trying to fly. The sky darkened as tiny particles of molten ejecta pelted the water around him, striking with the hiss of a thousand snakes. The hot embers ignited the proa's sail, quickly bringing Lilokwa out of his stunned trance. Bits of hot stone seared his flesh, but he ignored the pain as he grabbed a plastic milk jug used for bailing and frantically threw water on the flames to extinguish them before they engulfed the canoe.

Twenty-seven miles away, the island of Maiana shuddered like a rung bell from the impact. Buildings toppled as if shoved over by the hands of an invisible giant. People flew through the air as the ground heaved and slid aside like a carpet yanked from beneath their feet. A fifty-foot-high wave of water swept outward from the point of impact, submerging the island of Maiana before the authorities could sound an alarm. Two thousand people perished in seconds. After the tsunami passed, only a few specks of naked coral, swept clean of its briny inhabitants, protruded above the ocean's roiling surface.

Lilokwa, his skin blistered and his hair singed, knew he was witnessing destruction on an epic scale. His heart raced as he joined Teto in paddling the proa. He channeled his fear into his arms, frantically digging the blade of the paddle into the water. He was a man of the sea. He knew currents, tides, and waves. He also knew tsunamis. Less than twenty minutes after the impact, twenty minutes in which his fear and his dread multiplied by the second, he saw the leading edge of the monster tsunami approaching, shaded by the ominous rising dark cloud behind it. It rushed toward him as relentless as a summer squall and as silent as a whisper. His heart sank with the realization that they would never make it home. Not until the wave reached the shallow water around the atoll did it produce a sound, a low rumble like the deep, throaty growl of an angry animal. Seconds before the wave struck, the water drained from the lagoon, emptying it and revealing wet coral, floundering fish, and the rusting hulks of WWII landing craft and bullet-riddled fuselages of downed Japanese Zeros. Now, another disaster, this time not manmade, but not one of nature's periodic tribulations, was visiting its wrath upon the island.

The receding water pulled his small proa toward the sharp-edged rocks of Buariki Island. Teto at the rudder struggled to angle the small boat away from the rocks, but the current was too strong. Lilokwa waited to be smashed into the coral rocks. He could see the roof of his home from the prow of his boat and wondered what his wife and daughter were feeling. Were they as terrified as he was? He should have been there with them.

The noise grew until it became a deafening roar. The tsunami wave swept into the lagoon, churning the sand before it like a bulldozer, tossing aside landing craft, Japanese fighters, and chunks of coral. It smashed into the windward side of the atoll with the force of a sledgehammer against a glass windowpane. Trees splintered into flying wooden shrapnel. The coral atoll cracked and disintegrated. Lilokwa had time for one quick prayer before the wave towering over him crashed down, smashing him, Teto, and his proa into the bottom of the reef.

The wave continued outwards from the impact point unfazed by its brush with the earth, submerging all of Tarawa beneath its inexorable advance, traveling south to the islands of Kuria, Apamama, Nonouti, and north to Abaiang, Marakei, Butaritari, and Makin. Seven hours later, fifteen-foot waves crashed against the rocky shoreline of Wake Island. Three hours after that, tourists on the beaches of Hawaii noticed an unusually large surf. Surfers reveled on the large curlers. Two hundred miles south of Hawaii, an ocean liner encountered a fifty-foot wave that damaged her engines, requiring her to radio for help.

The entire Gilbert Island chain, the center of the Republic of Kiribati, vanished in minutes. The Phoenix Islands farther south and east suffered massive devastation with thousands of casualties from a series of twenty-foot waves. In all, almost seventy thousand people died, with thousands missing or unaccounted for. The more eastern islands of Kiribati's Line Island chain fared better. Some people remained blithely unaware of the devastation that had visited their island nation. Others watched the strange lights in the evening sky and made wishes on a falling star. Their horror was yet to come and in some ways more terrible than that of those who had died instantly.

Five miles east of what had been Maiana atoll, the alien pod, over nine-hundred feet in length and so black it was almost invisible in the dark waters, slowly cooled beneath the surface, waiting.

2

Thursday, Dec. 14, 2130 hours   Fort Irwin, California –

Aiden Walker lay close to the ground, listening to the desert sounds around him. The sounds of the night were different from the day sounds, quieter, more subdued. A few yards away, a tarantula wasp scratched out a hole in the sun-baked earth to bury its paralyzed prey. It would deposit one egg on the tarantula, which would soon hatch, releasing a larva to devour the spider alive. It had no animosity toward the spider. To the wasp, it was food. A fringe-toed lizard hugged a boulder fifty feet away, trying to soak up the last remnants of heat the boulder had absorbed from the sun before returning to its burrow for the night. It failed to hear the faint flutter of a roadrunner's wings or the sound of its feet racing across the sand. Unlike the happy-go-lucky Roadrunner of the cartoons, this roadrunner was a desert predator. It leaped onto the rock and held the lizard down with its clawed feet, while its wicked beak made short work of the lizard. It ran off beneath the shelter of a Joshua tree to consume its meal. Like the tarantula wasp, the roadrunner thought in terms of predator and prey. The desert was a dangerous place, a land of kill or be killed. Now, men played the same game.

In spite of the chill of the night air, Walker was uncomfortably warm in his desert camo Ghillie suit. He had to urinate so badly his teeth ached, but he refused to move, even when a spider the size of his left testicle crawled across his hand. Nearby, the soft crunch of boots on gravel reached him. He smiled. *Finally*. His opponent was stealthy, placing his footsteps carefully and avoiding dried vegetation, but years of training allowed Walker to pick out the minutest noise that didn't jive with the natural sounds of the desert. He waited until the figure was almost upon him, and then held his breath.

The person was dressed in desert camo pants and shirt, and heavy boots. He wore a tan *shara* draped over his head bound in place by a simple knotted *egal*. In his hands, he carried an AK47. He approached to within fifteen feet of Walker's position, perfectly silhouetted by the rising moon behind him. He stopped and sniffed the air. He wrinkled his nose and turned to his left to look at the decaying corpse of a desert hare. Though it stank to high heaven, the hare had been there only a few hours, placed there by Walker. The horrendous odor of rotting flesh was just that, the juices from a decaying corpse, sprinkled liberally around the hare from a small vial Walker kept in his sniper kit. His opponent lowered his weapon and pushed back his *shara* to wipe away the sweat beading his forehead. It was the perfect moment to strike, but Walker remained motionless.

This isn't right, he thought. It was too easy. He could have killed the man in any number of ways, silently and quickly, but his sixth sense told him to wait. Less than two minutes later, a second person approached. This one was less silent. His heavy boots snapped dried twigs and crunched sun-baked earth, making no attempt at stealth. There was purpose in his long stride.

The heavier man walked up beside the first one and spoke briefly in Arabic, expressing his disdain for trekking through the desert and especially for the stench of rotting hares.

Walker made his move. He burst from the shallow depression he had dug in the dirt and took three quick steps forward, scattering pieces or creosote and yucca he had piled around him to camouflage his position. Even though he had flexed his muscles as much as possible during his lengthy watch, they ached from inaction. He shunted the pain to the back of his mind, concentrating on getting the job done. Both opponents turned at the sound of his attack, but it was too late for them. Walker gently squeezed the trigger.

"Bang, bang, you're both dead," he said.

"Damn it, Walker, you almost gave me a heart attack."

Walker smiled, leaned his Remington M24 sniper rifle against a boulder, unzipped his pants, and began urinating. A sigh of relief escaped his lips. After four hours lying immobile in the dirt, relieving himself felt better than sex. Sergeant Bill Costas watched the stream of urine splashing the ground, creating a yellow puddle that ran toward his foot. He cocked an eyebrow at Walker and shifted his position slightly to avoid the stream.

"I thought all black men were hung like stud horses. You got some cracker in your woodpile?" he asked.

Walker zipped up his pants and pulled back the hood of his Ghillie suit. The warm desert air felt cool against his baked skin. "More than ten inches is a waste of flesh."

Costas shook his head. "You'd better get a new tape measure, son. I'm surprised you can hit anything if you're using that as a measuring rod."

Walker eyed the huge Barrett M107 SASR Costas had chosen for the mock desert war games. The Special Application Sniper Rifle fired a heavy caliber .50 BMG round and weighed almost thirty pounds. In anyone else's hands, it would have looked obscene. Costas toted it as if it was a .22 caliber squirrel gun.

Walker nodded at the rifle. "I think someone's overcompensating. Were you planning on taking out a tank or something?" he asked.

"I like to know I've got the right tool for the job, whatever that job might be," Costas replied, stroking the stock of the SASR. He threw Walker a big grin. "I thought I had you a few clicks back, but it was just a damned lizard rustling the brush."

"If you weren't so heavy on your feet, I mightn't have heard you."

Costas picked up his foot, examined his size-twelve boot, and frowned. "Heavy? I'll have you know I can boogie with the best of them."

"Costas, even the one-legged fat women say you're clumsy."

Costas feigned a pained expression. He placed his right hand on his heart. "Now that hurts, Major. That just plain hurts."

Walker picked up his M24 and slung it over his shoulder. He preferred the M24 to the newer M110 sniper rifle. He had used one of the M110s before but didn't like the fact that it was a semi-automatic and had no forward assist to chamber a round quietly. In the field, silence could be the difference between life and death. He never carried his rifle with a round in the chamber. The M24 was trustworthy, accurate, and easy to maintain. Its powerful 7.62 mm rounds could knock a man down at a hundred yards, remove his head at two hundred, and punch a hole through his skull at eight hundred. On a windless day with good visibility, using his Leopold 10x42mm scope, he could kill at a thousand yards.

If he needed close-up firepower, he carried a FN Herstal Special Forces Combat Assault Rifle, the SCAR L-CQC with a 10-inch barrel instead of the standard 14.5-inch one and configured to fire 7.62 mm M118LR 175 grain ammo, allowing him to carry only one type of ammo in the field to save weight.

He looked at the sniper trainee, who was listening to the two veteran soldiers' banter. Walker took in his hairless chin and bright, innocent eyes, wondering if he had even been that young and naive. *Maybe before Vegas*, he thought, *before the Kaiju. Certainly not now.*

"This big lug used you as bait, you know," he said. "He wanted me to shoot you so he could fix my position."

The kid stared at Costas in disbelief.

Costas replied, "Love and war, kid. No rules." To Walker, he said, "You always said if the army wanted someone killed bad enough to risk a grunt's life, then sometimes a grunt was expendable." He jerked his thumb at the trainee. "I deemed him expendable."

"Thanks, Sergeant," the rookie replied. "I appreciate the consideration."

"Come on," Walker said. "I need a shower."

"Big date?" Costas asked. He wore a big grin on his face. He had been nagging Walker to ask out the sweet young lieutenant from the motor pool for over a week.

"No. Just grungy."

"What's the matter, turning gay? Lieutenant Wong is as hot as they come, and she can strip down a jeep faster than you can say your morning prayers."

Walker smiled at Costas' jibe at his being a Muslim. Even though they had spent a lot of time killing fellow Muslims in Iraq, his religion had not gotten in the way of their working relationship or their long friendship. "She's a hottie all right. She's also married. Didn't you see her ring?"

"Sure, but what's that matter? I've seen her staring at your ass, while I've been ogling hers of course. Her old man's back in Cleveland or somewhere boffing the neighbor's wife. You should go for it."

Walker shook his head. "I've got too much to do."

"Oh, I guess those new major's gold leaves weigh pretty heavy on you. You should use some of that 0-4 pay raise to buy her dinner and a motel room." He twirled his moustache with his finger. "We can double date. I know these two sisters who might like a bit of *ménage a cinq*."

"This isn't the al-Khaleej district in Baghdad."

"You're telling me. Whores cost a fortune in California. Must be a new sin tax or something the governor imposed." He started back the way he had come.

"Where are you going?" Walker asked.

Costas stopped midstride. "Just showing junior the way home."

The kid looked at the two of them, shook his head, and started the five-click hike north to Cowboy Drop Zone where a chopper was waiting for them.

"I parked about a click that way," Walker replied, and set out for his truck.

"Son of a bitch! Me and the kid hiked all over this damn desert looking for you. We even climbed halfway up Killer Escarpment for a better view of the surrounding countryside."

"That's why you're a sergeant and I'm a major."

They hiked down a narrow arroyo south past Bruno Cave to the spot Walker had parked his 2010 Chevy Silverado beneath the scant shade of a Joshua tree. The Mojave Desert sun didn't seem to know that it was almost Christmas. When he opened the door, the hot air trapped inside the cab him like a slap in the face. He cranked the A/C to full blast and waited for the cab to cool.

As he stripped off the Ghillie suit, he said, "There's a cooler with some *Dos Equis* in the back."

Costas raised an eyebrow. "Since when did you start drinking?"

"They're for you. Pass me a Gatorade."

Costas reached behind the seat and fumbled through the cooler. He tossed Walker a bottle of Gatorade. "Horse piss," he said. He fished out two cold bottles of beer for himself and twisted the cap from both bottles. He drained one and dropped it to the floorboard. "Damn I needed that," he said, smacking his lips loudly.

He drank the second beer more slowly while Walker carefully wiped down his rifle, cleaned the scope, and placed both in the form-fitted Samsonite case. Later, he would disassemble and clean it more thoroughly. Only then did he drink his Gatorade to quench his raging thirst. The needs of his weapon came before his own needs. His rifle could save his life. When Walker dropped the empty bottled behind the seat and reached for the gear shift, Costas stopped him.

"Why don't we sit here for a while and enjoy the silence?"

"Why, Costas, I didn't think you were a nature lover."

"Nah, I'm just not looking forward to the ride back. My kidneys can't take the punishment."

"Maybe you shouldn't drink so much beer."

"Alcohol is part of my religious experience."

Walker waited until Costas finished his beer and belched before putting the truck into gear and leaving. Even with the 20-inch lift kit and heavy-duty shock absorbers Walker had installed, the ride was torture with the truck bouncing one way and rolling another, slamming his ass into his seat like a bucking bull, as he maneuvered through the twisting arroyo. Costas groaned with every bump.

It was a bumpy thirty-minute ride back to Barstow Road and another twenty minutes to Ft. Irwin. Costas didn't let up the entire time. His insistence that Walker hook up with Lieutenant Wong or any available woman began to annoy him. He considered shoving him out of the truck to see if he bounced on the asphalt, but decided he did not want to deal with the paperwork. As they pulled up to the base gate and Walker prepared to show the guard his ID, a jeep screeched to a halt in front of them, blocking the road. A young corporal climbed out of the vehicle, walked over to Walker, and saluted.

"Sir, I was sent to locate you and Sergeant Costas and escort you both back to Colonel Hassert's office." He glanced at Costas. "Before the sergeant shacks up with a broad and a bottle of booze," he added. "The colonel said that, not me."

Costas smiled. "The colonel does remember me."

Walker's stomach twisted into a hard knot, just as it did before every mission. "What shit has hit the fan and where, Corporal?"

"It's another one of those things, sir, the alien pods. It landed in Kiribati less than an hour ago."

Walker's stomach crawled up his throat and took a dump in his mouth. After Vegas, he had thought it might be over. He should have known better. Gate Rutherford did. He had predicted just such an event.

"Where in Hades is Kiribati?" Costas asked.

The corporal shrugged. "I don't know. One of those islands in the South Pacific I think."

"Corporals don't think," Costas replied. "It's against the regs. Fucking Kaijus," he snarled.

Walker could only agree.

* * * *

Colonel Jonathan Emmet Hassert eyed the strange pair sitting across from him while he toyed with his cigar cutter.

"This solid silver *Prometheus* was a gift from President George W. Bush for my work training troops for the deserts of Iraq. I'm proud of this cigar cutter and especially proud of the engraving on its side." He read it aloud to Walker and Costas over the rim of his glasses. "From a Grateful Nation – George W. Bush, President USA." He laid the cutter on his desk and glared at them. "Anything that rocks my tightly run base upsets me, gentlemen, and two soldiers being given carte blanche by the Joint Chiefs of Staff bothers me even if one of them is a major who's killed a Kaiju."

He tapped the top drawer of his desk. "I've got a humidor full of *Cohiba Esplendidos* cigars in here. I want one so badly I could piss my pants. It rankles me that a colonel, the commander of a goddamned army base, I can't smoke in my own office. My wife won't let me smoke in the house. I have to sneak out back for a smoke like a goddamned buck private." He opened the drawer, removed three cigars from his humidor, and leaned forward his seat. "You would think that with normalized relations with Cuba, the price of these would drop, but they're still thirty-bucks-a-pop. A colonel's pay only goes so far. I allow myself one lousy cigar per week; two if it was a damned rough one, and gentlemen, this one is shaping up into a granddaddy, son of a bitch, ball buster of a week."

Walker was eager to get on with the briefing, but he knew the colonel was making small talk to ease his own mind. That meant whatever he was about to say made him uneasy. He said nothing as Colonel Hassert laid the cigars beside the cutter on his desk, carefully removed the cellophane wrapping from each one, and snipped off the tips. He handed two of the cigars to Walker and Costas.

"You've been doing admiral work here, Major; you and Sergeant Costas. Now, it's time to get back to what you're really good at, killing fucking Kaiju." He jammed his cigar in his mouth, pulled out a box of matches, and lit it. He smiled as he slowly exhaled a cloud of smoke.

In the two months he had been at Fort Irwin, Walker had never heard the colonel utter as long a speech or reveal as much about himself as he just had. *He's scared*, he thought. *Hell. So am I.* He didn't smoke, but he accepted the gift for what it was, a sacred rite between three soldiers about to go into combat where death was a glaring probability. He held the cigar in his hand as he spoke.

"What do we know about this one, Colonel?"

"The son of a bitch slipped in under the radar for one thing. No warning. NASA didn't see it coming, and they can't tell us if there are any more."

Walker wondered what Doctor Gate Rutherford was doing right about now. The NASA catastrophist had gone above and beyond when he had joined Walker's team delivering a baby nuke inside Kaiju Nusku in the desert outside Las Vegas, but then he had disappeared off Walker's radar screen. The phone calls became less frequent and then stopped altogether. Walker suspected he had undergone some kind of test of faith. Many people had after the Kaiju, even him.

Kaiju Ishom in California and Kaiju Girra in Indiana had wiped out San Francisco, Oakland, Chicago, Omaha, Des Moines, and a few other major U.S. cities. If not for the sacrifice of Astronaut Commander Erwin Langston in riding his Orion spacecraft into the communications nodule controlling the three creatures from the moon's surface, the trio of Kaiju would still be rampaging across the country.

"What are they calling this one?"

"Kiribati, pronounced *Kir-ih-bahs*, for whatever the hell reason," the colonel replied.

"I guess they ran out of them heathen gods to name them after," Costas quipped.

Walker shot Costas a dirty look to silence him. "Any current word from the area?"

Hassert shook his head. "Not much. They're moving some military satellites to fly over the area for a look see, and two subs, the *USS Colorado* and the British *Essex*, are a couple of hours out, but most of what we know is from a few survivors with ham radios or Sat-phones."

Walker didn't like going in with no Intel. "If the aliens operate on the same time frame as before, we have twenty-four hours before they come out of the pod. Of course, that's just conjecture. Doctor Rutherford said to expect a few surprises from the next Kaiju. We may be too late already. When do we leave?"

"That's the rub. Since the Republic of Kiribati is an independent sovereignty, we require their permission to go in. So far, we've heard nothing. We're going to fly you and Sergeant Costas to Pearl, where you'll join your fire team, and then fly on to Wake Island to wait for word."

Walker frowned as he fought back a flood of bitter memories. "I don't have a team, Colonel. They all died inside Nusku."

"You do now. Six men with experience doing mop up work in Girra under the command of Captain Ian McGregor will be waiting for you at Pearl. They're experienced and they volunteered. They'll have any equipment you might need. If you have any special needs, let me know and it'll be waiting for you in Pearl."

Walker didn't like working with untried men, but he had no choice. At least they knew what to expect. "I suspect we'll need SCUBA gear. I think this one landed in the ocean on purpose. I doubt we'll be using gliders this trip like last time."

Hassert opened his hands wide and nodded. "Anything you need, Major Walker."

Costas leaned forward in his seat, his unlit cigar jammed in the corner of his mouth. Before he could speak, Hassert added. "No booze and no broads, Sergeant Costas. Major Dire warned me about you."

Costas snorted. "He would."

The colonel handed Costas a box of matches. "Never use a lighter on a good cigar, son. It taints the flavor."

Walker smiled. Dire, codenamed *Postmaster*, was their handler in the Mideast. He had issued all their wet work sanctions in Iraq, choosing the targets and bypassing the usual military channels and local civilian authority, allowing them an added layer of anonymity that had been very useful to them in a country rapidly descending into chaos. The situation had only gotten worse since the Kaiju had come. Some mullahs had seen their arrival as a sign from Allah and encouraged their followers to double their efforts to conquer the country. Now, Iraq consisted of Baghdad, narrow strips of land bordering the Euphrates and the Tigris Rivers, and a semi-independent Kurdish province in the north. At a time when the country needed men like him and Costas over there, the administration was undecided about how to deal with ISIS. The Iraqis had failed to fight together as a country so many times they no longer had the heart to win. He was relieved they had pulled him out.

"How long?" he asked.

"The C-5 is warmed up and waiting on the runway. You've got twenty minutes to shit, shower, and stow your gear."

Walker sighed and nodded. The trouble with being the first person to kill a Kaiju was that they considered him the foremost authority on Kaiju slaying. He didn't think this one was going to be a by-the-book operation. If the aliens were intelligent enough to send bioengineered creatures to wipe out a planet's population, they would be smart enough to learn from their mistakes.

"What's the national drink of Hawaii?" Costas asked.

"For you, Diet Coke," Walker replied.

Costas frowned, slapped his right shoulder, which still bore the scars of the Wasp attack inside Nusku, and winced. "It's for the pain, mind you. You being Muslim and all, you wouldn't know about the miraculous pain relieving effects of good Kentucky Bourbon. Coke doesn't work for all of us. My religion doesn't forbid alcohol. In fact, it encourages it."

"Well drop by the PX on the way to the airfield and get you some aspirin." He rose from his seat and saluted Colonel Hassert.

Hassert returned his salute. "Good luck, Major. Sergeant, keep the major safe."

"Colonel, I've been watching his back longer than I care to remember, though now I'm wondering if it's been worth it."

Costas ignored Walker's look of consternation as he lit his cigar and tossed the matches back onto the colonel's desk. Walker shook his head sadly at the sergeant's irreverence and walked to the door.

3

Saturday, Dec. 16, 2:15 a.m.   *Radiant Princess*, South Pacific –

Mark Talent was the luckiest man in the world, at least as far as he was concerned, and in most instances, what concerned him was the only thing he considered worth bothering with. He always told people he had a talent for luck. It was a poor pun on his name, but Talent was not big on humor. He was not exactly humorless, but his wit ran slightly off kilter to societal norms. An internet meme of a cute kitten with a ball of string did not elicit a smile from him, but a woman hit in the ass by a closing door, or a politician caught with his or her pants down did.

Few people were even aware of that side of him, for Talent was not a gregarious man. At thirty-four, he was the typical layperson's image of a Prepper – a loner, quiet, rugged, and deadly serious about survival. Atypically, he had a four-year degree from the University of Arizona in Business Management and spoke three languages – English, Spanish, and his native Tohono O'odham.

His small, one-bedroom adobe home in Vopolo Havoka, Arizona, a small village in the middle of the Sonoran Desert on the Tohono O'odham Reservation, was his fortress against disaster, his *wickiup* of solitude. It was located seventy miles southwest of Tucson, twenty-seven miles from the reservation town of Sells, and nine miles north of the Mexican border. He had a deep well that provided good water, a few goats and chickens for meat, a small garden for fresh vegetables, and an ample supply of dried and canned goods stored in a wooden shed behind his house.

Talent especially enjoyed his view of 7,700-foot tall Baboquivari Peak, or *Waw Kiwulki* in his native Tohono O'odham language. Baboquivari Peak was the most sacred site in the Tohono O'odham Nation, home of *I'itoi*, the Creator. He did not really believe in a creator, neither *I'itoi* nor the Catholic God his parents had beat him over the head with as a child, but it made a good story when he sold guns and homemade flint-tipped arrows made from local flint at area gun shows. Gun shows and the occasional construction job kept him in folding money, and a small annual stipend from the Tribal Council from casino revenues and a yearly grant for his small, traditional farming methods ranch paid for his food and fuel.

However, none of that was luck, except being born Tohono O'odham. The rest he had achieved by hard work. Luck had stepped in at the most opportune time. A spur of the moment purchase of a lottery ticket in Sonoita had paid off. Hoping to win at most a few hundred dollars, he and a man from Rhode Island split a sixteen-million-dollar Powerball Jackpot. After taking the cash-out option and paying Uncle Sam his lucrative share, he had a little over three million dollars left. Three alien Kaiju stomping America's butt four months earlier had deepened his sense of the likelihood of an apocalyptic scenario. Even his Arizona desert retreat didn't feel safe enough. His people had it bad enough already. If a few hundred thousand Mexicans streamed across the border, things would only get worse, and his ranch was right in their path north.

Australia seemed the best place to start fresh. It had deserts, nine of them spread out over half a million square miles, covering most of the western two-thirds of the continent. That was twice as big as Texas, or as much area as the Four Corners states of Arizona, New Mexico, Colorado, and Utah combined, with Nevada thrown in for good measure. Except for the eastern edge, the entire continent was desert, mountains, or dry scrub. Ninety-seven percent of the population lived along the coasts. Australia was the Big Empty. They spoke English, of a sort, and as a Native American, he felt a special kinship with the Aborigines, especially the *Noongar* and the *Anangu* of the south and southwest. He couldn't bring in his guns though. Australians were a bit stricter on guns than the US, but he could join a gun club once he got there.

Talent was used to deserts. He felt a special kinship with shifting sands and wind-carved rock. He loved the clean smell of the air after a summer monsoon rain, the fragrance of saguaro blossoms and desert sage in April. At night, the desert sky came alive with stars that no city-dweller ever saw; so vivid and so close, it looked as though he could reach up and run his fingers through them, leaving rainbow trails of color.

Talent sold everything – house, weapons, food, supplies, even his clothes – for what he could get and bought new clothes in Phoenix. He drove his beat up '91Chevy pickup truck to Los Angeles, abandoned it in a Wal-Mart parking lot, and booked passage on the cruise ship *Radiant Princess*. Even though flying was faster, he would never fly to Australia. Planes crashed and he couldn't fly. Cruise ships were safer, or at least if the ship sank, he could swim after a fashion. All he had to worry about were Listeria food poisoning and drinking too much booze on the twenty-two day cruise.

Now that he was rich, Talent splurged for an outside balcony suite, the only real luxury whim he had ever acceded to, other than the cruise. It wasn't simply for the comfort, although his room was outstanding. He needed to see the sun in the day and the moon at night. Sun and moon – *tash* and *mashath* in his tongue – were important aspects of his life, his connection to the earth.

He was rich, but he didn't feel rich. In fact, he was decidedly uncomfortable during dinner with all the attention the waiter focused on him, even though he showed the same consideration to everyone else in his section of *Michelangelo's* restaurant. The close proximity of the other diners and the dull roar of conversation assaulted his senses, forcing him to flee before desert arrived. He leaned over the glass balcony railing of the ship's Piazza, designed to convey an air of spaciousness to the interior of the vessel, but it seemed claustrophobic to him. He wandered through the shops lining the Piazza, paying little attention to the clothing, the jewelry, or the souvenirs. He played a few slot machines in the casino while nursing a beer, but after the throng from the theater arrived, it became too crowded, too talkative. He retreated to the upper decks.

He strolled along the Sun Deck two levels above his cabin on Deck 14, enjoying the cool night air. The tang of salt water in the air was alien, the opposite of the dry, flinty smell of the desert. However, the moon was familiar, even if seen from a different angle and half shrouded by rain clouds. He bathed in its light, as one would bask in the sun after a long winter's night. As he walked, he overheard snippets of conversation between two passengers, an overweight American man in his mid-fifties and a lithe, attractive oriental woman about half his age, a mismatched couple if he had ever seen one. Normally, he would have ignored them, but the word Kaiju got his attention.

"They say it wiped out Kiribati," the man said, almost in a whisper, "or at least Tarawa and the Gilbert Islands."

"Oh, all those people. How sad," his companion replied. Though her reply expressed sympathy, her tone was flat and unemotional, as if the deaths of thousands of people she didn't know didn't affect her little world. "Are we safe?"

The man checked his watch. "It happened about three o'clock last night, or tomorrow," he added with a soft chuckle. "I'm not sure which side of the International Date Line we're on right now. Kiribati is in the Western Time Zone, but it protrudes into the eastern side of the line like a little thumb." He held out his thumb as a visual aid. "I wouldn't worry," he reassured her. "I'm sure the military is dealing with it. They took care of the first three creatures. Are you ready for that nightcap yet?"

"Sure, but just one." She covered her mouth with a delicate hand as she giggled. "I think I've already drunk too much wine with dinner."

They walked back into the ship arm-in-arm, leaving Talent wondering about their crassness over the deaths of thousands of people. He also wondered about the topic of their conversation. *Another Kaiju. I guess maybe I waited too late to emigrate.*

He kept a mental map of the ship's position based on the information displayed every day on the television in his room. The ship was currently about two-hundred-fifty miles north of the Equator. At twenty-two knots, they should cross the Equator around noon. They were midway between Tarawa and Kiritimati, also known as Christmas Island, right in the middle of the Republic of Kiribati. The other Kaiju broke out of their pods twenty-four hours after landing. That would place the ship somewhere northeast of Enderbury and the Phoenix Islands at that time, less than twelve-hundred miles from Tarawa. *Too close for comfort*, he thought.

He hoped news about the Kaiju didn't spread around the ship too quickly. The last thing he wanted was to be on a ship with three-thousand panic-stricken passengers. Cruise ship crews had a difficult enough time dealing with hundreds of sick passengers. They wouldn't be able to handle a frenzied mob of frightened men, women, and children demanding evacuation to some imagined safe area.

The lobster ragu over pappardelle he had for dinner began to churn in his stomach. He wasn't sure if it was due to the food's richness or the dire news. "Maybe I need a drink, too," he said to no one in particular and followed the mismatched couple into the bar.

* * * *

Saturday, Dec. 16, 0320 hours   *USS Colorado*, SSN-788, South Pacific –

Captain Travis Dent had shadowed Russian subs, Chinese subs, and even Iranian subs during his twenty-one-year career, but he had he received an order to search for an underwater monster. He turned to his exec, Elizabeth Haynes.

"Time and position, Lieutenant."

Her answer was immediate. "0320 hours, sir. We're two-hundred-twenty-four-miles southeast of Tarawa." She glanced up from her clipboard. "We crossed the International Date Line into Kiribati territory seven minutes ago."

"I don't think we need worry about the Kiribati Navy, Lieutenant, and the Aussies and Brits know we're here. Any chatter on the radio?"

"A few rescue pleas from stranded boats or survivors on the islands." She frowned, as if not responding to pleas for help bothered her. "No commercial or local traffic since 0130. We picked up a routine position check from the cruise ship *Radiant Princess* about 0110 hours, and a satellite transmission from the *Essex* to RFTG *Salient* near New Caledonia at 0116; then a second message to both RFTG *Salient* and Navy Command Headquarters at Whale Island, Portsmouth at 0215. Do you want transcripts?"

He was aware that a British Response Force Task Group had been patrolling the South Pacific in a joint effort with the Royal Australian Navy since the first Kaiju had appeared four on Earth months earlier. "Was there anything special in the message to British Navy Command?"

"It was a follow up on the first message, a routine report of the damage to the islands of Kiribati."

Dent furrowed his brow. "That's puzzling. If it was routine, why follow up with a second message and why cc Whale Island?" He thought for a minute. "What did it say?"

Haynes referred to her clipboard. "It reads: Damage to Gilbert Group total, Phoenix Group severe. Moving east top speed to assess damage to Line Group soonest."

"That's odd. Why didn't they survey the Line Islands on their way in as we did, and why soonest? He's a fool to push his boat top speed through all that floating debris still sinking."

"Do you think it's a coded message?"

Dent smiled, pleased that his exec had arrived at the same conclusion he had. He had chosen Haynes because of her 1610/2 FITREP, her 1616/26 Eval reports, and the fact that she had graduated the Academy top of her class, but those only told him she was qualified. Her former superiors had reported that she was intuitive and thought fast on her feet. That was the quality he was after in an exec.

"I think the captain of the *Essex* is chasing something east."

"A Kaiju? That wouldn't be very smart."

"No, Lieutenant, but it would be in line with how Captain Colfax thinks. He's old school like me, but he hasn't been bloodied yet. I have." He winced as memories of California rose to the surface. "Plot an intercept course for the *Essex*. Let's see what he's up to."

"Yes, sir."

Haynes was right. If Colfax were chasing a Kaiju, he would need help whether he wanted it or not. This wasn't a private war. If it was, the U.S. had first shot. America had been the aliens' primary target. He liked to think it was for a reason. If they wiped out America, the aliens could take out the remaining world powers piecemeal. It looked like the aliens had decided to try it again. In order to win the war, the world powers would have to learn to cooperate better than they had during the first attack.

He carried the mental scars of his first action against the Kaiju. Assigned to Admiral Grayson's task force, the *USS Colorado* had joined in the confrontation with Kaiju Ishom off the coast of San Luis Obispo, California. The *Colorado's* BGM-109 Tomahawk cruise missiles had bounced off the creature's impervious black armor like rocks thrown at a tank. Then the Wasps attacked the fleet. Their missiles depleted, he surfaced to assist a destroyer under attack by Ishom's squadrons of flying creatures with the two movable .50 calibers and the forward mounted retractable 20 mm Vulcan 61 six-barrel, rotating cannon. During the battle, he had lost four crewmen, including his original exec, Lieutenant Kyle Pettis, a longtime friend. It was a humiliating defeat. As much as he wanted payback, he wouldn't risk his crew for a personal vendetta. He hoped Captain Colfax wasn't playing a fool's hand.

Four hours later, the *Colorado* had closed to just within passive sonar range of the *Essex* eighty miles north of Enderbury Island. A blip at two o'clock on the sonar screen indicated its position. Captain Dent's gaze fixed on a second blip at two-thirty rapidly closing on the *Essex's* position. The blip faded, disappeared briefly, and reappeared, as if the sub's AN/BQQ-5E sonar was having a difficult time locking onto the object's surface.

"It's not another sub," Haynes noted.

"Not unless someone has built one almost a thousand feet long from bow to stern. I believe we're looking at a Kaiju. Sonar, what's its depth?"

"It's resting on the surface, sir, but its keel is at a depth of fifty fathoms, three hundred feet," Sonar operator Lee Bates replied with a touch of awe in his voice, tinged with fear. "The image keeps breaking up. Should I deploy the TB-16?"

Dent briefly considered the towable sonar, but dismissed it as impractical. He had read the specs on the Kaiju's armor and doubted sonar would give him a dependable image.

"No. Try the acoustic pickups." They were at the equipment's extreme range to pick up anything useful, but he needed something to guide him.

Bates tapped his headset. "I'm not picking up any normal biological noise, just a weird, undulating echo, like a power-line hum." A few moments later, he said, "She's switched from passive to active sonar."

Dent could hear the Essex's active sonar pings over the sonar operator's headphones.

"Is the *Essex* aware of the Kaiju's position?" Haynes asked.

"Oh, he knows all right," Dent replied grimly. "That's why he switched to active pinging. The *Essex's* making straight for it at full speed. He's going to mark the Kaiju's exact position to fire his torpedoes, but can the Kaiju hear him?"

"Two torpedoes in the water from the *Essex*," Bates announced. "Running fast and true."

Dent winced. *Too soon. What was Colfax up to?* "Distance to target?"

"24,000 yards."

Dent thought the captain of the *Essex* displayed a healthy regard for safety of his boat by trying a long shot. The British Spearfish torpedo was nineteen-feet long, tipped with 750 pounds of *Torpex* explosive. Propelled by a hydrogen peroxide turbine engine, it could reach speeds of eighty knots, but firing at a distance of twelve miles from target allowed the Kaiju ample time to detect and counter her torpedoes.

"Time to target?" he asked Haynes to verify his quick mental calculations.

"Six minutes," she replied.

Dent started counting down the time. At six-minutes-fifteen seconds, he glanced at Bates.

He nodded. "Both torpedoes struck. No apparent damage. It's still moving." Fifteen seconds later, Bates announced, "The Kaiju's firing back. Ten tracks headed for the *Essex*, no make that eleven. Estimated time to impact," he stopped and frowned, "one-minute-forty seconds."

Dent whistled softly. The alien missiles were traveling at Mach .9, just under supersonic speed. He would have said it was impossible for any submerged object to travel that fast, except the proof was on display on the screen in front of him. The *Essex* wouldn't even have time to turn or initiate her anti-torpedo defensive measures.

"Sir!" Bates yelled.

"What is it, son?"

Bates glanced up at him in shock. "Six objects headed our direction. Estimated time to impact is two-minutes-fifteen seconds."

Dent turned to the control crew. "Helm, set rudder seventy degrees to starboard. Ahead flank speed. Crash dive! Crash dive! Take us to 1800 feet. Rig for collision. Battle stations."

As the battle stations alarm and dive klaxon fought it out, Dent tried to think of a way out of dangerous the situation he had gotten them into.

One-minute-thirty-seconds later, Bates announced, "No explosions on the *Essex*, sir, but distinct sounds of metal tearing and air bubbles escaping. She's dropping rapidly nose first toward the bottom. Whatever those things were, they ripped her open."

Whatever they were. Given the alien propensity for organic weapons, he suspected a heretofore-unknown living or cyborg self-defense mechanism protecting the Kaiju, a marine version of the Wasps. He glanced at the depth gauge – 1200 feet. They weren't going to make it. 1800 feet was below the suggested operating depth for a *Virginia-Class* submarine, but he had no choice but push the boat to its limits. The objects were moving too fast to outrun. If they had a depth limit, maybe he could out dive them.

"Engage *Shade*. Launch *Subsut* and *Scutter*."

He didn't think the Advanced Defense Suite would work. The devices employed acoustic and electronic countermeasures to trick enemy torpedoes into chasing false signals, and then detonating their warheads in the enemy torpedoes' paths. The aliens preferred living weapons systems. Animals were smarter than most machinery. He wondered if they operated on a sense of smell or by using biological sonar, like whales and dolphins. He had to throw them off the scent.

"Reduce speed to 15 knots. Bring rudder twenty degrees to Port."

Twenty seconds later, Bates confirmed his worst fear. "No good, sir. The objects ignored the countermeasures. Impact in twenty-three seconds."

"Communications, send a Priority One message to USPACOM. Tell them … tell them the Kaiju has broken through into the Pacific."

He reached out and lightly caressed the cold metal bulkhead of his ship, his last command. He hated going out with a score of *Kaiju*-1, *Colorado*-0. His ship deserved better than that. His crew deserved better. He looked at Haynes.

"I'm sorry I won't be able to recommend you for a ship of your own, Lieutenant."

"It's been an honor, Captain," she replied. A smile flickered on her lips, and then she saluted.

There was no explosion, but whatever the Kaiju had launched at them struck the hull like buckshot fired at an aluminum can. The boat slewed sideways in the water under the brutal impact. Dent slammed into the bulkhead, breaking left his arm, barely retaining consciousness when his head bashed against a console. His head spun and pain throbbed up and down his arm. The sharp odor of hydraulic oil from a ruptured pipe mixed with the scent of AFFF from hand-held fire extinguishers, as crewmen raced around the stations putting out small blazes in control panels. The control room was dark except for the dim red glow of the emergency lights. Most of the instruments were dead and unresponsive.

Lieutenant Haynes hadn't been as lucky as Dent. He looked down at her lifeless body lying on the deck, her eyes open but unseeing. A deep gash oozed blood from her forehead. *What a waste,* he thought.

He forced the image from his mind. "Damage report," he called out.

"Missile room flooding. Engines offline. They're working on battery power."

He glanced up at the dull-gray rounded object that had ripped through the control room bulkhead wondering why it had not exploded. None of the objects had exploded. Were they merely projectiles whose purpose was to puncture the hull and disable the sub? Seawater under immense pressure sprayed around its edges. The jet of water had sliced the helmsman in half. The upper part of his body lay across his console, his hand still gripping the control stick. His lower extremities lay on the deck, partially submerged by the rising water. The object shifted position, opening gaps along the edge. More water sprayed into the control room. The cold seawater rose above Dent's knees. He held on as the sub rolled to port, weighted down by the inrush of water.

He checked the depth gauge – 2100 feet and increasing rapidly. The sub was in an uncontrolled dive.

"Blow all ballast tanks," he yelled.

The sub shuddered as air under pressure forced water from the bow tanks, but the gauge continued to climb. Not all the tanks had responded. The sub was plummeting to the bottom. He examined the object that had gutted his ship through the red haze of mist filling the control room. It had not exploded, at least not yet. *If it has a delayed timer*, he thought; then, four glowing eyes he had mistaken for gouges on the object opened. The eyes formed a square at the top of the creature's oval head, moving independently of one another as they scanned the room. A slit below the eyes opened, revealing a mouth filled with hundreds of tiny gleaming razors. Long tentacles forced their way into the room through gaps around the body. One swept across the room, grabbing a damage control crewman putting out a fire and slamming him into the bulkhead, crushing his body. The rip in the hull widened as more tentacles emerged and the creature pulled its way into the ship. The shrill screech of ripping metal sounded throughout the ship as the creatures gutted it. Dent got one last look at the creature crawling through the opening before the dark water rose above his head.

The *Colorado* and her crew of 132 officers and crew passed 2500 feet and continued her death plunge to the bottom. Steel bulkheads crumpled like aluminum beer cans under the immense pressure. The bow broke away and raced the rest of the submarine to the bottom. Their task completed the Kaiju attack creatures abandoned the dead husk of the

Colorado and returned to their host. Hours later, a brief rain of metallic debris showered the craggy bottom of the Pacific Ocean sixteen-thousand feet below.

4

Thursday, December 14, 11:05 p.m. CST   Johnson Space Center, Houston, Texas –

Doctor Robert Wingate Rutherford, known as Gate to most of his friends, accepted the news of the Kaiju landing in the South Pacific with stoic fatalism. He knew it had been inevitable that the aliens would try again. He had hoped for more time to unravel the mystery of the Kaijus' origins, but at the rate he was going, that could take years. The aliens were not going to wait that long.

His mind conjured a vivid image of the impact and ensuing tsunami rolling outward from the impact site. He automatically added the numbers – impact speed, blast kilo tonnage, water displacement, wave speed, and estimated deaths immediately after impact. The data came to mind as readily as a NASCAR driver estimating to the last gallon how much fuel needed to reach the finish line, but he was no longer a NASA catastrophist. Predicting the number of casualties and dollar values for the destruction caused by astronomical events was no longer a clinical, theoretical study to him. The three Kaiju that had devastated large parts of the West Coast and the Mid-West had proven his calculations all too accurate. Many others were more capable of taking up his discarded mantle, people who had not watched one of the great, lumbering creatures emerge from its impact crater like an ebony demon from the fiery pits of hell and devour humans; people who had not crawled through the guts of one of the alien killing machines. Now, the numbers had faces; flesh and blood people instead of line graphs on a chart.

His rash impulse to join Captain, now Major, Aiden Walker's team inside Kaiju Nusku had, if not scarred him, humbled him, and set his mind on a new course of endeavor. His thirst for revenge was still burning inside him, a smoldering flame that time could not extinguish. He had dusted off his old astronomy textbooks and became a working astronomer once again.

He was determined to locate the source of the Kaiju. Unlike many of his colleagues, he did not think their origin was interstellar space, the Oort Cloud, or the alien home planet. Wherever the aliens' home world was located, they needed a base of operations closer to Earth. The aliens could wage a war of extermination with a months' long timeframe between launch and arrival on Earth, but the logistics of years or decades between events defied logic. The aliens communicated with the Kaiju. The communications node on the moon that Colonel Langston destroyed proved that. Gate did not believe in FTL communication. No, the aliens, or at least an advanced party, were much closer, watching, listening. The most recent Kaiju landing in Kiribati only four months after the first seemed to prove his point.

His bet was on the Kuiper Belt, a mass of small TNOs, Trans-Neptunian Objects, orbiting the solar system from 30-50 AUs from the sun. 4.5 -7.5 billion kilometers sounded like a great distance, especially for a race that had only recently sent a probe that far out into the fringes of the solar system, but for an alien species that had crossed unknown light years, it was a hop, skip, and a jump.

Photos taken by the New Horizon probe that had reached Pluto in 2015 lay scattered across his desk and spilled into untidy piles on the floor. The public's intrigue by the exciting revelation that Pluto was geologically active had died quickly, as events around the globe took precedence, but to astronomers, the excitement continued. Pluto had an atmosphere, if only a thin mixture of methane and nitrogen. It was a living world, worthy of further study, but his interest lay in a smaller body beyond Pluto – Haumea, one of only a handful of bodies in the Belt large enough for the designation of planetoid.

Haumea, surrounded by icy chunks containing volatiles – methane, hydrogen, ammonia, carbon dioxide, and sulfur dioxide – was the ideal location for an alien base. Readily available frozen volatile gases would provide building blocks for more complex compounds, such as those recently discovered in the Kaiju tissue. Another reason he had focused on Haumea was the fact that the New Horizon probe mysteriously stopped sending data after it passed around the dark side of the planetoid. His colleagues offered countless reasons for the probe's failure, all plausible, but Gate did not like coincidences.

For the hundredth time, he calculated the trajectories of Nusku, Girra, and Ishom – his Unholy Trinity – based on data supplied by NASA satellites. Unfortunately, the data was spotty. The DRS satellite had picked the objects up only hours before impact. Most of the trajectory was pure speculation, his interpretation of the best available information. The spaghetti graphs he derived from the satellite images resembled a hurricane path prediction five days before landfall. Lines went everywhere. Even so, enough of the projections intersected Haumea's orbit to reinforce his initial belief. The aliens were there.

Unfortunately, no spacecraft the U.S. or any other country possessed had the capability of reaching them at such a distance. The Orion was the most advanced spacecraft in existence, but it would take years to reach the Kuiper Belt. If they could find a crew willing to invest a decade of their life to the journey, the Orion still could not carry enough fuel, food, water, and oxygen for the journey.

Gate brushed his hand through his sandy brown hair. He had allowed it to grow much longer after his Kaiju Nusku event. He had no time for haircuts. His tall, lanky frame, once well-muscled and toned from regular exercise, now more resembled a gangly scarecrow. Food, when he took time to eat, had no taste. He slept most nights on the sofa in his office, awoke after a couple of hours of restless, nightmare-ridden sleep, and went directly back to his calculations. His search was not a passion. It was a compulsion. He was on a holy quest.

Kaiju Kiribati's arrival in the South Pacific had fulfilled another of his dire predictions concerning the aliens. Given the defeat of the first three creatures, he had warned government officials that the aliens would next seek a remote location for an ocean landing where terrain and political divisions would hamper the military's ability to bring resources to bear quickly. His first two choices had been either Indonesia or Malaysia. Many parts of both nations were sparsely populated, undeveloped, and torn by political strife. Kiribati was his third choice. The landing there validated his point.

Kaiju Kiribati had broken the pattern of the earlier creatures. It had become active within a few hours rather than the usual twenty-four hours the military thought they had to prepare. It landed in a remote location, but his scenario predicted it would head for a heavily populated area, such as Australia. So far, his predictions were chillingly precise. The aliens were not fools. They had utilized the data provided by the first three Kaiju and incorporated it into the new design. Given the travel time from the Kuiper Belt, even at speeds well beyond the capabilities of human technology, the aliens had worked quickly to prepare this Kaiju. He was certain this creature would have several surprises in store.

Being certain that he knew the origin of the Kaiju and convincing anyone in authority were two different things. Washington had proven slow to act and even slower to consider scientific data. The military insisted on clinging to a conventional warfare mindset that had not changed even with the futility of previous attacks on the creatures. The baby nuke that Walker's team delivered inside Nusku had worked only because Langston had destroyed the communications node, rendering the Kaiju immobile and the host of creatures inside confused. He had heard rumors of a new weapon the biologists had developed from Kaiju tissue, but killing the creatures one at a time was pointless. The aliens were determined to wipe humans from the face of the planet and take it as their own. This Kaiju was a test. If successful, they would continue to send improved Kaiju to Earth in numbers too large to defend against. The Kaiju and their alien creators had to be defeated at the source.

He splashed water on his face, glanced at his disheveled appearance in the mirror above his bathroom sink, and sighed at the dark circles ringing his eyes. His cheeks were hollow and his skin had a sickbed pallor. He looked more like a refugee than a distinguished scientist. His status as hero for his small part in the defeat of Nusku had opened a few doors for him initially, but that fame had quickly faded when he began hounding anyone who would listen to his pet theories. They were in no mood to consider what was to come. The Kaiju were dead. Long live the victors! He would not sway generals or senators looking like a mad scientist. It was time he discarded his notoriety as a recluse and rejoined the world while he still had one to join.

He still had a few friends willing to stand by him. Director Carl Caruthers, head of NASA, kept him apprised of the latest news that did not reach the media. It was through him that he had obtained the New Horizon photos and the depositions of the surviving members of the ill-fated *Lunar One* mission. If anyone could get him into the loop on the new Kaiju, it would be Caruthers.

This time, he would not go to Kiribati. He had seen Kaiju more intimately than he ever wished to again. He had fought Wasps. He had witnessed firsthand the destruction of Chicago. He could close his eyes and recall the stench of burning cities and decaying flesh, the stink of Wasp blood, and the miasmic reek of alien smells inside a Kaiju. He wanted no more adventures. Instead, he would remain close to home and channel his energy, his inquisitiveness, and his anger into less dangerous pursuits. If mankind could not locate the source of the Kaiju and develop a means to defeat them, he would face danger soon enough without seeking it out. He did not quaver in his belief that mankind could win if he was determined enough. The one thing Gate Rutherford had not lost was his dogged determination.

5

Thursday, Dec. 14, 2315 hours   Bicycle Lake Army Air Field, Fort Irwin, California –

Walker quickly found out Colonel Hassert had not been kidding. As soon as he and Costas stepped out of the jeep and onto the dry lakebed that served as Fort Irwin's airfield, two crewmen grabbed their gear and rushed it up the lowered tail ramp into the enormous belly of the Lockheed C-5 Galaxy. The two-hundred-fifty-foot-long C-5 looked like a pregnant submarine with wings. The four GE TF-39 turbofan engines whined their readiness to take off, kicking up a cloud of dust from the gravel runway. A harried-looking loadmaster escorted them to their seats, and then checked after them to make certain they had secured their safety harnesses correctly, as if this were their first trip on a cargo plane.

"We take off in one minute," he informed them, and then disappeared into the crew cabin. Only the two crewmen who had loaded their gear remained in the cargo bay with them. One of them smiled at Walker and threw him a quick thumbs up signal.

The cavernous interior could hold seventy-five men and cargo, but he and Costas were the only two passengers, a testament to the importance of their mission.

Costas leaned over and said, "I never liked these things. They don't look like they can get off the ground. I would have preferred a nice commercial flight with a hot stewardess and cold cocktails."

"They're called flight attendants now, and quite a few of them are males."

Costas frowned. "I don't want to see no dude in a short skirt, even if he is as handsome as me."

Walker shook his head. Costas was as non-PC as they came. His mouth engaged much faster than his brain. If it could be insulted, Costas could piss it off. He understood gays and lesbians, but still had trouble with the concept of transgender, transsexual, and gender uncertainty. To him, it was still dudes, dykes, and dames or worse, babes. The noise of the engines ramped up, and then plane shuddered as it began taxiing down the runway. "I hope they finished that runway extension," he yelled at Costas above the roar of the labored engines and the crunch of gravel beneath the C-5's 28 wheels.

Costas, alarmed, jerked his head toward Walker, and wrinkled his brow. "Why?"

"The old runway was only 8,000 feet. A C-5 needs 8,500 feet to take off."

Costas frowned and craned his neck in an effort to see outside. When he looked back at Walker, Walker was grinning ear to ear. "You're jerking my chain."

"Just a little gallows humor before the flight. A C-5 only needs 6,000 feet of runway."

Costas continued to glare at him as the lumbering C-5 lifted from the lakebed; then, he closed his eyes and settled back for a nap.

* * * *

Friday, Dec. 15, 0530 hours   Wheeler Airfield, Oahu, Hawaii –

The C-5 made the twenty-five-hundred-mile journey in just over five hours. The lights of Honolulu blazed brightly below them, but the dark, misty hulk of four-thousand-foot Mount Ka'ala looming to their right drew most of Walker's attention. It seemed as if the wingtips of the big plane brushed the clouds shrouding the mountain's peak. He forced himself to relax. The pilot knew his job. He banked sharply and pointed the plane's nose straight down the Oahu Plain. He reduced power to the engines and lowered the landing gear. The C-5 touched down so smoothly it didn't even rouse Costas snoring next to him.

Walker nudged him with his elbow. "Welcome to Wheeler Field, Oahu."

Costas yawned and grinned. "I know this bar in Honolulu, the *Pua Pua*, where the babes are primo and the booze ain't watered." He kissed his fingers and opened them. "Bitchin'! What say we grab a taxi and head that way?"

Walker wasn't listening. His focused his attention on the five-ton truck rumbling down the runway toward them. As it pulled up, six men jumped out of the back, carrying their gear in hard-shell, waterproof polyethylene cases. He was surprised to see the men wore Navy S.E.A.L. patches with Special Forces tabs on their uniforms. "I don't think we'll have time for sightseeing," he said.

A seventh man, tall and thin but well-muscled, stepped down from the passenger side of the cab. The creases of his uniform were so crisp they could cut glass. His immaculately polished boots shone even in the dim glow of the truck headlights. With his rugged good looks and neatly trimmed moustache, he looked like recruiting poster. He walked up to Walker, spent a few seconds giving him the once over, saluted, and then announced, "Captain Ian McGregor reporting with *Fire Team Bravo*." He made a quick jerking motion with his hand and two of his men ran inside the C-5 and grabbed Walker and Costas' gear. "If you two gentlemen are ready to go, we'll walk across the field for our ride."

Walker scanned the airstrip and saw no vehicles other than the truck and the C-5. "Where are we going, Captain, and in what are we riding?"

At that moment, a V-22 Osprey shot above the rear of one of the hangers and edged across the field to a spot two-hundred feet from the stationary C-5. The pilot tilted its twin nacelles and hovered for a moment before setting down.

"There's our taxi now," McGregor yelled over the roar of the Rolls Royce T-406 engines. Smiling, he added, "Compliments of the Navy."

Walker eyed the Osprey, whose maximum thousand-mile-range would push the aircraft to its limit to reach Wake Island without an in-flight refueling. "What's our ETA to Wake?"

"Sorry, sir. There's been a change of plans. We're headed to Kiritimati, Christmas Island, in Kiribati."

"How convenient with Christmas only ten days away," Costas remarked dryly. "Are we looking for anything in particular or just picking up a little shiny something for the Joint Chiefs?"

McGregor didn't acknowledge Costas' caustic humor. "We're rendezvousing with the *USS Mississippi* one-hundred-fifty miles northwest of the island."

Walker's sense of disaster began hammering at him again. Even well-planned assaults presented an inordinate amount of risk. This mission was circling the toilet bowl like a Kaiju-sized turd. Though he dreaded the answer he might get, he asked, "What's this all about, Captain?"

"We've lost track of the *USS Colorado*. The captain reported contact with a Kaiju shortly before communications ceased mid-transmission. They also reported the British sub the *Essex* destroyed."

Two subs lost. Walker didn't like the way things were going – too many surprises. First, the aliens slipped a pod onto the planet undetected and wiped out an island chain. Then, the Kaiju popped out of its pod early and sank two nuclear submarines. Now, he was undertaking a mission with Navy S.E.A.L.S with whom he had never worked, one of them a spit and polish captain.

"Do we have a location?"

"Navy's *Cyclops* reconnaissance satellite picked up a black object on the surface north of Enderbury Island. It's size, shape and spotty radar image indicates a Kaiju, so they're assuming that's it."

"So we ferry to the *Mississippi* on the Osprey. What's the plan after that? I would kind of like to know since I'm supposed to be leading this mission." Walker's tone left no doubt about his feelings on his omission in any change of plans.

McGregor shifted uncomfortably under Walker's glare. He didn't like being in the middle of a tug of war. It was an untenable position. "That's the catch, sir. Washington decided international cooperation was called for. They hastily organized a combined task force of U.S., Australian, and British forces after the subs disappeared. They're still hammering out the details even as we speak. Just between you and me, Major Walker, I think this is a shitty way to run a war."

"You and me both." He turned on his heel and stalked off toward the waiting Osprey. "Let's get this Bizarro Circus on the road, Captain." He paused. "Who came up with the designation *Fire Team Bravo*?"

"Don't know, sir. It was listed as such in my orders."

As he climbed into the Osprey, Walker wondered why not *Fire Team Alpha*? The military liked things neat, orderly, and as numerically ordered as possible. Why go for the next designation?

* * * *

Saturday, Dec.16, 0930 hours   80 Miles north of Kiritimati Island –

The V-22 Osprey could transport twenty-four men, but the nine of them were sitting in the cramped, metal fold-down seats in the six-foot-wide cargo space just behind the cockpit. Their pile of gear filled the space between the rows of seats. Three 800-gallon auxiliary fuel bladders needed for the return flight filled the remainder of the twenty-four-foot-long cargo space, loaded on pallets through the folding rear hatch. There had been no time to set up an in-flight refueling, and the extra fuel doubled the Osprey's thousand-mile range, allowing it to return to Wheeler Airfield. Most of the long flight had been devoted to weapons checks, weapons cleaning, and catching a few winks before they reached their destination. It was unlikely they would have an opportunity later.

During the last leg of the trip to Kiritimati Island, Walker tried to learn a little something about Captain McGregor, his new second-in-command. He had worked with Costas for so long that they operated as a closely-knit team. Sometimes he thought the big, burly sergeant could read his mind. McGregor undoubtedly had the same tight relationship with his S.E.A.L. fire team. Now, Walker had to relay orders through McGregor until he learned something about the men assigned him. He had no problem with Navy S.E.A.L. training or in their abilities. He had worked with S.E.A.L.S in Iraq and had found them to be equal to any task. The differences between S.E.A.L. training and Army Special

Forces training were slight, but those few differences could cause major rifts during a firefight, and men could die.

Walker knew how McGregor must feel. He had successfully led his team for several months. Now, thrust into a subordinate position and working with a commanding officer he did not know, he could be harboring some resentment. The longstanding Army-Navy rivalry didn't help matters. They had no time to feel each other out. They both had to hit the ground running.

He wasn't sure how easily Costas would accept the situation. His outspoken sergeant's disregard for authority was the main reason he was still a sergeant, although he had reluctantly accepted a promotion from Sergeant to First Sergeant for his effort in the Nusku mission, but only after Walker explained about the extra three-thousand dollars a year in pay – booze money, Costas called it.

"Captain, I hear you and your men were the first team inside Girra after Langston stopped the Kaiju. What did you think?"

McGregor took a long moment to consider his answer. "I think these alien bastards are some vicious mothers. To them, everything is food for something else. The concept of using your enemy to fuel your attack creatures is goddamned sick. I don't believe they consider this a war as we do. To them, it's just exterminating the indigenous population of vermin to claim the planet as their own." The edges of his mouth curved up in a slight smile. "They might have a higher opinion of us now."

"That's what I'm afraid of," Walker said. "Before, we were fighting organic exterminator units – planet cleaners. Now, we may be facing their military might."

"Hey," Costas piped up, "how did you like those Ticks?" His eyes were hidden behind a pair of aviator shades, but Walker suspected they had a typical Costas mischievous twinkle.

McGregor frowned. "I didn't like them at all. They left me with a nasty scar on my right leg and three weeks in the base hospital from a goddamned allergic reaction to the venom."

"You should have seen them before the Kaijus went immobile. Hundreds of them coming at us like Nips in a massed kamikaze charge."

Walker shook his head. "Japanese, Costas, not Nips. How many times do I have to warn you about racial slurs?"

"Well, I got over the towel-head Arab thing, didn't I?"

"It took you two years."

Costas turned to the man next to him, Private Watts, a slim, dark-haired boy who looked eighteen, but had the hard eyes of someone much older. "I took one of the Ticks home with me as a pet. Trained it to sit up and roll over."

"What do you feed it?" Watts asked, half-believing Costas.

"Privates' privates." Costas' loud guffaw could be heard throughout the plane over the roar of the twin Rolls Royce AE 1107C engines.

The young private grinned.

McGregor looked at Walker, and then glanced away. After a few seconds, he turned back to face him. "You're a Black Muslim, right?"

Walker smiled. He had been expecting the question in some form or the other the entire trip, certain McGregor had read his FITREP file, just as he had read McGregor's on the flight from Fort Irwin. "No, not a Black Muslim. That's Louis Farrakhan's Nation of Islam or York's slightly more bizarre Nuwaubian Nation with its ties to Egypt and ancient aliens, among a few others. I'm a follower of the true Islam faith as taught by the prophet Mohammed, and before you ask, no, I don't like what's happened to Islam by the radical mullahs. To me, Islam is a religion of peace and tolerance, not one of conversion by the sword."

McGregor nodded. "My parents were members of the Kirk, the Church of Scotland, but they brought me up Roman Catholic when we moved to the U.S. That's when I was young. I guess I'm more of an agnostic now." He paused. "With the aliens, the Kaiju, and all, it's kind of hard to put any faith in a religion that preaches that mankind is made in God's image and that we are his chosen people."

"That's the Jews, Captain," Costas said. "The rest of us heathens are just trying to get by best we can."

Walker threw Costas a dirty look, but he shrugged it off.

"I need religion to stay focused, Captain. Faith is a personal thing, but I feel we're all a little less human if we don't have faith in something."

Costas refused to remain out of the conversation. He grinned and said, "I got faith in this." He patted the M107 SASR 50 BMG lying on the seat beside him. "And this." He grabbed his crotch. "In this life you gotta be good with both."

"Then you should become a Muslim," Walker said. "Remember, a devout Muslim receives seventy-two *houris* and an eternal erection when we reach *Jannah*." Walker said it with a grin. Even as a devout Muslim, he had a little trouble believing that particular tenet of his religion. It equated women as chattel, and as an African-American, he had a particular dislike for the concept of owning people. It wasn't his idea of Paradise.

Costas, who had questioned Walker at length many times over the years about his religious beliefs, snorted in derision. "Paradise? Virgins? Now, if it was seventy-two licentious ladies of the night, I might be interested. I ain't got time to break in a bevy of amateurs. Besides, if an erection lasts more than four hours, you should call your doctor."

The last statement elicited a chuckled from Private Watts. Specialist Perez's face turned bright red, but Walker caught a brief smile.

McGregor jerked his thumb at Costas. "Is your sergeant always like this?"

"Our sergeant," Walker reminded him. "No, sometimes he's a real pain in the ass, but you can't find a better man in a fight."

McGregor looked doubtful, but said, "I hope so. I think we'll need him."

One of the flight engineers signaled for Walker's attention. "Fifteen minutes, majorMajor."

Walker glanced at his wrist comp – 0930 hours. It had automatically changed the date to Saturday when they crossed the International Date Line. Nothing looked any different outside; still the flat expanse of sea he had been staring at for four hours except for a small smudge on the horizon, Kiritimati – Christmas Island. The Osprey banked sharply to the left and began circling an empty patch of ocean that looked like every other square mile of ocean. Two minutes later, the faded black, rounded bow of a nuclear submarine broke the surface, followed by the sleek conning tower.

He frowned when he saw the bright white mini-sub secured with six tie-down straps near the sub's stern atop one of the sub's two aft lockout hatches. Walker recognized it as a DSRV, a Deep Sea Rescue Vehicle, used to rescue trapped sailors, but this one was not U.S. Navy. It was British. He scowled at the presence of the unwieldy rescue vehicle. Capable of only a snails pace speed of four knots, the mini-sub was a lousy choice for a delivery vehicle for his fire team, especially one painted bright white. They might as well have painted a big red target on the side. He was beginning to think the brass was determined to sabotage his mission.

As soon as the sub leveled off, four sailors popped out of a hatch just aft of the conning tower. The Osprey slowed, as the twin nacelles with their thirty-eight-feet diameter rotors began converting for a vertical landing. They stopped and locked at 88 degrees. The Osprey dropped like a rock until the pilot pulled up and leveled the aircraft fifty feet above the sub's deck.

"We're landing on that?" Specialist Perez asked. "Can the pilot land between the conning tower and the DSRV?"

The curvature of the hull greatly reduced the width of the submarine's thirty-four-foot beam, leaving a narrow level area that ran the length of the stern.

"No, son, we're jumping," Costas said.

The pilot expertly lowered the Osprey until it hovered ten feet above the deck, just clearing the DSRV, and held it steady. With the forward cargo door of the Osprey open, members of the team unloaded gear and dropped it to the waiting sailors, who promptly passed it down the sub's open hatch. Walker led the way, sliding down the ropes the short distance to the deck. He slammed into it a bit harder than he intended as the sub rode the waves, but he recovered quickly and stepped back to make room for the others.

"This way, sir," one of the sailors, a young female yeoman, said.

Walker climbed down the hatch ladder into the engine room. A clear plastic sleeve prevented seawater from ruining delicate electronics gear during rough seas. He expected the loud roar of diesel engines, the clatter of pistons, and the hiss of escaping steam. Instead, it was eerily quiet, especially after the deafening roar of the V-22's engines drumming in his ears for four hours. The sub's S9G reactor below his feet provided power for the twin 30,000 horsepower turbines that, in turn, powered the sub's stealth pump-jet propulsor, replacing the usual screw-type propeller. In an emergency, the auxiliary diesel engines could take over.

Costas noticed the bright red and yellow radiation hazard placard on the bulkhead and quickly cupped his hands around his crotch. "Is this the reactor? Do I need a tin foil cup to protect my boys?"

The yeoman laughed and handed him a radiation dosimeter badge. "Pin this to your clothing. If it reaches 50 rads, you might want to check on that aluminum foil jock strap. We'll stow your gear in the missile room, forward, sir," she said to Walker. "We set up sleeping quarters for you and your men in the forward torpedo room."

"We won't be sleeping, yeoman. We'll stay with our gear. I need to see your captain."

She smiled and nodded. "Commander Murdock asked me to bring you to him as soon as you were aboard."

"Certainly, yeoman."

"Great," Costas grumbled, "stuck in a radioactive sardine can with a bunch of Navy boys. What a way to spend Christmas." Costas turned to the yeoman and grinned broadly. "Meaning no disrespect, ma'am. Present company is a welcomed exception."

"Play nice, sergeant," Walker warned.

The yeoman grinned. "No problem, Captain. In the Navy, we eat wolves like the sergeant for breakfast. There are one-hundred-thirty-two men aboard this boat, and we've been at sea for four months. Ask any of them why they leave me alone."

This drew a chuckle from Electronics Specialist M. Perez, earning a hot glare from Costas. "You think that's funny, soldier?"

Perez reached up a slender, long-fingered hand and removed the cap covering a head of curly red hair. "Kind of, Sergeant."

Costas' jaw dropped. "On my saintly mother's grave," he coughed. "You're a dame."

She shook her head until the hair fell just above her shoulders. "I'm a Navy S.E.A.L., Sergeant, and if you don't close your gaping mouth, I'll close it for you."

Costas' mouth snapped shut like a Venus flytrap around a bug. "I'll be damned. We've been coeded."

"No doubt about that first part, Costas," Walker said.

Actually, Walker was as surprised as Costas to find a female S.E.A.L. on his fire team. He knew the Navy had graduated quite a few, but he had never met one. Most S.E.A.L. teams were reluctant to include a female, a misogynistic holdover from the 'men are men and women stay home' days. He had traded rounds with enough female ISIS fighters to ignore the weak female label. He knew the S.E.A.L.S would not graduate anyone who could not cut the mustard, regardless of sex.

Walker waited for McGregor. "See that the men are situated in the missile room. I'm going forward to see if the captain knows what the hell is going on."

During the four-hour flight, the only message they had received were the coordinates for the rendezvous with the *USS Mississippi*. He needed current Intel. It troubled him that McGregor seemed to know more about the operation than he did. He was not going to sacrifice his men while the brass in Washington dickered over coffee and doughnuts about whose penis was the biggest.

It was SOP to maintain the lights at a low level in a sub at sea to accommodate off-duty crewmembers sleeping in their berthing racks, the tiny eleven-square-foot cubicles lining the corridors. Behind the drawn blue curtains, the only privacy available, he heard snores and muted snatches of music leaking from headphones plugged into the ships entertainment system. He went down two flights of stairs and entered the control room.

The sub's nerve center looked more like a control room for a factory or a hydroelectric power plant. Crewmen in blue, one-piece overalls sat behind high-tech consoles or stood beside banks of dials with clipboards jotting down readings. Only the two control yokes manned by two drivers, previously known as , betrayed it as the heart of a fast attack nuclear submarine. There was no periscope. A photonics mast in the conning tower, or Sail in the U.S. Navy and Fin in European boats, fitted with advanced video cameras and filters, relayed images to the control room monitors via fiber optic cables. This ensured the integrity of the hull and eliminated the need for the *Mississippi's* control room to be located directly beneath the Sail. It was located forward and near the sub's widest point to for more room.

Commander Murdock looked too young to skipper a nuclear submarine. With his bright-blue eyes, wavy sandy-colored hair, dimpled cheeks, and solid-framed athletic build, he looked more like a tennis pro than a man with his finger on a nuclear trigger. At thirty-one, he was young for a commander, well below the average age of a boat captain. The silver oak leaves on his epaulets were a match for Walker's and looked just as new.

"Welcome aboard, Major Walker," he said as Walker entered the control room. "I hope your gear is stowed and your team is situated. We're getting under way in five minutes. I don't like sitting on the surface." He turned and scanned a clipboard handed him by the sonar officer. He signed his initials and faced Walker. "If you heard about the *Colorado*, you'll know why I'm a bit jumpy." He shook his head. "One-hundred-thirty-five men and women down into to the briny deep. It sounds poetic, but it's a damned disaster."

"I heard about the *Colorado* and the *Essex*, but that's about all I know. I've been hustled from transport to transport since I left Fort Irwin ten hours ago. I still don't know the details of my mission. Do you?"

Murdock picked up a manila envelope lying on a table and handed it to Walker. The look of sympathy he offered Walker told him the news was not good. "The details are in here. In short, my orders are to approach the Kaiju to what they term 'an acceptable distance' and drop your team in the water. We're not to surface. Large swarms of Wasps have been attacking the small islands of the Kiribati chain. Malden Island got hit just under an hour ago. We flew a recon drone over the island. I watched people dying real time until a Wasp deliberately collided with the drone and crashed it. It was a slaughter. As far as I can tell, there were no survivors on the island. You can view the video if you like. Just tell my executive officer." He nodded to the XO, a short, dark-complexioned man leaning over a chart table.

"Lieutenant Commander Dobbs will assist you in every way possible." Murdock checked his watch. "I estimate we rendezvous with the Kaiju in one-hour-forty-five minutes. If you want some sack time, I suggest you grab it now. I'll get your crew as close as I possibly can, but I won't risk my boat. An acceptable distance, my ass," he snarled. "USPACOM is leaving it up to me. They're afraid to pull the trigger on another boat."

The sub captain turned and strode down the corridor to the sonar room, leaving Walker standing there with more unanswered questions. Seeing his plight, the XO walked over.

"Don't think too badly of him, Major. He's under a lot of strain. Our orders are unclear and we're not certain exactly what ships are available to back us up, if any. Communications between U.S., British, and Australian units is all routed through USPACOM. We play hell getting timely updates." He glanced toward the sonar room. "His younger brother was a warrant officer on the *Colorado*."

Walker nodded. "I see. We've both been left standing with our asses in the breeze. Please offer him my condolences. My men could use some chow. No time for sleeping." He looked at the manila envelope marked 'Top Secret.' "Have you seen my orders?"

Dobbs nodded. "I have and I wouldn't blame you for taking an Article 92 instead. An Australian C-17 Globemaster did a low flyby four hours ago and airdropped a container for us. It's in the missile room awaiting your inspection."

Walker's curiosity got the better of him. If the XO thought a court martial for refusing to carry out an order might be preferable to completing his mission, it must be one for the crapper. "What is it, a baby nuke?"

Dobbs cleared his throat. "It's an NBC all right," he replied using the term for Nuclear, Biological, or Chemical weapons, "but not a nuke. It's a chemical called K-2, a nerve toxin derived from Wasp venom. They discovered that in concentrated doses it's as deadly to the alien tissue as it is to humans. Some asshat in a lab coat decided to mix it with Novichok A-230, a Russian acetyl cholinesterase inhibitor. It escaped their testing room and killed fourteen people. It's some deadly shit. The captain is not happy about having it aboard. Neither am I. You'll be delivering two canisters containing tiny nanites infused with K-2." At Walker's raised eyebrow at the word nanites, he explained, "They're microscopic organic robot factories, viruses really, that make more K-2 from the Kaiju's own tissue. Theoretically, you simply set the timers on the canisters and run like hell. The nanites will infiltrate the creature's body via its bloodstream."

"They couldn't have designed this weapon for this specific Kaiju. They're assuming the aliens aren't making improvements based on any data the previous creatures transmitted before Langston took out the communications node on the moon. They're just sending us in hoping they're right."

Dobbs' face clouded. "The alternative is a nuclear strike. It might kill the creature, but it could just as easily precipitate a war. Countries like

Iran and Korea are itching to push the button, hoping to add to the chaos and pick up what real estate they can grab in the aftermath. China has issued warnings that it will consider a nuclear detonation anywhere in the South Pacific as a Western attack on Micronesia and will defend its island neighbor comrades with all its might. I'm quoting there," he added.

"Aliens are trying to destroy the Earth and countries are still trying to out-piss one another. I hope one of these bastards lands in downtown Beijing in the middle of Red Square and stomps some commie ass."

"We can always hope. Major Walker, I agree with you about your mission. The chances of success on your first Kaiju mission were equally dismal; and yet, you succeeded. I'm betting on you."

"The three of us who survived escaped only because of Commander Langston's sacrifice. This one doesn't have a control module; at least NASA hasn't discovered one yet. It's autonomous, therefore capable of making decisions based on its environment and any threats it encounters. It's more dangerous than all three previous Kaiju combined." He crunched the envelope in his hand. "This is a death warrant for my team, and Washington expects me to deliver it."

"But you'll deliver it," Dobbs said.

Walker sighed. "What choice do I have? Someone has to try it. I've been inside one of those things. I know what to expect, and what I expect is that the aliens are one step ahead of us this time."

"Good luck, sir."

"Lieutenant Commander, I'll take all the luck I can get."

By the time he reached the forward missile room where his team was waiting, he had built up a head of steam at the callous manner in which the brass was using his team. He slowly looked them all in the eyes. Costas, who could read his moods, frowned. Walker held out the envelope for them to see. Their gazes followed its movement as he waved it around.

"Here are our orders." He wadded the envelope and tossed it to the deck. Several pairs of eyes followed the envelope's path to the deck. "Most of you, perhaps all of us, won't be coming back from this one. I won't bore you with details or try to sway you with tales of heroic sacrifice and do-or-die efforts. You're all volunteers. This is the mission they've assigned us, and we will perform it to the best of our abilities. However, if any of you feel your lives are too important to waste trying to save the world, step forward, and I'll release you for other assignments, no hard feelings. Hell, I might join you."

Captain McGregor shifted in his seat, appearing slightly uncomfortable with the tone of Walker's speech.

"You've all been inside one of these creatures. You know what it's like. I can only add that in a fully sentient Kaiju, the creature's biological security system is ten times worse. I'm sure you've viewed the video Doctor Phillip Rutherford filmed during our little venture inside Nusku." A few heads nodded. "That's the equivalent of watching a battle on TV rather than participating in it." He paused to let that sink in. Whatever resistance the S.E.A.L.S had met inside the dead Kaiju Girra, it had been undirected, random attacks. "The aliens are smart. We don't know where these Kaiju pods originate or how long they've been in transit. This one could simply be number four in the series, identical to the others, or more likely, they've made a few adjustments to compensate for us obstinate humans."

He directed their attention to the two unlabeled black neoprene canisters, each the size of a quarter-barrel beer keg, sitting conspicuously in the center of the room. "Gentlemen, let me introduce you to our Kaiju killer."

Before he could begin, the ship's intercom, the 1MC, came alive. "This is the captain. We've picked up a distress call from the cruise ship *Radiant Princess*. The same creatures that sank the *Colorado* have attacked her. She's sinking. Despite my orders, I will not allow a civilian vessel to go under without trying to rescue as many passengers as possible and protecting the rest until more rescue ships can arrive to assist. Major Walker, will you please come to the control room? I have a mission for you and your team."

Costas smiled. "Lock and load, boys! Looks like we got some Kaiju ass stompin' to do."

6

Saturday, Dec. 16, 6:15 a.m.   Kiritimati Island, Republic of Kiribati
_

Teana Moss was confused. She had walked from her home in Tabwakea to her job at the Beach House Fishing Lodge only to find the doors locked. She saw the owner, Kema Tebura, peeking furtively out the second-story window at her, but he wouldn't answer her repeated calls, only lowered the shades. It was a lousy job, answering telephones and booking guests, but it was better than being a housekeeper at the Captain Cook Hotel or working with her father at the copra groves. At twelve years old, she had seen herself living in New Zealand or Australia by the time she was eighteen, attending a university. Now, at twenty, she knew her dream would never happen. She would never leave Kiritimati.

On the way back home, she noticed how deserted the beaches were. Usually, in December, tourists lazed in the sun on the sugar-white sand or cast their lines in the surf for fish. Some chose to wade in the shallow offshore flats to fish for bonefish, trevally, or giant triggerfish. She saw no one. Had she missed a holiday? Unlikely. On an island as tiny as Kiritimati, any holiday was a cause for celebration. She supposed by Kiribati standards, Tabwakea was populous with twenty-three-hundred people living there. In fact, Kiritimati comprised seventy percent of all the land area of the thirty-three islands of the Republic of Kiribati.

She left the path and cut across the shrub-covered grassland to her home, sniffing the fragrant white blossoms of naupaka and bay cedar shrubs. Butterflies fluttered around the naupaka tasting their sweet nectar. She tore off a thick, succulent naupaka leaf and rubbed the oil on her hands to soften her skin. Fresh holes in the dirt showed where feral pigs had been rooting for grubs beneath some of the plants, exposing their roots. She raked the dirt back over them with the side of her shoe.

She suspected something was wrong when she saw old Chun Lao sitting on his porch smoking one his awful-smelling Chinese cigarettes. Chun took his small boat out very day, rain or shine, to catch trevally or crab for the hotel's kitchen. Only something dreadful would keep him off the water. She was hesitant to approach him. Although she had been born on Kiritimati and spoke Gilbertese as fluently as she did English, he still didn't consider her a true I-Kiribati. Her grandfather had been a member of the American 102nd Infantry Regiment stationed on the island during WWII. He had fallen in love with the island and its people, married an island girl –her grandmother – and never left.

Chun Lao glanced up at her as she approached him and laid his still burning cigarette on the edge of the porch.

"Why is the Beach House closed?" she asked.

"Haven't you heard?" he asked in his low rumble of a voice.

"Heard what? Our television is acting up. I can't get a signal."

"One of those Kaiju things smashed into Maiana yesterday evening. It wiped out all the islands around it. Tarawa's gone."

Her heart pounded against her ribs beneath her breasts. The air suddenly seemed too thin to breathe. She clasped a hand to her chest and pressed against her sternum to quiet her runaway heart. Her legs turned to jelly. She plopped down on the porch beside Chun. She had heard a noise like distant thunder in the night, but thought it was a passing storm. She had known it was the screams of thousands of people dying.

She noticed Chun's double-barreled shotgun lying on the other side of him. He claimed he used it to hunt feral pigs and to shoot nosey sharks that got too close to his boat, but she had heard rumors that he had been known to take pot shots at people he thought were raiding his crab traps. He seemed the type of person who would shoot at another human being, cold, always on the verge of anger.

"Tarawa gone?" she asked when she found her voice, hoping she had misheard Chun.

He nodded. "The tsunami swept over half the islands in the Phoenix chain too. Didn't you hear the surf pounding last night? We had five-foot waves crashing on the beach."

She shook her head. "I went to bed early because I had to work today."

"I think everyone took the day off," he said as he stared to the west. "I did."

"What's the shotgun for?" she asked.

He frowned. "When Kaiju attacked the U.S., the flying monsters carried people off and fed them to the Kaiju." He patted the shotgun. "It's not happening to me."

She stood. "I have to go home. My parents …"

She turned and raced away. When she arrived home, her father had already left for his job as supervisor at the copra groves. He mother met her at the door, her face ashen. Her eyes darted to the sky to the west.

"Mrs. Pelu was just here. She said …"

"I know. Chun told me. What are we going to do?"

"Pack a bag. Quickly!" she added when Teana stood there staring at her. "We're going to the airport and leaving the island."

"Where …?" she began to ask; then shook her head. It didn't matter where they went. "We have to go to the grove and get Father first."

"He didn't go to work. He's at the airport buying tickets. We'll meet him there. Hurry!"

Her mind was in a fog. She didn't know what to pack. She stood in her room and surveyed her life's possessions. Her CD player and collection of CDs, her television, her seashell collection, her photo albums – she had room for none of them. She settled on two pair of shoes, a good dress, a few pair of shorts and shirts, and underwear. After a moment's hesitation, she threw her iPad, her hairbrush, and a handful of toiletry items into the overstuffed bag.

Her mother was waiting at the door, a large suitcase in each hand, and her purse slung over her shoulder. "We'll take the canoe across the lagoon," she said. "It's too far to walk carrying heavy luggage."

They tossed the bags into the small outrigger canoe pulled up on the beach and pushed it into the water. Teana paddled as fast as she ever had in her life, picking the most direct path through the coral reefs and small inter-connected lagoons. They reached the far side of the lagoon in fifteen minutes. She didn't bother beaching the canoe. She leaped into the shallow water and grabbed her suitcase. They carried one of the large suitcases together to share the burden. They hurried through the town of Banana, seeing hardly anyone on the streets. The shops were closed, the shutters pulled tight. Even the bus from the town to the airport wasn't running. It sat empty and driverless on the side of the road.

Cassidy International Airport had three airlines – Fiji Airways, Air Kiribati, and Coral Sun Airlines. Most of the latter's planes were large enough for local hops to Tarawa or Canton, but Tarawa was gone, possibly Canton too. Fiji Airways operated a Boeing 737 into Kiritimati from Nadi, Fiji, for the crowds of fisherman visiting the island. The big 737 sat on the runway preparing to leave.

Her family wasn't the only people wanting to leave the island. The small terminal building buzzed with the noise of the frightened crowd. It seemed as if half the island was there. She knew many of the people but didn't recognize their faces. Instead of their normal island serenity, they wore masks of fear and anger. The harried ticket clerk behind the counter argued with three people simultaneously, as they attempted to buy tickets by shoving handfuls of cash at her. Most of the crowd was islanders.

The fishermen had purchased round-trip tickets. They were standing outside apart from the crowd, waiting to board the jet. She spotted her father by the door waving to them.

"Teana! Soria!" he yelled.

She and her mother rushed over to him.

Her father's normally placid mien was twisted into anger and disappointment. He nodded at the strident crowd. "Look at them. Animals! There are no more tickets available. I bought the last three. People are paying all they have for tickets to anywhere on anything leaving the island. I don't know where they think they're going. Most of these planes don't have the range to get them anywhere safe."

The fear was a virus, contagious, affecting everyone it touched. The islanders had always thought themselves safe secreted thousands of miles from the troubles of the world, but overnight, they had become the center of a crisis, a second alien attack. Not since the bitter horrors of World War II, or the second horror of forced displacement during the nuclear tests, had they felt so helpless and so lost. The earth had been pulled from beneath their feet, leaving them floundering in the murky waters of apprehension.

Teana knew, because she shared their terror. It had no taste, color, or smell. She could not point to it and say, "That is what I am afraid of." Most, like her, had not seen the Kaiju in America even on television. Their sheltered lives had no room for the misery and misfortunes of others. Hurricanes, tsunamis, poor fishing, poverty – these they knew and understood. Tales of monsters were for frightening small children. Now, they knew the monsters were real.

As soon as the boarding ladder rolled up to the 737 jet, the people waiting with tickets rushed the plane, fighting for a place on the steps. The stewardess didn't look at the tickets or check their names against her passenger list. She stood aside as they thrust their tickets and boarding passes at her. The crowd inside the terminal saw the plane loading and started for the doors as well.

"Come on," he father yelled.

They raced toward the 737 with her father waving their tickets in the air. Behind them, the frightened islanders – their neighbors and friends – had become a frenzied mob fighting to exit the building. The press of the crowd shoved the people at the forefront into the glass doors, crushing them against the glass with the weight of the crowd. Finally, the glass doors and adjacent window wall smashed and shattered. The people pressed against it fell, trampled beneath the feet of the mob.

Teana reached the steps ahead of her father and mother. Above the noise of the 737's engines, another sound, more ominous for its unnaturalness, like the flapping of hundreds of sails luffing in a changing wind, filled the air. Teana glanced up and saw a cloud of giant winged creatures descending on the island from the west. Their black and orange bodies gave them the appearance of bumblebees, but all resemblance to earth creatures ended there. They swooped and hovered on double pairs of leathery wings. Vicious, razor-edged talons tipped their eight, multi-jointed legs. A three-foot-long stinger protruded from the rear of their abdomen.

A section of the swarm broke away and dipped down among the houses of the village of Tabwakea. They rose into the air again moments later grasping struggling people in their forelegs. They turned west toward their master, the Kaiju, laden with their human offerings. Teana heard Chun's shotgun fire twice in the distance and then went quiet. She waited, hoping he reloaded, but it remained silent.

The largest part of the swarm, numbering in the hundreds, continued across the island toward the airport. She stood transfixed in horror, as the swarm split again. Scores of creatures attacked Banana, repeating the grisly process they used in Tabwakea. They were near enough to see the blazing orange strips of their eyes and to hear the dying screams of their victims. The people around her finally began to comprehend the danger. Many of them raced for the jet, while others either ran back toward the safety of the terminal building or raced across the runways toward the surrounding trees.

Close up, the creatures, Wasps, she now remembered their names, were even more terrifying. They were savage, mindless creatures serving one purpose: providing fuel for the Kaiju. Jagged rows of teeth like the edges of band saw blades filled their mouths. Their stingers dripped drops of viscous, milky venom and were long enough to skewer a human body. They dove toward the tarmac.

"Hurry!" her father yelled.

She turned to run up the steps. A wing slapped her in the face as a Wasp plucked the man in front of her from the steps and flew away. She looked into his terror-filled eyes as he struggled and screamed, and watched those eyes go empty and lifeless when the creature's stinger repeatedly stabbed into his chest until his screams stopped. More screams erupted around her. A woman clutched by a Wasp grabbed onto her husband's outstretched hand, who struggled to hold her down. The Wasp slashed her with its talons until her body split in two, spilling her intestines over her hapless husband. Her lower body fell to the tarmac, dragging him with it. Before he could rise, a second Wasp plucked him from the ground to join her.

The Wasps dove into the dispersing crowd, chasing down stragglers. More of the creatures flew into the terminal through the shattered door, slaughtering the people seeking shelter there. Farther down one of the runways, a De Havilland DHC-6 turboprop taxied for a takeoff against the wind. Its twin Pratt and Whitney engines struggled to lift the overloaded plane from the tarmac. Its wheels bounced several times before they left the ground less than fifty feet from the edge of the runway. Teana knew that with its limited range, the De Havilland might make the small airstrips on Teraina or Tabuaeran north of Kiritimati, but doubted it could reach Malden Island or Starbuck Island, the closest islands to the south. The De Havilland had room for the crew and a maximum of nineteen passengers, but it flew heavily and awkwardly, as if loaded far beyond its capacity.

It mounted slowly above the treetops and circled the field, as the pilot tried to decide on a destination. His indecision and the plane's slow speed spelled its doom. One of the Wasps flew directly into the starboard engine's spinning propellers. The blades ripped the creature to shreds, but its hard ebony carapace sheared off the blades. The engine stalled and died. The plane veered right in a steep dive. The pilot struggled to add power to the port engine, but it was a futile gesture. The plane was too close to the ground to recover. It struck a grove of palm trees near the beach and cart-wheeled into the surf where it exploded in a ball of flame. A billowing streamer of black smoke rose from its grave. Wasps followed the plane's path and picked through the burning debris for the passengers; then flew away with still-smoldering corpses. Any flesh, living or dead, was food for the Kaiju.

Teana looked away from the grisly scene. She reached the top of the stairs and stepped toward the door of the 737. The pilot had witnessed the demise of the De Havilland and was not waiting. He gunned the engine and began taxiing down the runway. Teana lost her balance and fell forward as the boarding ladder slid down the side of the moving fuselage. She grabbed onto the rail to regain her balance, as the gap between the steps and the door widened.

"Jump," the stewardess urged.

Teana hesitated; then, felt hands lift her and propel her forward across the gap, barely reaching the outstretched hand of the stewardess, who yanked her through the open doorway. She looked back to see her father and mother standing at the top of the steps, moving farther away as the jet gained speed, heedless of the people crushed beneath its wheels or blasted across the tarmac by the wash of the powerful engines.

"Daddy!" she screamed.

He smiled at her and wrapped his arm around her mother. His smiled vanished when a Wasp stinger pierced his chest. His arm fell away her mother's shoulders as the creature yanked him from the platform and flew away. Her mother followed him a few seconds later. As the stewardess sealed the door, she caught one last glimpse of the Wasps flying away with their burden of humans. Few people remained from the hundreds that had thronged the terminal.

The stewardess looked down at her with a tear in her eye, her face awash with pity. "You're safe," she said. "You're safe."

As the 737 lifted from the end of the runway and shot away from the island faster than the Wasps could follow, she didn't feel safe. She felt numb. She allowed the stewardess to help her to a seat at the front of the jet. She noticed with dismay that the cabin was barely half-full. There was room for so many more. As the jet banked west for a southern heading to Fiji, she looked down at her home from the window by her seat. Buildings burned in the cities and wrecked automobiles lined the roads. Hundreds of Wasps circled the island, rounding up and carting away all stragglers. *Two of those bodies are my baba and toba*, she thought. *My father and mother dead, my home destroyed. I am truly butirawa – homeless.* A few minutes later, she saw a black dot on the ocean below her with a line of Wasps flying between it and her island. *The Kaiju*, she thought. Anger swelled up inside, but she had no release for it except through her tears. She pulled down the shade on the window, closed her eyes, and wept for her parents and her friends, all dead because of the aliens.

Then she wept for herself.

7

Saturday, Dec. 16, 7:30 a.m.   *Radiant Princess*, north of Enderbury Island –

Mark Talent knew something was amiss when the steward failed to deliver his breakfast to his room as he had every morning of the voyage promptly at 6:15 a.m. He waited an additional forty-five minutes before deciding to venture to the Horizons Courtyard. The choices offered by the enormous breakfast buffet were less limited than those of room service, but his standing order of toast, butter, jelly, crisp bacon, and two scrambled eggs was more than sufficient to start his day. The Horizons was a last resort. Sharing breakfast with hundreds of passengers, many of them children, did not appeal to him, but at least it offered the option of grabbing something and returning to his cabin to eat in solitude.

He stepped out of his cabin into a hornet's nest of activity. As he feared, word about the Kaiju attack on the islands of western Kiribati had already spread. Frightened passengers crowded the corridors, whispering so they wouldn't frighten the children, who already knew something was amiss by the pallid faces and furtive mannerisms of their parents. Rumors triumphed over fact. One story he overheard announced two Kaiju appearing in Washington. D.C.; another rumor had multiple Kaiju ravaging parts of Europe.

One young woman whose cabin was two doors down from his and with whom he had never spoken cornered him by the elevator. Every time he had seen her, she had taken great pains to make herself attractive with judicious applications of lipstick, eyeliner, rouge, and makeup. However, today her hair was unkempt, and she wore no makeup. Her clothes looked thrown on in haste.

"Are they turning the ship around?" she demanded. "They should turn the ship around."

"I have no idea. I wouldn't think so. It's almost twenty-four-hundred miles back to Hawaii."

She tugged at her pale, lipstick-free lower lip. "Where's our Navy? Why aren't they here to protect us?"

Before he could respond, she shook her head and wandered back down the corridor. By the time he threaded his way through the speculating crowd and reached the fresh air of the Lido Deck, Kaiju had destroyed Hawaii, all of Kiribati, and the Philippines.

The air of celebration that had previously suffused the ship evaporated like water spilled on a sidewalk in a hot Arizona summer. Now, the passengers were merely frightened, milling about in confusion. Next, after their apprehension mounted and the rumors grew even wilder, they would panic. After that ... He didn't want to think that far ahead.

He spotted several harried crewmembers harangued by crowds of insistent passengers, as if they thought a steward or a housekeeper would be privy to some private information they didn't have access to from the television or the internet. He felt sorry for the poor crew, but not sorry enough to intercede – not his circus, not his monkey.

On the Lido Deck, no one was in the pool. This in itself was an ominous sign of the mood aboard ship. People scurried to and from the Horizons Courtyard like a line of carpenter ants bent on defoliating a forest. They buzzed by him with trays laden with food. The selections were random, as if any food in sufficient quantity would see them through whatever impending crisis they imagined might occur. Talent took one look at the melee inside the buffet and reconsidered his options for breakfast. The bag of potato chips, a can of macadamia nuts, and two apples in his room now looked good. As he stood there, one overweight man clad in plaid shorts and a brightly colored Hawaiian shirt, looking back over his shoulder to see if his equally overweight wife and child were following, slammed into Talent, sending the tray of food he carried flying across the deck. The man glanced up at Talent and sneered.

"Asshole!" he shouted. "Look where you're going."

"I wasn't going anywhere," Talent replied calmly. "I was standing here." He didn't want to give the overwrought man a heart attack. His face was as bright red as the blob of cherry Jell-O quivering on the deck. "But excuse me anyway." He stepped aside to let the man pass.

Hawaiian-shirt man refused to accept Talent's apology. He noted Talent's long, black ponytail beneath his Stetson, his cowboy boots, his ruddy complexion, and the Tohono O'odham Man-in-the-Maze symbol on the horsehair clasp of his bola tie and frowned. Instead, he decided to show his young son how a real man handles a situation.

"They shouldn't let Indians on this ship," he said in a voice loud enough to cause heads to turn in his direction. "You're all drunks and thieves."

Talent was willing to give the man a little leeway. Since the advent of Facebook and social media, people believed they could say anything they wished with impunity. It wasn't the first time someone had called him out for being Indian. He held his temper and turned to walk away. The man rushed around in front of him to continue his tirade. "I'm not through with you," he said. "I'm going to report you to the captain. I paid good money for this cruise, and I shouldn't have to deal with the likes of you."

Talent replied, "I paid eleven thousand dollars myself. Now, why don't you go get your family some more food?"

He stepped around the irate man and continued walking. From the corner of his eye, Talent saw Hawaiian-shirt rush up behind him, swinging his fist at the back of his head. Talent ducked aside, and shoved the man in the back as he overshot his target. The man stumbled across the deck and slammed into a stack of folded deck chairs. He fell, and the pile of chairs collapsed around him. Talent stared at him for a moment, judging whether the man would try to escalate the altercation, but the anger had left him, replaced by embarrassment.

Talent left the man where he lay to consider his rude behavior. His wife rushed over and attempted, unsuccessfully, to extricate him from the tangle of deck chairs. The crowd, more concerned with their own fears than with the momentary spectacle, broke up. Before Talent reached the elevators, a ship's officer with two gold bars and the word Security on the epaulets of his white uniform barred his path. Talent looked from the man's nametag, which read *Nils Ivers – Security*, to his face, stern and frowning.

"We don't want any disturbances aboard ship," he warned. "We will not tolerate such behavior from passengers."

"I agree. Perhaps you should speak to him." He pointed to the Hawaiian-shirt man just now getting up from the scattered deck chairs.

"I was passing by when the incident occurred. I saw you shove him."

Talent quickly grew weary of the security officer's arrogant manner. As a Native American, he had been on the receiving end of too many authoritarian diatribes over the years. He had not liked it from the police; he certainly refused to tolerate it from a ship's security officer, not for eleven-thousand dollars.

"He confronted me, and then insulted me. When I attempted to leave, he attacked me. I'd say he came off damned lucky."

The officer took a step closer to Talent. "You embarrassed him in front of his family."

"No, he embarrassed himself in front of his family. Maybe he'll learn from his experience. Perhaps you'd better concern yourself with bigger problems."

"What bigger problems?"

"Look around, Ivers. These people are ready to explode. They're afraid, and no one is telling them anything. The truth would be less harmful than rumors."

Ivers shifted nervously. "There's no cause for alarm."

While they had been conversing, the atmosphere of fear among the passengers had grown worse. Talent pointed to people grabbing liquor bottles from the pool bar and rushing off. "Then you had better tell them that. They might believe you. I don't."

"I'll be keeping an eye on you."

Talent laughed. "Don't try to intimidate me. You do a piss poor job at it."

Ivers scowled, reached out his hand, and grabbed Talent's bola tie. Talent immediately seized the security officer's thumb and twisted it behind his hand. Ivers yelped in pain and struggled, but Talent's grip was too strong to break.

"Don't ever lay hands on me," Talent growled. "You might intimidate frightened passengers or women and children, but to me you're just a glorified mall cop in a white uniform."

He released the security guard's hand. Ivers reached for the whistle hanging around his neck by a chain to summon help.

"Before you can blow that whistle," Talent warned, "you'll be lying on the deck choking on it." Ivers hesitated. In a softer tone, he said, "Good. You accused me of instigating an incident with no facts and without questioning any of the two dozen witnesses. You made a mistake. Don't make another one that you might regret. I don't want any trouble, but I won't back away from it."

"We have a brig on this ship," Ivers warned, trying to regain some of his lost dignity.

"You might have enough men to put me in it." Talent narrowed his eyes and glared at the security officer. "But you won't be in any condition to see it happen." He backed away from Ivers, giving the man the personal space to calm down.

Inside the Horizons Courtyard, the food had run out. Passengers began yelling and fighting for the few remaining scraps. The fact that there were fourteen dining rooms, grills, cafes, and bars aboard ship, as well as room service, was lost on them. In their fear, they had abandoned rational thinking for frenzied mob mentality. Tensions on the ship were ready to explode.

"I'm returning to my cabin now. I think that in a few minutes, you're going to be too busy to bother with me."

Ivers stared over Talent's shoulder at the growing fracas in the courtyard and his face paled. Without another word to Talent or a backward glance at the crowd, he raced to a door marked Personnel Only and disappeared through it. Talent thought it was time for him to disappear as well.

As he hurried along the outside corridor to the aft elevators to avoid the crowds, he saw people pointing out to sea. He glanced to see what had caught their attention. At first, he thought it was a whale – he had seen a few on the voyage – but as he realized how far away the object was, its true size became apparent. It was low in the water, as black as the inside of a mineshaft, and headed directly for them. A chill coursed through his body as he recognized it as a Kaiju, the one that had wiped out Kiribati.

As he watched, scores of lines appeared in the water between the Kaiju and the ship, like torpedoes fired from a submarine but traveling much faster than any torpedo he had seen in the movies. Within seconds, they had closed to within a few hundred yards of the ship, close enough to make out details. They were gray and long, but they weren't torpedoes, at least not any type of torpedo he had seen. The portion of the objects visible above the waterline was at least ten-feet long. Their movement seemed more organic than mechanical, as if propelling themselves with tentacles or long, thin fins. He wasn't sure what they were, but was certain they meant trouble.

He crossed to the port side of the ship to place more distance between him and the objects in case he was wrong and they were torpedoes. Screams erupted all around him as people became aware of the Kaiju and the strange objects. Now their unfocused fears had a target upon which they could vent. Panic became a stampede.

The 113,000-ton ship shuddered from the impact when the projectiles struck starboard amidships. Talent grabbed a doorframe and hung on as the ship canted several degrees to port. When the ship resettled, he rudely elbowed his way through the crowd and raced down two flights of stairs to his cabin just a few doors down from the aft stairwell. He opened his door, went immediately to the balcony, and stared out. What he saw froze his blood in his veins. They had not been torpedoes, as he had feared. They were aquatic alien creatures, and they looked like they meant business.

He rushed to the open closet by the bathroom, pulled a gift-wrapped box from the shelf, and ripped off the bright red and green paper. He laid the box on the bed and opened it. Inside, wrapped in two souvenir tee shirts, lay a leather sheath holding a *kukri*, Nepalese machete with a curved thirteen-inch blade and a *Becker BK7* combat utility knife with a seven-inch blade. He thanked Hawaii's user-friendly knife laws. He didn't know if Australia would allow him to bring the weapons into the country, but he had felt naked without some kind of self-defense protection. He wished he had one of his guns.

The Gurkha kukri machete was a tourist souvenir, cheaply made with a dull blade. The first thing he had done after purchasing it was to apply a liberal amount of superglue to the space between the metal tang and the wooden handle and pound the rivets tighter. Then he wound a long, thin leather strip around the entire handle to pull the two pieces together tighter. Afterwards, he attacked the dull edge of the blade with a rattail file and a whetstone until it was sharp enough to draw blood from his finger pressed against the fine edge. The Becker utility knife blade only required a few strokes with the whetstone to remove the steel burrs. A machete and a knife against alien creatures hardly qualified as an even match, but it was better than no weapon at all.

He went back out on the balcony with the kukri in his hand. Looking down and to his right, he saw several of the creatures chewing through the metal hull below the waterline as if it were cardboard and disappearing inside the ship amid a flurry of whipping tentacles. Others used their long tentacles to pull themselves from the water and crawl up the side of the ship. At first glance, they resembled giant squids with tubular bodies rounded on the end with eight tentacles twice their body length, but as they left the water, their streamlined bodies expanded and broadened until they became shorter and twice as wide for greater stability on land. They employed four of the thicker tentacles to grip the metal hull. Instead of suckers, the tentacles bore lines of sharp barbs that sliced through the steel as easily as a church key through the top of beer can.

One of the creatures focused its four, bright orange iridescent eyes on Talent. He could see intelligence behind the gaze, or at least a sense of purpose. It opened its maw, revealing a mouthful of razor-sharp needle teeth. Slits on the sides of its neck puffed out, exposing rows of crimson gills, indicating its adaptability to either air or water. It began trilling a high-pitched undulating whistle that rattled the glass of the balcony balustrade, as if saying, "Everyone back off. This one is mine."

Faced with fleeing or fighting, Talent chose to fight, not from any Quixotic sense of adventure or from an inflated egotistical estimate of his skill and abilities, but because he knew there was nowhere on the ship to run from a creature that could chew through steel easier than he could eat an overcooked flank steak. He did a little shuffle dance on the deck, aiming the tip of the kukri at the creature. "Come on, you bastard!" he yelled at it. "Come get some of this Tohono O'odham bad boy."

Accepting his challenge, the creature changed direction, angling crablike across the hull toward his balcony on the four thick appendages, its four, thinner, whip-like tentacles doing a frenzied dance in the air like dreadlocks in a high wind. The creature left a trail of ragged puncture marks in the hull in its wake. Talent waited, feet planted firmly on the deck, as the first tentacle as big around as his thigh whipped over the side, shattering the glass balustrade. He dodged aside as the leathery appendage whipped about wildly. As it withdrew, he attacked the arm with his kukri. The blade barely penetrated the dense, dark gray flesh, but it dripped with yellow ichor as he yanked it out. A second tentacle shot over the side of the railing to join the first. He ducked, barely avoiding a savage blow to his head. The tentacle smashed into the wooden panel separating the balconies, splintering it into kindling.

A shard of wood lodged in his right shoulder, but he felt no pain. He was riding a dopamine high, as his body converted the amino acid tyrosine into dopamine. Acting as a neurotransmitter, the dopamine increased his motor control and coordination. Dopamine, the reward part of reward-motivated behavior, was nature's way of encouraging the fighter, much to the consternation of the pacifist. In nature, the pacifist became food. The tentacles, once a blur of motion, slowed until they became a deliberate dance of alien flesh, one he could match step for step. Oxygenation from his rapid breathing converted the dopamine into adrenaline, slowing his pancreas' production of insulin to allow more synthesis of sugar for quick energy. He moved faster and thought more rapidly than he ever had before. The hormones coursing through his bloodstream made him a fearless fighting machine. He wondered if his ancestors had felt as he now did during a battle. He sensed the spirits of his grandfathers watching him, heard their victory song urging him on. Euphoria replaced fear.

Two more tentacles joined the first two. One wrapped nimbly around a chair and drew it over the side of the ship, crushing it. He picked up the second chair and threw it at the retreating tentacle.

"That's *my* chair," he yelled, using his voice as a weapon, willing his anger into the words.

Glass shattered on the balcony two doors down from him, as one of the creatures broke through the balcony doors. Two feminine screams quickly followed. He tried not to let the screams distract him as he prepared himself for another opening. He dodged tentacles, weaving among them like a dust devil dancing through a patch of creosote plants. The creature's head crowned the balcony deck, staring at him with hunger in its four alien eyes. He leaped at it with the kukri gripped tightly in both hands. Using his body weight, his fury, and the strength of his upper arms, he drove the blade through the resilient alien flesh just above the upper left pair of eyes.

This time, the blade bit deeply. A stream of putrid yellow ichor ran down into the creature's eyes. A bellow like a constipated moose erupted from the creature's throat. Talent held on as the creature thrashed its body in an effort to dislodge the machete, slamming him repeatedly into the remaining partition on the opposite side of the balcony. He braced his boots against one of the metal posts of the demolished glass railing and thrust the blade deeper, wiggling it back and forth to break the suction of metal to flesh. Finally, the blade pierced bone or cartilage and slid in to the hilt. A dark fluid gushed from the wound.

The creature loosened its grip and slid back into the water. He wrenched the machete free just before the creature yanked him over the side with it. He fell back to the deck gasping for breath. The creature's foul-smelling dark blood drenched his arms and chest. He wiped it from his face and lips with the sleeve of his shirt, amazed he was still alive. He knew he had not hit any of the creature's vital organs, only wounded it, but it was enough to send it running. It was as if it had never experienced pain, and the new sensation confused it. It would soon get over that.

He felt like yelling out a war cry but refrained. There were other Squid around and he was too exhausted to fight off another attack. Now that the adrenaline rush was fading, his chest and arms ached and his hands shook uncontrollably. He had counted coup, marked his opponent. He peered over the edge of the balcony. Several of the Squid had returned to the water, but unlike his attacker, they carried numerous bodies enmeshed in their tentacles, some dead and mutilated, others still alive and struggling. Their struggles would end quickly, as the creatures began submerging for the return trip to the Kaiju.

He had witnessed the Kaiju's grisly feeding habits on video newscasts and read the report of the scientist who went inside Kaiju Nusku. It was better that the hapless people died before they suffered that horrific fate.

The entire battle had taken less than five minutes. Talent rubbed his bruised side where the creature had slammed him into the wall in its frenzied effort to dislodge the Kukri. He winced as his fingers probed tender flesh. He yanked the splinter of wood from his right shoulder, biting his lip to keep from screaming. It was the size of a Popsicle stick but had not penetrated deep. He ached, but he had broken no ribs or serious injuries. His streak of luck still held, but he doubted he would be as lucky next time.

Screams and the sounds of commotion continued to fill the corridors for half an hour as the remaining Squid prowled the bowels of the ship. One of the creatures passed by his door as it pursued a passenger fleeing down the corridor. Unlike an octopus or squid out of water, the alien Squid moved quickly on their motile tentacles, much faster than their fleeing human prey. The walls shuddered as the flailing tentacles ripped into the deck, walls, and ceiling to gain traction. By the blood-chilling yell, the creature caught whomever it was chasing. Finally, the screams faded.

The ship was no longer moving. The barely detectable throb of the propellers had stopped. He flicked the light switch experimentally, but no lights came on. The ship was without power and dead in the water. *That can't be good*, he thought. Then, when an apple rolled off the coffee table, he noticed the ship was listing a few degrees to starboard. It wasn't an appreciable amount yet, but judging by the size of the holes the creatures had punched in the ship's hull below the waterline, the ship was doomed.

He knew modern ships were built better than the supposedly unsinkable *Titanic*, but steel didn't float; steel wrapped around a volume of air did. Between the relentless pull of gravity and the inexorable weight of infilling water forcing out the air, the *Radiant Princess* was destined to join the hundreds of other 'unsinkable' ships littering the bottom of the ocean. The thought of being cast adrift in the middle of the ocean frightened him more than the creatures, but he waited a while longer before venturing out of his cabin.

The rampaging Squid had ripped numerous oak panels from the corridor walls and ceiling, exposing the ship's electrical wiring and plumbing. Water poured from a broken overhead pipe, soaking the carpet. Only the emergency lights functioned, with many of them damaged or missing altogether. Even in the dim light, he noticed streaks of blood smearing one section of the wall.

Five or six cabin doors wrenched from their hinges by the Squid lay blocking the corridor. Talent moved one of the doors aside as he made his way toward the stairs. Then, he noticed daylight flooding the corridor from an open door two doors down from his, the cabin of the young woman who had confronted him earlier. Curious, he pushed his way past an overturned housekeeping cart, stepped over the wet sheets and towels that had spilled from it, and ducked under a cabin door half-embedded in the wooden paneling opposite the room. He paused outside the door listening, but heard nothing from inside. He peeked around the edge of the doorway and peered inside the room. He wished he hadn't.

When he saw the extent of the carnage inside the room, his empty stomach threatened to heave its pitiful contents. Then, the stench of the alien creature and the sharp coppery tang of human blood hit him. Twin pools of blood marked the spots the cabin's two occupants, the girl and her roommate, had died. One of them had almost made it safely out of the cabin. A pool of blood stained the carpet just inside the door. A bloody handprint slid along the wall until it abruptly shot up the wall and into the crushed ceiling, as if the creature had yanked her off her feet and deposited her body by the door.

Shards of glass from the shattered sliding balcony door littered the sitting room where the second occupant had died. A loop of small intestine lay coiled in the center of a long, bloody smear in the carpet. A smashed glass coffee table and overturned chair mingled with the remains of both televisions ripped from the wall and squeezed with great force until they had folded in half. Linen, articles of women's underclothing, and souvenirs swept from the bed during the melee filled the space between the bed and the wall.

The tattered curtains formerly covering the balcony door lay in a jumbled heap across the sofa. A woman's leg protruded from beneath the curtains. He knew she was dead – there was too much blood present for survivors – but he had to be certain. He picked his way across the room through the devastation and pulled aside the curtain. The lower half of a woman's leg, torn off just below the knee, lay on the blood-soaked sofa cushion. He fought down the gore rising in his throat. He had not known either of the women's names and couldn't recognize to which the leg belonged, but being able to put a face to the carnage brought home the reality of the macabre scene. He folded the curtain back over the dismembered leg and left the room.

Outside in the hallway, his stomach rebelled. He puked up the previous night's dinner, retching until his stomach was empty. The bile left a vile taste in his mouth, but he had nothing with which he could rinse his mouth. He gripped the machete tighter at a noise coming from a cabin farther aft and crept to investigate. His blood was up. His battle with the creature had been a matter of self-defense. Now, he was angry and wanted revenge for the massacre whose aftermath he had just examined. The girl meant nothing to him. She was just one of the thousands of passengers he had tried hard to ignore, but in death, she became a symbol of the aliens' disregard for human lives. If one of the creatures remained on board the ship, he wanted to get in a few more licks.

The door of the cabin was ajar but intact. He pushed it open and peered in. A middle-aged man dressed only in a white ship's bathrobe sat on the edge of the bed muttering to himself, a bottle of liquor in his hand. His hand shook as he raised the bottle to his lips and took a long swallow. He stared at the smashed balcony door. The brackish smell of seawater and the stink of the alien creature suffused the room. A Glock G25 .380 semi-automatic rested on the bed beside him. Talent walked into the room. He glanced at Talent and held out the bottle.

"Here, you look like you could use a nip, too."

Talent accepted the half-empty bottle of rum, took a swig, rinsed his mouth, and spat it into the hallway. He took a longer swallow and felt the alcohol burn as it slid down his throat. He handed it back and nodded at the balcony door. "Did you fight it off?"

The man shuddered. "Hell no, I was in the shower when the ship heaved over." He gingerly touched a bloody gash in the back of his head. "I think I knocked myself out for a minute or two. I heard the thing trashing my cabin when I came to. By the time I threw on a robe, it was gone. I peeked out the window and saw it. I wish I hadn't. Those people." He looked up at Talent and wrinkled his brow. "What the hell was it, some kind of sea monster?"

"Kind of. They came from a Kaiju."

He paled. "God, another one of them?" He took another swig of rum, and then offered the bottle back to Talent, who decided he had best keep a clear head and refused. The man eyed the machete in Talent's hand and the splashes of yellow and dark purple blood staining his shirt. "It looks like you did some damage."

"Not enough, but I'm alive."

While the man continued drinking, Talent walked into the bathroom and returned with a wet towel and a small first-aid kit he found in the man's travel bag. He wiped the blood from the wound with the towel and inspected it.

"It's not deep. I'll wrap it." Talent cut a piece of gauze, folded it, and placed it over the wound; then, wrapped gauze around his head to hold it in place. When he finished, he said, "You'd better slow down on that rum."

The man looked at Talent as if deciding whether to heed his advice or ignore him, but then set the bottle on the floor at his feet. "My name's James Owens of Chicago … formerly of Chicago. Those Kaiju bastards destroyed my home, hell, my whole city. Now, they're after me again. It's like they've declared a personal vendetta against me."

"Against the whole human race I think," Talent said. "My name's Mark Talent. Were you a cop in Chicago? I noticed the Glock G25. That model is for law enforcement only."

Owens raised an eyebrow. "You know your guns."

"I was a gun dealer back in Arizona."

"Yeah, I was a detective on Chicago's North side for nineteen years. Still have my badge. That's how I managed to bring my weapon with me aboard ship. I'm on my way to Australia to take a job as security chief for a friend's import-export business." He snorted. "Nineteen years on the force and now I'm a friggin' security guard." He waved his hand at the contents of the cabin. "He paid for this cabin and most of this. After Chicago, all I had left was my suit, my two guns, and a bad attitude."

Talent's ears perked up. "Two guns?"

Owens pointed to a dresser drawer. "I've got a .357 Ruger and a box of .357 SIG cartridges in there. You're welcome to it, although it looks like the action is over."

"Not yet. I'm afraid it gets worse. The Kaiju is headed this direction, and the ship is dead in the water. Look, I'm going on deck to see what's happening. You game to come along, or are you going to sit there and finish that bottle?"

Owens tipped the rum bottle over with his bare foot and let it soak into the carpet. "I think I've been drinking a little too much of that lately." He looked up at Talent. His steel gray eyes were those of a sad puppy, but the grim look on his face was that of a bulldog. "Let me get dressed."

While Owens dressed, Talent tried the telephone. As he expected, it wasn't working. "Do you have a cell phone?" he asked Owens.

"I do, but I don't have a signal."

"The ship's communications system must be down. That means no one's coming to help us. We're on our own."

He picked up a piece of gauze, dipped in the rum on the floor, and shoved it between the wound in his shoulder and the shirt material. The bleeding had stopped but the alcohol would reduce the chance of an infection.

Owens stepped out of the bathroom looking a little better. He had dressed in khaki slacks and white Polo shirt, and he had run a comb through his hair. He wore a Chicago White Sox baseball cap to cover his bandaged head. His Glock rested in a shoulder holster tucked under his left armpit. He opened the dresser drawer and removed a locked black case. He fished a key from his pocket, opened the box, and removed a Ruger SP101 .357 six-shot revolver. Its unblemished stainless steel body and pristine black rubber handgrip marked it as seldom used. Its lack of an external hammer, the double-action trigger to prevent accidental discharge, and short three-inch barrel made it the perfect concealed carry weapon. In the box was a nylon holster with two Velcro straps for securing it to the lower leg, two boxes of SIG .357 ammo, and a speed loader. He handed the weapon to Talent, who hefted it in his hand.

"Nice balance," he said.

"I carried a Smith and Wesson .25 automatic as a backup piece for years, until I actually needed it." He shook his head. "Not the weapon you want in a dark alley gunfight. I bought the Ruger instead. It'll knock down a horse."

Talent didn't need to conceal it. He loaded the Ruger, holstered it, and shoved it in the pack pocket of his jeans. He took one box of ammo and the speed loader and shoved them into his front pocket.

"Are you ready?" he asked.

Owens nodded, took a last look around his cabin, and walked out into the corridor.

As they walked toward the aft stairwell, they could hear people talking, or in some cases sobbing, inside their cabins. Owens knocked on a couple of doors, but the occupants were too frightened to answer.

"They could be injured," Owens said to Talent's questioning look, as he stood outside one door waiting for a response.

Talent knew it was the cop in Owens still wanting to protect and serve, that prompted him to check on the passengers. It was a noble gesture, but he had no sympathy for people who cowered behind locked doors. Sometimes you had to stand up and fight, no matter the odds.

"There are three-thousand passengers on this ship," he reminded Owens. "We can't check every cabin." He began walking away.

Owens scowled but followed him down the corridor. When they reached the aft elevators and stairs, to Talent's surprise, the elevators were working. That gave him some hope. If all the power wasn't out, the ship might have sent a distress call. In the well-traveled waters of the South Pacific, the odds were good that some ship was close enough to reach them before they sank. Then he remembered that having a ship nearby hadn't worked out so well for the *Titanic*.

"Do we walk or ride?" Owens asked.

Normally, Talent would have shunned the elevator during an emergency, but his battle with the Squid had left him exhausted.

"Ride," he suggested.

They rode in silence to the Skywalker's Nightclub on Deck 18. Both men drew their weapons and aimed them out the elevator door as it slid open. Talent expected the worst. He was pleasantly surprised to find the club empty of both Squid and corpses. The Squid had been there and had done a thorough job of ransacking it, but the club was not open in the early mornings. Three of the floor-to-ceiling windows were missing, and shards of broken glass littered the carpet. It looked as though a hurricane had blown through the room. The Squid had smashed tables and chairs and tossed them aside. Talent picked a path through the broken glass and debris to look out one of the windows facing the ship's bow.

An alarming number of dead bodies lay in two rows near the pool on Deck 16 just forward of the club. Blankets covered some of the corpses, but others remained uncovered, as if the job of covering them had proven too emotionally difficult. People sat in deck chairs or milled about aimlessly. Some wore the clothing they had slept in. Others wrapped themselves in beach towels or blankets. A handful of white-uniformed ship's officers and an equal number of crewmembers moved among them serving coffee, handing out bottles of water, and tending to wounds. An air of having passed through the storm lay over the survivors, but Talent knew they were simply in the eye of the hurricane. The worst was yet to come, yet the passengers sat around the pool as if at afternoon tea.

As they descended the stairs at the rear of the club, Talent spotted a mutilated corpse floating in the Terrace Pool four decks below them. A swirl of red water encircled the body, as if targeting it for the next wave of creatures from the Kaiju. Talent had no doubt there would be more. The goal of the first attack was to cripple the ship, allowing the Kaiju to harvest the passengers at its leisure.

"The fools need to go below deck. The inside cabins might offer some protection."

"They're suffering from shock," Owens reminded him. "They need time to get their heads on straight."

"They won't have to worry about heads if the Wasps come, and they will."

Owens grimaced. "You're right, of course. Let's talk to one of the ship's officers."

They moved forward along the Sun Deck, passing a few passengers moving in a daze amid the wreckage of wooden lifejacket lockers, tangles of deck chairs, and the glass of broken windows like war refugees after an aerial bombardment. Some clutched a few pitiful personal possessions to their chests, while others dangled lifejackets from the shoulders.

When he and Owens reached the pool, Talent noticed two ship's officers standing outside the fitness room entrance conferring with two crewmen. He skirted the pool and crossed the deck toward them, ignoring pleading glances from frightened passengers. He could offer them no consolation or words of comfort. He wanted to shout at them, to get them up and moving, but decided to leave that to the ship's officers.

One of the officers wore three stripes on his epaulets, the ship's purser. He watched the pair approach, eyeing the pistol in Owens' hand and the kukri strapped to Talent's waist with suspicion.

"You shouldn't have that weapon, sir," he said to Owens.

Talent noted the drying pool of blood beneath the purser's shoes and waved his hand toward the line of corpses. "After this, I would think you would have passed out every pistol on the ship to the crew," Talent replied.

"Only the captain or the first officer can issue firearms."

Talent pointed toward the west and the dark speck of the Kaiju that had grown much larger since the attack. "That's not an island out there. It's a Kaiju. We're dead in the water and sinking fast."

The purser licked his lips nervously. "The lower levels are compartmentalized to prevent sinking."

The purser's denial of the obvious annoyed Talent. He was literally standing in a pool of blood and claiming all was well. Talent recognized bullshit when he heard it. "How many levels are flooded?"

The two officers exchanged glances but didn't reply. One of the crewmen, a maintenance man whose uniform was wet up to his waist and with oil streaking his face, spoke up. "The bilge pumps are out. The lower level of the engine room is flooded. Water is a meter deep in the second level amidships engine room corridors. I don't think anyone made it out of the engine control room." His lips quivered. "I heard screams. The starboard diesel tank ruptured, emptying into the sea. Water is pouring in to replace it. We're down almost three meters at the stern. We tried to seal the leaks, but they're too big and there are too many of them. Some of those creatures ate their way through the hull, and then chewed their way back out again, as if their aim was to sink us."

The purser frowned at the maintenance man. "It's not your place to report to passengers. The captain will make an announcement soon."

The other crewman spoke up. "The bridge isn't answering any calls."

"Have either of you checked in with the bridge?" Talent asked the two officers.

"I thought it more important to calm the passengers and to offer medical treatment," the purser replied.

Talent looked around. "There are maybe twenty people here. There are three thousand hiding in their cabins, minus the dead ones, of course. You need to redefine your priorities."

Owens tapped Talent on the shoulder. "Come on, let's go the bridge. These two dickwads don't have a clue. They'll still be standing here when water crawls up their asses."

The purser, seething at Owens' comment, straightened his back and stared down his nose at Talent. "The captain will determine if and when we abandon ship."

"Abandoning ship isn't a good idea," Talent told him. "Unless I miss my guess, the Kaiju will send something else at us soon, probably Wasps. It just wanted to slow us down. Eighteen fiberglass lifeboats crammed with passengers might look like tasty treats to them. At least on the ship you could secure a few areas and move the passengers there. You might want to tell the captain that, if he's still alive," Talent said as he walked away. "Personally, I wouldn't count on it. The bridge is essentially a big glass box; not very good at keeping out giant alien Squid."

"How long do you think this tub will stay afloat?" Owens asked as he rushed to catch up with Talent.

It was good question; one Talent wished he knew the answer to. He should have asked the only person who seemed to have a clue about what was happening aboard ship, the maintenance man. "I'm no expert on ships, but once the water reaches a certain level, it'll go down fast."

"Maybe we should go stake out a claim on a lifeboat. You know, beat the rush."

"I don't know if a Kaiju sees in color, but floating around like a bright orange and white snack doesn't appeal to me. Let's save that option as a last resort."

Just as they entered the spa, the ship shuddered and groaned, and then rolled a few degrees farther to starboard. Water splashed over the sides of one of the spa's hot tubs and poured in a fast stream across the tiled floor toward them. The ship's stern was settling deeper in the water.

"Maybe it's time for that last resort," Owens suggested.

Talent agreed that facing more of the creatures in a lifeboat beat drowning, but he wasn't ready to call it quits. "Not yet. We need something better than pistols to face down a swarm of Wasps. Maybe someone on the bridge can supply us with something bigger."

Seconds later, the ship's signal horn sounded six short and one long blast.

"Son of a bitch! That's the abandon ship signal," Talent noted. "Someone's alive on the bridge, and he panicked."

Talent took the steps up to the bridge two at a time. He didn't need to open the door. The door and a section of bulkhead adjacent to it were missing, leaving a ragged opening. Three men stood amid the wreckage of electronic equipment and clutter of shattered glass. Almost every piece of equipment on the bridge, from the gyrocompass to the state-of-the-art navigation systems, bore varying degrees of damage. The only commonality was that none of the dozens of screens at the long row of consoles beneath the windows was illuminated. Coagulating blood covered a black leather captain's chair wrenched from its base and tossed beside the door. More blood streaked the carpet and the jagged edges of one of the broken windows. Electronic equipment dangled from the overhead by a tangle of cables and power cords.

One of the men on the bridge, a short and wiry Filipino, had two stripes on his sleeve, the ship's second officer. He eyed the intruders with obvious hostility.

"Who are you?" he demanded. "I need you to leave the bridge immediately and go directly to your lifeboat muster station."

"Easy, slick," Owens said. "We're here to help."

"Where are the captain and first officer?" Talent asked.

The second officer winced and waved his hand around the demolished room. "They were on the bridge when those things attacked. Where do you think they are? Those creatures swarmed aboard and smashed into the bridge. They're gone. They're all gone, the entire bridge watch."

The second officer's voice grew more strident and his hands more animated as he spoke.

"Get a grip, second officer," Talent snapped, calling him by his rank to remind him who he was. "Why did you sound Abandon Ship?"

He jerked his eyes starboard. "Because of that."

Talent looked toward the Kaiju. It seemed to have stopped moving, but a black cloud swirled around it. He knew it was not smoke.

"Wasps," Owens said, correctly identifying the cloud as a swarm of Kaiju Wasps. "We're fucked."

Facing another attack on a sinking ship offered few options. "How much longer will this ship remain afloat?" Talent asked.

The officer glanced around the bridge nervously. The equipment upon which he relied to tell him exactly what was happening throughout the ship lay in pieces on the floor, now worthless junk. He had to rely upon his training, his instinct, and his experience.

"Three hours at most. We can't control the flooding and each section of the ship that fills speeds up the process."

"What about rescue vessels?"

The second officer's face looked stricken. "Communications are out. We have to abandon ship."

Owens scowled. "Son, I've seen those Wasps pull doors off patrol cars. They won't have much trouble with those fiberglass canoes."

The second officer was out of his comfort zone. He had trained for emergencies, but the reality of this one had left him floundering. His normal duties included Navigation, Watch Keep officer, updating the bridge logs, and monitoring safety and bridge equipment, none of which applied to the situation in which he now he found himself.

"We can't stay here," he said.

Talent kept his voice quiet to keep the second officer calm. He looked at his name badge. "Lieutenant de le Rosa, you need to arm as many men as you have weapons and move the passengers to the theater. We can block the passageways with whatever we can find and shoot anything that comes through."

He glanced out the window at the Wasps. A line of them ran from the Kaiju toward the northeast. He figured one of the nearby islands was their target, but they wouldn't ignore a nice big, juicy, cruise ship for long, especially after the trouble they went to in crippling it. "We might not have much time."

De le Rosa hesitated. "I don't know. The captain ..."

"You're the captain now," Talent snapped. "The lives of your passengers are in your hands. You don't have much time to think about it."

De le Rosa nodded his head. "Okay." He turned to the warrant officer beside him. "The ship's intercom is out. Pass out the portable walkie-talkies and inform the crew to move the passengers to the Princess Theater. Locate any other officers you can find and have them meet me in the Wheelhouse Lounge in ten minutes."

Having made a decision and committed himself to its outcome, Talent noted that de le Rosa regained some of his self-assurance.

"Now, you two gentlemen accompany me and Able Seaman Pratang to the weapons locker to help arm the security personnel."

"Now you're taking," Talent said.

"Do you have shotguns for skeet shooting?" Owens asked.

"Yes, twenty of them. They're in a locker in the entertainment officer's office. I'll send someone for them."

It's a start, Talent thought. "We'll need any weapons we can scrounge up – pistols, fire axes, hell, even butcher knives from the kitchens. This is going to get messy."

Talent wished he had brought his arsenal of weapons with him. He felt severely under armed with only a borrowed .357, a kukri, and a knife. "You go with de le Rosa," he told Owens. "I want to keep an eye on the Wasps."

"Yell if you need help," Owens said.

Talent looked out at the line of Wasps and frowned. "If I need help, it'll probably be too late to yell."

8

Friday, Dec. 15, 11:30 a.m. CST   Houston, TX –

While Mark Talent was worrying about Saturday's breakfast aboard the *Radiant Princess*, with the nineteen-hour time difference, Doctor Gate Rutherford was sitting down to Friday's lunch with Carl Caruthers of NASA, Director of the Johnson Space Center. At 6'1'', Caruthers was just as tall as Rutherford, but where Rutherford was thin and wiry; the director was as broad-shouldered as a pro linebacker was and big enough to box as a heavyweight. He tore into his 18-ounce rare T-bone steak with gusto, while Rutherford picked at his barely touched poached salmon. Caruthers cocked his head slightly and pointed his fork at Rutherford's plate.

"You'd better eat that, Gate. If you lose any more weight, we can strap a parachute to your ass and stick you on top of an SLS vehicle as the escape system."

Rutherford, freshly shaven and groomed for the occasion, tried to smile at the director's jibe at his appearance, but it emerged on his lips as a grimace. As usual, Caruthers was immaculately dressed, looking as if ready to act as NASA's public spokesperson at a press conference. Gate was uncomfortable in his best grey suit that now fit him like a funeral shroud, drooping from his shoulders and billowing outward from his chest as he leaned forward across the table. He pushed the plate aside and answered with a curt, "I'm not hungry. I need your help."

"You need a keeper," Caruthers' answered, and then laid his fork warily on the edge of his plate and sighed. "Okay, I get it, no more remarks on your appearance. What can I do for you?"

"I need a foot in the door, yours."

Caruthers frowned. "You burned a lot of bridges with your accusatory tirades. Some very important people got the public spotlight shined on them. They didn't like that."

Rutherford snorted. "I can't help that. No one would listen to me. Now, they will. I was right."

"I'll grant you that, but politicians and generals have longer memories than elephants. Hell, they have staff just to keep up with the names of people on their shit list. You're Turd Numero Uno on most of them. Okay, the Kaiju landed where you predicted it would, and the aliens have changed patterns just as you said they would. You're batting a thousand so far. What do you need from me?"

Rutherford had considered the question carefully before asking the director for the meeting. He had even suggested the director's favorite steakhouse to set the mood. He needed to keep his wish list short or risk alienating the only person who still had faith in him. Even truncated, his list had some heavy items on it. "First, I need access to the NEOWISE Infrared Near-Earth Orbiting Body telescope. I need a closer look at Haumea."

Caruthers paused; then nodded. "I think I can arrange for you to access NEOWISE for a few hours."

Rutherford shook his head. "I need it for forty-eight hours at least."

"Two days!" Caruthers bellowed, drawing a few hard glares from restaurant patrons and eliciting a concerned look from one Stetson and black jeans-clad waitress. "Hell, I had to sell my soul to bring it out of hibernation when the first Kaiju appeared. The Near-Earth Orbiting boys would carve out my liver if I tried to co-opt their bird."

"I need a look at both sides of Haumea. That might take a while."

Caruthers cocked a bushy eyebrow at Rutherford. "Sure of what?"

Rutherford hated to reveal so much so soon, but he knew Caruthers would demand details before risking his career. "I believe the alien base is on Haumea." Before Caruthers could protest, he added, "I know I suggested it months ago, but the DRS satellite data points to Haumea as the origin of the Kaiju pods. If they are there, Infrared will spot any heat signatures."

Caruthers hung his head and shook it slowly. "My God, Gate. You don't ask for much, do you? I'll see what I can do. They're NASA boys after all and they're team players, but they're also tight-assed SOBs just like you. They'll want something bright and shiny in return for two days of dedicated observation time."

"Tell them that if I'm right, NASA will be sending a probe to Haumea ASAP. They can have all the access they want to search for asteroids."

"A probe? You're pretty free with NASA's budget."

"If the aliens are there, the military will gladly open their pocketbook to bankroll a probe. They'll just buy one less aircraft carrier or something to cover the cost."

"There's that. Okay, I'll put the deal to them. They'll probably drool on their pocket protectors for more asteroid-searching capability. They might just go for it."

Rutherford smiled at the waitress who was still eying them suspiciously to assure her that her two guests weren't mad men, at least one wasn't. "There's one more thing."

Caruthers stared at him. "Jesus, Gate. You don't want much, do you?"

"I need data from the GEMS."

Caruthers' face clouded and he narrowed his eyes. "The Gravity and Extreme Magnetism Small Explorer mission was cancelled six years ago. You know that."

"I also know the Air Force revived the mission and launched GEMS on a Delta IV Heavy two months ago, along with a new, improved version of *Janus*. Sam Ahern and Sanjay Patangan are running the GEMS operation from Goddard."

"How the hell did you … That's classified information, Gate. I wouldn't let just anybody know you know about it. How do you know by the way?"

"I know a nuclear payload tech. He spent three days at the Cape working on a top-secret Air Force satellite. I guessed from his involvement, it had something to do with warheads. The military bitched about *Janus's* failure for months after the Kaiju arrived. Then, they went silent. Sometimes it's not what you hear but what you don't hear."

"How did you know they sent up three nuclear warheads? Even I wasn't in the loop on that one. I only found out because they needed a manned mission to correct a faulty alignment thruster. For that they needed Johnson."

Rutherford grinned. "Three? I didn't know how many. I just assumed they wouldn't be satisfied unless they built it bigger and better. Why waste the opportunity to spend taxpayers' money with Congress so eager to assure its constituents it's doing everything in its power to thwart the alien invasion? I'm surprised they settled for three missiles."

"How did you learn about GEMS?" He scowled. "Did Patangan blab? He always was a talkative bastard. If he cornered you at a conference or a party, you couldn't get away from him. You just had to smile, nod your head politely, and pray someone came to rescue you."

"No one talked, Carl. Sam Ahern has been working for Bell Labs since they pulled the plug on GEMS six years ago. Three months ago, he suddenly took a sabbatical. By itself, it meant nothing, but then he immediately went to Goddard. His specialty is black hole detection by measurement of gravity distortions. I drew a straight line between point

A and point B and got GEMS. I assume the military is scanning the Oort Cloud for an alien ship. They won't find one there."

"I'm glad to see you back behind a telescope, but I think your real talent lies in espionage. I'm guessing you'll go public if I refuse."

Rutherford rolled his eyes. "You know me better than that, Carl. No blackmail. I'm just letting you know what I know to cut through all the bullshit and the red tape. I don't have time for Senate sub-committees or chain-of-command decisions. We can keep this in the NASA family and keep the military out."

Caruthers snorted. "Good luck with that. The military has had their collective noses up my ass since the Orion fiasco."

Rutherford understood the director's reluctance to bypass the military. Although publically touted as a hero for destroying the alien communications pod on the moon, Commander Langston's deliberate act of crashing the Orion *Lunar One* spacecraft had ruffled a few feathers. NASA had excluded the military authorities from the decision-making loop, and because of the manner in which the military hierarchy worked, they couldn't believe that the director had not abetted or at least given his tacit approval to Langston's actions.

"If I can pick up gravity distortions around Haumea, we'll know for certain if the aliens are there." He decided to play his hold card. "If we can detect gravity wave distortions between Earth and Haumea, we could have months advance warning of another inbound Kaiju instead of a few days, or no warning at all, as with this last one. That should make the military happy. They're going to send more Kaiju. You can bet on it. I know how the aliens think. I wouldn't be here begging hat in hand if I didn't think I was right."

He sat back and studied his friend's face, searching for something in the NASA director's troubled eyes that offered a glimmer of hope. He had spread all his cards on the table. He had counted on their friendship to get this far, but he knew Caruthers would not allow personal feelings to sway him. Any change of procedure or sudden shift in focus of the GEMS or the NEOWISE satellites could set back their research for years. If he was wrong, there would be serious hell to pay, and Caruthers would be the first one to suffer, but he wasn't wrong. He couldn't be.

Finally, Caruthers cleared his throat. Rutherford was so tense, the sudden sound made him jump. Caruthers spoke slowly. "I can't make any promises, Gate, but you have an uncanny sixth sense about these things. That's what made you such a good catastrophist. I'll go out on a limb for you one more time, but I don't know how much weight my word carries."

"Tell the military that I'm certain another alien pod is headed this way even now. We need to know where it's going to land."

Caruthers wrinkled his brow, reached for his wine glass, and drained it in one gulp. "Are you that certain?"

"Why send a single Kaiju to such a remote location? I know I predicted it, but I assumed they would send more than one. What can a single Kaiju do in a territory as large as the Southern Pacific Ocean? It's there for a reason other than wiping out the human population one island at a time."

Caruthers shook his head. "You scare me, Gate, you surely do." He pushed his half-eaten steak away from him and looked disdainfully at his empty wine glass. "I think I just lost my appetite."

"Now you know why I can't eat."

Caruthers raised his glass and caught the waitress's attention. "If you're right, Gate, you may be announcing the end of mankind."

Rutherford sighed. He knew he was right, but his certainty offered no consolation. "Now you know why I can't sleep."

The waitress rushed to the table with a bottle of wine. As she re-filled the director's glass, he said, "I hope you're in no hurry. I may need a few of these."

9

Saturday, Dec. 16, 10:00 a.m.   *Radiant Princess,* north of Enderbury Island –

For Talent, the waiting was harder than facing more of the creatures. Inexplicably, the Kaiju had approached no closer. It sat there like a lump of coal floating in the ocean. A steady stream of Wasps continued to fly to the nearby islands and return laden with a cargo of human bodies. He was thankful the creature was too far away to witness the feeding process close-up. He was spared that particular horror. He had read the reports – humans, some still alive, dropped into that giant tentacle-encircled maw, multiple rows of serrated teeth grinding the bodies to a pulp, and depositing them in a lake of acid to digest and feed the myriad of creatures living within the Kaiju's body.

The ship's crew, the two-hundred-fifty or so remaining from the original twelve hundred, abandoned lowering the lifeboats. They rounded up the passengers and directed them to the Princess Theatre. Upon learning that they were not evacuating the ship, many passengers chose to remain on the open decks or returned to the imagined safety of their cabins. A few refused to leave their seats in the lifeboats, fearful the boats would leave without them.

Most of the sixteen-hundred seats in the dimly lit theater were empty, a far cry from the crowd packing the theater during one of the musicals he had attended a few nights earlier. It had been a review of 60's rock, including a Beatles medley, his favorite group. Those two hours of pleasure now seemed a lifetime away, as distant as the Golden Age of rock and roll itself. Some of the crew and a few of the passengers carried pistols, shotguns, or fire axes – anything that might offer a defense against the return of the Squid or an attack by Wasps. Many of the hastily armed people looked uncomfortable with the responsibility of defending the passengers thrust upon them. Some had probably never fired a gun at anything but paper targets, skeets, or beer cans.

The ship had settled another six feet deeper in the water in the last hour. Talent had ventured below decks to Deck 3 and watched the water steadily creeping up the stairs. If the Wasps didn't attack soon, they would have to abandon ship or go down with it into the briny deep. He hoped that wasn't the Kaiju's plan all along, to separate them from the ship for easy pickings. He hated to think that the creature was that smart.

They had barricaded the corridors leading to the theater from the elevators and the Wheelhouse Lounge on Decks 6 and 7 with tables, chairs, desks, cases of booze from the bars, and anything else that could fill a gap in the defensive wall. They had blocked the smaller side doors and the doors to the backstage area with stage scenery, wheeled carts, forklifts, costume racks, and boxes of merchandise stripped from the boutiques. In spite of the preparations, an air of despondency lay over the gathered crowd so thick Talent could taste it. With only a few emergency lights working, they sat in the dark like frightened children who had switched off the lights to hide from monsters, or like settlers huddled in the fort waiting for the Indians to attack. This time, Talent was not rooting for the Indians.

Owens walked over to him carrying a twenty-gauge shotgun taken from the sports equipment room. He and Talent had removed the useless birdshot from several boxes of shells and replaced them with steel ball bearing scrounged from one of the ship's machine shops. They had not had time to do more, but Talent doubted they would use even those few. If an army couldn't stop them, how much resistance could a group of untrained passengers offer against the creatures? Unlike most of the people in the theater, Owens seemed at ease. Like Talent, he knew that if any of the creatures broke through the barricades, they would all die a horrible death, but he was eager to inflict some damage before he died.

"Walking forward along the deck is like walking uphill," Owens groaned, noting the ten-degree incline toward the ship's stern. "It's going to be hard to hold on to a seat with one hand to keep from sliding downhill and fight off the Wasps with the other."

"I'll see if I can find you a seat belt," Talent replied.

"That would be nice. By the way, have I told you I can't swim?"

It was the second time Owens had mentioned the fact to him. Talent suspected he was telling the truth. "I don't think I've got time to teach you, but I wouldn't worry too much about it."

Owens sighed. "I wish they would hurry up and come."

Talent arched an eyebrow at Owens' odd remark, but he knew how the Chicagoan felt. Every groan of the sinking ship, each time the ship suddenly lurched and shuddered as another area flooded, drove home the fact that their refuge was rapidly becoming useless. Inside the theater, they could bring several weapons to bear on individual creatures as they came in through the chokeholds of the doorways. If forced to evacuate the ship, as seemed imminent, they would have only one or two armed people to defend the one-hundred-sixty or so passengers cramped into each lifeboat.

"Patience is a virtue," he told Owens.

Owens sneered. "I've never been very virtuous. Let's get it done."

"Are you in a hurry to die?"

Owens' face turned cold and hard and his tone was bitter as he said, "I died when Chicago died. I've just been marking time since then."

"Don't check out too early on me," Talent said. "You're the only person I trust to have my back on this ship."

Owens smiled and rested the shotgun across his shoulders behind his head. "Oh, I've got your back, all right. If one of those things grabs me to haul me off, you'll do the honors, right?"

Talent nodded. "No problem."

De le Rosa walked over. After his initial moment of panic, he now seemed calm and collected. Talent figured most of it was a show for the passengers. Inside, he was as frightened as Talent was.

"We bypassed the dead comm tower and jury rigged an antenna to the radio. I'm not sure of the range, but we managed to send out an SOS. A nearby freighter acknowledged and is on the way here."

"Great," Talent replied. "How long?"

De le Rosa's cool façade waver a little. "Three hours."

Talent's hopes faded. "We don't have three hours. We might not have three minutes."

A walkie-talkie burst into life as one of the crewmembers that the third officer had stationed outside in the corridor reported in. "They're here," he yelled.

Overhearing his report, the noise level of the crowd rose tenfold as the first fingers of panic began to ripple through the crowd. People wept or prayed individually or in groups. Most had not witnessed the earlier Squid attack or watched videos of previous Wasp attacks in the U.S. Their fear, however badly it gripped them, would become overwhelming once the carnage began. Talent hoped the people selected to defend the crowd would not be among the first to cut and run.

"I had better see to the passengers," de le Rosa said, and then tuned, and walked away.

The crewman who had reported the Wasps' arrival burst through the door a few moments later. Two other crewmen quickly shut the door behind him and barred it with a steel pipe wedged through the handles. It was the best they could do, but Talent knew the makeshift lock would not hold for long against a Wasp onslaught.

Owens glared at the door and pumped a shell into the chamber of the shotgun. Talent made sure the reloader for the .357 was ready to go. He set it and the open box of cartridges on the seat beside him within easy reach. He had chosen a spot on the starboard side of Promenade Deck on the theater's upper level. The Kaiju was off the starboard side of the ship, and he figured the starboard side offered the Wasps the easiest access to the theater. If the Squid returned, it would not matter. They could bore right through the hull and enter the theater from any place they chose.

Owens moved across the aisle to the far side of the door. Between him and Talent, stood two crewmembers armed with a pistol and a shotgun and a nervous passenger armed with a shotgun. Farther back spread out across the top of the stairs, half a dozen passengers armed with fire axes and boat hooks waited. Although from different backgrounds, ethnicities, and countries, each person had one thing in common, a look of dread anticipation in their eyes; all, that is, except for one of the crewmembers, a short Filipino bartender about twenty-five years old standing next to him. She gripped the pistol with both hands as if she knew how to use it, her legs braced and bent slightly at the knees for balance. Instead of fear, her face was a mask of burning rage. Talent thought that was a good thing. A little honest rage could make up for a lack of courage or scarcity of skill. She glanced at Talent and noticed his scrutiny of her.

"Those bastards killed my roommate," she said. "We've been together for five years. Now, she's gone. I'm going to kill at least one of them before they get me. I have to watch it die."

The sound of shattering glass filtered through the barricades. The creatures were breaking through the outside doors into the elevator lobby. Passengers began fighting their way down the main staircase to the lower level, running toward the stage away from the doors. The frenzied mob trampled people too feeble or too slow to keep up and shoved others over rows of seats or down the steps in their eagerness to escape. Talent tried to ignore the crowd, but he knew the stampeding passengers would limit the armed defenders' fields of fire, thereby reducing their effectiveness.

The rising din of the crowd and the scent of blood from injured passengers fed the Wasps' fury. They attacked the last barricades with increased zeal. It had taken the passengers an hour to erect the barriers, but the alien Wasps demolished them in less than five minutes.

Talent got his first up-close view of a live Wasp as it pushed its head through a gap in the pile of rubble. If he had not already confronted the Squid, the sight might have disheartened him. In the confined space of the corridor, it had folded its wings across its back. It scuttled down the corridor on its two pair of hind legs, reaching out the two forward pair to grasp the handles of the doors. The razor-edged talons at the tip of the appendages looked like four scythes. The door rattled but held until a shotgun blast shattered the glass door. He glared at the Malaysian cook who had fired his shotgun.

"Wait until they're inside, fool! You're wasting ammunition."

Chagrined, the cook nodded, licked his lips, and pointed the shotgun at the entrance; then, realized he had forgotten to pump a fresh shell into the chamber. He glanced at the others in embarrassment and reloaded. They didn't have long to wait. The first Wasp yanked at the door until the hinges bowed and then snapped. A salvo of bullets and shotgun pellets killed it as it burst through the open doors. Its demise was more a matter of luck than the result of a well-aimed fusillade.

Another Wasp clambered over its comrade's corpse. The defenders rushed out of its way, still firing at it. It finally went down with several large holes in its head, but not before slicing into a passenger's chest with one of its long, curved talons. The man's expression was one of disbelief and horror. He clutched at the gaping wound with his hands as he fell. Both Wasp and passenger hit the floor at the same time. Talent had no time to check on the man, but he judged by the size of the gash in the man's chest, and the amount of blood slowly spreading around him, he didn't have a chance.

More of the creatures entered the theater from other entrances. A flapping sound like sails in a breeze filled the theater as Wasps took to wing in the open space. Now the defenders had to think in three-dimensions to avoid death from above. Gunfire exploded in all directions. Talent was amazed they weren't shooting each other in a Wild West crossfire. He and Owens directed their fire at a Wasp that had cornered two older women. The ex-Chicago cop began striding toward the creature as Talent reloaded. His face was grim and his lips twisted into an angry snarl. He pumped shells into the shotgun and fired until it was empty, and then produced his pistol and continued firing. The overeager detective blocked Talent's line of fire.

"Damn!" Talent yelled, and turned his attention to a second Wasp attacking the Filipino bartender. True to her word, she didn't run. Her anger and thirst for revenge fueled her desperate assault. Her bullets were finding their mark, but the small caliber pistol couldn't penetrate the creature's overlapping plates of ebony armor covering the nine-foot-long orange-brown body. As the Wasp moved, small gaps appeared between the plates, but she was firing wildly without taking aim, and the bullets were bouncing off.

"Aim between the eyes," he yelled at her. "Shoot at anything that's not black and shiny."

She nodded and took careful aim at one of the eyes. It took her two shots to hit it, but the creature reared in pain, exposing a gap in its armored abdomen. Talent shoved his pistol into its holster with his right hand and pulled the kukri from its sheath at his waist with his left in one fluid motion. He ducked beneath a deadly flailing forelimb and landed on his knees. With a double-handed grip on the machete's handle, he sliced into the belly along the gap in its armor. The flesh was tough and unyielding. It was like hacking into a six-inch-thick piece of dried jerky, but his anger sparked an adrenaline surge that lent him strength to force the tip of the blade deeper into the alien flesh. Using his body weight, he pulled the kukri downward and across the creature's belly.

An explosion of hot, yellow ichor drenched his arms and chest. The creature flung its body down to crush him, but Talent rolled between two rows of seats that held the creature's weight off him. While the injured Wasp attempted to extricate itself from the tangle of seats and railings, Talent released the machete, grabbed the .357, and emptied it into the open wound. He had no idea where the creature's vital organs were located, but his luck held. The Wasp hissed loudly, shuddered, and went still. He yanked free the machete and reloaded the pistol.

As he crawled from beneath the Wasp, he spotted the bartender going head to head with a second Wasp. She wore a smile on her face as her barrage of bullets forced the creature to retreat, but she failed to see a third one diving from the ceiling toward her. Before Talent could shout a warning or bring his own weapon to bear, the hovering Wasp clasped her body to its chest and rammed home the stinger. The sharp barb exited just below her right ribcage amid a spray of blood. She glanced down at the object protruding from her midriff and raised the pistol to her head. Talent assumed she was seeking a quick way out, but to his surprise, she lifted the pistol higher and fired one last round into the creature's face. Then, it yanked her from the floor and flew away to join a growing line of Wasps bearing similar packages of dead or sedated passengers back to the Kaiju.

Her courage and final act of desperate defiance gave him goose bumps. He vowed to go out the same way, kicking ass and taking names. Although he was a full-blooded Tohono O'odham, he had always identified with the more aggressive Southwestern tribes, such as the Apache or the Comanche, than his historically peaceful people. The warlike Apache had called the Tohono O'odham *Papago*, a derogatory term meaning tepary bean eaters, a name the Spanish Conquistadors kept alive for centuries. His refusal to be a traditional tribal member had earned him the name *Lobo*, a lone wolf, a name he had embraced with pride. He had used his reputation as a lone wolf to become a recluse, to avoid mingling with people of his own tribe or Whites, except on business.

Why then, he wondered, *am I ready to die for strangers*?

The number of defenders fell rapidly, as the Wasps systematically attacked anyone with a weapon with abandoned frenzy. They began pouring through the entrances as the remaining defenders fell back under the concentrated onslaught. Two of the ship's officers, standing out even in the muted light in their white uniforms, directed a stream of passengers out one of the side exits, many of them dropping their weapons as they fled. Talent shook his head in disbelief. Where did they think they were going? Alone and out in the open they would present easy targets.

He didn't have time to dwell on their fate. One persistent creature forced him backwards down the side stairs to the lowest tier of seats. It had learned from watching the demise of its brethren. It kept its head low to avoid exposing any weakness in its underside armor plating and continuously bobbed its head to foil any shot to its vulnerable eyes.

Talent felt the wall at his back and cursed. He had allowed the creature to back him into a corner. Suddenly, the Wasp turned and thrust its stinger at him like a Bengal Lancer. The barbed tip ripped splinters from the wooden wall as it withdrew. He parried the second thrust with the kukri he held in his left hand but the force of the blow numbed his hand. As the creature edged closer, he dropped over the balcony railing and landed on the raised walkway crossing the theater. When the Wasp leaned over the railing in pursuit, he fired into the soft tissue inside the creature's open mouth. It reared, bellowed, and collapsed with the upper part of its body flung over the railing, missing his head by only a few inches. When one of the legs twitched, Talent placed the barrel of the pistol beneath a gap in the armor and fired one more shot into the side of its head to make certain it was dead.

He sought refuge in one of the balcony boxes to reload and catch his breath. As the feeling slowly returned to his left hand still, he discovered he had sprained his wrist. He flexed it experimentally and groaned as a sharp, stabbing pain lanced through it.

"This sucks," he groaned.

The carpeted deck beneath him shuddered three times in rapid succession, followed by the loud screech of tearing metal. He cursed under his breath. The sound could mean only one thing; the Squid had returned to join the Wasps in the attack. They were hastening the ship's demise by punching more holes in the already compromised hull. His fighting platform was rapidly sinking beneath him. It was time to abandon ship and take his chances at sea.

His reloader rolled across the floor as the ship suddenly listed several degrees to starboard. He lunged for it, missing it by inches. It rolled off the edge of the balcony to the floor below. He cursed and began reloading one cartridge at a time. Owens had disappeared during Talent's fight with the Wasp. He searched the room for the detective and saw him standing beside a man wielding an axe at the corner below the stage. They were defending a small crowd of passengers against one of the Wasps. As he watched, the man with the axe went down, slashed almost in half by a swing of the creature's forelimb. A passenger tried to climb up onto the stage; only to have her back ripped open shoulder to waist by the same creature.

Owens was weakening. The barrel of the shotgun sagged to the floor between shots. Each time, he lifted and fired more slowly, leaving himself exposed. If not for the easy pickings of panicked passengers around him rushing within reach of the creature's jaws and legs in their haste to escape, it would have killed him already.

Talent watched with disgust as one man dragged a young girl in front of him as a shield when the Wasp lunged at him. The girl died; he lived. Talent was so enraged that he almost shot the man, but decided to save his ammo. He felt a sense of cosmic karma when a second Wasp flew overhead, ripped the man's head from his body, and continued toward the exit with it dangling from its talons.

The emergency lights went out, leaving the theater in complete darkness except for the minute scraps of light filtering in down the corridors and through the doors. The faint light created long, deep shadows, making it more difficult to target the Wasps. The Wasps, on the other hand, seemed to have no difficulty in finding their prey in the dark.

The theater was clearing of Wasps as the creatures killed and carted away the passengers that hadn't already fled in panic. The muffled screams and scattered reports of gunfire from outside the theater confirmed his belief that the creatures were waiting for just such a foolhardy attempt to reach the lifeboats. He spotted an opening in a side door that would take him down the corridor to the exit and felt an overwhelming urge to go through it, leaving the remaining passengers to fend for themselves. He had known Owens only a few hours; and yet, felt closer to the Chicago cop than most of the members of his own tribe.

It was likely they would all die together, but he decided to give Owens a fighting chance.

Wires from the overhead stage lighting ripped out by the Wasps dangled from the ceiling, providing the quickest way down. The balcony was higher than the stage. He quickly judged how much cable he needed and jammed his pistol down the front of his jeans. He grabbed the cable with both hands, being careful of his injured wrist, and wound his leg in the cable. With a running start, he dropped over the side of the balcony. The cable jerked as he reached the end of its slack, sending shooting pain through his wrist, but he held on.

The arc of his swing carried him across to the stage. He stifled the urge to emit a Tarzan yell. In the dim light, he misjudged his landing and released too late. He dropped six feet to the stage and skidded to a stop on his boot heels. He pulled his pistol from the waistband of his jeans with his left hand, leaped from the stage, and landed astride the Wasp's back just in front of the first pair of wings.

Clinging to one of the wings with his good right hand as it was were the bull rope he used to stay atop bucking bulls in Tucson's *La Fiesta de los Vaqueros*, he fired a round into a small gap in the creature's ebony armor just behind the head with his left hand. Cocking the hammer and squeezing the trigger brought agony to his wrist, but he bit back on the pain and fired two more rounds. The giant Wasp bounced and twisted its body in its attempt to dislodge him, but he had always done well in the bull riding and bronco riding events at rodeos. The certainty that bucking off would mean his death kept him clinging to his precarious perch. Seizing the opportunity Talent had presented him, Owens rammed his shotgun into the creature's throat and pulled the trigger. Talent jerked his head back just in time to avoid a geyser of ball bearings and gooey Wasp blood shooting from the fist-sized exit wound. His alien steed stumbled and collapsed on the floor. He slid off and faced Owens.

"It's time to go," he said.

Owens looked at the few remaining passengers around him. "They're coming with us."

Talent figured the odds of reaching a lifeboat and lowering it into the water before a Wasp or a Squid got them was slim to none. Riding herd over a group of frightened passengers lowered their odds even further, but he knew Owens would never abandon them. He nodded. "Okay, but we're going to have to move quietly. These things have excellent hearing."

They climbed onstage and passed through a side door into a corridor filled with costumes and stage props. There were no emergency lights. Owens used the light of his cell phone to pick a path through hanging racks of sequined tights, gold lame dresses, feather boas, and rows of hats. Gunfire outside punctuated the muted screams of people and the screeches of the creatures. Talent smiled as he recognized the familiar bark of an Mk46 Squad Automatic Weapon.

"Sounds like the cavalry has arrived," he said to Owens.

He pushed through the tangle of costumes toward the exit. Just as he reached for the knob of a second door leading into the main corridor, the sound of heavy caliber weapons erupted just outside the door.

The door pushed open and a grim-faced black man clad in military camo stared at him. "Don't just stand there. If you want to live, you'd better get your ass in gear and come with me."

He turned and disappeared back into the corridor. Talent glanced at Owens. "I say we follow him."

Talent's luck was still holding.

10

Saturday, Dec. 16, 1000 hours   *USS Mississippi,* eighty miles north of Enderbury –

When word of the sinking cruise ship reached the *USS Mississippi,* Commander Murdock defied his orders and set a course to rendezvous with the *Radiant Princess.* He couldn't order Walker to help. Fire Team Bravo's mission was more important than the rescue of a sinking ship, but Walker applauded Murdock' decision. Like the captain, he wasn't going to let three thousand passengers die. He had seen enough death in his lifetime. His orders required them to make contact with the Kaiju. If it was near the cruise ship, conducting the rescue mission offered a win-win scenario.

It would take the *Mississippi* over two hours to reach the stricken cruise ship. Murdock radioed the V2-Osprey and ordered it to return to the sub. After reaching the surfaced sub, the pilot had once again shown his skill at hovering by keeping the landing gear barely touching the sub's foredeck in the rolling sea. This placed the side door within an easy leap, saving the time required to climb ropes. The pilot didn't mention his low fuel situation, but Walker knew the Osprey would never make it back to Hawaii if it continued on to the cruise ship. The pilot would have to take his chances on finding fuel at one of the small airfields on one of the nearby islands and hope he didn't find Wasps waiting for him instead.

When they reached the *Radiant Princess,* Walker noticed the ship's stern low in the water. He also noted the swarm of Wasps buzzing the ship. He spoke to the pilot.

"Hover over the Sun Deck. We'll rope down to the Lido Deck beside the pool. Once we're down, make one pass with your weapons to cover us while we set up; then, get the hell out of here."

The pilot nodded.

"Good luck," Walker called to him.

The pilot gave him thumbs up and grinned.

They approached on the ship's port side. As they got closer, Walker saw several lifeboats already in the water. Wasps had ripped the fiberglass roof from one of them and were busy plucking passengers from the lifeboat. A second lifeboat had suffered a similar fate and had capsized. The pilot made one pass along the length of the cruise ship, giving the crew chief a clear shot out the open side door with his M240 machinegun. He killed the two Wasps attacking the lifeboat, but the sky was full of the creatures. Reluctantly, the pilot abandoned the lifeboats to their inevitable fate and returned to the cruise ship.

He waited until he was almost over the ship before cutting back on the power and converting the nacelles for hovering. He expertly edged the Osprey into the confined space between the ship's communications towers and the deck railings. The engines' backwash scattered towels and chairs across the deck. Walker took the first rope down. As soon as his feet touched the deck, he took a position to cover Costas with his 7.62 mm SCAR. Costas hit the deck behind him two seconds later and moved to the opposite side of the Osprey. Simultaneously, Captain McGregor and Corporal Hightower descended the second rope. As soon as all four were in position, Walker signaled the remaining five members of the fire team to join them.

So far, the Wasps hadn't spotted them on the deck, but they had noticed the arrival of the V-22 Osprey. The vehicle had spent exactly eighteen seconds hovering above the deck to disgorge the team before the pilot rotated the nacelles and zoomed away. As soon as the Osprey took off, the camera-operated Gau-19 minigun on the Osprey's belly opened up on the creatures, swiveling back and forth in tight arcs as it ripped into their bodies with a stream of .50 caliber bullets. Two Wasps died instantly. Another fell into the sea with shredded wings. The crew chief fired bursts from his M240, adding a flurry of 7.62 mm bullets to the fray.

Instead of the single-covering pass Walker had requested, the pilot made three daring strafing runs across the deck of the sinking cruise ship, killing at least a dozen Wasps. On his outward leg, he passed over the lifeboats, offering what protection he could to the hapless passengers before lack of fuel forced him to break off and head to the nearest island. Walker hoped he made it.

When the roar of the Osprey's engines faded, Walker heard small-arms fire coming from inside the ship toward amidships. A line of Wasps converged on the area a few decks below them. His face turned grim at the bodies the Wasps carried as they winged their way toward the Kaiju. Memories of the digestive pool inside Kaiju Nusku's head were still too vivid to talk about. His written and his oral reports to the military had been the last time he had discussed the horrors he had seen with anyone. He turned to Costas, who cradled his .50 caliber Barrett M107 SASR in his arms as he peered around the corner.

"Costas, take three men and move aft down the port side. I'll move down the starboard side with the others. We'll meet in the elevator area amidships. That seems to be where the action is."

Costas looked at the bodies lying around the pool, some covered with blankets, others lying in the open. "Looks like they had some action here."

Captain McGregor motioned to Walker. He pointed to his eyes and lifted two fingers. They were about to have some company.

Walker motioned to Privates Wiggins, Stimson, and Sergeant Rhoades to join Costas. McGregor, Corporal Hightower, Specialist Perez, and Private Watts would accompany him. The men needed no prompting to spread out and take cover. McGregor had trained them well. He hoped the Wasps were simply inquisitive and would pass them by. Any firefight would slow them down and draw the attention of more unwelcomed guests. The Wasps might not have spotted them, but they smelled the corpses and the blood smearing the deck and came closer to investigate. Walker waited until both creatures were fully out of sight of their brethren before signaling to fire.

Hightower, a 6'1', 255-pound bruiser from New Jersey, cut loose with his M134 mini gun. Six rotating barrels spat a swarm of its own, hurling 7.62 mm bullets toward the nearest creature at 2,800 ft/sec. The lightweight version of the minigun he carried weighed half as much as the larger version, but he held the 41-pound minigun like a water hose spraying death and destruction at the Wasps. Spent shell casings bounced across the deck, as the deadly hail of bullets ripped into alien flesh. Chips of ebony armor and globules of icterine yellow blood flew from the creature's body and head. Each new chink in its armor exposed more flesh. Hightower, in a state of murderous ecstasy, emptied the 5,000-round belt in just over a minute, and then slipped another into the weapon from the four he wore crisscrossing his chest.

The remaining members of the team concentrated on the second creature. 5.56 mm rounds from redheaded Sergeant Rhoades' Mk46 SAW and the combined firepower of HK MP5s firing Smith and Wesson .40 caliber rounds produced the same effect on the second Wasp. Within two minutes, both creatures were lifeless hulks, their bullet-riddled bodies staining the decks with alien blood.

A shadow fell over Walker. He glanced up to see a Wasp crouching on the Sports Deck above him watching the display of firepower. It hissed loudly and bounced up and down on its front legs. Walker didn't know if the creature was angry at the death of its kin or eager to eat him. He raised his SCAR L-CQC and poured a clip of 7.62 mm rounds into the creature's head. Injured but still functioning, the Wasp unfurled its wings and leaped into the air. Costas brought it down short with three quick .50 caliber rounds from his SASR. He grinned at Walker.

"It's like shooting skeets," he said.

Walker knew Costas would soon have plenty of opportunity to shoot skeets. The noise of the weapons fire had alerted the Wasps to their presence. A dozen of the creatures peeled off from the stream of inbound Wasps and aimed directly at them. They didn't have time to do a casual search along the deck. They needed to get to the passengers quickly and keep the Wasps at bay until help arrived. Splitting up was no longer an option. He pointed to the stairs on either side of the bar.

"Everyone down the stairs," he shouted, "and conserve your ammo. We wasted too much just then in a useless killing frenzy. If we run out, we're dead."

McGregor snorted a dissent at Walker's rebuke, but signaled his team to follow him down the stairs, while Costas and Walker covered their descent. The windows and walls of the Lido Deck offered some protection against the Wasps outside the ship, but those inside came at them from all sides drawn by the sound of gunfire and alien pheromones released by the dying Wasps. One of the creatures, intrigued by the smell of hot dogs and burgers, was busy dismantling the kitchen of the Trident Grill, using its powerful forelimbs to yank griddles, deep fryers, and storage cabinets from the wall. It turned at their approach. Costas threw the creature a surly sneer and opened up with his M107.

"Eat this, bitch," he yelled as he concentrated his fire at the Wasp's head. He was working on putting out its fourth eye, when it collapsed over the counter, smashing the glass of the warming box. He stopped long enough to grab mustard from the condiment bar and squirt it over the dead Wasp's head. "Order up!" he yelled. He looked at Perez. "Sorry about the bitch thing."

Perez grinned, aimed her weapon at the dead Wasp, and fired a short burst into its head. "No need to apologize. She gives bitches a bad name."

Watts and Stimson took down one Wasp that stood over a partially consumed body in the wading pool, adding its yellow blood to the red swirls of human blood in the water. Creature by creature, they removed the obstacles in their path until they reached the main stairs and elevator lobby. Walker yanked his weapon aside just in time to avoid shooting a steward running up the stairs.

"They're in the theater," he yelled, waving his arms wildly. His white jacket was in tatters, and a large bloodstain marred its front and right side.

"Who is?" Walker asked.

"The passengers, the creatures … they're all dying."

Walker pointed to the bloodstains. "Are you injured?"

The frightened steward stared at him uncomprehending for a moment, and then bolted for the door before Walker could stop him. Costas started to follow, but Walker called him back.

"We can't save them all," he said.

It was a grim statement, but all too true. If they attempted to round up every stray passenger along the way, they would never reach the theater seven decks below them where most of the passengers had taken refuge. It was a numbers game. As they continued down the stairs, they encountered signs of slaughter everywhere – patches of bloodstained carpet, smears of blood on the walls, and grisly bits and pieces of human flesh on the stairs. Confirmation of the Wasps' strength was evident in elevator doors peeled apart like aluminum foil, metal stair railings wrenched from their supports and curled like confetti, and doorways pushed inward until the bulkheads around them split apart. Walker had seen Wasps in action before and knew firsthand of their capabilities. However, McGregor and his men had only faced solitary Wasps and the smaller alien creatures comprising the Kaiju internal bio-system. The captain stared in awe at the bent metal doors.

Walker ignored the sounds of Wasps in the surrounding corridors and concentrated on reaching the theater as quickly as possible. Passengers would be safer in their cabins than huddled in a group. They could round up stragglers later. Rescuing the besieged passengers in the theater was his first priority. Twice, they encountered Wasps using the stairs to prowl the bowels of the ship in search of prey. Corporal Hightower's minigun made short work of them, singing its own high-pitched song as its rotating barrels spewed deadly lead into their bodies. Walker had hoped to reach the survivors without incident but that was proving impossible. To the Wasps, gunfire meant human activity, and they would soon home in on the sound. He pushed the pace.

When he heard noises on the landing below, Walker raised his hand and clenched his fist to halt the men behind him. *More Wasps or just another passenger?* he wondered. He edged around the corner and came face to face with a man wielding a fire axe. The man held the axe over his head ready to deliver a blow, his face a mask of fear and rage. His eyes widened in surprise when he saw Walker. He gasped and fell back against the wall to catch his breath, resting the head of his axe on the floor. Walker noted the fresh Wasp bloodstains on the warrant officer's white uniform, surprised that he had fought off at least one of the creatures armed only with an axe. The five passengers with him, three women of various ages, a young boy in his mid-teens, and a man in his seventies, surged forward.

"Are you here to rescue us?" the axe-wielding man asked between gasps of air.

"Please help us," one of the women pleaded.

Walker surveyed the passengers for wounds but saw none. "How many are in the theater?" he asked.

The warrant officer shook his head. "I don't know … forty, fifty maybe." He suddenly lurched forward and grabbed the front of Walker's fatigues. "There were hundreds of us. The creatures … they got in. They're everywhere." He glanced back down the stairs as if expecting a Wasp to attack at any moment.

Too late, Walker thought, bitter at the delay above deck that might have cost so many lives. Ten minutes might have made the difference. Now, hundreds of passengers were dead and his team was at greater risk.

"Where were you going?" he asked.

The warrant officer pointed up the stairs. "To the lifeboats. The ship is sinking."

"The Wasps are on the decks above. It's dangerous out there."

"It can't be any worse than down there. It's a slaughterhouse. I'd rather die on deck than go down with the ship."

Walker knew he couldn't allow them to throw their lives away. He was too late to save the passengers in the theater. He would have to do it the hard way, a few passengers at a time. He sighed in frustration.

"The lifeboats are on the Promenade Deck," he pointed out. "That's two levels below us."

The warrant officer looked back down the stairs and stared at him in shock. "I … I got turned around. The blood …" His voice trailed off.

"McGregor, take these people to the lifeboats. Take three men with you. I'll send any stragglers your way. Keep them there until we make our break."

He looked into McGregor's eyes and saw the captain was thinking exactly what he was thinking – they would be sitting ducks in the lifeboats – but they had no choice. They could not afford to wait for a rescue vessel, and the Osprey could not land on the ship to pick up survivors.

"Costas, Rhoades, Perez, Watts – come with me."

He pushed past the startled passengers and hurried down the stairs. Just as they reached Deck 8, the ship shuddered with half a dozen hard impacts from below. The low groan of sheering metal vibrated through the hull. It might have been the ship settling deeper in the water, but he doubted it. The creatures that had sunk the two submarines and holed the cruise ship had returned to finish the job. Instead of hours, they might have only minutes before the ship went down.

As they continued deeper into the ship, they encountered a trickle of passengers fleeing the theater and directed them to McGregor's group. Walker was dismayed that they met so few survivors and so many Wasps. They didn't have time for a proper sweep. They killed the Wasps blocking their path and those attacking passengers, but ignored the rest. He also tried to ignore the screams echoing down the corridors and rising from deeper below decks, but with little success. They filled his head like the tolling of the bell for the dead, one ring for each dead passenger. It would take a long time to ring out three thousand times.

On Deck 7, the passengers had erected barricades from anything they could find to seal the entrances to the theater. The flimsy obstacles proved no match for the determination and strength of the Wasps. The creatures had pushed the barricades aside like a toddler wading through a pile of building blocks.

When he turned a corner and saw a Wasp with a struggling human grasped in its forelimbs, Walker's battle concentration lapsed for a moment, and his anger burst forth. He raced at the creature firing his weapon at the creature's head. The Wasp refused to drop its prey, instead trying to back away down the corridor. He backed it into the lounge. When his SCAR clicked on empty, he pulled his 9 mm Beretta and continued firing from point blank range. The Wasp bit the passenger's head from the body, discarded the headless corpse, and lunged at Walker. A burst from Rhoades' Mk46 cut short the creature's attack. Walker stared at the creature's corpse, cursing himself for his stupidity. He tried to refocus and regain his battle calm. Unbridled anger served no purpose in the heat of battle. Any lapse of concentration could prove deadly, had almost been his downfall. Mistakes could kill. He took a deep breath, nodded his thanks to Rhoades, and continued.

The theater was a gore-ridden feeding zone. The stench of alien spore and human blood and guts assaulted his senses. The emergency lights were out, creating deep shadows that could easily conceal Wasps. He flicked on the flashlight attached to the barrel of his weapon. The beam revealed corpses and parts of bodies everywhere – lying across seats, on the stairs, in the aisles, even strewn across the stage. Pools of blood, amputated limbs, and piles of human entrails from eviscerated corpses dotted the floor and seats. Wasps fed on some of the dead, while taking others back to feed the Kaiju. Two or three small groups of survivors huddled in corners fending off attacking Wasps any way they could, with empty shotguns, axes, and pieces of broken railings.

He motioned for Rhoades and Watts to take the starboard side, while he, Costas, and Perez took the port side as they fanned out across the upper level. Perez, seven inches shorter than Costas, looked every bit as deadly with her MP5 as she knelt behind a trashcan.

"What does the M. stand for?" Costas asked her, nodding at her nametag.

"Mad Dog," she answered, and then bared her teeth for effect.

"No, really," Costas insisted.

"Maddy. Magdalena Rosa Perez, but Maddy will do."

"Flirt on your own time, Sergeant," Walker told him.

They each picked targets, and at a signal from Walker, began firing. Walker took aim at one Wasp circling the theater just below the ceiling, loosed three quick bursts from his SCAR, and watched its bullet-riddled corpse drop from the sky onto the floor. It thrashed about for a few seconds and went still.

Strangely, the Wasps inside the theater offered only token resistance. Most chose escape over attack, a decided change in their normal behavior. His team proceeded down the staircases and quickly dispatched the few remaining creatures. As soon as they had cleared the theater, the survivors rushed toward them. Many still wore life vests. All were frightened and exhausted from battling the Wasps, but their eyes shone with renewed hope. Walker hoped it wasn't misplaced.

"Rhoades! Perez! Escort this group to join Captain McGregor." He tapped the PTT, the push-to-talk button Velcro strapped to his wrist to activate his radio. "McGregor, I'm sending Rhoades and Perez back with more survivors. If we're not there in ten minutes, don't wait for us. Launch the lifeboats. Save as many as you can."

The ship rolled to port and bobbed as it sought balance. Rhoades glanced at Perez and the pair hustled the survivors toward the exit.

"Costas, Watts. We'll take the corridor. If I were hiding from Wasps, I would go backstage."

Descending the steps and exiting through the side door, they moved toward the backstage area. Sounds of scraping drew his attention to the door they had just exited. Suddenly, the door crashed open and a Wasp burst through. Costas turned his M107 on it, concentrating on the unprotected flesh just beneath its throat exposed when the creature raised its head. It reared toward upwards as the .50 caliber rounds struck home, bringing down a section of ceiling on top of it. Costas continued firing until the creature stopped moving, and then placed a round in its head for good measure.

Walker hesitated before the backstage door when he heard more noises behind it. Fearing another Wasp, he cast an uncertain glance at Costas, who shrugged his shoulders and shoved a fresh ammo clip into his weapon. Walker turned the doorknob and threw the door open wide, his weapon leveled at whatever he might find inside. Instead of Wasps, his flashlight illuminated a tall man with long black hair tucked beneath a Stetson. He turned his head aside to avoid the blinding light. The man's cowboy hat and cowboy boots were oddly out of place among the sandals and deck shoes of the several other survivors with him. The Gurkha kukri he carried in his left hand and the Ruger .357 caliber pistol he held in the other separated him from the other passengers. The man's expression was one of amusement rather than fear.

"Don't just stand there," Walker said. "If you want to live, you'd better get your ass in gear and come with me."

He didn't wait to see if they followed. They had little choice in the matter. The alternative was drowning. He could feel the ship sinking with each step he took, as if the floor was in a slightly different place each time he set his foot down. Costas eyed the young man, giving him the once over. Noting the .357 he carried, he asked, "You know how to use that thing, Cowboy?"

Talent nodded; then opened the cylinder to show Costas his last three rounds. "I could use some ammo. Got any?"

Costas pulled his 9 mm Beretta from his holster. "Here. Use this." He flicked on the flashlight attached to the Picatinny rail under the barrel and smiled. "Let's you see what you're shooting."

"Name's Talent," he said, as he took the pistol, cocked it, and flicked off the safety. "A M9A1 Beretta 9 mm. Nice." Costas handed him two extra clips. He shoved them in his front pocket and passed the .357 to the man behind him.

Costas smiled at him. "I see you know your weapons. Make me proud, Cowboy."

Talent grinned at the nickname. "I'm Tohono O'odham. I would be the one on the other side during an attack by savage redskins."

"Go Redskins," Costas said.

Walker cautioned them to silence as they came to the stairs. A deep trilling wafted up the stairwell from somewhere below. It reminded Walker of the ululations of Iraqi women mourning their dead. An answering trill came from somewhere above them.

"Squid," Talent said.

Walker looked at him questioningly.

"It's what I call the things that attacked the ship. They look like giant squid, but more badass with razor-tipped tentacles that slice through metal like a box cutter through cardboard. You don't want to fuck with them."

Walker nodded. "We'll go around." He pointed to the casino. "Through there."

The casino was in shambles. With no power, the machines' continuous electronic tunes were silent, and the bright blinking screens were dead. Walker had never seen a silent casino. Casinos used noise to generate invisible partitions between gamblers, creating the illusion of privacy where they could lose without public shame or dance triumphantly amid the cacophony of musical heraldry and the admiration of fellow gamblers when they won. Silent, the room reminded him of a machine graveyard. Like disgruntled losers, Wasps had wrenched many of the slot machines and electronic poker machines from their pedestals and tossed them across the room in an orgy of destruction. One had landed halfway through the glass cashier's window. A scattering of paper currency littered the counter and the floor. Costas picked up a fifty-dollar bill and shoved it in his shirt pocket.

At Walker's look of reproach, he said, "What? It's to pay for the valet parking."

Crystal chandeliers and lighted glass mosaic panels were now piles of broken glass. Three corpses formed a neat pile against one wall, as if the Wasps had stacked them there for later retrieval.

"Looks like the Temperance League has been here," Costas quipped, as he kicked aside piles of poker chips. He grinned when he spotted a box of cigars sitting on the counter at the cigar lounge. "*Makaleha* Hawaiian cigars," he noted appreciatively as he unwrapped one, stuck it under his nose, and sniffed. "Ah! Smells like Kona coffee." He stuffed a handful of cigars into one of his pants pockets, laid the fifty-dollar bill on the counter, and continued moving forward.

The rear door of the casino burst inward behind them, slamming into an upended electronic poker machine and shattering the glass screen. A Squid stuck its head inside the casino. When it caught sight of the humans, it opened its mouth, revealing rows of jagged teeth reminding Walker of a lamprey eel from hell. It puffed out its neck, exposing rows of slits on each side. The frilled gill slits began vibrating, and an undulating trill that sent shivers up Walker's spine spilled from its open mouth. Using four of its tentacles, it pulled its body inside the room, and then rose on the four larger appendages to tower above them.

This was Walker's first look at a Squid, and he was duly impressed. With its twenty-foot-long whip-like barbed tentacles, the aptly named Squid was a formidable foe. Unlike Kaiju Ishom, which had landed in the ocean just off the coast of San Francisco by mistake, Kaiju Kiribati was equipped for a water environment. The aliens had learned from their first effort and were hitting humans where bringing sufficient weapons to bear was more difficult – the ocean.

"I'll handle this," Watts said. He fired a burst from his MP5/40 at the Squid, hitting it in the head. The bullets drew blood, but the Squid ignored the wounds. It stretched its body to present a smaller profile and scuttled around the room on its tentacles. Watts, infuriated that his shots had no effect, cursed and moved closer to the Squid.

"Watts, hold your position!" Walker yelled, but it was too late. The Squid shot forward with a surprisingly graceful fluid motion and loomed over Watts. Almost too quickly for the human eye to follow, one of the tentacles whipped out and wrapped around the surprised S.E.A.L.'S arms and chest. He screamed in agony as the sharp barbs dug into his flesh. The humerus bones of both arms and his ribcage cracked as the powerful tentacle squeezed. The creature lifted him from the floor and flung him across the room. He crashed into the wall with a sickening crunch and laid still, blood spilling from his open mouth. His MP5/40 skidded across the floor and came to rest beneath a pile of wreckage.

Owens pulled a Glock from the shoulder holster under his left arm and began firing at the Squid as he crossed the room to check on Watts. When the pistol clicked on empty, he reached down and removed Watt's Mossberg 500 12-gauge shotgun from his dead body. The shotgun had no safety and a shell was already in the chamber. He immediately began firing slugs into the creature. Just as Walker was about to join him, Talent took two steps toward the Squid fired the 9 mm at one of the creature's eyes.

Walker turned to Costas and said, "Keep them moving," and then joined the two men. Together, the three of them poured lead into the creature's head, rupturing two eyes and forcing it back into the corridor where it ripped at the walls with its writhing tentacles. Finally, one of their bullets, or a combination of them, struck a vital organ. It staggered and collapsed. They had bought a couple of minutes of extra time for the others, but the dead Squid had already summoned its companions. He didn't have time to examine the creature.

He grabbed Owens and pushed him toward the stairs. "Let's go, old man."

Owens scowled. "Name's Owens, Sonny Boy."

"Let's go, Owens." He turned to Talent. "You too, Cowboy."

Talent grinned and raced up the stairs behind Owens. Walker stopped and looked at Watts. He knew immediately the young S.E.A.L. was dead. Watts' chest was concave, crushed inward by the brute force of the tentacles. The shattered bones of his arms punched through the skin. He had been dead before he struck the wall.

Walker panicked when he didn't see McGregor or the survivors on the deck. Then the bone conductor speaker on his headset mic boomed with McGregor's voice. "We're on the starboard side of the ship. The port lifeboats are useless because of the ship's list."

They reversed course and passed through the ship to the starboard side, where McGregor waited with about thirty passengers.

"Is this it?" Walker asked, eying the small number of survivors.

"There are probably more below decks, but searching for them will take time. It's your call, Major." McGregor stared at Walker as he waited for Walker's order.

Walker's training argued for him to search for survivors until the last possible minute, but the deeper they went below decks, the more time it would take get back out, and the ship was sinking fast. They could not leave the passengers with them unprotected, and splitting up his team again was a bad idea. Fire Team Bravo had a more compelling mission – the Kaiju – and he had already lost one man. There was no backup. He made his call.

"We have to go. We'll take two lifeboats and prep a couple more in case someone makes it out behind us."

McGregor nodded. Walker didn't know if that would have been McGregor's call, but he didn't argue. "Get the boats ready," McGregor called out to his team. He glanced at Owens holding Watts' shotgun. "Where's Watts?"

"Watts didn't make it," Walker answered. "A Squid got him."

McGregor's face became hard. He fixed Walker with his gaze as if he were staring down the barrel of a rifle. His voice was cold, as he said, "You lost one of my men?"

"He's one of my men," Walker snapped. "Watts stepped up when he was needed and went down fighting. He was a good soldier."

McGregor was not interested in platitudes. He glared at Walker. "You lost your entire team inside Nusku. Are you trying to kill mine now?"

Costas overheard and took a menacing step toward McGregor. Corporal Hightower, muscles bulging from carrying the heavy M134 minigun, stepped between them. Costas, always ready for a fight, grinned at him.

"Bring it on, Navy," he growled.

"Back off, Costas," Walker ordered. "Captain McGregor, we're all expendable. If you have a problem with that, I suggest you find another line of work. We've got a job to do, and I won't make any promises." To the others, he said, "Lower the lifeboats."

Upon hearing that they were leaving, one of the passengers cried out, "My wife is still below decks somewhere. We became separated in the confusion."

Walker looked at the man, so distraught he was shaking. "What deck was she on?"

"The Plaza Deck, Deck 5." The man's eyes pleaded for help. He was clearly too frightened to go after her alone, but didn't want to leave his wife behind.

Walker sympathized with him, but his plight did not sway him. He could not risk the other survivors and his team for one passenger. "I'm sorry. I have to get these people to safety. If you want to try it alone, I'll lend you my weapon, but we can't wait for you."

The man deflated. He glanced away ashamed and humiliated by his crippling fear. He shook his head slowly, and joined the others. Walker's decision tasted bitter on his tongue, but he couldn't save everyone. The way things were going, he would be lucky if he could save the rest of his team.

11

Saturday, Dec. 16, 11:30 a.m.   *Radiant Princess,* adrift north of Enderbury Island –

Talent thanked his luck for once more saving his ass. The arrival of the Special Forces fire team had been providential. Faced with only three bullets left in his pistol and Owens' Glock down to its last clip, things had looked bleak. Beyond all logical reason, trapped below decks with Wasps and Squid on a sinking ship, he was still alive. Unfortunately, he still had plenty of time to die.

Deck 5 was now awash from the stern to amidships. Furniture floated out of broken windows partially submerged by the rising flood. Adding insult to injury, water from the swimming pools on the decks above them cascaded down over their heads as they prepared the lifeboats for launching. The ship was listing to starboard almost fifteen degrees, making it difficult to lower the boats. Talent feared the ship would roll onto its side before they managed to get the lifeboats into the water.

The lifeboats operated on a gravity-fed davit. Once one of the survivors, a deckhand, demonstrated the procedure, it was virtually a hands-free operation. Walker divided the survivors into two groups. Captain McGregor and four members of his team took charge of one group, while Walker and three others took the remainder of the passengers in his boat. He wondered at Walker's reasoning behind the division. He had watched the confrontation between the captain and Major Walker with great interest, ready to offer his input concerning the soldier's death if asked, but no one did. It was a classic test of wills between two equally determine men, but Talent considered it bad timing and a poor choice of venue for a pissing contest. He was surprised that Walker didn't pull rank on his subordinate. The overly neat captain needed slapping down a notch. He didn't trust a man who spent too much time on his appearance. It spoke of narcissism.

Talent pulled Owens aside. "I think we should go with the major."

Owens was puzzled. He removed his cap and ran his fingers through his thinning hair, wincing as they brushed the tender flesh around the knot on the back of his head. "Doesn't matter to me, but why?"

"I've got a bad feeling about the captain. He seems a little insecure for a Navy S.E.A.L."

Owens studied McGregor for a moment as McGregor helped load passengers into one of the lifeboats, and then shrugged. "Seems sane to me, given the circumstances, but I'll go with your instincts." He threw Talent a big grin. "We've still got each other's backs, right?"

"Right."

While three S.E.A.L.S kept watch for Squid and Wasps, the rest lowered four boats from their overhead positions until they were even with the deck. The ship's list left a yawning chasm between the deck and the lifeboats' doorways. Two of the S.E.A.L.S used wooden life-jacket lockers to bridge the gap. Walker left a hastily scribbled note explaining the lowering procedure for any survivors that might follow. He also ordered his men to rush up and down the deck lowering more boats all the way to the waterline. At first, Talent was mystified, but then realized the major was providing decoys for the Wasps to attack, improving their chances of escaping undetected. As the boats lowered down the side of the ship, Talent noticed the deep gouges in the hull from the Squids' keen-edged claws. The larger holes they had ripped in the hull were below the waterline flooding the interior.

As they passed a line of portholes, Talent found himself staring into the distraught face of a middle-aged female passenger trapped in her cabin. She pounded on the glass with her fists, shouting something unintelligible through the glass until the lifeboat passed below the window. The sight made Talent sick to his stomach, but he could do nothing. The window was too narrow for egress even if he broke it out. He turned away and tried not to dwell on the hundreds of other passengers in similar situations scattered throughout the ship, too frightened to flee the safety of their cabins until the water reached their doors. By then it would be too late.

Once in the water, the cables detached automatically from the lifeboats. Rather than immediately starting the engines, Walker allowed the boats to drift slowly away from the ship. As they passed through the wreckage of demolished lifeboats from earlier attempts to flee the sinking ship, Talent saw the wisdom in Walker's actions. He had hoped some of the lifeboats had gotten away, but by the degree of destruction and amount of debris floating in the water, it looked unlikely. He hoped his group had better luck.

In all, thirty-seven passengers and crew manned the two lifeboats in their group, a small showing for the ship's four-thousand passengers and crew. He wondered why the Kaiju had bothered with a single cruise ship. Why float around in the ocean, inviting retaliation, simply to eliminate a ship that posed no threat and harvest the human cargo it could have obtained more readily from another island? After wiping out an entire island chain, expending its efforts on such a small target seemed an enormous waste of energy. Then, it struck him – energy was what the creature was all about.

He had read that the Kaiju's ebony armor was not only impervious to any explosives mankind had thus far thrown at it – even the nuclear bomb exploded inside Kaiju Nusku had not destroyed the shell, only the organic matter inside – the shell was also photovoltaic, a massive, highly efficient solar panel providing energy to the creature. It absorbed all forms of energy, conveying it to the giant power storage organ deep inside the creature. Humans were simply another source of energy to keep the creature moving forward in its mission of destruction. The last two days had been cloudy. No matter how efficient the creature was at converting sunlight to energy, no sun meant less energy.

The thought that his fellow passengers had died simply because the creature needed a light snack soured his stomach. The creature and its alien masters infuriated him. He knew it was insane, but he hated the Kaiju. He had never hated anything more than he now hated the creature and the aliens. He was beginning to understand Owens' thirst for revenge. A Kaiju had destroyed Chicago, his home. Everything he esteemed, everyone he knew, was gone. The attack had been a personal affront and had become even more personal when it attacked the ship.

Talent could not claim that kind of personal vendetta. The Kaiju attack in America had not endangered him in any way, merely inconvenienced him. Even the Kaiju attack on the cruise ship had not elicited more than fleeting sympathy in him for the plight of the passengers. His interest in saving them had not been personal. Even his initial interest in Owens had been because of Owens' second pistol. If he could have rescued himself by ignoring them, he would have. Only later had he found himself inexplicably entangled in Owens' crusade to protect the passengers. What had he gotten himself into?

After twenty minutes of drifting, they had placed less than three hundred yards between them and the ship, which continued its death slide to the ocean's bottom. The bow was riding high out of the water, and waves lapped against the cabin walls of the Promenade Deck. Only three other lifeboats had left the ship after theirs, and the occupants had ignored Walker's written warning about using the engines. Some of the passengers in Walker's boat watched the other lifeboats speed past them with envy.

One of the passengers decided to make his views known. He stood up and cried out, "Start the engines, damn it! Those things will come for us."

"Sit down and shut up before you attract their attention," Walker told him. "If you make any more noise, I'll toss you overboard."

At first, the man looked defiant, returning Walker's glare as if he weren't used to someone speaking to him in such a manner. For a moment, it looked as if he were going to continue to protest, but Costas pulled his knife from its sheath and laid it across his lap. "In case you splash when you hit the water," he said to the man and drew his finger across his throat.

The man eyed the long blade, licked his lips nervously, and sat back down, sullen but silent. Talent liked the pair's no-nonsense attitude. They were determined to save as many as they could in spite of people's worst instincts during an emergency. He didn't have the patience to play savior. He had already invested more effort in being a caring human being in the last few hours than he had in the past ten years. It had been his experience that most people who promoted altruism over self-preservation were invariably the recipients of said altruism. People who never made plans for emergencies often held those who did in self-righteous contempt and overt disdain, even as they cried for their help when a disaster occurred, a troubling human failing for which Talent had no sympathy.

Two of the last three lifeboats to leave made it less than fifty yards beyond them before the Wasps descended on them en masse. Walker did not need to explain his reasoning again after the passengers witnessed the slaughter of their fellow passengers. The third lifeboat, seeing the wisdom in silence, cut its engines and drifted. For now, the Wasps ignored them as they concentrated on ferrying the corpses back to the Kaiju. Talent did not expect the lull to last long.

"How far away is the rescue ship?" he asked.

Walker stared at him for a moment before answering, "The freighter is about fifty miles from here. It's making about 20 knots. The lifeboats can do maybe 6 knots. Once we start the engines, we should reach it in just over an hour, but I'm hoping for a little unexpected help."

Behind them, the *Radiant Princess*, all 110,000 tons of her, hissed and groaned its death song before disappearing beneath the roiling water. The few remaining Wasps now focused their attention on the drifting lifeboats. The third of the last boats to leave, drifting slightly ahead of them, came under attack by two Wasps. The passengers were unarmed, and the Wasps made quick work of them, ripping away the roof and killing the screaming passengers like a ratter after a nest of rodents. Talent wished he hadn't witnessed the grisly sight. It would haunt him for the rest of his life. *Which may be a short one*, he noted, when the two Wasps left the mangled corpses in the lifeboat for other Wasps to leisurely carry off to the waiting Kaiju and moved toward the remaining boats.

Walker spoke quietly into his headset to the other boat. "Stay low, but keep your weapons handy." He looked at the passengers, frightened and cowering in their seats. "Anyone without a weapon, try to find something to hide behind or crawl under. You others, be ready."

None of the armed passengers looked ready to fend off Wasps. In fact, they looked like Christians waiting for the lions in a Roman arena, but with less piety. Their desperate eyes searched for somewhere to run, but they had nowhere to go. Talent hoped fear would give them the courage to fight back. He glanced over at Owens. Except for a few cuts and bruises, the former detective seemed eager to fight. For an ex-cop whose job had been protecting citizens, Walker figured Owens' inability to protect and serve was gnawing at his guts. To Walker, who had never been one for joining in on the reindeer games, fighting to save strangers was a new experience for him. Surprisingly, it suited him better than he had imagined.

No, it's just my Indian blood stirred up, he consoled himself. *I still despise people.*

He watched the Wasps methodically demolish one of the empty decoy lifeboats, taking it apart a piece at a time in search of prey. The next boat suffered a similar fate. Now, the only two boats were Walker's and McGregor's. Talent tightened his grip on the 9 mm and watched Walker, waiting for a sign to open up on the creatures as they approached. He had to give the major his props. He was as cool as a frosty pitcher of margaritas as he watched the Wasps drawing nearer. Then he spoke softly into his headset.

"Start your engines and pick your targets."

As soon as the diesel engine of their lifeboat cranked, the Wasps homed in on the noise. Talent broke out the window beside him and laid the barrel of his Beretta on the sill. Owens took a window on the opposite side of the craft with his Mossberg 12-gauge shotgun. Costas chose the forward windows of the upper level. He stood with his .50 caliber SASR cradled in his arms and pointed at the windows. Walker covered one door with his 7.62 mm SCAR L-CQC, and Private Stimson covered the other door with his MP5/40 caliber.

Specialist Perez stood in the middle of the boat ready to put out fires where needed. Talent was surprised when the S.E.A.L. unbuttoned the top buttons of her shirt to extract a tiny silver cross, revealing the cleft of her cleavage. He had heard of female soldiers but not S.E.A.L.S. Her sex did not change his opinion of her abilities. He had seen her in action. She gripped her MP5 in one hand, while she kissed the cross she held in the other. She muttered a quick prayer and shoved the cross back down her shirt. She glanced at Talent and winked at him. Then her face went grim as she stared out the window.

Besides the armed S.E.A.L.S, him, and Owens, two passengers had fire axes and one had Owens' .357 with only three shots left. *Good enough for a gang fight,* Talent thought, *but a spit in the ocean against a swarm of Wasps.*

The lifeboat shuddered from the impact of a Wasp landing on the roof. Perez fired a short burst through the underside of the roof into the creature's belly.

"Place your shots carefully," Walker yelled. "Conserve your ammo and aim for exposed flesh or the wings. Hit the eyes if you can."

When the same Wasp stuck its head over the side of the boat on his side, Talent placed the barrel of his pistol against one of its eyes and fired. The creature roared in pain at its shattered eye, but it had three more eyes with which to identify the source of its agony, and it focused all its energy into reaching Talent. It began ripping at the fiberglass hull around the window with two forelimbs, while thrusting the other pair through the opening at him. Their curved talons were twin deadly blades slicing the air. Talent leaped aside as one sharp talon slit open the seat cushion beside him, releasing a cloud of cotton batting that filled the air like snowflakes. Avoiding the slashing talons in the confined space was difficult. One wrong move could kill him.

Walker slid open the lifeboat door, leaned outside, and fired into the base of one of the creature's four wings. On his second burst, the wing blew away from the connecting musculature. The Wasp withdrew to the roof and began hissing a shrill, multi-timbred tone that pierced the air even over the sound of gunfire. The call summoned a second Wasp. It joined the first, scurrying along the side of the boat, slashing at the thin fiberglass hull in a mad frenzy. Suddenly, all hell broke loose on the lifeboat, as the two Wasps coordinated their attacks on one section of the hull. Talent did not have time to keep track of those around him. He was too busy firing, reloading, and firing again. He heard a scream and turned to see one of the passengers gasping for breath, a disbelieving stunned expression on his face, as he stared down at a Wasp talon thrust through the thin hull, skewering him. The man raised his arms and stared at Talent, silently pleading for help, but it was too late. The Wasp jerked the talon upward, splitting the man's chest wide open.

Infuriated, Perez yelled, leaped up on one of the benches, and fired her MP5 into the creature's head. Most of the bullets bounced off the dense armor, but enough of them found flesh to force it back. Talent took careful aim at the spots where Perez's bullets had penetrated, marked by splotches of yellow blood, adding his firepower to that of the S.E.A.L. specialist. It took his last clip of ammo, but their concentrated fire finally produced results. The Wasp bellowed in rage, pounding on the hull with its four front limbs, and then tried to fly away. Its wings fluttered once; then it fell into the water and slowly sank beneath the surface.

Perez yelled, "Yeah! That's how you do it."

Talent wanted to high-five her, but they had no time for end-zone celebrations. They had killed one Wasp, but more drawn by the gunfire swarmed in to join the attack, and he was out of ammo. He took a deep breath and pulled out his kukri. One of the passengers, the man who had left his wife behind, his face pale from fright, handed Talent the axe he held with trembling hands. He had been sitting next to the dead passenger, and the dead man's blood splattered his face.

"Y-y-you can handle this better than I can," he gasped.

Talent sheathed the kukri and reached for the axe. The man was so frightened his hands refused to release the handle. Talent gently peeled his fingers away from the wood. The man sat back down and lowered his face into his hands, sobbing.

Gunfire erupted from the second lifeboat, as the M134 minigun and the MK46 SAW picked out flying targets. Even the combined firepower of the two heavy weapons was barely a deterrent. As soon as one Wasp died, another took its place. A woman's terrified scream pierced the sound of gunfire as a Wasp dragged her through one of the windows. Corporal Hightower's minigun made short work of the Wasp, but the Wasp and the woman, both now dead dropped into the water beside the boat.

Talent didn't have time for more observations. The remaining Wasp began digging at the top hatch of their lifeboat, ripping out chunks of fiberglass. Costas turned, and holding the heavy M107 in one hand, fired several rounds into the creature's throat as it shoved its head down through the opening it had made. The .50 caliber opened a hole the size of a grapefruit in its neck, spraying the ceiling with its yellow blood, but still it refused to die. A passenger whose inquisitiveness got the better of him craned his neck to see what was happening. His curiosity was untimely. With a single swipe of one of its thrashing forelimbs, the Wasp decapitated him. His head rolled across the deck to land at Talent's feet.

Talent stared down at the man's head, mouth open in stunned surprise and dead eyes staring up at him. He grimaced in disgust and kicked it out of the way.

Wasps had completed their destruction of the decoy lifeboats. Now, they converged on the only two boats under power. Owens emptied the magazine of the 12-gauge shotgun at one Wasp hovering outside the window, cast the weapon aside, and began firing his Glock. As several of the creatures began shredding the lifeboat, peeling the thin fiberglass away in long strips, Talent cocked his fire axe above his shoulder. It appeared to him that his move to the Australian deserts would end on the sea.

With a loud groan, one of the metal posts supporting the roof began to buckle under the weight of the Wasps on the roof. The weakened ceiling sagged, and then gave way. A Wasp fell through and landed among the passengers. Private Stimson turned his MP5 on the creature, which was almost as stunned as Stimson was by its sudden appearance inside the craft. The Wasp immediately began doing what Wasps do, attacking anything that moved. In the close confines of the boat, Stimson had nowhere to move and little room to fire his weapon without endangering passengers. The creature backed him into a corner. He began hammering the Wasp on the head with the butt of his weapon. Suddenly, the Wasp whirled, thrusting its three-foot-long stinger at Stimson. He dodged the first thrust, but the Wasp was too fast. The stinger stabbed into the left side of his abdomen and exited through his spine. Even before the stinger began pulsing venom, Stimson was dead.

Owens was standing opposite Stimson. When the Wasp swung around to sting Stimson, its head now faced him. He emptied his Glock into the creature's face. Almost at the same time it stung Stimson, it lunged at Owens. He ducked behind the partially collapsed metal pole to avoid the snapping jaws. Talent noticed Owens' predicament and raced to help. His only weapon was the axe. He brought it down with all his might on one of the leg's articulation points. To his surprise, he severed the leg. It fell away, shuddering on the deck. His attack produced the desired results. The Wasp turned away from Owens and faced him.

When it whirled on him, it withdrew its stinger from Stimson. Stimson's body slid from the stinger onto the deck. Talent threw the axe at the Wasp's head and rolled under its body. He snatched up Stimson's MP5, praying it wasn't empty. Lying on his back staring up at the Wasp's belly less than a foot above his face, he chose a narrow gap in the ebony armor that widened slightly as the creature breathed, and fired pointblank. As the .40 caliber slugs tore into unprotected flesh, the Wasp tried to trample him with a seven-legged shuffle. Then, it suddenly stopped moving. He rolled beneath a bench as the Wasp's legs began splaying outward. Moments later, the dead Wasp thudded to the deck, splintering the bench above him, but the metal frame held.

As Talent crawled from beneath the bench and rose to his feet, one of the windows behind Owens crashed inward. A Wasp dug two of its scimitar-tipped legs into the detective's back. One of the talons protruded from his right chest near his shoulder. The second, more serious wound came from the second talon piercing his left lung. The Wasp dragged the stunned former detective backwards across the deck. He stared at Talent in shock, frothy blood dripping from the corner of his mouth. He moved his lips to speak, but was unable to force out the words.

The dead Wasp's body lay between Talent and Owens. He knew he would never reach Owens in time. His stomach tightened into a hard knot, as he raised the MP5 and aimed at Owens' head. Owens, realizing Talent's intent, nodded. Talent squeezed the trigger and placed one round into the detective's forehead just before the creature jerked him through the window.

Anger exploded inside him, a burning rage that coursed through his veins like molten lava, burning away all caution, all thought of protecting others. His consuming fury stripped away the thin veneer of civilization with which men draped themselves to disguise their love of violence, leaving only the primitive instincts of the hunter. He despised himself for what he had done to the closest thing to a friend he had, and he hated the Wasps for making him do it. The desire to lash out blindly, kill as many Wasps as he could before they killed him, drove away all thoughts of self-preservation. If necessary, he would rend their bodies with his bare hands, or gnaw on their alien flesh with his teeth.

He searched for his next alien Wasp victim, and saw Walker staring at him. Walker's face was grim as he recognized the madness overwhelming Talent. He yelled something, but the words were lost in the all-consuming roar of Talent's berserker rage. Ignoring Walker, he slung the MP5 over his shoulder, and using the dead Wasp's body, scrambled through the gaping hole onto the remains of the roof. It took him several moments to realize that the roaring was not his blood thundering in his ears. The sound grew louder as an object flashed by above the lifeboat. Expecting yet another alien terror, he raised the MP5 and waited. A loud whoop of delight from Sergeant Costas, who had followed him onto the roof, took him by surprise. Then, the object began firing at the Wasps.

"Go get 'em, sailor boys!" Costas yelled, dancing a jig the roof, heedless of the ragged hole inches from his size twelve boots.

Talent looked up and saw several objects circling the area. He threw Costas a questioning look.

"They're Harpy MQ 1B Predators with 25 mm, swivel-mounted Gau-12 Gatling guns in their noses."

Slowly, the fog of the primitive hunter lifted from his mind. As his blood cooled and his faculties resumed control of his body, he recognized the drones' V-shaped rear stabilizing fins and swept-back wings. "Where did they come from?"

"From the *Ortega*, a U.S. by-God escort carrier about four hundred miles from here."

He recognized the name. The *Ortega*, one of the navy's newest small escort carriers at just over four-hundred-feet in length, was the perfect delivery vessel for ferrying helicopters, V/STOL aircraft like the V2-Osprey and F-35 Lightning, and unmanned aerial drones into hot spots.

Technicians safely ensconced in their video game-like air-conditioned consoles at Creech AFB, Nevada, five thousand miles away, controlled the five Harpies using satellite imagery and fast data links. They adroitly maneuvered the drones among the Wasps using their *Rotax* 914F turbocharged engines, spewing 25 mm death from their Gatling guns at 4,200 rounds per minute, in a carefully coordinated aerial ballet, avoiding both the lifeboats and each other with their crisscrossing lines of fire. The drones zeroed in on the Wasps, ripping them to shreds in a hail of lethal ordinance. To Talent, it was a sight worth savoring. He only wished they had arrived five minutes sooner.

Seeing the Wasps dying or retreating, the passengers emitted cries of joy, hugging and kissing each other in enthusiastic shows of relief and gratitude. Talent didn't feel like celebrating. His talent for luck had kept him alive one more day, but it had not extended to Owens. In the few hours he had known the detective, he had felt in him a kindred spirit, a man beaten down by life but fighting to remain above dirt one day longer than Death wanted. That he had been the one to end that life, even at Owens' last request, did not sit well with him.

He climbed back down into the lifeboat, avoiding the congratulatory hugs of the passengers, and leaned back on one of the benches, resting his head against the hull with his appropriated MP5 lying across his lap. He knew he should get up and strip Stimson of his extra ammunition in case the creatures returned, but he was too bone-weary to move. He had been operating on adrenalin and caffeine since dawn. Now that the danger was past and his berserker rage had subsided, he felt like he had been ridden hard and put away wet.

Perez stood staring down at Stimson's body for several minutes. Finally, she knelt beside him and closed his eyes with a tenderness that spoke of more than simple camaraderie. Her fingers lingered on his face for a moment; then, she sighed heavily and methodically removed his extra ammo and his dog tags. She stuck the dog tags in her breast pocket, walked around the Wasp corpse, and dropped the ammo onto the bench beside Talent. Then she walked away without saying a word.

Slowly, as the drones forced the Wasps back toward the Kaiju, the two lifeboats slipped away from the scene of carnage. The machinegun fire of the Harpies faded into the distance. The passengers continued their celebration. Walker communicated briefly with Captain McGregor in the other lifeboat. Talent overheard him mention six dead passengers. Walker had lost three passengers and a member of his fire team, with one of the passengers being Owens. Despite the harsh taste of reality, they had been lucky.

Talent hoped each one of the twenty-eight remaining survivors of the ill-fated *Radiant Princess* understood just how lucky they were. Over three thousand of their fellow passengers had not survived the alien attack. Hundreds of thousands more had died on the islands. He glanced at Costas lighting up one of the cigars he had liberated from the cruise ship. *Let them all enjoy this brief respite*, he thought. He was certain the alien Kaiju was just getting started.

12

Saturday, Dec. 16, 10:15 p.m. CST   Johnson Space Center, Houston, TX –

Director Caruthers had called in debts, made under the table deals, and possibly sold his soul to the devil, but by eight p.m., eight hours after their lunch meeting, Gate Rutherford had his first photos from the newly positioned NEOWISE satellite spread out across his desk. The images were fuzzy, even with computer enhancement, but the tiny dot more than 4.5 billion miles away and one-third the size of Pluto was clearly visible, as were its two moons, Hi'iaka and Namaka. Named after a Hawaiian goddess of fertility, Haumea, or more properly, *136 108 Haumea,* was an ellipsoidal minor dwarf planet in a long trans-Neptunian orbit. Probes were planned for a closer survey, but Rutherford could not wait seven years until the proposed 2025-launch date or the sixteen years the journey would take using a Jupiter-assisted orbit. The NEOWISE Infrared photos would have to do.

The images were interesting, but the accompanying data attached to each photo were what drew his attention. To a layman, the strings of numbers meant nothing. To Rutherford, even after years away from the telescope as a catastrophist, they told a compelling story. Haumea itself was icy cold, close to 50^0 on the Kelvin scale, slightly above Absolute Zero, 0^0 K, which converted to -273^0 Celsius or -523^0 Fahrenheit. That gave the tiny planetoid a surface temperature of -225^0 C. Any water vapor or volatile gases became ice crystals deposited on the frozen surface like fallen snow. It was a highly inhospitable environment. A low gravity world with vacuum for an atmosphere, but if he were right, he suspected the aliens had not chosen Haumea for its charm or beauty but for its ideal location. The nearby icy chunks of volatile compounds orbiting the planetoid, held in place by Haumea's weak gravity, were a valuable source of power and organic building material.

One small spike stood out on the IR wavelength graph. Its location was at the very edge of the planetoid, almost hidden behind an eclipsing

Namaka. At 289^0 K, it was much warmer than the rest of Haumea. The casual, trained observer could have easily dismissed it as a computer glitch or a photo anomaly, but the number struck a chord within Rutherford. Its resonant vibration dredged up a deep-seated fear that he had attempted to tamp down since the arrival of the first three Kaiju four months earlier. He quickly rifled through the data sheets seeking a different viewing angle, but the planetoid's slow rotation precluded a better look for another six hours.

289^0 K equated to 16^0 on the Celsius scale, the average mean temperature of the Earth. The anomaly was too much for mere coincidence to explain. The aliens were there on Haumea, and they thrived at Earth temperatures. That explained their attack. They were not merely interested in Earth's resources. They wanted the planet to colonize, and humans stood in their way.

Hunger and dread brought on a dizzy spell. He grabbed onto the edge of his desk before he fell; then, sat down heavily in his chair. His hands shook so badly he could not dial the director's number. After a few moments thought, he decided crying wolf now would not help his cause. He could see it, but others might see only a broken man's desperate attempt to salvage his reputation.

Was that what he was, a broken man? It was a certainty that he was not the same man he was before the Kaiju came. He sounded the same. For the most part, he looked the same. However, he did not feel the same inside. Witnessing so much death and destruction and crawling around inside a giant alien monster had done something to him, changed the core of his being. Before, he had been unemotionally detached, though not cold, content to calculate the impact of catastrophic events and live a simple life. Now, he hated. The barely contained rage that drove him was an uncomfortable growth, like a fiery cancer, burning away at all that had been Phillip Wingate Rutherford, leaving only a charred shell that thought of nothing but bringing the fight to the Kaiju's alien masters.

He reached over and turned on the iPod docking station on his desk, rarely used since his return from Nevada and his encounter with Nusku. Soon, the smooth jazz sounds of Spyro Gyra floated throughout the room. He closed his eyes and tried to lose himself in the fluid saxophone and roving bass line, but the IR image from Haumea haunted him, twisting the melody into the trampling of a dozen Kaiju legs smashing cities. The shrill trills of the saxophone became the screams of the dying. He slapped off the iPod and sighed into the empty silence it left. Not even music brought him any joy.

He longed to reach for the bottle of scotch in his top desk drawer. For the first month after his return, which he jokingly labeled 1 A.N. for Year

One After Nusku, the bottle or one like it had been his constant companion. Even in his worst drunken stupor, he knew alcohol was not the answer and had slowly weaned himself from the bottle. It would not be the answer now.

He needed access to the GEMS satellite. His hand was now steady as he dialed Caruthers' number.

The director answered on the third ring. "I was expecting your call," he said.

"I need the GEMS."

"Did the NEOWISE photos help?"

"They were … inconclusive. It'll take six hours for the rotation to offer a clearer image."

Caruthers paused. Rutherford imagined him leaning closer to the phone. "You saw something, Gate," he charged.

"Yes, but it would be foolish to go to anyone with it now. Six hours; then I'll know for certain."

"I appreciate your candor, Gate, but I need to know. Goddard has closed ranks on me on GEMS. Maybe I can throw the fear of God into them."

Rutherford glanced at the telltale photo atop the pile and sighed. "They're there all right, and they thrive at Earth-norm temperatures."

"You're frightened. I can hear it in your voice."

Rutherford snickered over the phone. "Damn right I'm frightened. You should be too. We all should be scared shitless."

Caruthers sighed. "I'll get you that feed from GEMS. I'll call you back in an hour."

Now he had set the wheels in motion. Once Caruthers had sunk his teeth into a project, he was persistent and persuasive. That was why he was the head of NASA. Goddard Space Flight Center and Johnson Space Center were both NASA and worked too closely to allow petty jealousies and professional rivalries to stymie any effort to identify the source of the Kaiju. Astronomical observations took back seat to saving the planet. If the director could convey his fear to the researchers at Goddard, he would have his access.

* * * *

It took Caruthers two hours, but Rutherford had his link with Goddard in Maryland. The researchers in charge of GEMS, Ahern and Patangan, were distant and cool toward him, but not outright hostile as he had expected for disturbing their routine. In return, he was polite and offered to keep them in the loop. He waited impatiently for the satellite to reach its new position. Using an instrument designed to detect gravity distortions caused by black holes light years away was different from detecting distortions within the solar system. Each planet created its own gravity well that bent light. Sifting through the streams of data for one particular line of numbers or an anomalous spike in a graph was slow, painstaking work, but by three a.m., he had his answer, and it surprised even him.

"Do you see it?" he asked the Goddard technician who had drawn the short straw to work with him.

The video link was fuzzy, but her weary expression and tired eyes stared at him with undisguised skepticism. She studied the point he had indicated for a long moment; then, brushed her long auburn hair away from her face and leaned closer to the image on the screen.

"It could be an anomaly," she finally replied.

"Moons don't dance. Namaka shuddered as it passed into Haumea's shadow. Something grabbed it and shook it."

"A gravity distortion?" She still was not convinced, but at least she had not dismissed him as insane, seeing aliens in the shadows.

"It would take a gravity field five times the strength of Haumea's to cause that kind of shift."

"It could be a micro black hole. We think we've discovered—"

He cut her off midsentence. "It's too strong for a micro black hole."

"It would explain the sudden loss of signal from New Horizon two years ago."

He was beginning to lose patience with her. She was almost as stubborn as he was. "So would deliberate destruction."

"Doctor Rutherford, jumping to conclusions based on a single observation isn't going to help your case."

He took a deep breath to calm himself. "I'm sending you the latest feed from NEOWISE. The IR spike on the surface and the source of the gravity anomaly originate from the same area."

He waited while she compared the two photos. She still was not ready to concede, but her protests lacked her earlier certainty. "It doesn't preclude a natural inclusion on the planet – a heavy metal asteroid or a micro black hole."

He confused her by replying, "You are absolutely right. I can see you need more convincing, so let's widen the field, see if we detect any more anomalies in the region."

She nodded her head. A half-smile creased her lips. "I'll need more coffee first."

Unlike her, he was riding an adrenaline surge, created by certainty and fear. Caffeine would only bring him down. "Will you please refocus the satellite to widen the field first? Then, perhaps you need a break.

You've been working very hard and have been more than patient with me. I'll continue to observe while you re-caffeinate."

She blushed. "Some here think you're too driven, Doctor Rutherford. I think you're a hero."

It was his turn to be embarrassed. He was glad the video link was fuzzy. People had called him a hero before, but he did not like the title. A hero does what he or she does without fear and regardless of the consequences. He had been scared to death the entire time he had followed Girra's path of destruction and traipsed around inside Nusku.

"I'm no hero. I'm just a scientist searching for answers."

"We'll find them." She rose from her desk. "I'll reposition GEMS, but then I need lots of coffee."

The first images from the newly positioned satellite showed nothing, just empty space. After refining the image, the distortion on Haumea reappeared in the same location.

"It's not an error or an anomaly," she told him. "Something is definitely there. While you were going over the data, I pulled up old images from New Horizon. The object couldn't have been there for more than two years. If so, it would have affected the orbits of the nearby Trans-Neptunian objects more severely. Stranger yet, when I checked for other gravity spikes, I found three evenly spaced at twenty-four hours apart dated four months ago."

Rutherford's heart went cold. She had not yet made the connection, but he had. The numbers were etched into his brain. "That's a perfect match for the three Kaiju."

Her expression changed from bemused fascination to fear as the color drained from her face. "You were right," she gasped.

"I take no joy from it. The aliens are much closer than everyone thinks. They can react more quickly than we anticipated."

"You anticipated them," she pointed out.

"It was my job to imagine the worst case scenario and extrapolate possible outcomes. This is as worst case as it gets."

She looked at him with a puzzled expression. "When I was running the newer data, I found this."

She placed an image on the screen. It was just empty space, but the numbers indicated something was there. The object was invisible against the blackness of space, revealed by the distortion of the light waves of the stars behind it. Only a very massive object or one possessing an unnaturally high density could cause such distortions. *Or one using an alien gravity drive,* he thought.

"We need to estimate its speed. I don't have to check its destination. It's headed for us."

He heard her sharply indrawn breath. "I have to contact Doctor Patangan. He will want to be here."

"You get him there while I contact Director Caruthers. Unless I underestimate him, I think we'll soon have all the help we need."

He should have been elated to discover proof that he had been right. The months of ridicule had hurt him deeply, and there had always been the nagging doubt that they were right and he was wrong. Vindication should have tasted sweet in his mouth. Instead, all he tasted was stomach acid from his churning stomach.

13

Saturday, Dec. 16, 1530 hours   *USS Mississippi*, Southern Pacific –

The passengers on Walker's lifeboat went wild when they saw the submarine surface less than two hundred yards off their starboard beam. After their harrowing ordeal, the *USS Mississippi* represented safety. To the Americans on board the *Radiant Princess*, it represented a piece of home. The sight of the American flag on the mast drove many to tears. To Walker, the sub's appearance meant he could get back to his original mission – killing the Kaiju. The atmosphere on deck was somber as the crew gazed into the dazed faces of the innocent victims climbing aboard the submarine. Some, in a state of delayed shock, could not get their limbs to work. Members of the crew carried them from the lifeboats as gently as they could. Walker could see it in the crew's faces: they thirsted for revenge. So did he, but he now had a greater respect for the danger the enemy represented. The aliens were learning.

He climbed from the lifeboat weary and worn out. He waited until the passengers disembarked before helping the crew remove the dead bodies. Enclosed in black body bags, they went into the sub's freezer. All except Stimson. His body went into the Sail awaiting a Navy burial at sea. Perez walked beside the stretcher bearing Stimson with her hand resting on the body bag. McGregor glared at Walker across the deck, and then disappeared inside the Sail.

Talent climbed aboard the sub one-handed, favoring his injured left wrist. His shoulder was bloody where the fight with the Wasps had reopened his wound. He looked as if he carried the weight of the world on his shoulders, shoulders stooped and eyes focused on the deck. Costas had informed Walker that Talent had shot his friend Owens as a Wasp carried him away. He knew from experience that a mercy kill was a hard thing to do and even harder to live with.

"You should see to your wounds," he told Talent.

"Yeah, after a cup of coffee." He eyed the open hatch with distaste. "Can't I ride up top?"

Walker patted his uninjured shoulder. "Come on. It's not so bad once you get used to it."

With the addition of the survivors, the number of people aboard the submarine suddenly increased by twenty percent. Making space for them required a wholesale shifting of personnel and a little Navy ingenuity. The crew relinquished their bunks to the weary passengers, tending to them as honored guests. Fire Team Bravo offered their bunks in the missile room to displaced sailors and made do with fold-out cots scattered throughout the missile bay. The ship's doctor went around patching up their physical injuries, which were mostly minor in nature – cuts and bruises, a few gashes from close encounters with Wasp talons, and exhaustion. These he could remedy with aspirin, Band-Aids, antibiotics, and sedatives, but their mental scars would remain with them for the rest of their lives. These were beyond his limited scope.

Most heart wrenching of all were the faces of the nine children, the sole survivors of the hundreds of children aboard the ship. Some of the younger ones clutched dolls or toys as if lifelines to their so recent past. The older ones seemed to shrink into themselves, becoming hollow-eyed children, Lost Boys in an alien Never Land. The lucky few were with their parents, clinging to them as they never had before. Most were now orphans, thrust into the midst of strangers by events they barely comprehended. The crew took it upon themselves to entertain them with songs, feats of amateur magic, and storytelling. It was a heartwarming effort, but despite the occasional bursts of laughter or fleeting smile, the children's sad faces quickly resumed their original blank masks of withdrawal.

Walker wasn't sure how to deal with his subordinate, Captain McGregor. McGregor blamed him for the deaths of the two Fire Team Bravo members, Watts and Stimson. While as team leader their deaths were indeed his ultimate responsibility, he knew he could have done nothing differently to save them. He knew because he had gone over every detail of the encounter in his mind during the wait for the *Mississippi* to arrive. There is one axiom a leader cannot ignore – in battle, men die.

It was a basic dark law of military physics. Every action produced an equal and opposite reaction. No one knew that better than he did. Survival was an immutable equation based on the absolute truth of numbers. Like a Las Vegas odds maker, during a battle every soldier calculated his or her chances of dying versus that of the enemy. It was a roll of the dice, and sometimes the dice came up snake eyes. The deaths of two men and nine passengers did not make for a glowing report. He felt his failure deep in his weary bones. He could deal with it, but could McGregor?

Ensconced in the missile room, the fire team performed the normal post-mission routine of cleaning weapons and restocking supplies, but now McGregor's men sat on one side of the room, and he and Costas on the other. They worked in silence, the only noise the soft clicks of rounds loaded into ammo magazines. Specialist Maddy Perez, who had been on the lifeboat with Stimson and had witnessed his death, sat slightly apart from her comrades. She felt honor bound to side with her team members, but did not agree with their condemnation of Walker.

He was not worried about their actions under fire. They were U.S. Navy S.E.A.L.S. In a fight, they would do their jobs to the best of their abilities. What concerned him was their attitude. Once they reached their destination, inside the Kaiju, he could not take the time to explain every order or to win their trust. Some of them would likely die on the mission, perhaps all of them. The attack on the cruise ship was just a taste of the enemy's power. They could not comprehend the tenacity of the creatures inhabiting the Kaiju under full Kaiju control. They had to obey his orders without question, regardless of their opinion of him. Anything less could mean mission failure and all their deaths.

He could replace McGregor to avoid the inevitable confrontation, but that would be a career ender for the young captain and could further alienate the team. He would just have to ride this one out.

Mark Talent proved another quandary. Although Talent was a passenger on the *Radiant Princess* and a civilian to boot, he had guts and skill with a weapon. He had shown something of his character during the fight against the Wasps, using a 9 mm, a kukri, and an MP5. He was cool under fire and had an innate sense of leadership for a man who claimed to be a loner. His berserker rage after killing Owens, if properly focused, would not be a hindrance. In fact, Walker preferred a little genuine hatred for the enemy to simply getting the job done. An angry soldier took more chances, and sometimes that made the difference between success and failure. A soldier should never waste his life, but should be ready to spend it if needed.

Now, down two team members, he could use Talent's help, but he wasn't sure if Talent was willing to risk his life again. As a civilian, he would most certainly face resentment from the other members of Fire Team Bravo who would see his presence as an affront to the memories of their two fallen comrades. He thought Talent could deal with that. The larger question was if Commander Murdock would allow a civilian onto the team. While it was technically Walker's team and his mission, rescued civilians at sea came under the sub captain's jurisdiction.

His mind was still in turmoil from the mission. He decided to perform his evening prayers. His ritual ablution before *Maghrib* was a quick one. The addition of the survivors and his fire team placed an extra burden on the sub's limited recycling capacity. The brief rinse had washed away the visible blood from his face and hands but not from his mind. Looking down at his hands, he could still see traces of blood from the rescue mission, mingled with layers of bloodstains deposited over the years. It was invisible to others. Only he could see it, but that did not make it less real. He feared his hands and his soul would never be free of the bloodstains of his victims.

As a sniper, he had done his duty. He had no qualms about killing the enemy, even fellow Muslims if it meant saving more lives, American lives. His superiors assigned his targets, but the call to make the shot always remained his. He knew the first time he failed to pull the trigger would be the last day he would be of any use to himself or to his country. One that day he would resign.

He chose a quiet corner in the missile amid the instruments death away from prying eyes. He hoped for a taste of tranquility, but inner peace, like peace in the real world, proved elusive. Often he had no opportunity to perform the required rituals for *salat,* the daily prayers. Many times his prayers were just a few silently spoken phrases to remind him there was a God and that Allah was his name. He knew any Imam would consider him a lapsed Muslim, but it was the heart that mattered, not the ritual.

The juxtaposition between his locale and his goal was not lost on him. He too often recited his prayers with his weapons by his side. With no Imam to read aloud the first two *rak'at* verses, he performed the third *rak'at* by quoting silently from the first book of the *Qur'an.* He sought absolution, but forgiveness hovered just beyond his reach, taunting him. Finally, he gave up. He would try again during his *Isha'* evening prayers before retiring, if he had the opportunity to sleep.

He felt the throb of the pump-jet propulsor through the deck. The commander was pushing his boat's engines for every rpm he could squeeze out them in pursuit of the Kaiju. Shortly before they had rendezvoused with the *Mississippi*, the Kaiju had turned south, submerged, and increased its speed to 130 knots. The sub's top speed was 30 knots. Catching it was impossible, but still they followed. Its straight-as-an-arrow path would take it near several island chains, but Walker was betting on Australia as its goal. Brisbane and Sydney were on the east coast of Australia; Melbourne and Adelaide were on the south coast. All were heavily populated. Hobart on the island of Tasmania south of Melbourne was Australia's main navy base. All would present tempting targets for an alien invader set on creating turmoil and chaos

As Walker's passed through the overcrowded forward crew's quarters on his way to the galley, he avoided looking at the faces of the passengers. He had suffered their heartfelt thanks too many times since boarding the sub. Their gratitude made him uncomfortable. He did not think he deserved it. Huddled in rows of sleeping cubicles stacked three high on each side of a narrow corridor, they looked like forgotten people filed away in a cabinet, their only separation from the hubbub and noise of submarine life a flimsy curtain.

He found Talent in the galley drinking coffee. Here, the air smelled of caffeine, fresh baked bread, and grilling meat, masking the odor of perspiration, engine oil, and the smell of fear permeating most of the sub. The clatter of pots and pans in the background was more subdued than the sounds of battle. They drowned out the sound of the engine room, but the throb of the pump-jet propulsor was a constant pulse felt through his feet and his elbows resting on the table.

Talent glanced up from his coffee as Walker sat down. A half-eaten sandwich sat on a plate in front of him. The sight of the sandwich roused a low growl in Walker's stomach, but like Talent, he didn't have much appetite in spite of his gnawing hunger. Talent was a complete mystery to him. He considered himself a good judge of men, but Talent kept his thoughts to himself, and Walker had trouble reading his stolid face.

"So you're going after this thing, huh?" Talent asked.

Walker wasn't sure if he detected awe or disbelief in Talent's voice. "That's my job."

Talent gazed at him over the rim of his cup with dark brown eyes edging on black that looked as if they had seen too much pain and suffering. The despair seemed to spill from the corners of his eyes onto his high, ruddy cheekbones. "Business is too good. Maybe you'd better find a new line of work."

Walker suppressed a smile and took a sip of his black and bitter. The boat's coffee was strong with no cream or sugar, just as he liked it, but it was a little too cold from sitting in the pot. "It comes with the uniform. Have you ever served in the military?"

Talent shook his head, swishing his long, black hair, now freshly washed and tied back in a ponytail. He had discarded his bloodstained clothing for a set of utilities. The blue coveralls donated by a sailor was a bit too large for his lanky frame, but then submariners tended not to run six feet tall. He still wore his Stetson and cowboy boots. Walker also noticed Talent had retained his kukri in its leather sheath at his waist.

"I'm not much of a joiner," Talent answered.

Walker had met many men like Talent, never seeking responsibility but accepting the heavy burden of decision making when circumstances thrust it upon them. He had interviewed some of the survivors. They all spoke glowingly of Talent's courage and his assumption of command when order had broken down on the ship. They were not as kind in their descriptions of the ships' officers.

"You're handy with weapons."

Talent shrugged. "I know guns." He chuckled. "I have a talent for them. People, I'm not so good with."

"I understand you were headed to Australia." He wondered if Talent was aware that Australia was the Kaiju's likely destination as well.

Talent's face soured and he shook his head. "It doesn't much matter now. I thought I could run away from the trouble, but I was wrong. You can't hide from these things. They're like a *haboob*, an Arizona sand storm, relentless and overwhelming. Anyone caught in one is going to come away dirty."

Walker knew what Talent meant. He felt dirty. Crawling around in a Kaiju's guts did that to a man. It left a cloying, alien stink that you could not wash off.

"No, you can't hide. They'll keep coming until we learn enough about the aliens to stop them." Walker paused for a moment, hiding his indecision behind another sip of too cool coffee. "My team is going inside this Kaiju to deliver a poison." He watched for some reaction from Talent, but his face remained expressionless, as if he already knew Walker's mission. "I'm down two men on my team with few prospects for replacements. Want to tag along?"

Talent set his cup on the table and leaned back in his seat regarding Walker with a wry smile on his face. "You trying to recruit me, Major Walker?"

"Something like that. I don't know that the brass will agree with me. If you refuse, I won't think badly of you. You'd be a fool to come really."

Talent chuckled. "You suck at selling."

Talent's laid-back attitude was beginning to put Walker more at ease. He decided he liked the Arizonan. "I won't shit you, Talent. I got the job because I know more about what to expect inside a Kaiju than most men would care to know. It is my considered opinion that we'll probably all die."

Talent didn't react to Walker's pronouncement of doom. Instead, he said, "Your captain doesn't share your enthusiasm."

Walker nodded. Talent didn't miss much in his quiet observations. "He's young and hasn't lost men under his command before. Some calls are hard to make."

"Meaning you're not afraid to send men to their deaths."

"I'm not afraid to *lead* men to their deaths if I think the results are worth the price."

Talent nodded his head, as if he had already made that same assessment of Walker. He leaned forward in his seat, pushed his sandwich aside, and folded his arms on the table. "My people, the Tohono O'odham, call me *Lobo*, Lone Wolf, because I don't play well with others." By the slight upturn in the corner of his lips, Walker believed Talent secretly enjoyed his status as an outsider. Talent paused for a few seconds before continuing. "Sometimes you have to go with your gut instinct. One day when I was young and restless, I went to see a *makai*, a medicine man, in Ak-Chin. He looked more like an old alcoholic uncle than what I imagined a medicine man would look like, but everyone said he was the real deal. He studied me for a while as I sat in front of him eager for advice. He mumbled a few prayers, and then told me I was born lucky. As it turned out, he was right about that. He also said I would gain a warrior's heart. He might be right about that too, although it's too soon to tell."

Talent sighed softly and sat back in his chair. His expression became somber, as if the words were difficult for him to say. "He finished by telling me I would die a warrior's death. Maybe it's time to see if he was right about that too."

"So you'll come?"

"Did you know I'm worth three million dollars?"

The abrupt change in topic confused Walker. He shook his head. "No, I didn't."

"It's true, but if these Kaiju take over, it won't buy a can of beans. Hell, maybe I can mount a bleached Kaiju skull over the door of my *hogan* on the reservation to ward off evil spirits. Yeah, I'll go."

Walker eyed the bandage around Talent's left wrist. "How's the hand?"

Talent flexed it and smiled. "Good to go."

"Good. I'll see that you're properly equipped."

"I want a BFG."

"The biggest friggin' gun you can handle."

"Good, it's settled. If I'm going to meet *I'itoi*, the Great Spirit, I want to go with a Kaiju scalp on my belt."

For a brief moment, Walker saw Talent as the fierce red warrior he considered himself. "It's not settled yet. The commander has to give his permission."

Talent's face became harder. "I don't think he can stop me, unless he wants to toss me in the brig. When are we jumping off?"

Walker rose from his seat, satisfied he had made the correct judgment call on Talent. "I'll let you know later. We're rendezvousing with the freighter that answered the *Radiant Princess'* distress call to transfer the survivors, and then we're going Balls to the Wall after the Kaiju. I have a hunch it will make a few stops for harvesting, but it has a big head start. Get some sack time. Once we're inside the monster, it'll be wall-to-wall trouble."

"It beats sitting and waiting."

The sub's 1MC speaker rang out five bells – 2, 2, and 1.

"1730 hours," Walker said. "By this time tomorrow we should know something more."

He left Talent to speak with Commander Murdock. He would have to summon all his persuasive powers to convince the sub's captain to go along with his request. It was unorthodox, one for the books, but strange times called for strange methods. He felt Talent's presence on the mission would be critical. It was nothing tangible, nothing he could point to as a definite reason to allow Talent to go. It was pure gut instinct. Now, he had to express his convoluted reasoning to Murdock without sounding crazy.

Commander Murdock was in the control room, looking as if had not slept in a couple of days, poring over a chart of the Coral Sea. He glanced up at Walker as he entered. His eyes were dark and rimmed by deep shadows. His wrinkled brow had gained a few more furrows overnight.

"That was a *Bravo Zulu* on the passengers, Major," he said.

The commander's unexpected praise stung Walker. "Twenty-eight passengers out of what, four thousand? More of a *Charlie Foxtrot,* sir. It was a clusterfuck from the time we hit the deck until the time you plucked us from the sea."

"It wasn't your fault you were too late, Major. You deployed as soon as we got the SOS."

"It didn't matter much to the people we left aboard ship." He didn't try to hide the bitterness in his voice. His mind supplied pleading faces to the possibly hundreds of passengers who had gone down with the ship, hiding from the Kaiju creatures and praying for a rescue that had been too little too late. He aimed none of his recriminations at the commander. Murdock had risked his career in ordering the rescue mission. Walker placed the blame squarely on his own shoulders. He had been too cautious, too slow.

"You saved who you could. The ship was sinking when you arrived, swarming with Wasps, and the Squid came back to finish the job they started. You saved twenty-eight people who would have certainly died if you hadn't gone. I'd call it a heroic effort even if it didn't go as well as expected. I'm getting some flak for even making the attempt, but that's my problem. Now, tell me more about these Squid. They're new."

Murdock' interest in the creatures was understandable. They had sunk two nuclear submarines and a cruise ship. "My encounter with them was brief but deadly. They're more difficult to kill than Wasps, faster and more intelligent. Mark Talent is the man you need to debrief on the Squid. He named them. Hell, he attacked one with a machete."

"He's got balls, for sure," Murdock said.

"I could use him."

Murdock became more pensive. "I can loan you a couple of good men, Major. I have several in Security. Allowing a civilian on a fire team mission …That's risky."

"With all due respect, sir, sailors are trained to fight from the deck of a ship or a battle station, not a stand up, face-to-face firefight like S.E.A.L.S. Besides, you're going to need all hands on deck when we catch up with the Kaiju."

Murdock frowned. "If we can. The damn thing's doing better than 200 knots. If it doesn't stop or slow down, it'll reach Australia days before we can make contact with it. We'll lose another hour transferring the passengers to the *Amata Maru,* a Japanese freighter bound from Guam to Tuvalu." He grimaced. "That can't be helped."

Walker saw that the thought of the additional lives lost while they pursued the Kaiju troubled Murdock. He was sure the commander was thinking, as he was, that if he hadn't attempted the rescue of the cruise ship passengers, Walker's team could have been in place inside the creature by now. However, it was a moot point. No one was going to leave helpless civilians adrift at sea.

"Can we rendezvous with any seaplane in the area that can expedite our insertion?"

"Negative. Australian military forces are preparing for the Kaiju, and anything we have is well north of us. Most local civilian air traffic is grounded because of the Wasps. The Wasps have formed a moving hundred-mile-diameter defensive perimeter around the Kaiju. No drones can get close to it. We're relying on satellite imagery to track its position."

Walker glanced at the chart on the table, a map of the South Pacific and the Coral Sea. Murdock had drawn a straight line from the *Radiant Princess* to Brisbane, Australia and marked circles around Vanuatu and New Caledonia, both neatly bisected by the line.

"You think Brisbane is its destination?"

"With a population of over two million, it presents a tempting target. From there, it's less than five-hundred miles south to Sydney. I think the aliens learned a valuable lesson during the last Kaiju attacks. We were quickly able to bring all our resources to bear on the three creatures on land. America was one country with one mission. Now, on the sea with each nation insanely adamant about retaining the sanctity of its national borders, it's more difficult to hit it with any concentrated, cooperative effort. If the aliens succeed in securing a large remote island, like Australia, and defend it with a ring of submersible Kaiju, they could establish a base on Earth to strike out at any continent, any coastline."

The commander tapped his finger on Australia. "That's why they use Kaiju, to wipe out the indigenous population of a planet and create havoc. If we fail to stop this one, the aliens can send dozens, maybe hundreds of Kaiju and control the world's oceans, eliminate international sea trade, and create an almost untouchable base of operations. Half the world's population would starve within a year."

He traced his finger along the circle around Vanuatu. "If the Kaiju has a weakness, it's its insatiable appetite. It could reach Brisbane and level the entire city before we could get close to it, but I believe it will stop in Vanuatu and maybe New Caledonia to harvest humans. God help me, I'm praying that it does." He grimaced as he dragged his finger along the length of islands of the Republic of Vanuatu; then, slammed the edge of his fist on New Caledonia, rattling the illuminated glass below the chart. "That's where we'll catch it and kill it."

Walker wished he shared the commander's optimism, but he had seen too many alien surprises to feel such high confidence. They were playing catch-up, not a great place to be when dealing with a formidable foe. However, killing the Kaiju was his mission, and he would do whatever it took to accomplish it.

"You get us there, Commander, and we'll kill it."

Murdock stared at Walker for a long moment that made him slightly uncomfortable. "About your request to take Talent with you, I don't think I can allow a civilian to take the risk. Admiral Holston would have my stripes. My authorization of the *Radiant Princess* rescue mission did not go over well. I'm sorry, Major. I'll get you and your team there if I have to melt the reactor doing so."

Walker detected a touch of hesitancy in the commander's voice. He knew Walker's team needed every advantage he could give it, but allowing a civilian to participate went against his training.

"Commander, I took a civilian into Kaiju Nusku, Doctor Rutherford. He had fewer skills to offer than Talent, and yet he proved invaluable in defeating the creature. Talent is willing to go. He knows the risks. I have a gut feeling about him. I think he'll prove useful."

"I'm sorry, Major. Talent goes with the other passengers."

It was blow to Walker's gut. He did not know why the commander's refusal hit him so hard, but he knew that somehow his chances of completing the mission just dropped.

Murdock turned to Lieutenant Commander Dobbs. "Lieutenant, will you please show the major our delivery vehicle?"

Walker arched an eyebrow at the XO, as Dobbs escorted him to the amidships airlock. "I assumed we would use the DSRV, and then swim in with as little noise as possible."

Dobbs smiled. "I think you'll like this S.E.A.L. Delivery Vehicle. The Globemaster dropped them off with the drums of K-2, two new MK-10 SDVs. Each one holds eight men or its equivalent in cargo, travels at 25 knots, and runs on brushless electric motors. It's almost undetectable on sonar."

Walker smiled. "It will make getting our equipment there a bit easier."

"The Navy aims to please."

Dobbs opened the hatch leading to the decompression chamber for the air lock. Inside sat two, twenty-foot long, black and white orcas.

"What the hell?" Walker exclaimed, as he eyed the two killer whales.

Dobbs laughed. "Whoever dreamed this one up decided using orcas as camouflage might allow you to sneak in. I guess they didn't realize the Kaiju is eating everything it encounters, including plankton and schools of fish."

"I'll give them an A for effort."

Dobbs pointed to a latch on the side of the vehicle near the orca's left pectoral fin. "This releases the cowling. There's a quick release handle inside to jettison the entire cowling in an emergency." He pressed the latch and lifted the side of the orca. Inside, four tightly packed seats spaced just wide enough apart to allow men wearing SCUBA gear took up the forward section of the vehicle, with tie down straps for cargo in the rear. A simple joystick with attached throttle controlled both the motor and the dive planes and rudder. "I'll leave you to get some sack time. I need to check in with Navigation."

As Dobbs left, Walker rubbed his hand along the smooth, rubberized surface of the fake orca. The material's dimpled surface was composed of thousands of tiny, multi-faceted projections that rendered the SDV almost invisible to sonar, the latest in stealth technology. If the vehicles allowed his team to slip undetected past the Kaiju's defenses, he could put up with the cramped quarters. Free swimming from the sub was too slow and exhausting, leaving them vulnerable when they arrived.

He shook his head and laughed. "A freakin' orca. What next?"

* * * *

Talent didn't much care for his confinement in the submarine. It was larger than he had expected when he first saw its sleek black form breaking the surface like a breaching whale, but the air felt stuffy and recycled, as if it had passed through too many lungs before reaching his. The air tasted of an odd combination of sea salt, sweat, lubricating oil, and a strange odor one of the crew told him was amine used in the carbon dioxide scrubbers. He had felt his first moments of trepidation climbing down the ladder through the narrow hatch into the sub's belly, glancing up at *tash*, the sun; as if it might be the last time he felt its warmth. He went reluctantly but with little choice in the matter. A few inches of steel offered a better defense against the Squid than did a thin layer of fiberglass. Of course, that was before he had learned of the demise of the British and American submarines.

The only place that felt remotely comfortable was the galley. The familiar smells of fresh bread baking and coffee brewing kept his mind from wandering the narrow, dim corridors and the miserable faces and accusatory glances of his fellow rescued passengers. None of them blamed him personally, but like most survivors of any dramatic upheaval, manmade or natural; they felt betrayed by those whose job it was to keep them safe. That entity varied from person to person – the government, the Navy, God – but idea that such destruction, such misery could be the result of a random uncontrollable event was as alien a concept as the aliens themselves.

Talent had little in common with the other passengers other than the circumstances of their rescue. The only people he had any contact with aboard ship – the prickish security officer, the third officer, the Filipino cook, and Owens – were all dead. He wanted off the sub, but did he want off badly enough to accept Major Walker's offer?

He wanted payback. He wouldn't kid himself by claiming it was in retaliation for the deaths of the *Radiant Princess* passengers. As gruesome and as senseless as their slaughter had been, he hadn't known them well enough to owe them vengeance. Nor was it to avenge any personal affront the creatures had caused him. He had survived. That was reward enough. No, perhaps for the first time in his life he understood allegiance to something larger than his small personal world. His people the Tohono O'odham understood. It was how they had remained a vibrant people throughout the chaotic years of the Indian Wars of the late 1800s. Now, he was beginning to comprehend the significance of their unity.

His status as *El Lobo* had blinded him to the essence of what had made the Native American tribes unique. Unlike the white-skinned *Toha* who pushed westward from the cities of the east, White Men with their strange White Man concepts, his people felt a close kinship with the land. They had no desire to conquer it or to own it, only to coexist with it. If the aliens wanted the Earth, the land, it was his duty to deny it to them.

Trading one confining environment for another, the interior of the Kaiju, seemed a foolish choice, but it was time he stepped up and rejoined the human race. For too long he had drifted along in a life parallel to but apart from the rest of humanity calling it independence. He was beginning to realize it had just been a different kind of fear.

He eyed the barely touched sandwich on his plate. The coffee had loosened the knot of fear in his stomach, but he didn't think it could handle food yet. He considered another cup; then, decided he was simply procrastinating. He had made his decision and rehashing his reasons wasn't going to change anything. He was going inside the Kaiju, and if his luck remained with him, he would come out again with a tale to tell. If not, no one would shed a tear for his demise.

He was glad Walker's team was not leaving immediately. His ribs ached where the Squid had slammed him around, and his shoulder itched from the three stitches the doctor had insisted on when he treated the puncture wound. The doctor had wrapped his sprained left wrist in gauze to relieve the strain. He hoped he had a couple of days to recover.

The galley was beginning to fill up as sailors filed in for dinner or to load up on caffeine for their night-duty watches. He felt uncomfortable in their midst. Their furtive glances reminded him that he was different, an Indian, as if any indigenous people ever needed reminding of their status. Then, one sailor smiled at him and raised his hand in a half-wave. He suddenly realized they were staring not because he was Indian or different, but because he was a new face among faces that had become too all too familiar. After three months at sea, any new face was a change of pace, an event worth noting. He returned the sailor's wave, kicking himself mentally for being too judgmental, a trait he detested in others.

He tried not to eavesdrop, but could not keep from overhearing snatches of conversation. They spoke of kicking Kaiju ass, but he detected an underlying current of fear in their bold boasts. Their voices were just a little too loud in an attempt to bolster their courage and mask their apprehension. Their fear didn't dismay him. They were the U.S. Navy. He knew when push came to shove they would be at their posts ready to fight.

He ambled through the ship seeking some place quiet away from the presence of others. He needed to think, to make a mental list of reasons to go with the major and reasons not to. He needed to compare the two columns, pro and con, to see if recent events had compromised his capacity to made sound judgment calls. The list itself did not matter. He had already made his decision, but a breakdown of his reasons would show him how far from sanity he was straying.

Peering into submarine's compartments like a Peeping Tom, he soon gave up on his search for a quiet retreat. By luck, he found the ship's library, a tiny room with two shelves of books, a few chairs, and a CD player with headphones. An officer sat in one of the chairs listening to music with his eyes closed, oblivious to his surroundings. His foot tapped out a fast rhythm on the carpeted deck. Talent picked up an old issue of *National Geographic*, trying to lose himself in the photos and an article about the chaotic life in Baghdad with ISIS controlling most of the country and terrorists killing scores of people each week in random bombings and suicide attacks. The tone of the writer suggested hope for the future, but the people interviewed seemed resigned to years of endless bloodshed. He wondered if a Kaiju landing in the desert would bring them together, or if it would just become a third-party participant in the slaughter.

A copy of *Neptune's Trident*, the ship's daily newsletter, lay on one of the desks. He wasn't interested in daily life aboard a submarine, but one large-print headline caught his eye: WHAT DO THE ALIENS WANT? *Good question*, he thought, *but in the end, it doesn't really matter.* The Red Man had asked the same question about the White Man as he encroached on traditional tribal lands, as if understanding them would solve the problem. They didn't fight back until it was too late or bother to unite as one people except for a few scattered battles, lessons from which mankind could learn. Whatever the aliens' intent, it didn't bode well for humans.

Finally, delayed exhaustion crept up on him. He had been running on adrenaline for so long he could taste it in his mouth. He had examined his assigned berth earlier; a narrow cot in the torpedo room slung between a berth below him and a row of pipes a few inches above his head, and decided it looked too much like a coffin. He laid down the newsletter, closed his eyes, and leaned back in his chair. In spite of the myriad of thoughts running through his mind, within minutes he was snoring softly.

14

Sunday, Dec. 17, 4:45 a.m.   Takara Landing, Efate, Republic of Vanuatu –

John Lini sat in his VPF patrol car off the side of the Ring Road near Takara Landing working on his second cup of coffee. He didn't mind the early shift. The island was usually quiet before five a.m. Except for the fishermen, most of the tourists weren't up yet, and the locals were preparing for work. The drunks had already gone to bed or were sleeping it off in a Port-Vila jail cell. In all his fifteen years on the Vanuatu Police Force, he had drawn his weapon one time and then had fired only a warning shot into the air.

Working the early morning shift left time for his favorite pastime, playing guitar twice a week with a local band on the island's hotel and resort circuit. A few island tunes, some country favorites, and a lot of old time rock and roll satisfied the tourists, the locals, and his need for recognition. Being a cop was a thankless job, but musicians got respect, even a mediocre picker like him. He knew he could never land a job with any decent mainland band, but on an island with a population of less than sixty-thousand people, he was one of the best pickers around.

At thirty-five, Lini still had all his teeth, his wavy blond hair, his tight abs, and his boyish grin, enough to land him in some lonely foreign female tourist's bed or a night with one of the locals. It was a good life, one that suited him.

As he raised his travel mug to his lips, the car shook, spilling a little coffee on his shirt. "Damn," he muttered, as he wiped the coffee off with a napkin stuffed down between the seats. "That's going to stain."

He glanced out the window but saw nothing, no traffic, no low-flying jet from Bauerfield Airport, no practical jokers shaking his car. A few seconds later, the car shuddered again, this time violently enough to scatter his paperwork across the seat and into the floorboard. *Earthquake.* Tremors were common in Vanuatu. Twenty-four volcanoes dotted the island chain. Some islands were nothing more than volcanic cones thrusting upward from the sea floor. Two volcanoes hadn't yet breached the surface, bubbling just beneath the waves. The last major eruption had been a decade earlier, but in 2015, Port Vila had rocked to a magnitude 6.5 tremor. He remembered waking up to his bed bouncing across the floor.

He searched the skyline south toward Yasur Volcano on Tanna Island, and then towards Ambrym and Lopevi to the north, the only active volcanoes in Vanuatu, but saw only the usual nightglow of molten lava in the cones, no plumes of smoke or ribbons of lava flowing down their flanks.

The car bounced violently again, throwing him into the steering wheel. If they had been working, he would have had a face full of airbag. It had to be an earthquake caused by one of the submarine volcanoes. He got out of the car and looked around but still saw nothing. He clicked on his radio.

"Car Six to base. This in Lini. Gracie, did you feel that quake?"

Grace Quai had radio night duty, a job he tried to avoid whenever possible. At least in a patrol car he could drive around the island. Sitting by the radio all night would drive him crazy. She answered.

"John, this is Gracie. Yeah, I felt the building shake. I think I'll ..."

Her voice cut off. "What, Gracie?"

Her contralto voice had picked up an edge of concern. "John, I just tried the land lines but they're out. I'm not getting anything over the fiber optic cable to Fiji either."

Lini checked his cell phone. It, too, was dead. "I've got no cell phone signal. Have you heard anything from TVL?" The local internet and phone provider was notorious for dropped signals and outages.

"Nothing, John. Do you . . ." Her voice dropped away as another tremor struck. Lini bounced along the side of the car, which danced from one wheel to the other think. The tremors were coming less than a minute apart, like pre-natal contractions. Lini wondered what was being born. Grace's voice came back on, "Do we have to worry about a tsunami?"

The tsunami after the earthquake of 1999 had caused severe damage to the island of Pentecost and inundated a few coastal businesses on Efate. He did not want to see that happen again, especially not on Efate. Without his cell phone, he could not get an update from Vanuatu Meteorological Service. VMS was responsible for tsunami and typhoon alerts. He cupped his ear toward the beach but heard only normal surf sounds, no pounding waves, or the roar of an incoming tidal wave.

For a brief moment, he linked the earthquakes with the Kaiju landing in Kiribati, but dismissed it as unlikely. Kiribati was two-thousand miles away, and the Kaiju had attacked a cruise ship near there yesterday morning. It couldn't be anywhere near Vanuatu in such a short time.

"I'll drive down to the beach and check the surf. Anything on the ship-to-shore?"

"It's dead too." After a few seconds, she said, "I'm frightened, John."

He rode out another tremor, and then answered, "You're Ni-Vanuatu, Gracie, a tenth-generation native islander. You're great-grandmother was a queen. You can't be scared."

"Well I am," she insisted.

He was too, but he was not going to admit it to her. "Okay. I'll drive back along the Ring Road and stop to check the surf in a few places. I'll be there in less than an hour."

"Don't stop for a swim."

He smiled. She knew him too well. An early morning swim was a great way to start the day. He always carried swimming trunks and a towel in the trunk of his patrol car. "I won't. Call if you hear anything. Lini out."

He replaced the radio microphone and leaned against the car. This time, the ground shook so violently it threw him to the ground as if someone had slammed in the back. He picked himself up off the sand and climbed into the driver's seat. He cranked the car, threw it into gear, and headed to the beach at Takara Landing. Twice, he fought the steering wheel as the road undulated beneath the wheels.

The beach was deserted in the predawn hours. The white sand gleamed in the early morning half-light like a ribbon of sugar. When the sun came up, the water would be deep azure and as clear as the bottom of a beer mug, inviting swimmers and snorkelers beneath its surface, or kite surfers taking advantage of the prevailing southwesterly winds. Now, the water was dark and mysterious. He took a deep whiff of blooming bougainvillea and frangipani, enjoying their sweet fragrances. Looking out toward the outlying islands, Emao, Pele, and Nguna, he at first saw nothing out of the ordinary; then, jerked his gaze back to a fourth island that shouldn't be there. To the right of Emao, a smaller black dot sat atop the surface of the ocean, too large for a ship and too narrow for the leading edge of a tsunami. The sand beneath his feet bounced with another tremor. He lost his balance and stumbled across the beach before righting himself. It felt as if the island was going to shake itself apart.

The mysterious dot got closer as he watched. *It must be a ship*, he thought. Suddenly, it rose from the surface, revealing a dozen long legs. *Kaiju*! His heart went numb and his throat became too dry to swallow.

He stood transfixed by the sight of the behemoth striding from the sea toward the island. *His island.* The thought of his island, his people in danger, melted the icy fear that gripped him. He raced back to his car as one of the massive legs struck the ground, creating another tremor that sent him reeling. A coconut palm, leaning away from the wind, lost its grip on the dirt and toppled across his path. He leaped over it and slammed into the side of the car. He ignored the pain in his right knee, yanked open the door, and slid into the driver's seat.

"Gracie," he yelled into the microphone, "Alert the VMF. Wake the Prime Minister."

The Vanuatu Mobile Force was the closest thing they had to a military, but he knew it would be no match for the alien monster.

"Is it a tsunami?" Gracie asked.

Better if it were, he thought. "No, worse," he answered. "It's a Kaiju."

* * * *

Jess Akuna's hands shook so badly he couldn't fasten the chinstrap of his helmet. He had worn the helmet a few times during full uniform drills, but he had never been scared to death before a drill. He wished he had a cup of *kava* to calm his jittery nerves, but it was too early for any of the stores to open. He glanced around the locker room and saw the other members of his Vanuatu Mobile Force squad staring at him, looking as frightened as he was. He shoved the helmet under his arm and faced them. They all spoke Bislama, the native Melanesian language, or French, or English, some all three. Bislama was his second language. He had spoken it since a teen when he moved to the island with his parents, but he addressed his men in English because his mind was too befuddled to think in Bislama.

"This isn't a war game. Our island, our homes are under attack. We have to go out there and do our duty."

One of the men held out his M1 carbine. "With this? What good is this against a Kaiju? I might as well piss on it."

Akuna knew how the man, Joe Chin, felt. Chin was a good barber but a lousy militiaman. In spite of the twice-yearly drills and hours at the shooting range, Chin could barely hit the target, much less the bull's-eye. "We can't stop a Kaiju, but maybe we can save some people from Wasps, or whatever else that creature throws at us. You can go home and hide if you want, but I don't think that's going to do much good. You've all heard about Kiribati?" A few heads nodded. "We don't have a choice. It's the VPF and us. No one's going to come to our rescue."

"Have we called anyone?" Tiami Regevanu asked. "What about Espiritu Santo?" Regevanu operated the restaurant at the Port-Vila

Country Club on Vila Bay where Akuna played golf every Saturday. Efate was the capital of the Republic of Vanuatu, but Espiritu Santo was the largest island of the seventy islands of the island nation, and everyone looked to them for assistance in an emergency.

"We have no cell phone or internet connections, and the cable to Fiji is out."

"Jesus Christ!" Robert Barbier called out. "Did that thing do that?"

Akuna had no answer for the short, overweight bus driver. "I don't know, Bob. It doesn't matter. No one's coming."

"There's a cruise ship in the bay," Seimata Kaltack pointed out. "Why don't we load up on it and leave?"

"All sixty thousand of us?" Akuna pointed out. "Besides, it pulled up anchor and sailed two hours ago."

"What about the airport, Jess?" someone asked. "I think …"

Akuna raised his voice. "Look, all this is pointless. There's no discussion involved here. We have our orders. The Kaiju will be here in less than an hour. We're evacuating the city, but they have nowhere to run except toward the Kaiju. Fourth Squad has set up its mortars at the edge of town. Second Squad deployed its two .50 calibers on the roof airport terminal. First Squad is on the roof of Parliament. We will deploy along Teoma Street to keep people moving."

"God help us," Tio Mataskelekele said.

Mataskelekele was a minister at the International Christian Church. Akuna hoped his word carried some weight with God. They would need it. With communications out, the Prime Minister had dispatched boats to the other islands, but what little help they could offer would be too late in coming.

The sun had risen bright and beautiful after two days of rain, but instead of a city basking in its warm, tropical glow, its austere light revealed a chaotic scene of mass exodus. The streets were jammed with cars and people on foot trying to leave the city. To where did not matter, only escape. The bay was astir with yachts and fishing boats loaded to the gunwales with people. Many would sink in the rough seas as soon as they left the shelter of the bay. A small Cessna flew overhead so overloaded it barely skimmed the treetops. People were in a panic. If they knew how little firepower the VMF had to resist the Kaiju, they would have been even more frightened.

Akuna lined his handful of men along the edge of Teoma Street. The heady scent of frangipani and gardenia filled the freshly scrubbed air, fighting the exhaust fumes of automobiles, but no one stopped to smell the air. Akuna's men waved their arms directing traffic, but their heads faced northwest, the direction from which the Kaiju would come.

The center of the island was a tangle of shrubs and dense growths of whitewood, kaori, banyan, and banana trees. Dozens of small streams and rivers ran to the sea from the slopes of the mountains and hills. He could see the hulk of Mount McDonald to the north. At twenty-one-hundred feet, it was the highest point on the island. Mount Tafa Ki Malao and Mount Putuet were smaller at seven-hundred and fifteen hundred feet respectively. Neither the island's rugged terrain nor the mountains would present a challenge to the nine-hundred-foot juggernaut bearing down on the city like a runaway freight train.

He caught sight of the Kaiju as it crossed a ridge near Mount Putuet near the old manganese mine. Its legs concealed by the trees, it glided across the landscape like a dark shadow cast by a cloud. Its darkness was a black hole absorbing the sunlight. With its hundred-foot stride, it hadn't even gotten its feet wet crossing the Epule River. The creature was over ten miles away and still dominated the skyline. It would be striding through the center of the city in half an hour.

His first thought as saw its entire bulk was of a gigantic, ebony cockroach designed by alien minds striding across the kitchen floor, except this cockroach walked on twelve legs. Razor-sharp protuberances lined the edges of each body segment. A nest of writhing tentacles ringed its enormous gaping maw. It was a horror from hell, a creature dredged from the darkest nightmares of a demented mind. He wondered if its appearance was a matter of design or purposefully constructed to strike fear into the hearts and minds upon the peoples upon which it had been unleashed.

The Kaiju itself wasn't the worst of their problems. The air around the creature was aswarm with the black specks of hundreds of Wasps. They could reach the city in minutes, but they were busy harvesting the people in the outlying homesteads and farms. To the alien creatures, humans, cattle, pigs, or monkeys – it made no difference. All were fodder to fuel the creature's inexhaustible appetite. He sighed with relief when the creature disappeared from sight behind another ridge, breaking the compelling spell it had cast over him. He knew it was still moving inexorably toward him, but better to fear the unseen disaster than be mesmerized by its gargantuan, ebony hulk.

An occasional shot rang out from the edge of the city as homeowners and ranchers wielding shotguns and hunting rifles tried to fend off the flying Wasps, but there were simply too many of them. He was torn between sympathy for the islanders' plight and grateful relief for the few extra minutes it gave the crowd milling around him to escape. The Kaiju reappeared, this time only a few miles from town striding along the Teouma River that emptied into the sea east of the city. A few minutes later, the louder reports of the mortar firing reached him from the village of Lololima just south of Lololima Falls. He glanced back at the crowded road and knew evacuation was impossible. The snarl of traffic and the clot of frightened people clogged the streets. If they had another four hours, it still would not be enough time.

"Get off the streets," he yelled at the crowd. "Hide in the buildings." He knew the flimsy buildings would not offer much protection, but it was better than standing in the open. When hardly anyone paid attention to him, he fired a burst from his M16 into the air to get their attention. "Hide!" he yelled to the startled crowd.

People scattered. They abandoned their vehicles and array of pushcarts and bundles, and raced to any shelter they could find. Some of his squad looked as if they wanted to join them. To their credit, they remained at their posts. The ponderous footsteps of the enormous creature shook the earth. Minutes later, the mortars went silent, their crews wiped out by the Wasps. The creature skirted the edge of the foothills of Mount McDonald and veered southwest toward the airport, as if destroying any method of escape was foremost in its alien mind.

He cringed with horror as a Gulfstream G450 twin-engine jet lifted from the runway. The pilot had made a serious error in judgment or in timing by taking off into the southwestern winds directly at the Kaiju. The pitch of the twin Rolls Royce Tay MK 611 engines increased to a shrill whine, as the pilot revved them to maximum speed to aid in banking the aircraft away from the creature. The Gulfstream had a sixteen-passenger capacity, but Akuna imagined the pilot had packed as many people into the craft as possible. It banked too slowly. At first, he thought the Gulfstream was going to crash into the Kaiju, but the pilot fought the controls for every ounce of lift the wings and engines could provide. The jet cleared the creature's back by fifty feet.

It wasn't enough. One of the Kaiju's hundred-foot-long tentacles lashed out from around its maw and struck one of the jet's wings, as one would swat an annoying buzzing mosquito. The right wing snapped off. The pilot sent all the power to the remaining left engine, but the jet veered left and lost altitude. It disappeared behind a ridge. Seconds later, the report of an explosion reached him, followed by a plume of black smoke rising behind the ridge. A handful of Wasps broke away from the creature to investigate the crash and search for bodies. The Kaiju continued its march toward the city.

Akuna had no time to mourn their deaths or wonder if any of his friends were among the passengers. Wasps descended on Port Vila. The foremost creatures flew over the city and attacked the boats in the bay or passing beyond the edges of it. A second dark swarm of Wasps flew toward the airport. The remainder swept down from the sky and attacked the people who still hadn't reached shelter. The sight reminded him of WWII dive-bombers attacking war ships. He had seen photos of Wasps, but these were different. Four oddly shaped lumps protruded from the Wasps' abdomens. As he tried to decipher what function they served, a Wasp flew six feet over his head and landed beside a woman clutching her young child to her breast. He smelled the sickening alien stench of the creature as it passed, like a flying abattoir. To his horror, the four lumps disengaged from the Wasp, extended four legs, and dropped to the ground.

The new creatures were tan in color, the size of small dogs, but very angular, almost pointed at one end. The rear legs were longer than the front legs and much thicker. He saw why, as the creature leaped into the air like a giant flea, covered the ten feet distance to the woman in one hop, and landed in front of her. The other three joined it, surrounding her.

The woman's scream broke his reverie. He rushed at the Fleas, firing his M16 wide to avoid hitting her. Most of his bullets missed, but several of them struck the creature to her right, killing it. He was surprised with the ease with which it died, but then realized their numbers, not their armor, was their strong point. If each Wasp carried four Fleas, there were thousands of them. He aimed carefully at the one between him and her and fired. His short burst ripped the Flea in half.

"Run!" he yelled at her as he struggled to replace his empty clip. He looked up as Seimata Kaltack joined him, firing his M1 at the other two Fleas. He killed one as it hopped at him. Akuna took out the fourth one.

"What the hell are they?" Kaltack yelled.

"I don't know," Akuna answered.

Hundreds of the Fleas hopped along the streets pursuing fleeing people. One man was down with three of the creatures on his back. With no neck, they drove their entire body forward, stabbing into his flesh with their sharp heads until he was dead. A long tongue emerged from their tiny mouths, licking up the blood. A Wasp swooped in to pick up and carry away the corpse, while the Fleas sought another victim. Fleas and Wasps formed a highly efficient killing machine.

"We can't kill them all," Kaltack said. "There are too many."

"We can try," he replied.

His fear slowly dissipated at the sight of the slaughter around him, replaced by a growing rage. He attacked the closest Wasp. His bullets found one of the creature's eyes, smashing it. It trilled loudly, as yellow ichor flowed down its face. He slammed a fresh magazine into the M16, pulled the bolt to send a round into the chamber, and began firing at the Wasp's head. Kaltack joined him.

His and Kaltack's combined firepower did some damage. The Wasp backed away, fluttered its wings, and tried to fly away, but Akuna has having none of it. He concentrated his fire at the creature's open mouth. Yellow blood began dripping from its mouth and showered the street as it shook its head. Somewhere among the hail of bullets he poured down its throat, one struck the brain. The creature's four hind legs folded, and it sat awkwardly on the ground. It attempted to crawl away using its front legs, but only moved in a circle when its hind legs refused to move, like a fly swatted and partially paralyzed by a fly swatter, refusing to die. Avoiding the thrashing talons on the tips of its front legs, Akuna walked up to it and fired a short burst into its remaining intact eye. The creature shuddered once and collapsed onto the street, dead.

Akuna's sense of self-satisfaction quickly evaporated when he saw the dozens of dead or dying people carted away by a steady stream of Wasps. A horde of Fleas darted among them, licking up pools of blood from the streets and sidewalks. The Fleas died easily enough, but he had used two clips of ammo to kill one Wasp out of the hundreds attacking the city. It was a numbers game and the numbers were stacked against him. There wasn't enough ammunition on the entire island to make a dent in the swarm of alien creatures.

The machineguns on the Parliament Building ceased firing one by one as their crews succumbed to the Wasps or Fleas. His squad was down two men. Regevanu and Mataskelekele were dead. He couldn't see Barbier, but heard his M1 barking from around the corner. He heard very little small arms fire from the other squads. During the battle, the Kaiju had gotten closer. Windows shattered and the pavement cracked with each footfall of the Kaiju's twelve legs, a staccato of tremors that strengthened in intensity with every step the giant took.

"We can't stay here," Kaltack said. "It's useless."

Akuna looked around them. There were few living people in sight. Wasps dominated the sky and Fleas commanded the ground. Kaltack was right.

"Okay," he replied reluctantly. His hot blood demanded more alien blood to sate his anger, but his senses pleaded for self-preservation.

They took shelter beneath a bus. From his low vantage point, he watched Wasp legs appear and disappear, as well as human legs vanishing from sight as Wasps took them. Fleas hopped in and out of view, attacking people in groups. He heard fewer screams as the crowd thinned.

The bus bounced around him. His fear of crushing by one of the bus's tires almost forced him from his hiding place, but dying beneath a bus's wheels seemed preferable to the ignominious death of becoming Kaiju food. He remained where he was, as an unnatural darkness replaced the early morning daylight. One of the Kaiju's hundred-foot long, boxcar-sized legs stabbed into a house a block away, skewering it with the knife-edged appendage. One the next step, the house exploded into shards of wood and concrete as the leg yanked it into the air, only to shower down moments later as debris. The Kaiju's writhing tentacles wormed their way into buildings and along the streets, probing for human prey as a woodpecker digs for insects. Tentacles withdrew with struggling people grasped in their deadly embrace destined for the creature's enormous open maw. He had thought the stench of the Wasps was bad. The Kaiju reeked of rotten flesh and coagulated blood. It stank of musty seaweed and sun-bleached fish.

A tentacle wrenched the bus from atop him and flung it aside like a child's toy. It crashed two blocks away amid the rubble of a school building. He rolled over onto his back and stared up at the belly of the creature. The Kaiju was as large as an aircraft carrier. Segmented ebony plates serrated like saw teeth along the edges covered its body. The head sat at the end of a short neck, but the head didn't have to move far. The tentacles around its mouth brought food to the creature's mouth. Three pairs of legs attached to the creature's forward section, while the remaining three pairs sat toward the creature's rear.

Akuna expected one of the legs to grind him into the pavement, but the Kaiju passed over him like a low-flying dirigible – exposing him to the Wasps and Fleas. He froze, hoping they would ignore him, but the creatures' vision, hearing, and sense of smell, developed by the alien bioengineers to seek out living flesh for the Kaijus, were too acute to miss a hapless human lying on the street. Several of the creatures circled the sky above him and Kaltack like vultures waiting for him to gasp out his last breath, but unlike vultures, they preferred live prey.

Kaltack's eyes grew wide with fright as Fleas began converging on their location. He stared at Akuna while raising his M1 and aiming at them. Akuna mouthed a wordless 'No' and shook his head, but his friend and fellow soldier had witnessed too many gruesome deaths, seen too much destruction. He looked away, rose to his knees, and fired into the nearest group of Fleas. As if his shot had been a signal, the Wasps stopped circling and hovered above them like nine-foot hummingbirds. Kaltack rose to his feet and continued firing. He killed two Fleas and howled in triumph. Unfortunately, he ignored the Wasps above him. Two of them dropped straight down at him. Each seized a shoulder with its deadly talons and lifted him into the air. His agony did not end there. Whether by purpose or simply a dispute over captured prey, the Wasps moved apart, ripping Kaltack in half.

His friend's blood raining down over him was the last straw for Akuna. Driven half-mad by rage, he raised his M16 and emptied the magazine into one of the Wasps that had slaughtered his friend. The Wasp tumbled from the sky and landed a few feet from him. The creature was dead, but killing it hadn't been enough to assuage his mounting fury. He reloaded and fired two more short bursts into its dead eyes.

As he stood there in the street, gulping breaths of air as his rage drained away, a shadow fell over him, reminding him how exposed he was. Reality set in and replaced wrath with caution. He wasn't certain why he wasn't dead already. The Fleas, momentarily distracted by another survivor choosing that moment to run from cover, ignored him. Akuna raced across the street to the rubble of a demolished building and cowered beneath a section of collapsed roof. A bellowing wail emitted by the Kaiju drew the Wasps away from the area and toward the city. The Wasps hovered a few feet from the ground, as the Fleas leaped up and reattached themselves to the Wasps' abdomens, and then flew away.

He glanced toward the city. The Kaiju had waded through downtown, a giant among pygmies, leaving a football-field wide swath of devastation. Fires started by severed gas lines erupted in a dozen buildings. With no fire brigade to extinguish them, the fires would quickly sweep through the rest of town, wiping it from the face of the earth like a fiery tsunami. The Kaiju now stood on its hind sextet of legs, using its front legs to hammer at the sides of the seven-story Grand Hotel. Each thrust of a pointed appendage ripped massive chunks of masonry from the building's façade. Like gutting a fish, within minutes the interior of the building lay exposed. White linen fluttered and floated around the creature like dandelion seeds blown by a puff of wind. People too frightened to evacuate promptly became food, as the massive writhing mouth tentacles snatched them from their rooms. It reminded Akuna of a giant alien spiny echidna ripping apart a termite mound and lapping up the exposed tasty termite treats with its long sticky tongue. The sight sickened him.

The Wasps, drawn to the creature by its feeding call, dove among the ruins like Brahminy Kites, harvesting people exposed by the creature's patch of destruction or driven from their hiding places by the heat of the raging inferno. Fleas swarmed over the rubble like rats. It became a hellish choice for survivors – roast in the flames or face the almost equally certain death from the Wasps, Fleas, or the Kaiju's probing tentacles.

The Kaiju, its destruction of the hotel and most of Port Vila complete, waded into Vila Bay toward the resort bungalows on Iririki Island. It scattered and sank ships and boats still moored to the docks or floating at anchor. With three strides, it was on the island, smashing wooden bungalows as if they were toothpick and glue constructions created for a school arts and crafts exhibit. The long tentacles lashed out at fleeing vessels, sending them to the bottom of the bay. Then, it turned back toward the main island. Akuna realized his hunch was right. The creature was methodically destroying any means of escape before settling down to wipe all trace of human life from the island.

He didn't know if Efate was the first island of all the islands of Vanuatu to suffer the creature's wrath or if his island had the bad luck of lying in the creature's path to more densely populated areas, such as Australia. His people, his friends, had been an opportune snack, a quick bite before lunch. He checked his weapon. He had half a clip left and no more ammo in his ammo pouch. Boxes of ammunition remained in the barrack's building near the airport, but he doubted the building still existed. He had even more doubt about his chances of reaching it alive.

To his surprise, Barbier rushed from across the street to join him. Smears of blood covered both chubby cheeks of his face, but Akuna saw no injuries. The severely obese bus driver was gasping for breath as he spoke.

"Are they gone, Joe?"

Akuna ignored his question. "Is anyone else from the squad alive?"

Barbier shook his head, flapping his jowls. "I don't think so. I watched Chin die. He didn't get off a single damn shot."

Akuna shook his head. *Eight men in his squad and only Barbier and he remained.* "No, they're not gone, Bob. They're busy cleaning out the city."

"What do we do?"

His city was gone, perhaps his whole island. He was no longer defending it; he was now simply one of the few lucky survivors. "If the Kaiju is headed to Australia, it might move on soon. If not, it might stay here until it eats every human on the island, unless the Americans decide to nuke it first."

Barbier's red face blanched at the prospect of nuclear annihilation.

"We head inland and hide in the jungle. We round up any survivors we run into and take them with us. That's our job now. If we're lucky, we'll live to see another sunrise."

A woman, her bloody clothes tattered, walked from the ruins of what had once been a home, and stared toward the Kaiju. He called out to her. She turned and looked at him with vacant haunted eyes.

"We start with her," he told his companion, "and anyone else we find."

With a new sense of purpose, he left his cowering spot and strode toward the woman. Barbier followed him. They weren't much of an army, but they still had a job to do. He could not say that he was no longer afraid; he was, but the fear was secondary, something he could deal with. What he was now was determined.

15

Sunday, Dec. 17, 0400 hours   *USS Mississippi* –

Walker had slept only three hours, but he awoke fully alert, as was his usual practice. Over the years, he had perfected the ability to drop into a deep sleep, quickly reaching REM stage and allowing his body to extract maximum recharge from every hour of sleep. It wasn't an optimum solution, but in the field, it often had to suffice. Around him, the rest of the fire team still slept soundly in their portable cots strewn among the forest of missile tubes. Costas' sonorous nasal rumblings matched the pulses of the pump-jet propulsor. He slept with one hairy leg thrown over the side of his cot, the rest of his body entangled in his blanket.

Walker detected a crisp, briny freshness to the air and the gentle rise and fall of the sub and realized they were running on the surface. Murdock was pushing the sub for every rpm he could coax from the engines to reach the Kaiju as quickly as possible. Every hour put them farther behind the behemoth. Despite his deep sleep, the fringes of Walker's mind still roiled with unresolved issues. He had not yet settled matters with his second-in-command, McGregor, nor had he decided how best to use Talent's skills on the team, if the Commander allowed it. Introducing a civilian to the teams' already delicate balance would be disruptive, but he sensed something in the young Arizonan that made him believe it would be worth the effort. To quiet the rumblings in his head, he decided to perform *Fajr*, his pre-dawn *salat* prayer.

The showers were deserted at 4:00 a.m. In preparation for his prayers, he stripped, ran a quick pulse of water over his body; and then, turned it off to save water as he soaped up. He turned the water back on and rinsed as quickly as possible. He dried off and changed into a fresh uniform he had procured earlier from ship's stores. He set his flashlight on dim, knelt on the deck, and quietly intoned the third prayer *rak'at* so that he wouldn't disturb his companions. He cleared his mind, waiting for holy inspiration that would not come. Instead, he saw the faces of the dead and the dying on the cruise ship interspersed with the faces of the men who had accompanied him inside Kaiju Nusku. After ten minutes of unanswered prayer, he gave up. He knew Allah would not fail him. Clearly, he had failed Allah. Perhaps the Imam were correct, and he was not a true and faithful servant of Allah. Was he trying to serve two masters – Allah and the U.S. military – and failing at both?

"I guess it's difficult being a Muslim in the Army."

Startled, Walker shot from his knees and whirled quickly at the voice from the darkness, his hand automatically reaching for the weapon on his hip that wasn't there. He had left them by his cot for his prayers.

"Whoa, Major! I'm one of the good guys."

He recognized the outline of Talent's absurd cowboy hat and relaxed. The lanky Arizonan moved closer, letting the dim red light from a missile tube service panel wash over his face, which bore a big grin.

"What are you doing skulking about this time of the morning?" Walker demanded. He wasn't angry at having his prayers disturbed. They had been in vain and a wasted effort. He was embarrassed that Walker had caught him off guard.

Talent shrugged his shoulders. "I'm not skulking; I'm exploring. I slept in a chair in the library. I couldn't cut those stacked shelves that pass for beds around here. A cute young yeoman came by and asked me if I wanted to go on deck for a while for some fresh air before we transfer to that Japanese freighter. At least the rain stopped. I was hoping to watch the sunrise."

He noted the sense of loss in Talent's voice, as if being below the surface away from the sun and sky bothered him. "Did the fresh air help?"

"It did until I climbed back down that hatch."

"It's going to be tight inside a Kaiju. Sure you still want to go?"

Talent arched an eyebrow at Walker. "I thought the commander put the kibosh on the idea."

"I'll work on him. I convinced him that I need you, but he's hesitant. He's just covering his ass."

"Aren't we all? Look, don't get me wrong, Major. I don't want to go. I'd rather find a quiet place somewhere and sit it out. That's been my philosophy for years. This isn't like a zombie apocalypse or a collapsing economy. A stockpile of canned goods and some ammo isn't going to do the trick. This is Biblical, end-of-the-world shit. There are no bystanders in this war. I'd rather die striking a blow than cowering on my knees. These Kaiju have pissed me off and I need some payback." He stared at Walker. "I'm just not sure why you want me to tag along."

What could he say? That he had a feeling about Talent, that an extra weapon could make the difference between success and failure?

"Sometimes I get hunches. Very often, they've saved my life or the lives of the men around me." *Except on my last mission*, he thought with bitterness. "I see something in you, Talent. I think you're a natural-born soldier, a leader of men. It's not something they can teach you in a military academy or in officer's candidate school. It's something here." He tapped his chest. "Some are born great, some achieve greatness, and some have greatness thrust upon them."

Talent smiled. "Are you quoting Shakespeare's *Twelfth Night* now? I thought you military types would be more into *Julius Caesar* or *Henry V*."

"It seemed a propos."

"How about 'Lord, what fools these mortals be?' from *A Midsummer's Night Dream*? Are we all fools for believing we can make a difference?"

"If I didn't think what I do makes a difference, I couldn't keep doing it."

"Yeah, I guess you're right. I just get maudlin early in the morning. Coffee will fix that."

"Bring me a cup and a doughnut when you go," Costas said from his cot, and then yawned. "If I can't sleep, drink, or have a woman, I might as well eat a friggin' doughnut." He sat on the edge of his cot, rubbed his eyes, and glanced up at Talent. "Morning, Cowboy. Is this a private meeting?"

Talent shook his head. "No, we were discussing fools."

"I thought I heard someone call my name."

Walker spoke up. "I've asked Talent to join us on the mission."

"I figured it was something like that. Glad to have you along, Cowboy. It might get lonesome sitting inside the belly of a Kaiju. Walker here knows all my stories. You'll be virgin ears."

"I can't wait."

Costas jerked his thumb over his shoulder at the sleeping fire team. "Should I wake them?"

Before sacking out, he had introduced them all to the SDVs they would use to approach the Kaiju, and together they had familiarized themselves with their operation, each one taking a dry run at the controls in case he or McGregor, who would pilot the two craft, became incapacitated. That and a primer on the safe handling of the drums of K-2 had taken hours.

Walker shook his head. "No, let them sleep while they can. What about you?"

"Oh, I slept some yesterday. I'm good." Costas shot Talent a broad grin. "Do you know how much fun we're gonna have inside that thing?"

He pursed his lips and shuddered dramatically for effect. "It'll be our own little slice of heaven."

"You've got a severe death wish, Sergeant," Talent replied, only half in jest.

"Go big or go home, that's my philosophy. They don't come bigger than a Kaiju."

"I'd settle for getting out alive."

"You've got to be willing to die to appreciate living. Life tastes sweeter after a victory."

"Don't let Costas kid you," Walker warned. "He's a survivor. Stick close to him and he'll get you out alive."

"You may have a few dents and dings, but nothing that won't buff out," Costas added.

Talent turned to Walker. "You said something about a BFG for me."

Costas grinned. "I've got just the thing for you, Cowboy."

He walked over to a stack of fiberglass cases, read the labels, and pulled a case from the stack. He opened the latches and stood back to allow Talent to look into the open case. Talent picked up Walker's flashlight and shined it in the case.

"This, gentlemen, is an M23 MGL, a 40 mm Multi Grenade Launcher. Its rotating magazine holds 14 grenades with an effective range of 400 yards. That's farther than from the Kaiju's mouth to its asshole." He picked it up and handed it to Talent. "It weighs just over fourteen pounds loaded, heavy but worth every ounce for killing power."

Talent hefted the MGL and grinned. "Now, this is what I was talking about. What about close up work?"

"For that, a nice HK MP5 will do the trick."

As Talent listened to Costas, now in teaching mode, explain the use and care of the M23 MGL, carefully noting the different types of grenades available, the men of the fire team roused and, one by one, gathered around them. Whatever differences the men had or whatever frictions remained among them, familiarity with their weapons was the key to survival and they took their jobs seriously.

"Now, boys and girls," Costas said, "remember that we will be in a tight space. Don't lob grenades or," glancing meaningfully at Talent, "go full Rambo with an MGL. Fragging your own men is frowned upon. I would reserve a special pissedness for anyone pricking my beautiful flesh with pieces of shrapnel."

Finally, the moment came that Walker had been expecting. Sergeant Rhoades pointed the knife he had been using to dig beneath his fingernails at Talent. "What's he doing here? Isn't he one of the passengers we rescued?"

"This is Mark Talent. He can handle himself pretty well. I asked him to join us."

"I ain't working with no amateur."

"Why not?" Costas retorted. "I will be."

Rhoades stood and glared at Costas. The big S.E.A.L. held the knife loosely in his hand, but like any member of a fire team, he could deliver a deadly blow with it from close up or from across the room with equal ease. Costas saw the knife but remained undaunted. Both were big men. Walker hated to take odds on who would come out on top in a fight, but he couldn't let it go that far.

"Both of you stand down!" he barked. After a few seconds, Rhoades backed away, but he did not resume his seat. "I've seen Talent in action. He's good. We're down two men. We need him."

"Yeah? Whose fault is that?" Rhoades asked. Several of the team muttered their approval of his question.

Before Walker could answer, Talent strode to the middle of the room. He looked Rhoades in the eye. "I saw both men die. Watts stepped in front of a Squid to save civilians and died like a man. Stimson died when a Wasp dropped through the roof of the lifeboat. Nobody could have saved him, right Perez?"

Perez winced, uncomfortable with her new position as a defender of Walker. Finally, she nodded. "Yeah, I was there. I couldn't stop it. It happened too fast. Talent jumped in like a champ and gutted the thing."

McGregor strode into the fray. He stood beside Rhoades and said, "Neither of them should have been in that position. Our mission was the Kaiju, not rescuing civilians. We lost two men for thirty civilians. At that rate, we can save a couple of hundred if we waste all our lives."

"Your life that precious to you, Captain?" Costas said. "Maybe you're in the wrong business."

McGregor ignored Costas and turned on Walker. "You could have refused the commander's request. It wasn't our mission."

Walker kept his growing irritation under control, as he replied, "I don't know about you, but I've seen too many people die. I'll save anyone I can."

"I for one thank you," Talent said.

McGregor whirled on Talent. "You've got no say in this."

Talent moved so quickly that no one had a chance to stop him. He spun McGregor around, pulled him against his chest, and jabbed the tip of a knife he seemed to pull from nowhere into the skin above the startled captain's carotid artery. Nobody moved, as all eyes focused on the bizarre tableau unfolding before them.

"Captain, I say what I think, and I think you're a fool." He pushed the knife a little harder. A drop of blood ran down McGregor's neck. "This man went inside a living Kaiju, fought the creatures inside, and came out alive. You and your team cleaned up a bunch of mindless, dying creatures after the Kaiju were dead. Now, which man do you think I want to follow?" He shoved McGregor forward and replaced his knife in the scabbard hidden inside the waistband of his jeans. "If the job's too big for you, step aside."

McGregor seethed, but held his tongue out of newfound respect for Talent's capabilities. Talent looked at the men sitting on the floor and said, "Who's up for some breakfast? I'm buying." He winked at Perez, and then turned his back on them and strode away.

Walker felt like shaking his hand. Talent had managed to put McGregor in his place, saving Walker from the unpleasant task of confronting him. "Well, gentleman," he said. "Shall we take him up on his offer?"

He brushed past McGregor and followed Talent down the darkened corridor. Behind him, he heard Costas say loudly enough for everyone to hear in his resonant bass voice, "I like that Cowboy. We're gonna have great fun together."

As he caught up with Talent, the 1MC announced, "One hour ago the Kaiju appeared on Efate Island in the Republic of Vanuatu. All communications with the island are out, but a high altitude *Albatross* surveillance drone dispatched along the Kaiju's likely route relayed photos of the capital city of Port Vila in flames."

* * * *

Talent listened to the tragic news over the intercom and felt no grief, no empathy for the dead on Vanuatu. He did not even feel anger. He was suffering from disaster overload. His mind could not digest the information and translate it into normal emotional context without shutting down completely. In a way, it was a blessing, but as he observed the tears and raw emotions of the sailors around him, even members of Fire Team Bravo, he questioned whether something was fundamentally wrong with him. Was he such a loner that he was incapable of human emotions? No, he had been angry when Owens had died, and he had barely known the ex-Chicago detective.

He picked at the scrambled eggs and bacon on his plate, but the food was tasteless and difficult to swallow. It lay like a cold lump in his stomach. He knew it was not the food. The sub's cooks were excellent. He pushed the plate away from him and took a sip of his coffee. The hot, black beverage drove away the chill enveloping him.

The R-21 *Albatross* was a solar-powered, lightweight drone capable of remaining in the air for days by using its solar batteries at night and recharging them by day. It circled the island of Efate at an altitude of ten-thousand feet, but its powerful array of interchangeable lenses revealed details as small as a stray dog. He heard several sharply drawn breaths and glanced up to see the galley's two television screens displaying a live feed from the *Albatross*.

"My God," Costas said, watching the Kaiju crush two single-masted yachts anchored in the bay with one of its legs. The once beautiful city of Port Vila was now nothing but piles of brick and mortar rubble licked by tongues of flame. Clouds of smoke partially blocked the view, but the drone's operator engaged the ultraviolet lens operating in the 350-nanometer wavelength, which pierced the smoke, revealing details of the Kaiju.

Talent cringed when he saw the line of Wasps bearing their grisly packages to the Kaiju's open maw, feeding it like a mother bird feeding its chicks. The horrors of his ordeal on the cruise ship and the lifeboat came flooding back, threatening to overwhelm him. He gripped the edge of the table with both hands, squeezing until the pain in his wrist pushed away the terror.

Walker noticed his discomfort. "The commander might be right. I shouldn't have suggested you come with us."

Talent shook his head. If anything, witnessing the Kaiju's rampage reinforced his need to accompany Walker's team into the belly of the beast. He could not live with himself if he simply walked away, became another refugee, a passive victim of the alien invasion.

"Too late. I have to go."

Walker nodded his head. "I thought you'd say that."

"How long will it take us to get to Efate?"

"About sixty-four hours, but the Kaiju will have moved on by then."

"Sixty-four hours?" He was not expecting it to be that long. He did not know if he could handle the better part of three more days in the tight confines of the submarine with so many bodies pressing in around him, so many voices. It was worse than the ship. "Can we catch up with it?"

"Eventually."

"You don't seem concerned."

A brief smiled flicked on Walker's lips. "You're wrong. I want to stop it before it kills more people, but we're sailing as fast as we can. We had no idea it was capable of such speeds. On land, the Kaiju lumber along at a snail's pace. It might reach the Australian mainland before we can catch up. We'll have to play it by ear."

Talent sighed. *So much for getting off the submarine.* "Is it always like this, your missions I mean?"

"Flexibility is rule number one for a sniper or a fire team. No mission ever goes quite as planned."

"There's something I've been meaning to ask. Just what is a fire team?"

"A fire team stands by to put out fires anywhere they're needed, usually by force of arms. Some are sniper teams, some are search and recover teams, some are black ops, and some, like Fire Team Bravo, are special mission."

Talent glanced over at McGregor and caught him staring at him. McGregor averted his gaze and forked a mouthful of bacon into his mouth, chewing it savagely. "I don't think the captain likes me."

Walker chuckled. "No, but after the stunt with the knife he sure as hell respects you."

"He rubbed me the wrong way." It was as close to an apology as he was willing to make to Walker. His attack on McGregor had been an impetuous act, one that he had immediately regretted. McGregor reminded him of too many people with whom he had butted heads over the years. One had been a snobbish IRS agent who refused to allow his deductions for his gun business. Another was a Pima County deputy who pulled him over for no reason and then proceeded to read him the riot act for wasting his time. The very worst was one of his very liberal professors who thought America had no business policing the world, calling America an Imperialist nation. Talent's rebuttal had earned a smattering of applause from the class, but the professor had failed him on principal.

He looked up at the television screen. The drone now swept lower over the city, showing Wasps dragging people from the ruins of buildings.

"That's something new," Costas said.

He peered at the spot Costas indicated and saw hundreds of small creatures hopping in and out of buildings like a warren of rabid jackrabbits. Their small size made distinguishing details difficult. Their angular bodies were about three feet long, ending in a point at either end. Their elongated rear legs made them appear much larger. The cricket-like legs propelled them high into the air with each powerful hop. He watched as three of the creatures took down a woman trying to take refuge in an automobile. They piled on top of her, stabbing her with their long proboscises, and then waited patiently until a Wasp came along to collect the corpse. To Talent's amazement, the hoppers attached themselves to the Wasp's abdomen and flew away with it.

"They're like goddamned airborne shock troops," Costas sputtered. "They ride the Wasps like fleas on a hound."

"Whatever those Fleas are, they're deadly," Walker said.

McGregor's eyes were wide as he watched the Fleas in action. "We didn't count on them."

"Squid, Wasps, Fleas, Ticks, and Pancakes – the Kaiju's infested with the little critters." Costas banged his fist on the table. "I say we delouse the bastard and send it back to hell."

Costas' bravado did not sway McGregor. "What other surprises does it have waiting for us?" He directed his question at Walker.

Talent waited for Walker to slap the captain down. Instead, he nodded his head. "Yes, this one is different. The aliens are getting smarter. That makes it imperative that we learn all we can about this one to prepare for the next one, and there will be more of them. You can bet on it. Until we can stop the aliens cold, they'll keep trying." He paused. "We volunteered because we've all been inside a Kaiju. We are among the chosen few who can claim that honor. If we don't do it, no one else will. If the K-2 works, we'll have a weapon against them. That's our job, delivering the weapon. Everything else is secondary. The welfare of the entire world depends on us completing our mission. Our lives aren't worth more than anyone else's. I intend to spend mine dearly."

No one spoke until Costas said, "Here, here."

Walker's speech had summed up what Talent had been feeling. Maybe it was survivor's guilt, a strange malady for a survivalist, but he felt he needed to make amends somehow with the ghosts of the dead on the *Radiant Princess*. They weren't his responsibility, but they needed someone to account for them. Like Walker had said. If he didn't do it, no one would.

He watched as long as he could, but when the conversation dropped into military technical jargon, he left.

Two hours later, they rendezvoused with the *Amata Maru*. He joined the line of survivors snaking their way to the hatch. Most seemed eager to leave the submarine, to get on with their lives. A heart wrenching few of the faces in the line still wore the empty haunted look they had when rescued. They stood silent, moved when directed to do so, as devoid of emotion as a store mannequin. They were the real victims of the Kaiju. He could not look upon them without feeling a twinge of empathy.

An ensign with a clipboard called out names. Talent answered when he got to his. The closer he got to the hatch, the more he knew he could not go with them. What would he do on the freighter? Get off at the nearest port and hop a plane for Australia? He could go anywhere he chose. He had the money. No place would be safe as long as the aliens kept sending their deadly Kaiju to Earth. He looked up at the patch sunlight shining down through the hatch, longing to feel it on his skin. Then, he cursed himself for a fool, and ducked through the nearest hatch.

Stowing away on a submarine was not easy. The close quarters of a submarine presented its own challenges to avoiding detection. His first task was removing his conspicuous cowboy hat and boots to blend in with the other sailors. He grabbed a pair of canvas deck shoes and a white 'Dixie cup' sailor's cap from an unlocked locker and stashed his boots and hat on a shelf. He tucked his long hair up under the cap, hoping he looked less like a six-foot-tall Indian and more like a sailor. At the last minute, he remembered his bola tie and slipped it beneath the overalls. Finally, he decided on the safest spot he could think of – the library.

He acknowledged the klaxon signaling the sub to dive with both relief and a touch of trepidation. Foolish or not, he had sealed his fate. He would either find a way to join Walker's team or spend the remainder of the voyage locked in the brig. He had spent time in jail before, a weekend in Maricopa County's finest lockup. A submarine brig couldn't be worse than that. At least he wouldn't share a cell with a meth-head junkie.

For five hours, he beat the odds. People came and went in the library, paying him little heed. With his cap pushed down over his eyes and a book across his lap, he looked like any other sailor killing time between duty rotations. The rumbling in his belly was his undoing. He hoped to make a quick run to the galley, grab a couple of sandwiches from the stack near the door, and return to his lair – a quick five minute trip. Unfortunately, he did not count on encountering Executive Officer Dobbs in the corridor outside the library. Dobbs, intimately familiar with every face on the boat, knew immediately that Talent was not one of the crew. In fact, to Talent's surprise, Dobbs knew who he was.

"Mister Talent, why didn't you transfer with the others?" he demanded.

For a brief moment, Talent considered running, but brushed the thought away as futile. He had nowhere to run.

"Sorry, I missed the bus."

Dobbs frowned. "Did Major Walker have anything to do with this?"

Talent removed his cap and let his hair fall down over his shoulders. "No. It was all my idea. I want to get in this fight."

Talent saw a brief flash of sympathy in the XO's eyes, but any hope of clemency faded as Dobbs keyed the intercom. "Security, please send two men to the library to escort a stowaway to the brig."

Talent held out his hands in mock surrender. "You got me, sheriff. When's the hanging?"

"We don't hang stowaways, Mister Talent, but we do make their stay with us … memorable."

They stared at each other in silence for the two minutes it took for the security detail to get there. Talent quickly learned he was wrong about the brig. They shoved him inside a small room the size of a broom closet and dogged the hatch shut behind him. Sitting on a hard metal bench covered by a paper-thin mattress, he barely had room to stretch out his legs. The only feature that made it better than jail was not sharing it with a crack head.

"Well, this worked out well," he said aloud to himself.

16

Sunday, Dec. 17, 2:00 p.m. CST   Johnson Space Center, Houston, TX –

Gate Rutherford's office was crowded with Director Caruthers, two NASA technicians, and Air Force Lieutenant Colonel Harold Stiltson standing around his desk as he received the latest data from the GEMS satellite. There was now no doubt that the gravity anomaly they had detected between Earth and Haumea was on a direct course for Earth. Three separate agencies had checked and corroborated his findings. All that remained was to determine the object's size and speed.

The open video link with Goddard revealed that they too had a military presence – a pair of armed Air Force APs with serious expressions. The female technician with whom Rutherford had been working, Sara Truesdale, had summoned Sanjay Patangan, and Sam Ahern had joined them thirty minutes later, accompanied by Colonel Stiltson and the two APs. He had no doubt an identical pair guarded the hallway outside his office. The Johnson Space Center was on lockdown.

"Here it comes," announced one of the technicians, a young man barely in his mid-twenties, freshly graduated from the University of Arizona. His voice betrayed his excitement. His infectious enthusiasm was shared by the second technician, several years his senior but equally pleased by the opportunity to work with new data. Rutherford feared that soon the magnitude of the new discovery and the jeopardy it would soon entail would settle in, and they would be as circumspect as he was.

Rutherford threaded his way across the room through the crowd and snatched the printout from the printer with a satisfying rip. Lack of sleep had only intensified his contempt for the presence of the military. Any intrusion by the military added layers of red tape and hours of delay as information filtered up and then back down the chain of command. It was time for a comprehensive policy and decisive, measured action, not a military boondoggle. He had no need to dwell on the string of numbers for long. They clearly indicated the object was moving. In fact, its speed was astounding.

"This can't be right," he said.

"What?" Colonel Stiltson asked, frowning as he looked at the page.

Rutherford ignored the colonel and directed his statement to Doctor Patangan. "The object is moving nearly .25 C."

The colonel's face projected his confusion.

"That's a quarter of the speed of light – almost 167 million mph," he explained for the colonel's benefit.

"How is that possible?"

"It is using a form of controllable gravity as a power source," Doctor Patangan spoke up over the video link. "Theoretically, it is possible. The aliens' science of propulsion must be far in advance of ours."

Rutherford added, "At that speed, the object will be here in 24 hours, but I suspect it will shed velocity as it approaches Earth, say another eight hours. This explains why we had so little warning of the first Kaiju."

"Is it another Kaiju?" the colonel asked.

Rutherford shook his head. "No, the object is less than fifty meters in diameter."

"Another communications pod?" Caruthers asked.

By its size, that would be the logical answer, but Rutherford did not think that was the case. "Possibly," he conceded, "but why would the aliens send a communications pod after the Kaiju arrives? So far, the Kaiju in the South Pacific has acted autonomously."

"Then what is it?" the colonel asked.

"We'll know more by tomorrow night when we can swing the Hubble around for a better view," Rutherford answered.

His evasive answer did not satisfy the colonel. He dealt in absolutes. "We need answers now," the colonel said. His firm voice shaped the statement into a command. "We need to devise a plan of attack."

"We'll work to pinpoint its likely landfall coordinates, but we can't be certain until a few hours before it strikes, Colonel. The object's speed is too variable. At this point, we would simply be guessing."

"That's not good enough."

The colonel's insistence on a definitive answer irritated Rutherford. Stiltson's heavy-handed military approach might work on his subordinates, but civilians, especially scientists who seldom ventured guesses, chaffed at someone breathing down their necks. Rutherford, who had dealt with the military for months after the three Kaiju were stopped, was especially resentful. "You can't stop it, Colonel, not with anything you have. Not even your revamped *Janus*," he added.

The colonel glared at him, and Caruthers silently cautioned Rutherford to shut up. It was too late. "What do you know about *Janus?*" the colonel demanded.

"I know no nuclear missile will come close to the object. It would be like throwing a baseball at a bolt of lightning."

"You don't have much faith in the military, do you?"

"I watched a Kaiju wade through our ground and air forces as if they weren't there. If not for Colonel Langston's sacrifice, we would still be fighting them. I also butted heads with a few of your ilk during my debriefings. They thought the threat was over and wouldn't listen to me. They took my data, filed it away, and shut me out. Forgive me for not jumping to attention and saluting when you bark."

"You don't know all our secrets, Doctor Rutherford," Stiltson said with a sneer. "We haven't been sitting on our asses these past months."

"Unless you've solved the artificial gravity equation using what's left of a Kaiju propulsion system, we're out of the aliens' league." To his surprise, the colonel had no snappy comeback. It seemed out of character for him. Rutherford stared at him, noticing the small uptick in the corner of his mouth, as if he was trying to smother a smirk. "You haven't solved it, have you?" he pushed.

The hard military shell snapped back into place. "That's classified information."

"Well, if you have solved it, you had better hope you're prepared, because whatever is headed this way is going to be different from anything else we've seen."

"Why do you say that?"

"The aliens are learning from their mistakes. They're not months away or even years. They're only light hours away. Using gravity wave communications, they have almost real-time access to whatever data the Kaiju transmit. From what we've seen, they can tailor a Kaiju to meet any new threat and get it here in months."

"What do you think the object is?"

Caruthers' eyes begged him not to answer, but he was tired of smug military self-assurance. They were essentially clueless but projected an air of preparedness that fooled no one. They faced each new threat exactly like the previous one. It was a foolish way to fight an alien threat.

"It's a super weapon," he said.

Caruthers swore under his breath. The colonel was equally stunned. He leaned in closer to Rutherford. "The Kaiju are weapons platforms. Why do you think this object is different?"

"The Kaiju are too slow. I think the aliens are growing impatient with their progress. They intend to wipe humanity off the face of the planet once and for all."

Colonel Stiltson glared at him. Caruthers covered his face with his hand. "Do you propose to incite panic, Doctor Rutherford?"

He shrugged. "I'm not proposing anything, Colonel. You asked me for my best guess. Personally, I'm panicking big time. You would be too if you had a clue as to what we're facing."

Stiltson walked to the door, opened it, and spoke briefly to someone just outside the door. Seconds later, two uniformed Air Police strode in. "These two gentlemen will see you off the premises, doctor. I believe Doctors Ahern and Patangan are quite capable of continuing from here."

Rutherford was incensed. "You can't shut me out, Colonel. I'm the one who discovered the aliens. Without me —"

"Precisely, doctor. From now on, we will proceed without you. You're still too . . . unstable from your distressing mission inside the Kaiju. We need cooler heads to prevail. This is not the time for panic."

"The hell it isn't." He turned to Caruthers, but the director's face was impassive. "I warned you, Gate. It's out of my hands."

One of the APs grabbed his arm. He tried to shrug him off, but the AP's grip was too tight. "Please come with us, Doctor Rutherford."

"You're making a mistake, Colonel. This isn't another Kaiju or a communications pod. If you continue to think of it as such, you'll be playing into the aliens' hands."

"That will be all, Doctor Rutherford," Stiltson said, as the guard closed the door behind them. "Please leave military matters in the hands of the military."

Rutherford turned to the guard who had spoken. "He's wrong, Sergeant."

"He's my superior, sir. I will obey his order, as will you."

Rutherford fumed. "Do you have a family, Sergeant?"

"A wife and son in Toledo."

"You had better call them and tell them goodbye."

The sergeant's hand squeezed tighter as he pulled Rutherford down the corridor past stunned NASA employees. At first, he thought they were carrying him to security, but they took the elevator to the parking garage and marched him to his car. Both guards rode with him to the gate, got out, and stood behind his vehicle with their hands on their weapons. With his options now zero, he slammed his foot down on the accelerator and sped away from the space center.

* * * *

Sunday, Dec. 17, 4:30 p.m. CST   Gate Rutherford's apartment, Houston, TX –

Rutherford worked furiously. They had kicked him out of Johnson, but they had yet to shut down his access to the NASA mainframe. That could come at any moment. He downloaded all the data from Goddard and established a backdoor link to the Disturbance Reduction System satellite. If he were lucky, no one would think to add additional safeguards to the DRS. Designed to detect gravitational waves on Near Earth Orbiting objects, the DRS was not powerful enough to scan Haumea, but would be sufficient to follow the new objects trajectory. Of all the satellites and telescopes in orbit, only the DSR had detected the Kaiju four months earlier.

He could have kicked himself for getting into a pissing contest with Colonel Stiltson. The outcome was inevitable. His only excuse was that he did not suffer fools easily. However, with the fate of the Earth at stake, he should have swallowed his pride and ignored the colonel. His deep-seated resentment of the military and, he admitted, his burning rage at the aliens, had combined to become a caustic chemical in his throat that spewed his words like machinegun fire. The tiny voice that normally self-edited his rancor was lost in the sound of gunfire.

He had let the director down, but most of all he had let himself down. He was right about the aliens, but now they would dismiss his theories as the ranting of a madman. The military fought each new war just as they had the last war. It took them years to change tactics. The aliens did not suffer from such human handicaps. They were in the species elimination business, and they adapted quickly to each new situation. He knew the new object headed their way was a weapon, an alien super weapon. He could feel it in his gut. They were through playing around. Now they were getting deadly serious.

The one sticking point in his conjecture was Kaiju Kiribati. If the aliens had a super weapon available, what need had they for another Kaiju attack? That question plagued his mind as he pored over the latest available data from GEMS. He compared the object's gravity signature to those of the first three Kaiju detected by the DRS satellite and found it to be much larger. The discrepancy could be that it was en route, traveling at a respectable percentage of light speed. The three Kaiju had already slowed to camouflage their re-entry trajectory as natural objects before the DRS had detected them.

A bitter churning in the pit of his stomach arose as Rutherford's struggling mind suggested the disturbing thought that the extremely high gravity distortions were inherent in the object itself, not in the gravity drive. The answer hit him like a kick to the groin. NASA was working on a nuclear-thermal propulsion system for a Jupiter probe because nuclear power was what they had to work with. The aliens had a gravity drive. It made a macabre kind of sense that they would base their weaponry on their gravity manipulation technology. Humans had developed nuclear weapons first, and then sought to harness its potential for space travel. Perhaps the aliens had followed a similar path.

Such a weapon carried with it the inherent dangers of miscalculation. Any mistake could prove disastrous to the aliens. To protect themselves, they would send it to Earth unarmed and arm it once it arrived at its destination, just as the military had the first atomic bomb used on Hiroshima.

The pieces fell together so neatly that his earlier obtuseness astounded him. The Kaiju was there to arm the bomb. None of the creatures within the Kaiju's internal ecosystem – Wasps, Ticks, Pancakes, or mice – possessed manipulative limbs or the intelligence to handle tools. Therefore, they had created, or utilized, Squid. Their delicately controlled tentacles, combined with at least ape equivalent intelligence, could perform such a task. They did not have to build a bomb. They simply needed to arm it, an undertaking that could be as uncomplicated as flipping a switch. The Squid were amphibious creatures, hinting at how they would arm the weapon – in the water.

One problem still bothered him: Why not send the bomb inside the Kaiju?

He was no physicist and could not venture a guess at the mechanics involved in creating, transporting, and triggering a gravity manipulative weapon, but he was an astrophysicist. Two gravity anomalies in close proximity created an unstable environment. Two massive bodies, such as planets, stars, or even entire galaxies, affected each other's orbits, tugging and distorting their masses in a dance of cosmic attraction through the solar system. Sending the Kaiju first eliminated that possibility with the added benefit of using the Kaiju to clear the target area of any threats to allow them the opportunity to arm it unmolested.

He needed help, but he needed to be careful. Even the hint of doing an end run around the military could bring down the full wrath of the military. Instead of banishment from Johnson, he could wind up in some military prison for the duration. Did civilians go to Leavenworth? He had no desire to find out. He needed someone with a theoretical knowledge of gravity drives, not an astronomer's knowledge of how gravity works. NASA's work with the warp drive involved gravity compression using dark matter to achieve superluminal velocities, but contacting anyone connected with NASA would set off alarm bells within the military. He would have to engage a coconspirator from outside the NASA fold.

His first thought was of Doctor Hugh Bartonelli, in charge of a Syracuse University project to develop a gravity propulsion system sponsored by Bell Laboratory. He had met Bartonelli twice at astrophysics symposiums, but both meetings had occurred over three years ago. Would Bartonelli even remember him, and if so, would his current reputation as a NASA crackpot impede any chance for cooperation?

He found Bartonelli's number on the Syracuse website, but got a polite recording asking him to leave his number and a message. His message was brief, describing their common interests and their last meeting in Albuquerque. He was pleasantly surprised to receive Bertonelli's return call half an hour later.

"Doctor Rutherford, it was pleasant to hear from you. I remember speaking with you at the last symposium. I read your paper concerning the Kaiju, a most interesting adventure." He paused. "Is this a social call or a professional one?"

"Professional. I need to pick your brains about gravity drives."

After a long pause, he asked, "Does this have anything to do with the Kaiju?"

Lying would not get their relationship off to a good start. "Yes."

"I assumed as much. I must warn you, Doctor Rutherford, I have been working with the Air Force on a project. Revealing any details concerning it might place me in an awkward position."

That was interesting news. Did Bartonelli's project have anything to do with Colonel Stiltson's reaction at the mention of a gravity drive? "My inquiry is more general. I have only two questions."

"And they are?"

He took a deep breath. Would Bartonelli hang up on him or report him to the authorities? "First, what is the possible effect of two gravity drives in close proximity, and second, in case of an accident, what would be the possible repercussions?"

He expected to hear a click as Bartonelli hung up, but he replied, "I assume you are asking as a catastrophist. If your interest were related to your recent dealings with the Kaiju, my obligation to the Air Force would not allow me to answer."

"Purely theoretical," he answered quickly. Was Bartonelli hinting that he suspected the reason for his call? "I'm, uh, preparing a new paper for NASA."

"In that case, I am at your disposal."

While they worked, he turned on the television without the sound and watched the almost constant CNN coverage of Kaiju Kiribati's rampage in the South Pacific, wincing each time they replayed bits of video of Kaiju Girra, Ishom, or Nusku or video taken inside one of the dead creatures. The visual assault was a constant reminder of things he would like to forget, but they had been etched into his mind using blood rather than acid. He used the barrage of images to spur his anger and to focus that anger into his search for answers.

The pair danced around the underlying reasons for their conversation like prima ballerinas, but an hour later Rutherford had his answer, and it frightened him. He had one more fact to check, the pod's trajectory. Using the GEMS data and his covert link to the DRS satellite, he deduced the object's speed and projected a strike mid-Pacific Ocean; then, he incorporated the previous reductions in speed recorded by the DRS in the Kaiju trajectories. Plotting his findings on the map, he approximated the strike zone as Latitude 23^0 and Longitude 166^0, a spot in the Coral Sea between Vanuatu and New Caledonia, well south of the last reported position of Kaiju Kiribati, but the close proximity was too much for coincidence.

He pored over the map for over an hour, wracking his brain to squeeze out a cogent reason for that particular area. It was on a line the Kaiju would take to reach Australia, which he deemed its likeliest destination, but why there? Why not closer to Kiribati where it landed or Australia, where a bomb would do the most damage? More importantly, why choose the Coral Sea? Why not target the vast empty ocean south of Australia?

Now, the reporter pointed to a map of Java. At first, he thought the Kaiju had attacked that island, throwing off his calculations, but her interest was a 5.6 magnitude earthquake centered in the nearby Java Trench. He paid little attention to the report or to the headlines scrolling across the bottom of the screen. He focused on the map of the South Pacific, trying to visualize the Kaiju's path. Then, the reporter switched to a different map of the area, one displaying the interconnecting network of submarine trenches and crustal plates crisscrossing the region. A CGI animation showed one plate sliding beneath the other and the resulting build up of geothermal pressure, resulting in a quake.

Her slender, well-manicured, and pink-nailed finger traced a line along the Java Trench, but his gaze froze on the New Hebrides Trench running between Vanuatu and New Caledonia. The alien pod strike zone placed it in the middle of the New Hebrides Trench. Was there a connection? He prayed he was wrong, but his training as a catastrophist immediately came to the forefront outlining the worst possible scenario.

To be certain he was right, he needed one more opinion – a tectonicologist, someone who studied plate tectonics.

By morning, he had his answer. At approximately 10:30 p.m. on Tuesday, December 19 – Monday, December 18 local time – the alien pod would strike the ocean one-hundred-eighty miles south of Efate Island, directly over the New Hebrides Trench. Once detonated, a bomb could release a gravity wave pulse powerful enough to trigger massive shifts in the underlying continental tectonic plates. The devastation would be unimaginable.

No, he thought bitterly, *I can easily imagine it. It was my specialty.*

Magnitude 8.5 or greater earthquakes would unleash tsunamis making the wave that destroyed the western Kiribati islands look like a ripple on the beach. Most of Polynesia, Melanesia, and Micronesia would vanish beneath the sea. The tsunami would inundate the eastern coast of Australia as far inland as the Blue Mountains. The tectonic shifts could expand across the entire Pacific region, striking California, the west coast of South America, and Southeast Asia, triggering a spate of volcanic eruptions. It would affect weather patterns. Such devastation would have a lasting impact on the global economy. More than one such bomb could wipe out all life on the planet.

And he could tell no one.

Anyone in authority would refuse to listen or dismiss his findings as scaremongering. Even his old friend Director Caruthers would be hard-pressed to give him one more chance. He had only one card to play – Major Aiden Walker. If there was a Kaiju, he was certain Walker would be in the vicinity, probably once again risking his life to stop it. He tried Walker's number but got no answer, and then realized that if he were on a mission, Walker would not have his cell phone handy. Using military channels to reach Walker was out of the question. He had only one option.

He would have to contact Caruthers and convince him to help. It was a daunting task. If he had not burned his bridges behind him, he had at least left them smoldering. He would have to humble himself to convince the director to help him. Thoughts of the enormity of the consequences of his failure would do that. If he failed, the world would die.

17

Monday, Dec. 18, 2100 hours   *USS Hatcher*, 150 miles northeast of New Caledonia –

Captain Clay Wilkins accepted his orders with the same stoic sense of duty his grandfather showed aboard the *USS Ticonderoga* in WWII, and his father aboard the *USS Wasp* during the Cuban Missile Crisis. In fact, his family had served aboard US warships as far back as the Civil War when great-great grandfather Elias Wilkins had helped sink the *CSS Alabama* during the Battle of Cherbourg on June 19, 1864 while serving as a gunner on the *USS Kearsarge*. Elias Wilkins had not survived that fatal encounter. Captain Wilkins fully expected not to survive this one.

Kaiju Kiribati had laid waste to Efate Island in Vanuatu, but then unexpectedly stopped atop the center of the New Hebrides Trench, a twenty-five-thousand-foot deep abyss between Vanuatu and New Caledonia. The Australian Navy requested his small reconnaissance fleet of three ships, the nearest available resource, to make contact with the Kaiju, observe it, and take actions to hold it there until the combined Australian-British fleet could arrive. He knew what that meant. His three ships were to sacrifice themselves if necessary.

The *Hatcher*, a Freedom-Class LCS, Littoral Combat Ship, and its two Ambassador Mark IV-Class Fast Attack Craft, the *USS Spindrift* and the *USS Amanda Gray,* were fast and heavily armed for their size, but were no match for a Kaiju. The *Hatcher*, a modified LCS replacing the Navy's Frigate-Class ships, was armed with an MK110 57 mm gun, a RIM 116 Rolling Airframe Missiles, and two MH-60 Seahawk helicopters. Its main defense was its stealth design and its 40-knot speed.

Originally designed to operate in small, enclosed bodies of water, such as bays, gulfs, and lakes, the open ocean presented a special set of hazards for the two Fast Attack Craft, especially in bad weather. At just over one-hundred-fifty feet in length and displacing less than two-hundred-fifty tons, twenty-foot waves could shake them to pieces. Unable to make the long passage to the South Pacific without numerous stops for refueling, the FAC's had been shipped in sections from the U.S. and assembled in American Samoa. Armed with eight Harpoon surface-to-surface missiles, an OTO Melara 3-inch gun, and a CIWS Block B Gatling gun, the FAC's could handle most threats. Capable of fifty knots, they could outrun anything on the sea. Except a Kaiju.

His small fleet had been serving double duty as reconnaissance vessels and acting as escorts for larger warships when dispatched to patrol the waters south of the Coral Sea. He had expected a boring sea duty. Now, he was on the front lines expected to fight a thousand-foot-long alien creature.

"Anything on radar, Lieutenant?" he asked of Lieutenant Phillip Druze, his First Officer.

Druze leaned on the shoulder of the radar officer watching the scope. "Not a thing, Captain. Do you think we're late for the party?"

Druze, at twenty-four, was young and eager for combat. Like most Americans, he was eager for payback. Wilkins, twelve years his senior, was more concerned with keeping his crew alive.

"Be patient, Phil. According to the last estimates, we're close enough to throw rocks at it."

Rocks might do as well as the weaponry we have on board, he thought to himself. He scanned the horizon with his binoculars, but the moon had not yet risen and finding a black-on-black object in the dark was almost impossible. His eyes were fatigued from searching. He rubbed them and tried again. A bright fireball to port less than two miles distant lit up the night sky.

"My God! Was that the *Spindrift*?"

"She's disappeared from radar," Druze replied. His voice broke as he spoke. "I've got the *Amanda Gray*, but the *Spindrift's* just ... gone."

"Battle Stations!" Wilkins called out.

As the claxon wailed and the crew rushed to their stations, he donned his helmet and lifejacket. "Set an evasive course away from the *Spindrift*. Inform the *Amanda Gray* to search for survivors but to join us as soon as they can."

He would lead the Kaiju away from the wreckage to allow the smaller FAC to slip in unnoticed. At least that was his plan. Beyond that, he had no idea what he would do.

"Send a message to USPACOM. Include a copy to the Australian Fleet. Tell them ... tell them we've made contact with the Kaiju and are about to engage."

Druze stared at Wilkins, his face growing pale. "What's our bearing?"

"South by southwest." He knew he couldn't persuade the Kaiju too far off its course, but if he could draw it a little north of its present course, he could bring it to the Australian fleet and let them deal with it. "We'll tempt it to chase our tail."

A few minutes later, the radioman announced, "Australian Command asks if we can occupy the Kaiju for another hour. It's sending a squadron of F-35's to intercept. The fleet is still three hours west of us."

Wilkins chuckled to himself. It was like asking the chicken to bait the fox. "Inform the Australians that we will do our best to keep our guest entertained, but if they want to join the party, they had better hurry."

For twenty minutes, they ran random zigzag patterns two-miles wide, but still they picked up no sign of the Kaiju on sonar or radar. Had the *Spindrift* exploded from another cause – a fuel leak or munitions mishap?

"*Amanda Gray* reports no survivors, Captain."

Wilkins drew in his breath and exhaled slowly. Thirty-five men and women gone in a flash. "Inform them to rejoin us but to remain astern and two miles off our starboard." In case of a fight, he didn't want to sink the FAC by accident with a stray missile.

He needed to widen the search area. "Send the two Seahawks aloft. Have them drop sonar buoys and link them to our sonar. That should give us a clearer picture of what's down there."

He had held the helicopters in reserve instead of using them in the search for survivors for just this purpose. Deploying several AN/SSQ-101 Sonobuoys would expand their acoustic receiving footprint and allow them to change RF frequencies to sweep for quiet targets, like the stealthy Kaiju. At the same time, it would make locating his ship more difficult, if the Kaiju employed any type of sonic detection. Ten minutes later, the two Seahawks were aloft and fanning out on either side of the *Hatcher*. At one and two mile intervals, they deployed the buoys. He joined Druze at the sonar station and watched the scope. After another hour of nothing, he was beginning to think they had missed the Kaiju altogether.

"I've got it!" the sonar operator yelled. "7,000 yards off our port beam." He looked up at Wilkins with a stunned expression. "It's at a depth of two-hundred feet, just sitting there."

So much for engaging it, he thought. "We can't touch it at that depth. Recall the Seahawks. The F-35's should arrive shortly. If they're armed with *Stingray* or Mark 24 *Tigerfish* torpedoes …" He paused. The airdropped anti-submarine torpedoes could reach depths of twenty-four-hundred feet, but they would only tickle the Kaiju. "We'll watch and wait," he finished.

They sat atop the Kaiju for the hour Australian Command requested. The F-35's showed up, but carried only conventional bombs and missiles, no anti-submarine weapons. With no target to attack, they circled the area until they ran low on fuel, and then returned to their carrier. Frustrated, Wilkins stepped outside on the deck for a breath of fresh air and a cigarette break. He leaned on the railing and stared out at the ocean. The waters looked calm and serene but two-hundred feet below, a storm was brewing. He could feel it in his bones. He was from New Orleans, brought up on gumbo, jazz, and voodoo. He didn't believe in voodoo, but he did believe in premonitions. The Kaiju had not stopped for a sightseeing tour or for a quick nap. It was there for a reason.

I wish I had some damned depth charges, he thought.

He almost missed the flash as an object pierced the cloud cover and struck the ocean three miles away. For a moment, he thought it might be a nuclear missile intended for the Kaiju, but no detonation followed.

"Just a shooting star," he said, but part of him did not believe in such coincidences. He finished his cigarette, tossed the butt in the ocean, and went back to resume his sonar vigil.

18

Wednesday, Dec. 20, 0120 hours   *USS Mississippi*, NNE of Efate, Vanuatu –

Talent remained confined to the brig for fifty-eight hours, during which time he re-evaluated his opinion of submarine brigs. They were indeed worse than jail. He lost all sense of time and at times, thought he was losing his grip on reality. They had taken his watch, his cell phone, and of course his kukri. They had allowed him his boots and hat, but not his bola tie. *Afraid I'll hang myself*, he thought bitterly. He was more likely to commit homicide than suicide. He was willing to do almost anything, accede to any demand placed upon him, to escape his dreary confinement and the boredom of his prisoner's routine.

He passed the time dozing or staring at the blank bulkheads. If he could have focused his anger, he could have burned a hole through the two-inch-thick steel plating confining him. The guard brought him food three times a day and left two bottles of water with each meal, but refused to speak to him. The food was good, much better than the slop they served in the Maricopa jail, but his appetite had left him.

He could not even use his meals to mark time. The guards delivered food at irregular intervals, whether by design or tied to shift changes, he could not say. Knowing the guards worked six-hour duty shifts, he created a crude mental calendar based on different guards, but he never knew if a guard had just come on duty or if his shift was almost over.

On estimated Day 2 of his incarceration, he considered going on a hunger strike, but decided no one would care. He ate to keep up his strength, but mostly just to have something to do with his hands. The morning of Day 3 dawned with him awake and pacing his cell. Twice a day, again at irregular intervals, they escorted him to the head and then directly back to his cell. He saw no one along the way. He decided they were deliberately clearing the corridors to keep him away from the crew. He could learn nothing about the Kaiju, but by the sounds of increased activity that filtered in through the air ducts, he suspected they were getting closer to it.

He welcomed the commander's summoning as a break in the boring routine. If nothing else, he hoped to learn something about the Kaiju before they shoved him back in his cell. He tried to look confident as he entered the commander's office, but the stern expression the sub's captain wore did not bode well for his future. He was not surprised to find Walker there as well. Walker flashed him a quick smile that vanished when the commander cleared his throat.

"You've presented me with quite a dilemma, Mister Talent," Commander Murdock began. "By the time we discovered you aboard ship, I couldn't spare the time to chase after the freighter to send you on your way." He glanced at Walker and then back at him. "I toyed with the idea of setting you adrift in a rubber raft and let you become someone else's headache."

Talent smiled. "I'm pleased you reconsidered."

The commander leaned across his desk and scowled. "It's not too late, Talent. Don't tempt me. It's only seventy-five clicks to the nearest island. You could make it before you ran out of food and water if you rowed real hard." He turned to Walker. "If I even suspect that you had anything to do with this, Major, I'll place you in the brig with Talent."

Talent spoke up before Walker could reply. "It was my idea, Commander, not Major Walker's. He informed me that you refused to allow me to join his team. I decided to take matters into my own hands."

"You're an obstinate bastard, Talent. I'll grant you that. Are you a fool as well?"

Talent nodded his head at Walker. "According to the major, I must be if I want to go with him."

Murdock averted his gaze and shuffled some papers on his desk, stacking them into a neat pile, as he said, "Well, that's not likely to happen. Walker's team is disembarking in one hour from the amidships deployment airlock." He laid the stack of papers in front of him, picked up a pen, and began signing them. Talent wasn't sure if the commander was through with him or not. He waited. He leaned forward to get a peek at the digital clock on the commander's desk, surprised to see it was almost 1:30 a.m., and that it was Wednesday. His mental clock had been off by almost six hours.

Murdock looked up at him and pointed the pen at him as if it were a weapon. "I'll allow you access to non-restricted areas until I can get you off my ship, but if you abuse your privileges or give me another minute's grief, I'll clap you in irons and feed you bread and water until your intestines explode. Do I make myself clear, Mister Talent?"

"Yes, sir."

"Okay then. You may leave. I suggest you recall your recent confinement before you make any decisions you might later regret. Walker, you will remain here. I have a few choice words for you."

Talent left the room, unsure of his exact status. Was he free or still a prisoner with a larger space to wander? It was true he wasn't going anywhere for the time being, but he was still stuck on the sub, and he was no closer to the Kaiju than he was before.

* * * *

After Talent left, Commander Murdock leaned back in his chair and smiled. "Do you think he'll bite?"

"If I know Talent, he'll be waiting for us at the deployment hatch."

"I hope you don't regret your decision. If anything happens, if this mission goes sour, the big boys back at USPACOM will stomp on you with both feet. I'll get a reprimand, a black mark on my record, but you'll bear the brunt of it."

Walker had considered that. If the mission succeeded and survived, he would have two dead Kaiju under his belt. Public opinion would shield him from anything too severe. If it failed or if he died, it did not matter anyway. They could say what they wanted about his cold corpse.

"Talent claims he's lucky. Maybe he is. We could use some luck. I just know that my gut tells me to bring him along. I have a feeling he's going to contribute something to the mission that might make a difference between winning and losing. If I'm wrong …." He shrugged.

"Well, the Kaiju hit Efate and moved on, but stopped in the middle of the Coral Sea. That's one bit of luck."

"Yes, but why?" Walker didn't like sudden changes in Kaiju behavior. They were agents of destruction. If it was just floating around, there was a reason.

Before Murdock could answer, the telephone on his desk rang. He picked up the receiver and answered. He stared at Walker as he listened and nodded his head. "You have a call from a Doctor Wingate Rutherford from NASA. Know him?"

"Gate? Yes. How the hell …? What does he want?"

"I'll put it on the speaker."

"Aiden, or should I say Major Walker?"

He recognized Gate's deep voice, but Rutherford sounded on edge. "Gate. How did you track me down?"

A soft chuckle came over the speaker. "It wasn't easy. Director Caruthers pulled a few strings, made a few calls. I'm afraid I have some rather disturbing news."

Walker sighed. It would take something extraordinary for Gate to make it through the layers of military protocol to reach him. Few people were even aware of his mission. "I'm sitting down."

"NASA picked up an object headed for your Military Grid Reference Coordinate 58LFL0844662651. It struck the ocean at $21^0 28$'South and $166^0 33$'East on Tuesday the 18th just after 2300 hours local time. I apologize for the delay, but stripping away the damned layers of red tape took time. Sorry I can't provide more exact coordinates, but I had to extrapolate the trajectory from very few fixes. We had to use a military satellite. They were not happy about that."

Walker cursed under his breath. "Another Kaiju?"

"No, it's too small for that. It's less than twenty meters in diameter."

Walker got the same feeling he had when he knew someone had him in their crosshairs. "That's smaller than the communications node. What's your opinion?"

Rutherford paused so long he thought they had lost the connection. Then he said, "I shouldn't speculate."

Walker knew Rutherford too well to accept that as his answer. He wouldn't have called if he didn't suspect something ominous. "Go on, spill it."

"Well, my sources told me that the Kaiju broke off its attack on Vanuatu and headed south; then, stopped moving."

Walker looked at the commander for permission to confirm. He nodded. "That's right. It stopped between Vanuatu and New Caledonia."

"Hmm. That's what I suspected. It's hovering directly over the New Hebrides Trench."

Walker had heard of the Marianas Trench, but not the New Hebrides Trench. "So?"

"The New Hebrides Trench connects with the Tonga Trench and the Kermandec Trench. The entire region of Melanesia is extremely geographically active. The Pacific Plate collides with the Australian Plate, squeezing the Caroline Plate, the North and South Bismarck Plates, and the Solomon Plates between them."

Walker sat up. As usual, Rutherford was taking a long time to make his point, but he was beginning to grasp where Rutherford was heading.

Rutherford continued. "Any major seismic disturbance could spread throughout the sub-oceanic region, causing sudden shifts in tectonic plates, creating enormous tsunamis, and invigorating a storm of volcanic activity. It would present a very promising target to a species intent on wiping out life on the planet."

The blood drained from Walker's face. Rutherford was describing an apocalyptic scenario, regional at first, but slowly spreading around the globe as shifting tectonic plates found new alignments. He was no geologist, but it sounded possible. "Could they do it?"

"I've conferred with a few colleagues in the proper fields – physicists, geophysicists, tectonicologists, and a specialist in gravity drives. The aliens' use of gravity drives in the Kaiju pods and directed gravity waves for communication indicate a conversant grasp of the technology needed. The geophysicists and tectonicologists agree that if they could generate a sufficiently powerful localized gravity blast, it could destabilize a large section of the New Hebrides Trench, causing untold damage to the surrounding mantle."

"So the Kaiju is waiting for the new pod before moving on? Why?"

He heard a sigh over the receiver. "I suspect the Kaiju was sent to arm the device or to place it in the proper spot. Using a gravity drive in the proximity of an armed gravity bomb might not be a wise idea. It now seems likely that the Kaiju was never headed to Australia."

"What do you mean?" Murdock demanded. "It has been on an almost straight-line course since arriving."

"Its goal has been to rendezvous with the pod. At first, it mystified me why the two objects arrived in such widely flung areas. Then I realized it would have expended a tremendous amount of energy on the journey as fuel for the gravity drive. Once it landed, it began to replenish its store of energy."

"Then why not land in eastern Australia near Sydney or Melbourne?" Walker asked.

"The aliens are learning. The Kaiju face less opposition in a remote area. My original projections were correct in that. However, the rest has crumbled under circumstances. Even I did not expect such a dynamic shift in focus of their efforts."

This time Commander Murdock posed a question. "How do we stop it?"

"I wish I knew. Triggering the bomb before it is in place would cause less damage than allowing it to reach the depths of the trench, but the resulting blast would still destroy the surrounding islands and, of course, anyone in close proximity."

Murdock shook his head and growled in frustration. "That sounds like we're damned if we do and double-damned if we don't."

"I'm sorry, Commander. We don't know the mechanism of the device, so disarming it is unlikely."

"It'll be damned hard to wrestle it from the Kaiju."

"Aiden, I'm sorry to deliver this ghastly news. I hoped I was wrong, but too many people better acquainted with the field of gravimetrics and geophysics concur. The aliens are trying to initiate a cataclysmic event.

If they succeed … well, you're a military man. You can better guess their strategy from there."

"They'll carpet bomb the entire planet with gravity weapons, wipe out every living thing. They can then come in and strip the planet of its minerals."

"Or plant a colony," Rutherford added.

Walker had not thought of that. If the aliens wanted to colonize the planet, they would leave no one alive.

The telephone crackled loudly. "I think I'm losing the satellite connection. They warned me this might happen. I'll speak quickly. You must somehow prevent the aliens from triggering the device or seize it and take it to a land mass to explode. That might reduce the bomb's effectiveness."

Walker considered the implications of delivering the bomb to Vanuatu, New Caledonia, or even Australia. The U.S. would soon be at war with more than the aliens.

"That will still leave the Kaiju to deal with, but I'm sure you have a plan for that or you wouldn't be there. One more thing …"

The connection failed.

Murdock leaped up and keyed the intercom. "Communications, can we reestablish the connection with Doctor Rutherford?"

"Negative, sir. He was calling from Houston. The NASA satellite he was using passed out of range. There are no geosynchronous communications satellites in the immediate area. The next satellite won't be within range for four hours. Even then, it might be difficult. It's an old I-3 satellite launched in 1996 by INMARSAT. The technology is outdated. It's past due for decommissioning."

Murdock sighed. "Son, I received my commission in 1996." He collapsed in his seat and stared at Walker, who was equally aghast at the foreboding news from his friend. "What the effin' Jesus Christ do we do?"

"My mission hasn't changed. If Gate is wrong, which he never is, we still have to stop the Kaiju. It's unlikely to remain in the area of the blast."

"That thing has already sunk two subs. Now, I'll have to risk my boat. Short of going kamikaze on it, I don't know what I can do that hasn't been tried already."

"The device is smaller. Maybe it's more vulnerable," Walker suggested.

"It's like tap dancing on a landmine." He slapped his palm on the top of his desk. "Oh, well. As you said, it's my responsibility. I'll think of something. Maybe your friend Rutherford can tell us more when we reestablish contact with him."

Walker was wondering about the 'one more thing' Rutherford had not had time to finish. Was it a warning or a suggestion? "If anyone can figure this out, it's Gate. He's become a ..." He hesitated, "a driven man since Nusku."

Murdock nodded. "An alien invasion can do that to people."

"No, it's more than that. Gate was a catastrophist. He made predictions about disasters. It was all facts and figures to him, lines on a graph. Then, he saw death and destruction close up and personal. He volunteered to go inside the Kaiju. That took guts, but it changed him. He has a hatred for the aliens that's eating him up inside. He's determined to defeat them. That's good for us. He's smart enough to pull it off, but I'm afraid it's going to burn him up like gasoline on a fire. That's a shame. He's my friend."

"If this war goes on much longer, everyone will suffer from PTSD. You take care of the Kaiju. Leave the bomb to me. We're not beaten yet."

Walker nodded his assent, but deep inside, he wondered.

19

Wednesday, Dec. 20, 0130 hours   *USS Mississippi*, New Hebrides Trench –

Three things puzzled Talent concerning his meeting with Commodore Murdock. First, that the sub's captain had released him at all. If the punishment fit the crime, why not simply keep him confined until they reached a port? The commander's threat to set him adrift struck home. He didn't have the personnel to keep a twenty-four hour watch on him, and yet that was exactly what the commander had proposed.

Secondly, why release him at 1:30 in the morning? He knew submarines operated on a twenty-four hour schedule, but it seemed odd that he had not simply waited until morning. He suspected he knew the answer to his third question – why had Major Walker been present at the meeting? Murdock's thinly disguised dressing down of the major in front of him had not fooled him for a moment. Waiting almost three days to admonish him was pushing the envelope. The commander seemed a strictly by-the-book officer. If he believed Walker had helped him stowaway, the major would have been sitting in the brig with him, impending mission or not.

Unless Walker's team was rendezvousing with the Kaiju by air, the sub must be closing with it. He closed his eyes and visualized a map of the South Pacific. If the *Mississippi* had maintained the same speed the entire time he was in the brig, they were somewhere near Efate Island. The Kaiju had devastated Efate Island three days ago. It should have already reached Australia, meaning the Kaiju had stopped moving. Why? Whatever the reason, the delay gave Walker his chance.

The galley was busy for 0130 hours, as sailors enjoyed a quick breakfast before the sub reached the Kaiju. He had retrieved his familiar Stetson and cowboy boots and most of the crewmembers recognized him as he entered. They were also aware of his stowing away. He expected scowls or jeers, but surprisingly, a few flashed him smiles or nodded their head in greeting. One young torpedoman shook his hand.

"Anyone willing to go to so much trouble to join the fight it all right by me," he said.

In the food line, the server offered to prepare him a fresh omelet any way he liked it and offered to bring him a fresh batch of biscuits straight from the oven.

"No, that's okay," he said as he added a biscuit from the hot line chafing dish to his plate. "These look fine." He added a spoonful of gravy and a sausage patty.

The crew's attitude mystified him, but put him at ease for the first time since he had boarded the submarine. Even the food seemed to taste better free of his jail cell. He wolfed down his meal and considered seconds, but decided against it. He did refill his coffee cup.

One bit of information the commander had let slip concerned Walker's team leaving via the deployment airlock. With a little searching in the ship's library, he uncovered a plan of the submarine and the location of the deployment hatch near the missile room. He intended to be there when Walker left and join Fire Team Bravo. To stop him, security would have to restrain him physically. At this point, he had nothing to lose. He would go big or go home, except he had no home to go back to.

At the appointed time, he worked his way to the airlock through the missile room, avoiding crewmembers on duty. To his dismay, Walker's team was suited up in wetsuits and SCUBA gear. He hadn't expected to swim to the Kaiju. He had seen the white submersible attached to the sub's hull and assumed they would use it. The closest he had come to diving was an afternoon of snorkeling in Rocky Point, Mexico. Talking a deep breath to help calm his nerves, he stepped through the door.

Walker glanced up at him, pointed to a pile of gear on the floor, and said, "I was wondering if you were going to show up."

While he stood there trying to figure out what was happening, Costas tossed him a pair of stubby swim fins. "Here's a pair of Force fins."

Talent eyed the fins with concern. They looked nothing like the awkward long fins he had worn snorkeling. These were short with split toes like frogs' feet and fit like sandals, leaving his heel and toes free. His confusion showed in his face. Costas mistook his concern about the fins for nervousness about the dive.

"Don't worry. It's just a short swim. Even you desert rats can make it. We're riding to the Kaiju in style."

Bewildered by his reception, he asked, "You were expecting me?" He had been anticipating a fight with little chance of actually going on the mission.

"I knew something as minor as the brig wouldn't keep you out of this," Walker said.

"But the commander …."

"Technically, you're still a stowaway. It might look bad on his record to have a prisoner escape the brig. If we survive, you'll receive a stern reprimand from the commander for your escape, but his hands are clean."

"What about your hands?"

Walker winced. "Hmm. My hands haven't been clean in a long time. I'll take what comes."

Talent was touched. "I won't let you down."

"I know you won't. Now, let me show you how to use a SCUBA rig."

As Walker explained the proper use of the equipment, Talent stripped, donned the black pants and shirt in a neat pile on the floor, and wriggled into the wetsuit. His delight in succeeding in his quest faded as he noticed Captain McGregor's intense glare focused at him. He knew that before the mission was over, he and the captain would have to finish what they had started.

The SCUBA equipment the fire team wore was unlike any Talent had ever seen. The mask covered the entire face and resembled a WWI gas mask. It was cumbersome, but Walker assured him it was more comfortable than biting down on a rubber mouthpiece. The SCUBA gear was an *Inspiration* rebreather, an enclosed system that reduced the chance of nitrogen narcosis and eliminated bubbles, which were very acoustically active underwater, perfect for covert operations. After Walker helped him strap on the gear, its almost 60-pound weight surprised him. The rebreather tank, belt weights, and other gear strapped to him weighed half as much as he did.

"How can you walk around in this get up?" Talent asked as he struggled to stand up.

"It's not designed for walking. In the water, you'll have neutral buoyancy. If you had to carry a bailout tank and extra tanks for decompression, then you'd have something to complain about."

"Decompression?" Talent asked, alarmed at the sound of the word.

"If we exit the Kaiju too deep, we won't have enough oxygen to reach the surface without stopping to decompress to allow the nitrogen bubbles to reabsorb into our tissue. It could kill us."

"That's a cheery thought."

"Don't worry," Costas bellowed, "you can list me as your beneficiary on your death benefits package. That way, if your head explodes, I'll go to the Bahamas and lay on the beach in your honor."

"I don't have a death benefits package. Should I have signed a paper or something?"

Costas shook his head. "Too late now. That's too bad."

Walker slapped Talent on the shoulder. "Don't listen to the sergeant. I don't have time to acquaint you with the rebreather's operation. It comes with a ninety-seven-page manual if you find a few minutes to read it. Breathe normally. Stay close to me."

Talent swallowed and nodded, unsure of what he had gotten himself into. Walker gathered up Talent's boots and his Stetson and handed them to one of the crewmen helping them.

"You don't want to risk getting it dirty," he said. Then he picked up Talent's socks and a pair of army boots and placed them in a plastic bag. He pulled a 9 mm from his waistband and added it to the bag. To Talent's surprise, he also added the kukri machete before tying it to Talent's weight belt. "Just in case. Okay, let's go," he called out to the others.

They filed into the deployment hatch. Wearing their rebreathers, they squeezed together like sardines. Talent felt a moment of panic when a crewman shut and sealed the door. The cold water started pouring in, and he fought the urge to pound on the door to let him out. He closed his eyes as the water rose over his head.

He remembered to breathe normally. It sounded easier than it was, but he didn't die immediately. The outer hatch opened, and they all swam out. It was daylight, but the water absorbed most of the light. The surface was a faint silvery smear high above him. *How high?* He wondered. He remembered the depth gauge on his wrist – 90 feet. It didn't seem so bad. Then he looked down into the inky depths below him. *25,000 feet below,* he remembered. Vertigo climbed up his spine like a drunken monkey climbing a coconut tree. His hands shook so badly he had to make fists and clutch them to his side. Walker switched on his helmet light, and then switched on Talent's. Floating just a few yards away were two black and white orcas. Before the fear of becoming orca food could loosen his bowels, he noticed the open canopies and assumed they were the SDVs, the S.E.A.L. Delivery Vehicles. He wouldn't have to swim after all.

Walker motioned for him to swim to the closest SDV. He floundered for a moment, falling behind the group until he figured out how to use his fins by watching the others. He took a seat in the vehicle and buckled in. Watertight crates strapped behind him contained their weapons and extra gear. He wondered at the purpose of a black drum that looked like a small beer keg.

Walker spoke to him through the mask's built-in communications system. "The Kaiju is now on the surface. The *Hatcher* reports the small nodule is a hundred feet below it with six Squid surrounding it conducting some kind of operation through an open panel."

A smaller alien pod? Talent wanted to ask about it, but then decided not to. *Maybe I don't want to know*, he thought to console himself.

"The Australians have pulled back ten clicks. The *Hatcher* and the *Amanda Gray* are two clicks away monitoring the situation with an *Albatross* aerial drone and a *Guppy* underwater surveillance drone. They report Wasps circling the Kaiju but they haven't attacked any ships. They seem to be guarding the Kaiju. The *Guppy* hasn't detected them, but we can assume there are more Squid in the water, so we'll approach slowly."

"What if we're attacked?"

Talent recognized McGregor's voice even through the tiny headset speaker.

"We split up and try to reach the Kaiju. Last ditch, abandon the SDVs and swim. Priority 1 is the K-2 devices."

Talent turned his head as far as he could turn his head strapped in the rebreather harness and glanced at the *Mississippi* floating like an enormous gray whale, barely visible in the faint glow filtering down from the surface. Then, someone closed the hatch and he could see nothing. The SDVs were much faster than he imagined. They covered the two miles to the Kaiju quickly. Walker brought the one he piloted to a halt. Glancing through the tiny window in the front, Talent could make out the Kaiju very faintly ahead of them.

"I'm picking up nothing but the nodule below the Kaiju," Walker informed them. "The Squid are sonar invisible when not in motion. We proceed as if they are there."

He eased the SDV forward. Talent braced for the impact of a Squid slamming into the side of the tiny vehicle. He had seen what they could do to a steel hull. They would have no trouble with a fake neoprene orca. He began to feel dizzy until he realized he was holding his breath. He relaxed and tried to breathe slowly. To his delight and surprise, they reached the Kaiju safely. The SDV nuzzled up against the monster and attached itself by a suction cup like a remora fish attached to a thousand-foot whale. Walker waited a full minute before popping the hatch.

A single line of blisters, the openings along the creature's flanks through which the Wasps and Squid emerged, lay just above them. Talent followed Walker, swimming awkwardly trying to look all around him for Squid, while the others unloaded the cargo. The second SDV anchored twenty yards away. Just as he began to wonder how they were going to enter the closed blister, Perez, recognizable by her shorter stature, swam to the edge of the blister, attached a small device to one corner, and flipped a switch. An electrical current tickled what passed for a muscle in the alien creature, and the blister popped open, sliding upward into a recess.

Next, she struck an underwater flare and dropped it inside the cavity. Talent was delighted to see the blister was empty. No creatures were waiting for them. Illuminated by the flickering green glow, Perez uncoiled a twenty-foot-long flexible antenna and attached it to a second black box she placed just inside the open blister. This was the repeater to boost their headset comm signals to the *Mississippi*. Finally, Perez pulled a pistol-sized spear gun from her weight belt and positioned herself to the rear of the cavity to stand guard. The high-pressure six-inch darts it fired would be effective against sharks or barracuda, but Talent doubted it offered much protection from alien Squid.

"All clear," Perez reported.

"Move out," Walker announced.

Walker hustled the team through the opening with the cargo and waited until everyone was inside before following. He entered just in time. The blister closed behind him with a sudden snap. If one of the team had been beneath the blister when it closed, it would have cut him in half.

Trapped! Talent's mind yelled at him. He hadn't bothered to ask how much breathing time the rebreather allowed. *Too late now*.

"What about the antenna?" he asked. If the antenna were severed, how would the sub know when to pick them up? It was a big ocean.

Perez answered. "The cable is neoprene reinforced with woven tungsten fibers. The antenna core is less than a millimeter thick. Our signal is going out."

Satisfied, Talent examined the cavity in which they huddled. The blister was a snug fit for the eight of them and the four crates and two drums. They swam a dozen yards deeper into the creature along a narrow tunnel until they reached a second chamber, slightly larger than the blister. A fleshy curtain sealed one end. Perez removed her black box and repeated her operation. A second curtain irised from the wall behind them, creating an airlock. For a brief panicked moment, Talent was in absolute darkness. Then, Perez ignited another flare. Seconds later, the water began draining away and the distant flap opened.

Walker glanced at his wrist computer and raised his thumb. "Air's okay. Remove your tanks but carry them with you. We'll leave them in the corridor beyond this one. It runs the entire length of the creature."

The last statement was for Talent's benefit. The others were aware of the internal structure of a Kaiju. Walker was pointing out the exit sign for him. He wore a similar miniature computer on his wrist, but not being computer savvy, he barely knew how to turn it on. He removed his mask and wished he hadn't. The air was good; at least it was breathable, but a heavy smell like damp rotting wood permeated the air. Mixed with that cloying pall was an entirely alien odor, stronger than the stench of Wasp blood, more pungent and biting. It reminded him of a dead bighorn sheep he had stumbled across out in the desert, four days dead. Compared to the reek of the Kaiju, the rotting sheep carcass smelled like roses.

He realized the others had almost stripped off their wetsuits and hurriedly joined them. Costas and Perez began passing out weapons from the crates, as he sat down to lace up his boots. He took the HK MP5 and the grenade launcher from Perez and slipped the grenade launcher over his shoulder by its strap. It felt heavy and reassuring on his shoulder. He kept the HP5 out and ready to use. Lastly, he slipped on the Kevlar helmet. He wished he had his Stetson, but the helmet provided more protection than a flimsy felt hat.

Costas passed out four clips each of 5.6 mm ammo for the SAW and 7.62 mm for the SCAR. He tossed Talent half a dozen clips of .40 calibers for his MP5, and then handed Hightower two belts of 7.62 mm for the M134 minigun. "This here is something new. I'm not sure how they do it, but basically, it's pieces of chipped up Kaiju armor dissolved in concentrated Kaiju stomach acid, kinda like acid reflux. Then they desiccate it, put it in molds, and form bullets from the powdery residue. When it hardens, it becomes tiny pieces of Kaiju armor with a gunpowder kick." He held up a black-tipped .50 caliber bullet for his M107 SASR. "This can blow a Wasp to hell and back, but we don't have much of it, so use it wisely." He handed Wiggins and Perez each a box of shells for their 12-gauge shotguns. "These are loaded with double-ought Kaiju buckshot."

Wiggins and Hightower wrapped coils of thin nylon rope around their shoulders and clipped metal quickdraws, carabiners, and cinch belay devices to their belts. Talent had discovered a climbing harness in his pack, essentially three strips of nylon held together by three even smaller strips with metal rings attached for the carabineer. He had tried rappelling once with an experienced mountaineer on Mount Lemon outside Tucson but found the experience unpleasant at best. Dangling in space held in place only by a thin clothesline seemed more risk than sport. Some people enjoy the rush. He preferred both feet firmly on the ground. He was not looking forward to this second outing.

"We move toward the mouth," Walker said.

Talent noticed new worry lines on the major's face and appreciated that Walker took his responsibilities seriously. Costas, on the other hand, was his usual self.

"In case of emergency, let the bastard swallow you and shit you out the other end." He looked at Talent. "Don't worry. Shit floats."

In spite of his nervousness, Talent laughed. "Are you ever serious, Sergeant?"

Costas narrowed his eyes, patted his weapon, and said, "As serious as a bolt of lightning when I need to be."

"Mic check," Walker called out.

Each one of them responded through their comm link. Costas had to show Talent where the push-to-talk button was located. He moved the Velcro attachment to Talent's collar just below his chin where he could activate it with a simple nod if his hands were full. Sergeant Rhodes took the lead with Wiggins following. He watched the lights on their weapons bouncing until they faded into the darkness. Costas and Hightower trailed as rear guard. Talent clicked on his own flashlight. The brilliant white beam did not reflect from the ebony material of the Kaiju. Instead, the alien substance absorbed the light, making it difficult to judge his steps. Each footstep felt as if he were stepping off into infinity. He felt comfortable sandwiched in the middle of the group, allowing them to guide him.

Perez wore one of the black drums strapped to her back. She had insisted on hauling it, and no one argued. Wiggins carried the other. Walker had informed him the drums contained a Kaiju poison delivered by an explosive device. Talent didn't know how large the explosion would be, but being somewhere else when it detonated seemed like a good idea.

Watching the others in action, Talent began to have doubts about his reason for being there. Walker had suggested he would be a valuable asset, but he was not sure what his contribution to the group would be. He could shoot well enough, but he didn't have the training or team experience the S.E.A.L.S and Spec Ops did. His biggest fear was that he would become a liability. To counter that, he decided to follow the fire team's lead and do what they did when they did it. He hoped that would be enough.

His real motivation for coming was more personal than altruistic. He wanted to strike a blow at the Kaiju. The image of the thousands of passengers on the *Radiant Princess* was never far from his mind. Their nameless faces would suddenly burst from his memory like a silent explosion, burning a hole in his brain. Faces he had not noticed in his private world aboard ship appeared in the minutest detail. He wondered if they were real or if his imagination provided the details much as a tombstone marks a grave as a reminder. He was thankful they were silent images. Sometimes at night, the nightmares were not.

He had never had trouble sleeping. Being active all day provided a natural sleep inducement. He seldom had nightmares, and they vanished with the rising sun. His dreams were the normal women, weapons, and wealth fantasies. That was before the Kaiju, before the *Radiant Princess*. Killing Wasps or Squid would never dispel the nightmares. Only striking at the heart of the problem, the Kaiju, would. Since he could not take the fight to the aliens themselves, helping to stop the Kaiju would be the next best thing.

"The nearest entrance is fifty yards ahead," McGregor advised. "I suggest we go directly to the blood-heat exchange pit to place the bombs."

"Negative. We'll deliver one bomb each to two of the closest hatcheries. Large arteries flow through them to feed the nursery cells. They're close to the surface and easily exposed. The bombs will be more effective and easier to deliver."

McGregor was not happy with Walker's decision and allowed his ire to surface. His eyes were cold and dark in the wash of Walker's flashlight. "The plan the Joint Chiefs approved called for the blood heat exchange as our primary target. Any change of plan should go through them."

"We don't have time for a conference call. The plan was based on old Intel. This Kaiju is more dangerous."

"Afraid, Major?"

"Captain, I haven't been afraid of anything since my high school prom. I was the only black kid in my school with a lousy sense of rhythm. It was my first and only date with Daisha Harper. I got over it."

"That doesn't answer my question," McGregor insisted. "My men are ready to do this. This isn't our first dance."

"I've seen your men in action, Captain, and I concur. Their training was excellent, but this has nothing to do with their ability or their readiness. The aliens modified this Kaiju from data the other Kaiju relayed before Commander Langston took out the transmitter; the introduction of the Squid and Fleas tells us that. They will have reinforced the obvious weak points and designed other safeguards. The deeper we go, the more resistance we'll face. I've seen the Kaiju's defense mechanisms in action. They're formidable, not the mindless, uncontrolled creatures your team dealt with in Kaiju Girra. Prolonged exposure inside the Kaiju lowers our chances of a successful delivery of the K-2 to the assigned location."

"So now you're concerned for the safety of my men."

Walker stopped so suddenly Talent almost slammed into him. "No, Captain. We're all expendable if the mission calls for it, but I won't waste anyone's life needlessly. While we're descending the shaft, we'll have to split into three separate groups – one at the top, one at the bottom, and those descending. That divides and weakens our firepower. The passages to the blood-heat exchange pit are narrow. It's a choke point. That limits the number of weapons we can bring to bear at any one time."

"Why didn't you bring up any of this earlier? And why did you bring him?"

To indicate Talent, McGregor pointed the barrel of his weapon at him, deliberately shining the light in his eyes. Talent shut his eyes and blocked the light with his hand. He had grown weary of the captain's resentment of both him and Walker. "Captain," he warned, "if you point that weapon in my direction again, I'm going to shoot you."

McGregor bridled at Talent's threat, but Walker stepped between them before the confrontation came to blows.

"I didn't bring it up because I wasn't informed of the nature of the weapon we were delivering. I assumed it would be a small tactical nuke, more effective deeper inside the creature. The object is to expose the K-2 nanites to the creature's flesh and blood. Both are abundant in the hatchery. One reason I asked Talent to join us is that we could use an extra weapon. The other reason is not in your need to know."

"Somebody better decide something fast," Costas yelled as he came running up from behind them. "I think we've got company."

The passageway was just wide enough for two men to walk abreast without scraping their shoulders and about seven feet high. There was no place to hide, nothing to use for cover. Loud hisses and the sounds of clawed feet scrambling on the hard ebony armor echoed down the tunnel.

"Wasps," McGregor growled at Walker, as if he had conjured them to defuse their confrontation.

"Two down, two up," Walker ordered.

Costas and Hightower turned and knelt. Walker and McGregor stood shoulder-to-shoulder slightly behind them, their weapons aimed over their heads. Costas' M107 .50 caliber and Hightower's M134 minigun made excellent first line weapons. Walker's SCAR and McGregor's MP5 could deliver concentrated firepower as well. Talent stood behind Walker, while Wiggins, Rhoades, and Perez faced the other direction covering their backs. Talent stood in the middle of the group, his finger lightly caressing the trigger of his MP5. He hoped the new Kaiju armor-penetrating bullets worked as well as promised.

The first Wasp appeared moments later. It barely fit inside the tunnel, even with its wings folded against its back, but framed by the black walls and illuminated by the multiple flashlight beams, it looked every bit the vicious killing machine he knew it was. Its stinger was useless in the narrow space, but its mouth and finely honed claws at the end of its forelimbs were just as deadly.

The roar of the minigun was deafening in the confined space. The creature's head almost disintegrated as the stream of bullets pierced ebony armor and dug out chunks of flesh. Yellow blood splattered the walls, ceiling, and floor of the tunnel. The first creature had no sooner struck the floor than the one behind it began ripping it apart to get past it. Slippery with alien entrails and blood, it looked as if the tunnel was giving birth to the creature. The second Wasp struck at them with even more ferocity than the first, its sense of hive defense heightened by the dead Wasp's pheromones. This time, all four men on the front line opened fire. Its fate was similar to the first creature only noisier.

Walker used the time it would take the Wasps to rip through the corpse barricade to good advantage. He ushered the team down the corridor toward the first hatchery at a run. When they reached the entrance, Wiggins and Rhoades automatically took up positions on either side, while the others rushed inside.

"Well, this is friggin' different," Costas growled, coming to a sudden stop just inside the chamber.

The hatchery, an enormous cavity eighty feet in diameter and a hundred feet high, resembled a fairyland cavern. Ten rows of shallow recesses in the irregularly shaped walls circled the chamber, rising tier after tier to the ceiling. The lower tier consisted of fifty smaller recesses. Each was less than four feet square. The uppermost tier's twenty-five cavities were twice as large, large enough to contain fully developed Wasps. Opaque crystalline lids covered each of the over a thousand nursery cells, glowing with its own internal light. The kaleidoscopic colors filling the chamber ranged from deep crimson to burnt-orange.

"It's almost beautiful," Perez commented.

Talent agreed, except he knew each cell contained creatures bent on killing humans. The chamber was no simple incubator. It was a living uterus. Each row migrated upwards as the creature within matured; the cell around it expanding to accommodate its growth, until it reached the top tier, and a fully developed adult creature emerged to join the ranks of killers protecting the Kaiju.

"It would be if there weren't hundreds more of these nurseries in the Kaiju," Talent replied.

The floor of the chamber pulsed with the Kaiju's powerful heartbeat, like the pumps of a massive water treatment facility, throbbing as blood flowed to the nursery cells to nourish the monsters growing inside. The strangely repulsive vibration in his legs reminded Talent that he was inside a living creature, albeit one comprised of manufactured parts, a gigantic alien cyborg.

However, it was not the display of colorful crystal nursery cells that had elicited Costa's surprised response; it was the horde of Fleas tending to the creatures ensconced in the bottom three tiers. The nursery cell lids were open, revealing pale, shapeless, wriggling forms within cocooned in a web of black tendrils and yellow fluid. The Fleas faced outward, excreting thick, black slurry from their rear ends into the bottom of each cell. As they moved away, the lids closed.

"My God! Is that liquid armor?" Perez asked in awe.

"They shit armor," Costas roared, and then raised his weapon and pulled the trigger.

The Fleas were intent on their nursery duties. The first few died quickly, but within seconds, they became aware of the human presence and entered attack mode. They were smaller and more agile than Wasps, hopping so quickly it was difficult to aim at them. Talent gave up trying to target a single creature and simply fired into the largest groups, taking no small measure of sadistic pleasure in watching the Fleas' bodies explode from his gunfire.

"Conserve your special ammo," Walker advised over the headset. "Switch to regular rounds in order, rear rank first. Eliminate the Fleas, and we'll place the K-2 drums inside the cells. The nanites will have direct exposure to the creature's blood supply."

His voice was barely distinguishable over the din, but there was a brief pause while team members took turns switching clips, and then the slaughter resumed. Anything further he had to say was lost in the clamor of weapons fire. Coordinating an effective defense strategy by vocal commands was impossible. Each soldier knew his job and assumed his assigned position, leaving Talent on his own. That suited him. He had no formal training. He fought on instinct, killing the nearest creatures first, but visually monitoring the others as they threatened fellow team members. It was eight private wars intersecting one another. Talent cleared his mind of all thoughts except killing Fleas.

Costas swatted one Flea that drew too close with the butt of his weapon and crushed it beneath his boot. He grimaced and wiped the gooey mess from the heel of his boot on the chamber floor.

The hail of bullets slowly began to turn the tide in their favor. Less than a score of the Fleas remained, enough to be an irritant like their terrestrial namesakes, but too few to breach the wall of bullets. Talent was beginning to think it would be a simple in and out mission – home by lunch. He should have known better. The upper tier cells opened, releasing twenty-five mature Wasps. They perched on the edge of their cells preening their new wings for the two minutes it took pumped blood to unfurl them fully.

Talent expanded his battle consciousness to include the new threat. In between firing into the diminishing number of attacking Fleas, the group managed to kill two or three Wasps, but the Fleas' persistence made ignoring them impossible. Just as the first group of emerging Wasps spread their new wings and took to the air, the lids on the tier below them opened, revealing another twenty-five Wasps. These did not wait on their immature wings to expand, intent instead on scrambling down the wall to join the fray. Things escalated quickly. Even Talent began to doubt Walker's wisdom in choosing the hatchery as a target. He switched out his empty clip with one containing the Kaiju armor-piercing rounds for the Wasps.

As if things were not bad enough already, the staccato rattle of Sergeant Rhoades' MK-46 SAW erupted from outside the chamber. Seconds later, both Rhoades and Wiggins backed into the chamber directing their fire out into the corridor. The new foe was not Wasps or Fleas. Writhing tentacles danced through the air, followed by a familiar grayish smooth body. *Squid*, Talent gasped silently. Of all the Kaiju creatures, he hated Squid the most.

The Kaiju-piercing rounds riddled the first few Squid with ease. Harder to kill than Wasps because of their thickened skeletons over vital organs, they still could not withstand a concentrated assault. Rhoades and Wiggins stood their ground. Talent was closest to them and turned his attention on the Squid. Unlike Wasps or Fleas, Squid were more circumspect in their tactics. They were fearless in their assault but less ready to spend their lives needlessly. As soon as a Squid died under the hail of weapons fire, another Squid used a pair of tentacles to hold the dead body erect in front of it. The Squids' long tentacles could then strike without warning from behind their flesh and blood shield. It was an effective ploy, forcing the fire team to waste precious ammunition.

The Squid, using their shields, edged closer. One twenty-foot-long tentacle whipped out, striking Sergeant Rhoades in the top of his head, cleaving both his helmet and his skull as easily as slicing a melon. He died instantly, but his death was not the end of the tragedy. Talent watched in mute horror as the lifeless sergeant slowly toppled to the ground, his dead finger welded to the trigger of the MK 46 SAW in a spasm of dying nerves and muscles.

One stray bullet tore through Wiggins' side. The stunned private lowered his weapon to press his hand over the wound gushing blood down his side. It was an instinctive move but it proved fatal. That single moment was all the Squid needed. They instantly surrounded the two men, shredding their bodies with the metal blades embedded in their tentacles. The black drum strapped to Wiggins' back broke free and rolled across the chamber floor toward Talent, coming to rest against the mutilated corpse of a Flea halfway between him and the line of Squid. One Squid puffed out the flaps on the side of its head, revealing deep red gills, and began emitting a series of sharp hoots. A second Squid rose to its full height on its extended tentacles and scampered after the drum. Talent emptied his MP5 into the Squid's chest, or the spot where he hoped its heart was located. It reeled, teetering on its tentacles like a drunken man on stilts, but continued toward the drum. Talent backed up a few paces up to reload.

Hightower had witnessed his comrades' deaths. Enraged, he leveled the minigun at the Squid's tentacles, pressed the trigger, and held it down. The lethal spray of Kaiju-piercing bullets dropped the Squid like kicking a man's legs from under him. It fell hard but struggled to raise itself on the shattered stubs of its tentacles, intent on recovering the drum. Hightower's second burst tore it almost in half. Slimy alien organs, most of them unrecognizable, spilled across the floor of the chamber. He then turned the weapon on the Squid's brethren, ripping holes in the dead Squid they used as shields, exposing the creatures beyond. He unleashed a stream of obscenities at them and laughed maniacally as bullets amputated tentacles and punched holes in flesh.

A few of Hightower's rounds pierced the black drum. Talent tensed, waiting for it to explode, grateful when it did not. Hightower's intervention gave Talent time to place more distance between himself and the Squid. He slapped in a fresh ammo clip and rushed to retrieve the loose drum. To his dismay, a Wasp swooped down from high above him and grabbed the drum in its forelimbs. Thick, black liquid dripped from the holes Hightower had made in it. He fired a burst into the Wasp's belly, killing it instantly, but it and the drum crashed to the ground beyond the wall of attacking Squid.

Walker had also witnessed the deaths of the two men and the loss of the K-2 bomb, but he had no time to lament their passing or evaluate the halving of their nanite weapons. He ducked a Wasp diving at him and loosed a short burst into its head. The bullets tore through the creature's mouth and into its brain. A geyser of yellow ichor sprayed him with sticky goo as it tumbled overhead in a death dive into one of the nursery cells, springing open the lid and exposing the immature creature inside. A second burst from Walker's weapon turned the juvenile into pulp.

More Squid hoots filled the chamber. The flying Wasps abandoned their attack on the fire team to form a living wall in front of the Squid, while the remaining Fleas pressed the attack from that direction, advancing quickly across the chamber, driving him and the others away from the hatchery and back toward the entrance and the waiting Squid.

The fire team was now trapped between Wasps and Squid and rapidly running out of ammunitions. They were also running out of options. The mission was in danger of ending before it had started. Talent glanced at Walker. He could see Walker's mind working furiously to extricate them from their predicament. Suddenly, Walker focused his attention on a narrow section of the wall between banks of nursery cells and began firing his weapon at the wall. Chips of black armor splintered away, revealing crimson flesh beneath it. Guessing his intention, Talent aimed his HP5 at the same spot and opened fire.

When a sizable expanse of alien flesh was exposed, Walker pointed to the M-23 grenade launcher on Talent's shoulder. Talent nodded. He had never exploded a grenade in a confined space, even one the as large as an Olympic-sized swimming pool, but death by flying shrapnel seemed infinitely preferable to being torn to pieces. He controlled his fear, ignoring the Squid rushing across the chamber toward him. He let his MP5 dangle from its strap, swung the grenade launcher into position, and clicked off the safety.

His first round was an M40 fragmentary grenade. He had not had time to practice with the weapon's attached M2A1 reflex sight. He trusted to his luck, estimated the distance, and fired from the hip. The grenade shot through the air in a perfect arc. For a brief moment, it looked as if an alert Wasp would intercept it, but to his immense relief, the projectile sailed between the Wasps legs and struck the exposed section of wall dead center. The explosion blew away a chunk of the ebony wall and crimson flesh beneath it, revealing a dark opening beyond. The intervening swarm of Wasps absorbed the brunt of the explosion and the flying shrapnel. Walker pushed his way through the few remaining Fleas, kicking them aside with his feet as he fired into them. Talent followed close on his heels. He had no idea where the dark, uninviting opening led, but it was an exit from the chamber of death.

20

Wednesday, Dec. 20, 0300 hours   *U.S.S. Mississippi*, New Hebrides Trench –

Fire Team Bravo was safely away and Mark Talent was with them. Relenting to Walker's request had gone against everything Commander Murdock had learned at the Academy, but fighting new enemies required new rules. Walker was convinced he needed Talent, and as the captain of the vessel delivering the fire team, he could not deny him every available asset necessary for the completion of his mission. His decision could quite possibly cost him his career, but that was the least of his worries. If Doctor Rutherford were right, the device the Squid were working on could wipe out half of Australia. He would have to let Walker deal with the Kaiju. His primary mission had now shifted to the destruction or the disarming of the alien gravity wave bomb.

Since he knew nothing about alien technology, disarming it seemed an unlikely scenario. Destroying it would be tricky as well. Accidently exploding the bomb and initiating the annihilation of Australia and the South Pacific nations would not look good on his record. He had the rough outline of a plan in mind to deal with the situation, but every variation he plotted ended in disaster for his boat. Somehow, he had to tip the odds in his favor.

His intercom crackled to life. "Captain, we just received a signal from Fire Team Bravo. They've entered the Kaiju."

He nodded his head. At least that part of the mission was a success. They were beyond his help now. "Notify USPACOM of the fact. Contact Captain Wilkins of the *Hatcher* and request that he keep his remaining Fast Attack Craft standing by to extract the fire team. Then inform the exec that I will meet him in the control center."

From the somber expression on Dobbs' face when he arrived in the control center, he had had time to digest the abrupt change of mission priorities, and it had soured his stomach. He was an intelligent man and an exemplary officer and had undoubtedly arrived at the same conclusion as Murdock. True to his nature, though, he did not protest.

"Lieutenant, luck has blessed us with the very equipment we need for the completion of this mission."

"You mean the LR5."

Murdock smiled; pleased he had not underestimated his executive officer. "I do indeed, Lieutenant. The Royal Australian Navy delivered the DSRV to the *Mississippi* in the hope that a rescue of the crews of the *Essex* or the *Colorado* might be possible. The nature of their sinking dashed that hope. I almost ordered it dumped over the side to gain speed. Now I'm glad I didn't. It's ideally suited for disarming the bomb. Its manipulator arm, under the control of a qualified operator, can perform wonders."

The bulky, white monstrosity secured to the hull of the *USS Mississippi* reduced her speed by an agonizing three knots. It made the submarine heavy in the stern and reduced her maneuverability to that of an inner tube with no paddle. He had considered cutting it loose when he began his pursuit of the Kaiju, over the loud protests of its two-man crew.

"You trained on the *Mystic* didn't you, Commander?"

Murdock smiled. "I did indeed. The Navy DSRV isn't that different from the LR5."

"The DSRV came with its own crew, sir," Dobbs pointed out.

"The diver will accompany me to operate the ROV. With its four video cameras, the *Scorpio 45* can keep an eye out for Squid, freeing me to tackle the alien pod. Between us, we might improve our odds. You, Lieutenant, will assume command of the *Mississippi* while I'm absent from the boat."

"I have to point out, sir, that your place is on the bridge. The Royal Navy diver is proficient at his job or they would not have sent him. I'm sure his assistant is equally qualified."

"They were sent to rescue downed submariners, not fight aliens. I am the captain of a fighting vessel. That makes it my job."

"Your dedication is admirable, Commander, and no one will question your bravery, but this sounds like a final goodbye."

Murdock winced. Dobbs' words were too close to the truth. "Better men than I have given their lives for freedom, and alien invader or communist threat, this is about freedom."

Dobbs stood straighter. "Yes, sir."

"The DSRV will undoubtedly attract the Squids' attention. You will load the forward tubes with the modified Mark 58 sonic compression torpedoes. Since the Squid offer no sonar profile, I will direct your fire visually. You will detonate the Mark 58s manually on my command when they close to within fifty yards. This should eliminate some of the Squid and might help mask the DSRV's approach."

"That's cutting it dangerously close, sir. You might catch the edge of the blast."

"That's a chance I'll have to take. With you clearing the field for me, I should be able to reach the goal line."

"What then?"

This was the tricky part. He had not yet gotten that far in his planning. "I'm not sure. I'll have to improvise as the situation unfolds. At the very least, I will take possession of the bomb for the home team."

Dobbs nodded. "Yes, sir."

He could see in his exec's eyes that Dobbs thought the plan was mad, and he was right. It was more a crudely drawn sketch scribbled on the back of a paper napkin than a true plan, but it was the best he could do. The Academy had not prepared him for battling aliens or defusing gravity bombs while fending off alien Squid.

His first instinct was to blast everything in sight, but that shotgun-assault approach could detonate the bomb. Like all modified Virginia-Class nuclear submarines, the *USS Mississippi* was a floating arsenal. Normally, her four forward torpedo tubes could deliver twenty-two Mark 58 and Mark 60 torpedoes, but two torpedo racks had been removed to make space for the survivors from the *Radiant Princess* and not yet been replaced. Her twelve missile tubes could launch over eighty Tomahawk cruise missiles, six armed with W76 100-kiloton nuclear warheads. The rest delivered thousand-pound conventional explosive warheads or BLU-97/B cluster bombs. An assortment of UAVs and ADM-160 MALD antisubmarine sensor drones could augment the boats defenses. For surface fighting, she carried a retractable 20 mm Phalanx M61 Vulcan Cannon positioned forward of the conning tower and mounts for two .50 caliber machineguns atop the Sail. Yet, for all practical purposes, he was reduced to hand-to-hand combat, using a one-armed rescue submersible.

Twenty minutes later, he sat in the uncomfortably small pilot's seat of the Australian DSRV. The thick Plexiglas windows below, forward, and above him allowed him a wide visual range. The control panel looked like any normal aircraft control panel with the addition of monitor screens for the video cameras and grips for the manipulator arm. Beside him sat Master Diver Lance Meyers, a twenty-four-year old former high school high dive champion from Adelaide. Meyers, at 5'6''and 145 pounds, looked more comfortable, but their elbows kept knocking in the cramped quarters. At first, Murdock's insistence that he would man the controls troubled Meyers, but after safely maneuvering the bulky DSRV away from the *Mississippi*, he relaxed.

"You handle her like a pro," he said.

Murdock smiled. "I know you're more qualified, but I need you to handle the *Scorpio 45* remote. This is going to be tricky, and we're not likely to get more than one chance."

He had informed Meyers about the alien gravity bomb before leaving – he owed him that much – but the young diver had taken it in stride.

"I could work better outside in the ADS."

The Atmospheric Dive Suit was a hard shell dive suit rated to 2000 feet used to clear away debris from downed submarine hatches.

"We're not rescuing sailors, son, we're disarming a bomb. The suit offers no protection against the Squid."

Using the forward video camera, he spotted the alien pod floating at a depth of 125 feet. His sonar screen showed only a blurry haze. The Kaiju was no longer there. Did its absence mean he was too late? He radioed the *Mississippi*. "Where is the Kaiju?"

Dobbs answered. "It got under way about three minutes ago, following its original heading. The Bluefin UUV drone picked up six Squid around the pod, two working on it and four spaced around it as guards."

"Are the concussion torpedoes ready?"

"Yes, sir. On your order."

"Stand by."

He positioned the DSRV a hundred yards from the pod and hovered, amazed that the Squid had not already attacked. He then fired a low-frequency sonic burst from the active sonar that was certain to get the Squids' attention. To Meyers, he said, "Send out the ROV. Take it to a depth of five hundred feet beneath the pod."

Meyers turned to the panel in front of him and flipped a switch. The *Scorpio 45* shot out of its bay and dropped below the DSRV. The top-mounted camera showed the white underbelly of the LR5 receding. Meyers panned the cameras to face the pod. The four Squid surrounding the pod ignored the ROV but homed in on the source of the sonic blast.

"Fire all tubes," Murdock ordered Dobbs.

The Squid could have covered the distance in seconds, but they took their time, first examining the DSRV with their array of sensors. They seemed perplexed that they detected no weapons on the miniature sub and were undecided about what to do. However, when they detected the first two modified Mark 58 torpedoes approaching at 70 mph, they went immediately into attack mode. One of the nineteen-foot long missiles shot by the DSRV's porthole, a black, red, and orange streak in the water. Six seconds later, two more torpedoes passed below the DSRV.

The modified Mark 58 conventional explosive warheads had been replaced with a low-frequency sound pump generator capable of emitting a low-frequency sound wave pulse at 200 decibels, deadly to humans and damaging to delicate electronic equipment. The generator directed the pulses forward and to the sides of the torpedo in an expanding cone-shaped pattern. Fifty yards behind the torpedo, he hoped the DSRV would be outside the lethal range. The Squid moved to intercept the first two torpedoes. When he deemed the torpedoes were far enough away from the DSRV for safety but near enough to the Squid to be effective, he spoke into the radio, trying to keep his nervous excitement under control. His entire plan hinged on the effectiveness of the torpedoes. If they failed … he didn't want to think about that.

"Detonate 1 and 2 on my command. Detonate 3 and 4 five seconds later."

He followed the track of the torpedoes on the sonar screen. When he had visual confirmation in the video monitor, he shouted, "Now!"

The pulse was too low to hear, but the rapidly expanding bubble of superheated water turned to steam by the acoustic blast struck the DSRV like an underwater tidal wave. It picked up the sub, rolled it onto its port side, and twirled it like a baton, leaving the nose facing the surface. Murdock fought the controls to right the small vessel as alarm bells began sounding. Half the lights on the panels went out. He barely slowed the vessel's spin when the second pair of torpedoes detonated. This time, the DSRV shuddered like a struck bell and dropped like a rock, passing four hundred feet before he got it under control.

"Bring up the pod on the video cameras."

Only one of the DSRV's two cameras still functioned. Meyers focused the image. Two of the squid were obviously dead. Their dismembered and cooked bodies floated in the water, surrounded by clouds of alien blood. Two more were intact but motionless. Murdock did not know if they were dead or merely stunned. The two Squid arming the bomb were farther away and had escaped injury. They continued to work on the pod. It seemed to Murdock that they had increased their speed to complete their task. He pushed the DSRV's control stick forward and edged closer to the pod.

"Bring the ROV up directly beneath the pod," he told Meyers. "I'll try to draw them away."

"What am I doing?" Meyers asked in a panicked voice. "I can't disarm a bomb."

"Shove the ROV's manipulator arm into the open panel to prevent it from closing. I'm betting that the open panel will compromise the pod's overall integrity. We'll use the ROV to drag it to the bottom and let the pressure at 25,000 feet crush it."

"Won't that detonate it?" Meyers asked.

Murdock did not answer. He was operating on pure speculation. He had no idea what would or would not set off the bomb, or if the ebony material of the pod had a depth limit. It was a spacecraft designed for travel through the vacuum of space, not withstanding enormous outside pressure. He could think of no other options. "We'll soon find out."

One Squid moved away from the pod and placed itself between the pod and the DSRV. It did not move closer, but began waving its tentacles in the water as if telling him to bring it on. Murdock brought the manipulator arm forward. The Squid's tentacles outnumbered him 8:1 and beat his reach by ten feet. The tentacles moved like lightning, while his manipulator arm, designed to move debris or heavy objects, was slow but powerful. If he were in a boxing ring, his opponent would plaster him with punches while he swatted air. He reminded himself that he wasn't going for a knockout punch, just sparring long enough for Meyers to make his move.

The Squid put on a burst of speed and raced toward the DSRV. At first, he thought it intended to collide with the sub as it had the two submarines and the cruise ship, but it halted ten feet away, matching speeds with the DSRV. It studied the mini-sub for a few minutes, and then shot one tentacle, grabbed the light bar across the front of the vehicle, and pulled itself forward. Suddenly, Murdock was staring into the four alien eyes of the Squid. There were no irises; it had no expression, but he thought he could see anger in the creature's countenance.

Then it opened its mouth, revealing the razor-sharp teeth capable of chewing through metal. He raised the manipulator arms like two beefy arms with fists coming together, and clamped the Squid's body between them. It squirmed free before he could increase the pressure. Another tentacle shot out and struck the thick Plexiglas porthole in front of him, leaving a spider web of fine cracks. The porthole could withstand the pressure at a depth of over 2,000 feet, but the Squid had almost cracked it like an egg. He switched on the outside floodlights and the Squid backed away.

As he kept an eye on the Squid, he also watched the monitor showing the ROV rising from beneath the alien pod. The second Squid now floated a few feet away watching the battle between machine and alien creature. It had not yet detected the ROV. The panel was still open, but

Murdock did not know how much longer they had. For all he knew, the bomb was already armed. Just as the ROV drew level with the pod, the Squid saw it.

"Now!" Murdock shouted.

Meyers shot the ROV's arm forward into the panel just as the Squid reacted. It touched a spot beside the panel, and the panel slammed down on the arm, leaving a four-inch gap. The Squid went on a rampage, attacking the ROV with all its tentacles. It stripped pieces of metal from the frame and punctured the two ballast tanks. The cameras died one by one, and then the lights, but for all the damage the creature did, it could not extract the ROV's arm.

"Take it to the bottom," Murdock told Meyers.

He pushed the power lever up to full but the pod did not budge. "It's not powerful enough."

His plan was quickly falling apart. They had prevented the panel from closing, but couldn't move the pod. Eventually, the Squid would succeed in yanking it free. It renewed its efforts on the ROV but the sturdy little vehicle resisted its attack. Finally, it settled for the next best thing. It wrenched the ROV free of the arm. Murdock watched the ROV sink out of sight.

Now, both Squid were free to attack the DSRV.

"Brace yourself," Murdock warned Meyers, as both Squid raced for the DSRV with a flurry of tentacles propelling them forward.

One struck the mini-sub head on, spreading the cracks in the porthole wider. The second latched itself to the bottom of the sub pounding at the belly hatch. Murdock knew they would either crack the porthole, flooding the DSRV, or damage the motors beyond repair. He pushed the vehicle forward toward the pod.

Meyers rose from his seat. "I'm going aft to check for leaks."

Murdock nodded. He was too busy tracking the Squid to discuss it. Meyers opened the hatch dividing the control cabin from the pressurized crew transport, stepped through, and dogged it shut behind him. When one of the Squid came at the porthole again, he raised the arms to block it, and then clamped them closed on one of the tentacles. He was now holding a tiger by the tail. It opened its mouth so wide he thought it was trying to swallow the DSRV whole, and chomped down on the arm chewing into the metal. He jerked the controls back and forth, singing the Squid around like a rag doll.

When he heard the hiss of the airlock cycling, he thought a squid had managed to open the hatch. Then he realized Meyers had donned the ADS and was leaving the DSRV. He yelled into the radio, praying that Meyers was on the same frequency.

"Meyers! Get back in here. What do you think you're doing?"

"I have a spear gun, a shark stick, and half a kilo of C4. I'll see if I can get their attention while you secure the pod."

Murdock shook his head. Meyers was foolish but brave. The spear gun was not powerful enough to do any damage. The shark stick held a shotgun shell at its tip, fired by shoving it into a shark's body to discourage them from becoming too nosy during a rescue. The C4 was used to blast any debris too large to move with the manipulator arm. "The shark stick won't detonate the C4."

"I know. The shark stick is just to get their attention. I've wired the blasting cap and C4 to the spear with a spool of wire running to my flashlight. I switch it on and wham – no more Squid."

"It's too risky. Get back in here."

He saw Meyers swimming twenty yards off the port side of the DSRV. "Too late. They see me."

A flash of gray Squid zipped by the porthole. He began to turn the sub toward Meyers.

"No, don't," he called out. "Finish the job."

Murdock hesitated, but then resumed his course to the pod. "Good luck, son."

The first Squid shot a tentacle toward Meyers. He jammed the shark stick into it and laughed into this radio. "Hurts doesn't it?"

The Squid backed off a few yards and studied him as it waited for its companion. Murdock saw him raise the spear gun, but he didn't have a chance to fire it. The Squid shot through the water like a torpedo and encircled him in its tentacles. Murdock heard his muffled curse just before he started screaming in pain as the creature tightened its grip. It pulled him toward its open mouth. Too close to use the spear gun, he yanked the spear from the barrel and jammed it in the creature's mouth. Murdock saw a brief flash of light from the flashlight, and then the C4 exploded, shredding the Squid's head. Squid and Meyers sank slowly to the bottom.

The diversion had allowed Murdock to get close to the alien pod, but the remaining Squid came at him in all its alien fury. He had just enough time to ram home the manipulator arm into the gap in the panel. Now he was irrevocably linked with the bomb. He set the controls to take both sub and bomb into the depths of the New Hebrides Trench. If he was right about its resistance to pressure, he had won. If not, he would never know what hit him.

The Squid attacked the sub and wrenched free the propeller, but Murdock had already blown the reserve air tanks. He and the pod were barely sinking, but he had one more thing he could do. He could flood the DSRV and sink it. He opened the hatch between the control cabin and the pressure chamber, sat back down, and began pounding on the cracked porthole with a tool. The noise enraged the Squid. It came to the front of the DSRV and dove straight at the porthole. The glass splintered. Water shot inside with three times surface pressure, not enough to kill, but the pressure was more than enough to quickly fill the DSRV cabin and flood the pressure chamber. The DSRV and pod began sinking faster.

Murdock held his breath though he didn't know why. He could never reach the surface without bursting his lungs. The Squid was not finished. It pulled its body through the smashed porthole and wedged itself inside the small control cabin. Its bulk pushed him into the bulkhead. He heard bones snap. The air spilled from his lungs, filling the water in front of him with bubbles. He stared the creature in its four alien eyes and smiled. Then he used his last breath to push the button, activating the underwater Oxy-arc cutter attached to the manipulator arm. The flame dug into the creature's body. He watched it writhe in pain before blackness took him.

* * * *

Lieutenant Commander Dobbs watched the DSRV sinking on the sonar screen. Instead of dismay, he felt a sense of pride. The *Mississippi's* captain had succeeded at the cost of his own life. There was still a chance the bomb would explode, negating Commander Murdock's sacrifice, but Dobbs hoped the universe did not work that way.

"I'm picking up noise of the pod imploding, sir."

Dobbs smiled and nodded to the sonar operator. Murdock's assumption concerning the pod's vulnerability was right. The world was safe – for the moment. There was still the Kaiju to deal with. He turned to the drivers. He preferred the old terminology.

"Helmsmen, take us out of here. Inform USPACOM that we are in pursuit of the Kaiju."

21

Wednesday, Dec. 20, 0320 hours   Inside Kaiju Kiribati –

Costas, Hightower, and Perez formed a lethal arc of firepower, holding the creatures at bay as they slowly backed toward the dark opening. Captain McGregor stood motionless staring at the mutilated corpses of Sergeant Rhoades and Wiggins as if waiting for them to arise miraculously from the dead. Talent wanted to shout, "We don't have three days to wait for their resurrection," but his half-forgotten Catholic upbringing curbed his blasphemy. Suddenly, in a fit of rage, McGregor raised his MP5 and, roaring obscenities at the top of his lungs, held down the trigger. He continued to yell even after he emptied the clip. Costas grabbed him by his shoulder, spun him around, and shoved him toward the opening.

"Move it, Captain!" he shouted, "Or I'll kick your sorry ass through the nice exit Talent just made for us."

McGregor tensed and fixed Costas with a deadly glare. Talent thought that he would have shot Costas if his weapon had not been empty. However, Costas was not intimidated. He pushed his face into McGregor's and repeated, "Move it." McGregor turned and walked calmly toward the narrow opening.

Walker and Perez waited at the opening, firing into the advancing Squid and Wasps to cover their retreat. Perez's Mossberg 12-gauge shotgun looked too large for the petite S.E.A.L. to handle, but she used it effectively, shredding flailing tentacles and shattering Squid eyes. Walker's 7.62 mm SCAR L-CQC sprayed Kaiju-killer bullets that ripped through ebony armor and gouged out chunks of alien flesh. Ignoring the threat of the armor piercing rounds, the Squid continued to press the attack. They seemed to understand just how much room they needed to utilize their multiple arms effectively. For every creature that died, another pressed through the entrance of the chamber to replace it. The

Kaiju seemed to have an endless supply of replacements, but Fire Team Bravo did not. With two members already down, they were hard-pressed to make an orderly retreat.

As soon as McGregor and Costas passed him and entered the opening, Walker yelled for Talent to fire three grenades into the midst of the tightly packed group of Squid. Talent popped off three quick rounds and ducked into the opening with Walker and Perez pressing close behind him. The grenades were standard issue, but were highly effective nonetheless, exploding in quick succession, spraying lethal shrapnel into the close ranks of Squid and the Wasps flying above them. Those creatures at the forefront of the attack became bewildered, thinking a new enemy had appeared behind them. They milled about in confusion seeking the new threat.

Seeing the disorder, Walker turned to Talent. "Fire a flash grenade."

Talent spun the drum to an M-84 flash-bang grenade, aimed through the opening, and fired. The grenade arced over the throng of Squid and exploded with a thunderclap so loud it shook Talent's insides. The brilliant burst of light that accompanied it spilled back through the opening. Talent closed his eyes, but the bright glow penetrated his eyelids, almost blinding him. He hoped it incapacitated the Squid as much as it did him. He rubbed his watering eyes, blinking until they cleared enough to see, and peered through the opening. No creatures pursued them, daunted either by the narrowness of the slit or by some instinct to guard the hatchery. They were safe for the moment, but they had lost two men and one of the K-2 drums. It was an expensive victory.

The space in which Talent stood was almost as narrow as the opening, a four-foot-wide gap between two towering crimson walls. He shined his flashlight upwards and saw mats of fibrous material dangling from protrusions in the walls as far up as the beam of the light would penetrate. The mats undulated in the slight, warm breeze. They were in one of the Kaiju's cooling ducts. The cloying, earthy stench of the hatchery was less obvious here, though a decidedly alien smell still permeated the air.

"Which way?" Costas asked.

Walker did not hesitate. He pointed his light down the right hand corridor. "This way."

"And do what?" McGregor demanded loudly.

Everyone stopped to stare at him. Washed in the glow of flashlights, the face beneath the helmet appeared demonic, pale flesh dominated by two dark eyes glaring at Walker, his mouth a rictus of anger set in his clenched jaw. His chest heaved in anger. Talent could understand his agitation. He had just watched two of his men die in a horrendous manner, making four casualties in his original six-man team, but Talent could not comprehend McGregor's insistence on focusing his anger at Walker. The remaining two members of his team – Hightower and Perez – looked on in confusion.

"Wiggins is dead," McGregor continued. "So is Sergeant Rhoades. Wiggins had one of the K-2 bombs." He shook his head. "Two more of my men are gone, and we're stuck in some … some Kaiju back alleyway nowhere near our assigned target. Just what do you intend to do, Major Walker – kill the rest of us?"

Both Perez and Hightower instinctively positioned themselves to back their captain, but his untimely outburst placed them all in danger. He was rattling the links of the chain of command, so integral to the core of their training, the glue that bound all soldiers together. McGregor was testing to its limits their loyalty to him, and it rankled them, especially Perez who shuffled her feet and shook her head sadly, looking as if she had rather be any place but there. Her conflict was evident in her tortured face.

Walker's reaction took the captain and the others off guard, even Talent. He pulled his M9 Beretta, placed the barrel against the side of McGregor's temple, and clicked off the safety. "I've had it with you, Captain," he said. His voice remained calm but his eyes matched his action, conveying the depth of his ire. "If you open your mouth one more time except to say, 'Yes, sir,' I'll put a bullet in your head. I've got no time to fight you and the Kaiju." He nodded his head down the passageway, his cold gaze never leaving McGregor's face. "This shaft leads to an intersection just above the passageway paralleling the blisters. I intend to use one of the transverse corridors to travel deeper into the Kaiju, find the shaft to the brain, and detonate the K-2. As the nanites eat away the control mechanisms, the Kaiju will be helpless, an unguided behemoth floating in the ocean. Once we reach the junction, feel free to blast a way through and leave." He turned to Perez and Hightower and his expression softened. "You two can go with him if you want. I won't order any man to follow me to his death."

Talent waited to see if McGregor and the others would respond. He did not doubt that Walker would pull the trigger if further provoked. A dark part of him hoped Walker would carry out his threat and shoot McGregor. Like Walker, he was fed up with the mealy-mouthed son of a bitch's insubordination. To his disappointment, McGregor retained enough of his wits not to test Walker's mettle. He remained silent. Neither Perez nor Hightower made any sudden move for fear of reprisal by Costas, who calmly kept them covered with his weapon from his position near the opening. Satisfied by their lack of response, Walker holstered his Beretta and went back to retrieve the pack he had left beside Costas.

It is said that disaster strikes when least expected. In Talent's case, that was doubly true. The tension froze time in the small corridor, but beyond the wall, time continued to flow at an alien pace. Without warning, the slit he had blasted ripped wider and half a dozen Squid tentacles shot through the opening, striking the wall. Walker dropped just in time to avoid decapitation and rolled away from their reach, as they snaked along the wall searching. Costas could not fire at the tentacles for fear of hitting other members of the team. He backpedaled away from the opening, dragging Walker with him.

To Talent's ears, the high-pitched squeal of Squid teeth grinding into the armored wall was worse than long fingernails raked across a chalkboard. He went to one knee, aiming his MP5 upward at the writhing tentacles, but withheld his fire until he was certain Walker and Costas were clear. Hightower was not as cautious. A shower of hot 7.62 mm shell casings sprayed over Talent's head and shoulders as the corporal stood over him and unleashed the fury of his M 134 minigun. Squid flesh and blood splattered the walls of the passageway as the stream of bullets ripped into the tentacles, but for every tentacle he severed, two more took its place.

Within minutes, the Squid had enlarged the hole sufficiently for the first Squid to squirm through it. It died quickly under a hail of weapons fire, but the tentacles of those creatures behind it dragged its corpse back. A second and then a third soon joined it, forcing the divided team away from the opening. Costas and Walker went one direction, and Talent and the rest of the fire team the other.

The Squid filled the narrow passageway so tightly there was no chance of friendly fire. Talent added his fire to that of the others. Beyond the creatures, he could hear Costas' SASR belching out .50 caliber rounds, but the sound diminished as the creatures gradually but relentlessly forced the two groups farther apart. Then, the Squid began to employ a new tactic. As the bodies of their comrades piled up, they scampered up the sides of the passageway as nimbly as they had the side of the *Radiant Princess* to come at them from above. Talent leaned back as far as he could, firing straight up at one particularly nimble creature. It presented an almost impossible target in the darkness as it scurried in and out of the beam of his flashlight. Finally, Hightower joined him and killed it with a blast from his minigun. The Squid fell from its perch and wedged in the narrow gap between walls, creating a temporary barricade.

Over the rattle of gunfire, Talent heard Walker's voice in his headset, but the signal was weak and difficult to make out.

". . . more Squid are attacking. Find a good location, set the timer on the K-2, and get out." A muffled yell in the background abruptly ended the transmission.

Talent did not want to abandon Walker and Costas, especially if they were under attack, but hands gripping his collar dragged him backwards down the narrow corridor, as the Squid set about methodically dismembering the Squid-corpse barricade. The tight confines prevented the Squid from overpowering them by superior numbers, but their tenacity forced the fire team to retreat, firing as they went, placing greater distance between the two groups with each step.

"Walker," he called over his headset mic, but heard only the soft hiss of static. He repeated his call until Hightower said, "Forget it. The Kaiju armor acts as a sponge, dampening any E-M signal."

The Squid had mysteriously abandoned pursuit. Talent was betting they had not forgotten them, but he was too tired to question their tactics. McGregor led the team forward in silence. Talent trudged along behind them, but continued to glance back for Walker and Costas. A dark depression descended on him. Such men who unselfishly risked their lives to save others deserved a more fitting fate – medals, adulation, and a long, happy retirement, Costas with a bevy of attending women.

As they marched, a wall of warm, moist air, fetid with alien smells, pushed down the tunnel into their faces, growing in intensity as they progressed. The mats of fringe flapped frantically in an attempt to propel the onrush of air down the passageway. With his head bowed to avoid the brunt of the foul wind, Talent began to notice patterns in the crimson walls, fine traces of black lines threading through the flesh just beneath the surface. He stopped and pressed the flesh with his finger, surprised by its softness. The area around his finger quivered and turned dark, as the black threads migrated to the pressure point. He removed his finger and the threads retreated to their original configuration. Fascinated, he wanted to experiment further, but McGregor's glare forced him onward.

For half an hour, they negotiated tight bends and squeezed through narrow enfolds of the passage that funneled the strong wind into a gale-force wind. It was with immense relief that they reached the junction Walker had described. Talent did not wait for orders or permission. He was too exhausted to care what McGregor thought. He collapsed against a wall to rest his aching muscles. Seeing him, McGregor motioned the others to join him.

The junction was a small chamber, the intersection of seven passageways forming an axis node. Two X-axis branches led left and right from the central chamber in which they stood, and two Z-axis branches split from the one they had just traveled, continuing forward, separated from each other by a thirty-degree angle and rose at a twenty-degree incline. One more branch bisected the chamber vertically, forming the Y-axis. The upward vertical shaft was not climbable, and they no longer had enough rope to attempt the descending shaft, a yawning five-foot-wide chasm in the center of the chamber. In addition to transporting the second drum of K-2, Wiggins had also carried most of the rope and climbing gear.

The chamber was composed of the same crimson flesh as the passageway, but here the dark threads were more numerous, so tightly packed they formed bands of black streaking the walls, especially at the points where passageways entered the chamber, where they formed thick orifices. As Talent watched, the orifice of one passageway began to expand, protruding toward the center until they met, sealing the passageway, and diverting the rush of air in a different direction. It was a vivid reminder that he was inside a living creature.

Talent's anger at McGregor bubbled to the surface when after only a few minutes' pause he roused his men and directed them down the right-hand branch. "What are you doing?" he demanded. "We can't leave. What about Major Walker?"

"Walker's dead."

The smugness of McGregor's answer rubbed Talent the wrong way. His hand rested on the hilt of his kukri, itching to plunge it into McGregor's heart, but he restrained himself.

"You're here on sufferance, Talent. Don't tempt me to leave you here. You heard Walker's transmission. We're placing the K-2 here and setting the timer for 30 minutes. The air will move it through the creature. The mission went FUBAR."

Talent scowled at McGregor. "I thought S.E.A.L.S were braver than this."

Before McGregor could deliver his rejoinder, disaster number three was upon them. From the two inclined shafts in front of them poured a score of mottled gray, bloated creatures the size of a javelina, but their closely set, heavily lidded red eyes made them look meaner than the ubiquitous native Arizona peccary. The four-foot long creature raced at them on at least eight pairs of short, spindly legs, each tipped with a vicious, sharp claw. They moved so swiftly, Talent was uncertain of the exact number. The castanet-like clacking of their foot-long mandibles was as unsettling as their loathsome appearance.

"Ticks," he moaned, recognizing them from Costas' vivid description. "*I'itoi,* give me a friggin' break."

Calling on the Tohono O'odham god of creation was pure instinct, on par with the adage that there are no atheists in foxholes. He had no more faith in the Tohono O'odham god than he did in the Christian God, and even less faith in McGregor.

"What's your plan now, Captain?" he spat at McGregor, as he fired into the creatures' midst.

The Ticks were amazingly agile despite their sluggish appearance. They raced across the chamber utilizing floor, walls, and ceiling and attacked the group with unbelievable ferocity, heedless of the volley of weapons fire aimed at them. Two of the creatures pinned Perez against the wall, their combine weight almost as much as hers. Their mandibles snapped together mere inches from her throat. Only her combat training and her upper body strength kept the creatures at bay, as she grabbed each one by the neck and hung on as she struggled to push them away. Other Ticks rushed to join the two creatures.

Talent saw her predicament, and without thinking, took out his kukri and lunged at the nearest Tick, driving the blade deep into its back. Because of its resemblance to a terrestrial tick, he expected to see red blood gushing out. Instead, a thick gray, malodorous sludge oozed from the wound, hardening so quickly it sealed the wound and gripped the blade. Talent yanked the blade free, taking a large chunk of Tick flesh with it. The smell almost gagged him. Tossing the useless kukri aside, he fired a burst into its head from inches away. The head exploded and the creature fell away from Perez, splattering her with gray sludge.

Before either of them could stop it, the second Tick slashed Perez's left shoulder almost to the bone. She screamed in agony and shoved the Tick away, but it clamped its mandibles around the drum and held on with bulldog tenacity. Talent killed it with a second burst.

Around him, the others were embroiled in a vicious hand-to-hand melee, fending off the sharp mandibles with rifles, feet, and hands. McGregor kicked one creature down the shaft in front of him, like punting a field goal. A second, he killed with his MP5. The six-barrels of Hightower's M 134 minigun hummed as they spun deadly fire into the massed creatures.

Perez's shirt was soaked in her blood. Gray lumps of Tick blood had sealed one of her eyes shut. Her left arm dangled uselessly by her side. Left-handed, the S.E.A.L. specialist could no longer fire her MP5 or the shotgun, but she kept a firm grip on her Beretta with her good right hand, shooting one particularly adventuresome Tick in the head. Talent took pity on the injured S.E.A.L. and shoved her against the wall; then, stood in front of her, cutting down any Tick that got too close.

Their numbers seemed infinite. They poured from the shafts like a gray flood, parting in the middle and dividing into two streams to navigate around the open shaft in the center of the chamber. Dead Ticks disappeared beneath the horde of freshly arrived Ticks, their bodies churned to mush by hundreds of pointed little legs. For the first time, even counting his first encounter with the Squid aboard the *Radiant Princess*, Talent expected to die. As if on command, the flap covering the hole in the floor closed, allowing the Ticks to surge back together into one mass and use the entire chamber to press their attack.

He continued firing until he exhausted his regular ammunition, and then switched to his last clip of Kaiju-piercing rounds. When that was gone, he pulled out his Beretta and fired the last four rounds in the clip. All he had left was the grenade launcher. Using it in the small chamber would be suicide, but it was tempting nevertheless. It would less messy dying that way than beneath the horde of Ticks.

Perez's hand shook as she struggled to pass Talent the Mossberg shotgun. Weak and one-handed, she could barely lift it. Talent admired her courage. Most people would have passed out from the shock of such a severe wound, but Perez was a S.E.A.L. More, she was a female, a minority within a minority. She refused to cry out or give in to her wounds. She continued to do her job.

The Mossberg held only five more shots in the eight-round clip. A quick mental count told him he would have to kill a dozen Ticks with every shot to stay alive. To conserve ammo, he waited until a Tick got too close to ignore. The battle had raged for less than three minutes, but to Talent it seemed half a lifetime. His life didn't exactly pass before his eyes, but he did remember incidents from his past he wished he had handled differently, but he could not see any path that would not have brought him to this place at this time. His prospects of ever reaching Australia grew dimmer by the minute.

When the head of one of the pair of Ticks he was fending off exploded, Talent looked up to see Walker and Costas running down the corridor. *Reinforcements*, he groaned appreciatively. Seeing Walker alive was like seeing a long lost brother. However, his relief was short lived as he took in the pair's battered condition. Splotches of yellow alien blood covered both men's tattered uniforms, as well as more than a smattering of their own blood. Walker's right wrist sported a bloody bandage, and a second one adorned his forehead, standing starkly white against his dark skin. His helmet was missing and gobs of yellow Wasp blood matted his black hair. Injured he might have been, but he waded into the Ticks with abandoned fury, scattering them left and right with powerful, angry kicks, shooting them with short bursts from his SCAR.

Costas had fared no better. The front of the sergeant's ripped-open blouse revealed a hastily applied bandage that only partially covered the series of parallel gashes running across his upper chest. Cuts and gashes of various depths and severity marked the flesh of his legs visible through his ripped trousers. He limped across the chamber favoring his left leg.

"You're alive," Talent said, almost gushing at the joy of the reunion, and then immediately regretted the obvious absurdity of his statement.

"Nothing can kill me, Cowboy," Costas replied, "not even bad booze or badder women." He fired a round from the M107 SASR that that went through one Tick's body and struck a second one, killing it as well. "Two for one!" he yelled.

"Sorry we're late," Walker said. "Our guests got a little rambunctious."

Talent nodded and fired a shotgun blast into a Tick trying to do and end run around him to get to Perez. Its head exploded with a satisfying popping sound. "I thought I'd have to kill this thing all by myself."

"I told you we'd have fun," Costas whooped, blasting holes in several Ticks charging him simultaneously.

"The K-2!" Perez yelled, scrambling on her one good arm and knees from behind Talent and across the chamber after the runaway drum, leaving a trail of blood behind. One of the creatures had succeeded in yanking the drum from Perez's shoulder by the strap and was rolling it across the floor of the chamber by butting it with its head. Injured, Perez made it only a few feet before collapsing.

Talent charged after Perez, now beset by two Ticks, emptying the shotgun into them, and hurtling over their dead bodies to catch up with the drum. Without the infected nanites in the weapon, their mission was over. Walker was two steps ahead of him. He lunged for the drum, blasting one of the Ticks pushing the drum as his body arced through the air. He tucked and rolled as he landed, bowling over Ticks like a Bocce ball. He succeeded in recovering the drum, but just as he lifted it from the floor by its strap in triumph, the closed flap covering the vertical shaft opened, creating a yawning chasm directly beneath him. Walker glanced at Talent with a bemused look of resignation on his face just before plunging down the shaft still clutching the drum to his chest. Then the flap snapped shut behind him.

Talent fell to his stomach and pounded on the edge of the flap in an insane effort to force it open, heedless of the Ticks surrounding him.

Costas dispatched the nearest threats, grabbed his shoulder, and said, "He's gone."

Then, as suddenly as they had appeared, the Ticks vanished back down the tunnels, leaving a vacuum of silence in their wake. Talent sat beside the shaft trying to catch his breath. It came in ragged gulps as he fought to control his rage. Men like Walker didn't die in some absurd quirk of alien physiology, an air duct opening or closing to divert a stream of air to cool an overheated Kaiju. They died in a blaze of glory – like heroes.

After a few minutes in which he silently railed against God, *I'itoi*, nature, and the aliens, he forced himself to his feet. He was accomplishing nothing sitting and brooding. He knew the Ticks had not left because they had beaten them. By all rights, he and the others should be dead. Something had called them back. Whatever that something was, it didn't bode well for him and the others, but he was too tired to care. He took advantage of the brief respite to remove Perez's ammunition and reload the MP5. Perez was slumped against the wall, nearly unconscious.

"They took the drum," she croaked out, bemoaning her failure as Hightower examined her wound and slapped a compression bandage over it.

"It's gone," Talent muttered, still not believing what had happened. "We have to go after it. We have to find Walker."

Hightower stopped what he was doing and stared at Talent. "You're insane," he said. "The drum's gone. The major's dead. The mission is FUBAR."

"The mission is over," McGregor said, walking over to stand above Perez, evaluating her condition; then, frowning. "We're leaving."

"No one's leaving," Costas growled.

"Just what do you intend to do?" McGregor asked.

"Like Cowboy said, we go after the drum." He pointed to the pack on Hightower's back. "We've got rope."

"Damn straight," Talent added, thankful for Costas' help.

"You are insane," McGregor said, addressing Talent instead of Costas. "You don't stand a chance."

Talent tried to remain cool. Instead of punching McGregor in the face, as every fiber of his being urged, he laughed. "That's been pointed out to me before. I was insane to fight so hard to join the fire team, and I'm surely insane to give a hairy rat's ass about the future of mankind. I'm not leaving until I kill this damn thing."

To his surprise, his words did not sound hollow to him. He wanted the Kaiju dead because it was a threat to civilization, not because he hated it or because it had taken from him the only two people with whom he had ever felt kinship. It was a strange feeling for him, but he found he liked it.

He turned away from McGregor, dismissing him as no longer relevant. He and Costas would complete the mission. Maybe that was why Walker had asked him along. He noticed blood seeping through Perez's bandage and knew she would die of blood loss long before she reached help. He picked up a piece of severed Tick flesh, ripped away the useless bandage from her shoulder, making her moan in pain, and smeared the creature's gray blood, which was already hardening, over the wound. Within seconds, the bleeding stopped. He did not know if the blood was as venomous as the bite, but in her condition, it did not matter.

"An old Indian remedy," he said to Hightower's look of astonishment.

"You're not my responsibility, Talent," McGregor replied. "Do as you wish." He turned to face Costas. "However, you are, Sergeant. We've lost both our K-2 weapons. You're pulling out with us."

"Fuck you, Captain," Costas replied, "respectfully, of course." He laughed. "I ain't ever pulled out of anything until I was done. Ask any whore in Bagdad. I ain't going nowhere until I see the major's dead body. Until then, this is a search and rescue mission."

McGregor leveled his MP5 at Costas. "I order you to evac with us, Sergeant."

Talent swung the shotgun up to cover McGregor, unsure if there was a shell left in the clip.

"Cover them, Corporal!"

Hightower raised the minigun and pointed it at both Talent and Costas, but he seemed unhappy about it.

Costas eyed the rifle pointed at his belly. "You going to shoot me, Captain? Because that's what it'll take to stop me."

"Don't do it, Captain," Talent warned. "I'll cut you in half."

"Shoot them both, Corporal," McGregor ordered.

Hightower shook his head and lowered his weapon. "No."

"What did you say?" McGregor snapped.

McGregor tensed. For several tense moments, Talent had been afraid the mission would end with Fire Team Bravo killing each other. *Hell of a way to end the day*, he thought. *As if the aliens aren't killing us fast enough.* Then, to his relief, McGregor lowered his weapon.

"Suit yourself." He dismissed Costas and Talent as if they no longer mattered. "Corporal, help Perez up. We're leaving."

"You can't just leave them here," Hightower argued. "We don't leave men behind."

"We're leaving Rhoades and Wiggins behind. We left Watts behind."

"No."

Hightower's refusal surprised Talent as much as it did McGregor.

"Don't compound your insubordination, Corporal Hightower. I'll overlook your refusal to shoot a fellow soldier, but not this."

"I'm not going, sir. I'm going to help the sergeant and Talent to complete the mission."

"I gave you an order, Corporal. You will comply."

"No, sir, I will not. I'm not leaving this beast until its black corpse is rotting in the sun. We've lost too many comrades to simply slink away with our tails between our legs."

"When we get back, I'll —"

"You'll do nothing, Captain," Costas said. "You have a man down. You and Corporal Hightower need to escort Perez back to the sub for medical treatment. Tick bites are highly venomous, as you know from experience."

"The K-2 is gone," McGregor said. "It's down there, with Major Walker." He pointed to the closed shaft. "It's sui –"

"Not another word, Captain," Costas warned. His rugged mien was chiseled from the same cold, hard stone as the faces on Mount Rushmore. It was as rigid and as unyielding as the impervious ebony armor of the Kaiju. All he needed was a fedora pulled low over one eye and he could have been mistaken for an old-timey Chicago gangster. McGregor took one look at him, saw the determination in his eyes, and closed his mouth.

Hightower took a step forward. "Sergeant, I'd like to complete this mission with you."

Costas' face softened as he answered, "I appreciate the offer, Corporal, but the captain will need help getting Perez out. She's too weak to walk. Leave me the rope and climbing gear." He turned to Talent. "I can do this alone, Cowboy. Maybe it's time for you to finish that trip to Australia."

Costas' suggestion stabbed Talent like a ten-penny nail in the heart. "You can't order me out, Sergeant. I'm a civilian. Besides, the Kaiju is headed for Australia. I thought I could save bus fare."

"This isn't going to go well, Talent. We're behind the eight ball. Walker suspected the next alien attempt would utilize everything they've learned about us from the previous Kaiju, but we didn't expect them to send intelligent creatures with it. Hell, for all I know, these Squid could *be* the aliens."

Costas' estimate of the Squids' capabilities stunned Talent. "They're smart, but intelligent?"

"Walker and I talked about that some on the way here. He gets a little talkative sometimes. That Wasp grabbing the loose K-2 drum and making off with it was no accident. The same thing happened here. The Ticks got the drum and suddenly lost interest in us."

Talent was so absorbed in thought considering what Costas had suggested, that the crackle of his headset made him jump. A second squeal quickly followed.

At first, the big grin that spread across Costas' face mystified him, but then Costas burst out, "He's alive. Walker's alive!"

"Impossible!" McGregor snapped.

"Two squelches means yes. He's alive."

For the first time since the sinking of the *Radiant Princess*, Talent felt a glimmer of hope. *Provided Costas isn't grabbing at noisy straws*, he added.

22

Wednesday, Dec. 20, 0345 hours   Inside Kaiju Kiribati –

The fall down the shaft did not kill him, but it felt like it as Walker made a mental inventory of the various aches and pains in his body. He had expected to die when the floor suddenly disappeared beneath him. Instead, like Alice down the rabbit hole, he bounced along the gradually sloping shaft before popping out into a strange chamber. He was sore, dizzy, and disoriented from his inelegant descent. However, the three Ticks that had fallen through the opening with him were not. They skittered around in the swath of light cast by the flashlight on his SCAR lying a few yards away out of reach. He pulled his Beretta and popped off two rounds into each of their heads.

He forced himself to his fee, wincing at the sharp pain in his leg, and retrieved his rifle. He shined his flashlight around the walls and ceiling, recoiling at the long, undulating fibers lining the wrinkled and folded moist flesh of the walls. As he watched, several strands of cilia reached out to snag a bit of material floating by on the breeze. The fibers curled around it, enclosed it in a network of strands, and drew it into the wall, which promptly secreted a glob of milky goo that trapped it. The flesh of the wall quivered like a bowl of pudding, and the object sank into the wall and disappeared. He decided to avoid contact with the wall and its alien air scrubbers. He had no wish to test the limits of the fibers or the digestive ability of the wall.

Larger tendrils dangled from the ceiling. These, too, were alive, lashing out at invisible objects, and then curling into tight balls, before extending once again, writhing like Medusa's serpentine hair. Even the floor was alive. It pulsed and shuddered, sending ripples of flesh spreading outward with his every step. It was as if the aliens had designed the entire nightmarish chamber to frighten human visitors.

He double-checked to see if the Ticks were dead. They were. As he watched, tiny filaments pushed up from the floor, wrapping around and forcing their way into the dead Ticks' flesh. He checked his boots, but no threads appeared. It seemed they only attacked dead flesh, or so he hoped.

Numerous opening of various sizes dotted the walls of the chamber. Most were too small to accommodate his body or too high on the wall to reach. He took stock of his body. He had escaped the fall itself with only a few extra minor scrapes and bruises on his arms and body to go with the gash in his wrist and the cut on his forehead, but the rim of the drum had landed on his right leg, slicing deeply into his calf. It was bleeding badly. He used the last bit of gauze in his med pack to wrap it, and then tested walking on it. The pain was excruciating but he had no choice but to continue moving. The Ticks or some other creature would come looking for him or the drum.

It concerned him that the Kaiju so quickly recognized the K-2 drums as a threat. That showed a marked increase in the limited intelligence displayed by the previous three Kaiju. They had operated on an instinctive level – kill, eat, destroy, defend itself against attack. Kaiju Kiribati seemed to be one step ahead of them. He hated playing catch up.

He checked his ammo situation. He had one clip of the Kaiju armor-piercing rounds in the magazine and one and a half clips of regular rounds in his ammo belt. He had two rounds in his Beretta and one extra clip, and he had his army knife. Arrayed against him were hundreds of Wasps, Squid, Fleas, Ticks, and numerous other alien creatures. *It's like playing rock, paper, scissors, lizard, Spock against a man with a cannon*, he mused sourly. He stumbled as the Kaiju lurched. It was a familiar sensation, one he remembered vividly from his ordeal inside Nusku. The Kaiju was moving. He was running out of time.

He longed to perform his afternoon *Asr* prayers, but he was certain that Allah would understand his urgency. His desire for inner calm would have to take a back seat to stopping the Kaiju. He recalled the story of Jonah and *al-hut*, the Great Fish, the Koran's version of the Biblical Jonah and the whale. It seemed somehow fitting to his present situation.

None of the openings looked appealing. He pulled up a schematic of a Kaiju on his wrist computer. He had cracked the screen when he injured his wrist, but by holding it at just the right angle, he could see the image through the spider web network of cracks. The teams investigating the dead Kaiju had managed to map a great deal of the creatures' interiors, but it was a slow, tedious process, made even more difficult as the organic parts of the creatures decayed rapidly after their deaths, leaving large voids filled with a stinking, viscous slime. The chamber did not appear on his schematic. He would have to trust his judgment and innate sense of direction to find a way to go deeper toward the center of the creature and forward toward the head. He would avoid the large central chamber containing the Kaiju shock absorbers. He didn't have time for a running battle with the flat, round, lubricating creatures that inhabited that particular section that Gate Rutherford had dubbed Pancakes.

He chose a branch leading more or less toward the acid pit. He was still determined to complete the mission. So far, it had been a cluster-fuck of the first magnitude, some of it his own fault. If he hadn't changed the target ....

"Stop this shit," he growled at himself. "Hindsight sucks hind tit."

He worried about Sergeant Costas. With the loss of both K-2 weapons, he was certain McGregor would abort the mission, but his stubborn sergeant was another matter. Not one to abandon a comrade, the big lug would undoubtedly jeopardize his career and his life in an insane attempt to rescue him. Costas was a good soldier, but a terrible romantic, despite his protestations to the contrary. He saw himself as a slightly tarnished White Knight with a .50 caliber lance. Walker hoped he didn't shoot McGregor in a fit of rage. He hoped Talent had sense enough to go with McGregor. He didn't need a civilian death on his already cluttered conscience.

He slung the K-2 drum over his shoulder and set off limping down the tunnel. If his life had been the only one in the balance, he would have detonated the bomb immediately. The Kaiju's air ducts would disperse the nanites throughout the creature almost as effectively as its bloodstream. However, he wanted to give the others time to escape. He might as well use the time seeking the perfect spot to attack the Kaiju – one last blow for mankind. He was not concerned about himself. He was not going anywhere anytime soon.

By the time he had traveled a hundred yards, he realized he had underestimated the severity if his injury. The top of his boot rubbed against the wound, adding to the pain, and sliding the bandage away from the cut, which was deeper than he had first thought. Blood ran down his leg and soaked his sock. He would have to apply a more permanent bandage soon or bleed to death.

No section of a Kaiju was safe. In fact, he was surprised he had not already encountered something designed to kill intruders. The aliens were nothing if not thorough, designing layers of defense throughout the creature. His only hope lay in the consensus of most scientists, the so-called Kaiju experts, that most of the creatures performed more than one function. With luck, they were busy with something as innocuous as polishing the woodwork and would leave him alone.

If Gate's theory was correct, and based on his personal observations it was, Kaiju Kiribati was more aware than the previous Kaiju. It suspected the black drums were a weapon and had taken steps to eliminate them. It would soon send some creature to seek him out and take it from him. Before that happened, he would detonate it and let the nanites do their job. If Allah willed it, so be it. He had come expecting to die.

The Kaiju lurched gain, slamming him into the wall. He leaped back before the cilia could latch onto him. "Take it easy out there, guys," he yelled, assuming the Navy was trying to slow the creature's advance. "I don't mind being shaken up a bit, but have some finesse. Remember, two to the chest and one to the head."

If the Kaiju was on the move, he hoped the bomb remained in place. If Commander Murdock succeeded in preventing the Squid from arming it, he would deal with the Kaiju. If the commander failed and Gate was right, the Kaiju might survive the resulting explosion, but he doubted anyone inside it would. The concussion would shake them like dried beans in a pair of maracas.

Two hours later, he realized he was hopelessly lost. Though the external design of Kaiju Kiribati and the arrangement of blisters along its flanks was a duplicate of the first three Kaiju, the internal structure did not correspond with his blueprint. The aliens had totally revamped the creature's design. He wondered what other surprises it had in store for him.

He stopped often to rest and reset his bandage, but the blood-soaked gauze simply wicked blood from the wound and down his leg. He knew next to nothing about the nanites he was carrying. He had no idea how long they needed to incapacitate the Kaiju once released. If the creature continued toward Australia at its earlier speed, he had less than two hours before it waded ashore. He had to do something fast. It was time to detonate the bomb. He hoped Costas was safely out of the Kaiju.

* * * *

After assuring themselves that McGregor, Hightower, and Perez were safely away, Talent and Costas followed Walker down the shaft. Talent struggled down the rope burdened with Hightower's appropriated minigun. He had relinquished the grenade launcher as too dangerous to use within the confines of the airshaft but felt more comfortable with some heavy firepower. When it came to aliens, there was no such thing as overkill. Unfamiliar with the climbing equipment, he dropped down the shaft in spurts and fits, slamming often into the hard surface of the shaft. He was glad to reach the bottom. Until he looked around.

"This place is from one of my nightmares," Costas said, dodging a tendril attached to the ceiling of the chamber. It writhed like a boa constrictor dangling from a jungle tree. He pointed to three lumps that might have once been Ticks. Fleshy tendrils from the floor encased them in a cocoon as it sucked them down into the floor. "Walker's been here."

"Which way?" Talent asked, examining the openings.

Costas checked his wrist comp and frowned. "This can't be right."

"What's wrong, sergeant?"

"This place ain't on the map. Should have picked up a Rand McNally at the last service station."

Talent did not like the confused look on Costas' face. "So what do we do?"

"Well, the major is a stubborn man. He would head toward the head. This thing has a control center for a brain. He knows it might take a while for the nanites to kill the Kaiju. If they started the job in the brain, it might slow it down or stop it." He frowned. "Problem is where is the brain?"

"Well, you said the head." Talent pointed down one of the shafts. "That's that way."

Costas eyed the M 134 minigun Talent carried. The 1,000-round belt was draped over his shoulder like a metal serape. "Be careful of that. It's the best thing GE ever built. It's made from old refrigerator parts, you know."

Talent hefted the forty-one pound Gatling gun. It was quite an armful. It had not looked so heavy in Hightower's big-shouldered arms. "Maybe it has a couple of cold beers inside, or a bottle of chilled white wine."

"Nah! White wine is for seafood or veal. This here Kaiju is dark meat, kind of spicy. You want a nice Italian Lambrusco or a French Red Zinfandel. Both are slightly acidic, low in tannins, and won't overpower the dish."

Talent was impressed. "Why sergeant, you're a connoisseur."

Costas looked embarrassed. "Don't tell anyone, but I took a sommelier course on one of my R and R's. People will think I'm a wuss."

Talent looked at the burly sergeant, broad nose slightly misshapen from too many brawls, his M107 SASR cradled in his arms, covered in alien blood, and laughed. "Oh, I doubt that, Sergeant."

Costas led the way. Talent followed close behind, keeping one eye cocked on the tunnel behind him. He wrinkled his nose. If he had thought the air in the upper air duct had reeked, he was now being schooled in just how rancid air could smell before it became a solid, fetid mass of putrescence. It smelled as if the Kaiju was already dead and rotting from the inside out. He noticed Costas' pained expression.

"What's wrong, Sergeant?"

"I've smelled that stink before. It's from the digestive pool in the head, where it dissolves its prey."

Talent stopped moving as Costas' words sank in. "You mean people?"

"Yeah, I mean people."

Talent fought down the urge to puke his guts out. He knew the Kaiju ate people, as well as anything else organic, but the knowledge had been peripheral, like knowing the contents of a can of Vienna sausages or what menudo was made from but eating it anyway. As horrific as the concept of alien cannibalism was, he could not help thinking, *Soylent Green is people.*

He began to notice a rocking motion that did not help matters in his churning stomach. "We're moving."

"Yeah, I noticed that. I hope that doesn't mean the alien bomb is armed."

Talent pulled up short, startled. "What alien bomb?"

"A new pod landed just south of Vanuatu. Gate Rutherford, he's one of our science buddies, thinks it's some kind of gravity bomb. The aliens intend to detonate it above the New Hebrides Trench and start up some kind of seismic event. The Kaiju was sent to arm it."

"Why didn't I know about this?"

"Well, Walker told me because I'm special. He didn't tell McGregor because he thought the bastard would turn tail and run, like he did anyway. I'm telling you because ... well, who are you going to tell?"

"So what's happening?"

Costas shook his head. "I don't know. Commander Murdock was going to attempt to disarm the bomb. The Kaiju's moving because either he failed and it's running the hell away from the blast zone to save its alien ass, or he succeeded and it's getting on with its job of killing people."

Talent tried not to let Costas see him quaking in his boots, as he slowly shook his head and started walking again. "I need to hang with a different class of people."

The fact that the aliens had upped the ante was disconcerting, but it fell under the category of Things I Can't Do Shit About, Talent's catchall category filled with a myriad of peeves and annoyances over which he had no control. An alien gravity bomb was high on the list but still three places down from *Sharknado 1-3* and any beer with fruit in it.

The airshaft ended at a wide tubular corridor that disappeared into the darkness in either direction. Numerous niches in the walls contained an array of tubes sprouting from the walls at different levels, the purpose of which mystified Talent. Costas ferreted out their use. He stepped on a pad directly beneath one of the chest-high tubes and received a squirt of thick, malodorous goop on the remains of his tattered shirt.

"Jesus Christ!" he growled. "This shit stinks." He eyed the contraption contemptuously. "It's a friggin' water fountain."

"Or a feeding station," Talent suggested. The horrific idea of aliens feeding on humans had not been far from his thoughts. He looked at one of the tubes almost six feet above his head. "What twelve-foot-tall creature uses that one?"

Costas wiped the goop from his shirt and looked at the high tube. "None I've seen. Whatever it is, I wouldn't want to meet it in a dark alley."

Talent glanced down the dark tube that looked as if it could run the entire length of the Kaiju. "You mean like this one?"

"Yeah. Come on."

They weren't alone in the tunnel. Talent spotted several small creatures around them. They came in all shapes and sizes, from insect-size millipede-looking creatures that scurried along the tunnel to creatures the size of desert tortoises that crawled at a snail's pace, stopping every few feet to deposit what looked like licorice jellybeans in small crevices in the floor. The jellybeans softened and flowed to fill the crevices, like a road crew filling potholes. They ignored the human intruders.

It was not long before they encountered a creature that made Talent's blood run cold. Even Costas seemed taken aback by it. They had found their twelve-foot-tall alien. It stood in the middle of the tunnel on four spindly, backward-bending legs with four equally long arms stretching across from wall to wall. The creature was bright red with black racing stripes. The creature's hands dug into the walls, extracting wads of immobile dark threads similar to the ones Talent had seen in the air duct walls. It deposited the wads in a pouch in its abdomen, and then removed handfuls of motile dark threads from a second pouch and inserted them in the previous threads' spots. It turned its bulbous head to stare at them with a pair of large, cream-colored lidless eyes; and then went back to work.

"It's some kind of maintenance creature," Costas said. He raised his weapon.

"No don't," Talent cautioned. "It's not attacking. Let's see if we can slip past it."

As he passed beneath its arms, he waited for the creature to attack, but it ignored them. Costas was amused. "It's bigger than a Wasp but docile. That's different."

Talent began to notice narrow bands of ebony armor encircling the tube at intervals. He had no idea what purpose they served, but one particular band with scratches drew his attention. Ebony armor did not usually scratch. No one had discovered any alien writing other than the flowing ultraviolet script on the communications node Commander Langston had reported that may have been writing, but to Talent the marks on the armor looked suspiciously like a word. These lines were not flowing; they were rigidly straight. He played his flashlight over the word.

It looked like a slanted capital N, followed by an A with a dot instead of a crossbar, a Z with double bars at the top and bottom of the letter, a vertical straight line like an I, and two horizontal angle brackets stacked atop each other facing opposite directions bisected by a straight line, like a Daliesque R.

He pronounced the word slowly, "NAZIR."

"What the hell is nazir?" Costas asked. He turned and saw Talent studying the wall. "Alien graffiti?"

"Could be. They found Egyptian hieroglyphs scratched inside the pyramids naming work gangs. People have been tagging things for years."

"Maybe a bored alien with time on his hands wrote it," Costas suggested. "Lots of down time in the military. Grunts get creative in filling the hours."

"It looks more deliberate, as if it was meant to be there."

"Hell, maybe it's the name of the aliens. Nazir – sounds like a good name for them. It has a nice alieny ring to it."

"The Nazir," Talent said experimentally. "It sounds better than 'The Aliens'."

"Then it's settled. The bastards are Nazir. Now, let's go kick some Nazir ass, or the alien anatomical equivalent."

As they continued along the corridor, they saw no more writing, but they passed numerous side tunnels. Each one looked much the same as the others, until Costas suddenly stopped at one of the tunnels. "Wait."

Talent tensed and tightened his grip on the minigun, expecting trouble. "What is it?"

Instead of preparing for an attack, Costas was smiling.

"What's so funny?" Talent asked.

"Can't you smell it?" he asked, taking a deep breath and exhaling slowly.

The stench had lessened somewhat or else, he had gotten used to it, but all Talent could smell was Kaiju. He took a cautious sniff and shrugged when he detected nothing different from the air ten yards down the tunnel.

"It's Walker's cheap aftershave. I could smell that rot from a mile away."

Costas' nasal discovery delighted him. Talent did not point out that it did not mean that Walker was still alive. Like Costas, he still held out hope of finding the major. Costas looked at Talent; saw the doubt in his eyes. He cocked his head to one side.

"Come on, Cowboy. Don't go all negative on me now. He's alive. I told you he wouldn't give up."

Costas started down the side corridor at a fast clip. Talent had no choice but to follow.

23

Wednesday, Dec. 20, 7:30 a.m.   Brisbane, Australia –

The Australian prime minister, Amanda Hyde, and the members of Cabinet breathed a collective sigh of relief when they learned that the Kaiju had stopped in the middle of the ocean after devastating Efate Island in Vanuatu. Every hour the creature delayed gave the military more time to prepare their defenses and civilian authorities time to evacuate reluctant residents from the Eastern seaboard. Benjamin Whitehurst, Minister of Defense, rose from his seat and addressed the Cabinet members.

"By God's grace, we have been given an extension on the life of our nation. I say we do not squander this precious time. The Americans undoubtedly have nuclear weapons. I propose we ask them to use them on the monster."

The prime minister was aghast. "Such an action flies in the face of our country's stance on nuclear weapons. Besides, we don't have the moral or legal right to detonate a nuclear bomb on another country's doorstep."

Whitehurst slapped his palm on the table. "If you mean New Caledonia, I say better them than us. Are you prepared to watch tens of thousands of our fellow countrymen die?"

"I'm not prepared to start WWIII." She had read the Chinese ultimatum.

Whitehurst waved his hand in dismissal. "The Chinese are bluffing."

"If they're not?"

"Then it will be the Americans they hold to blame, not us."

"Passing the buck, as the Americans say. In a war between China and the United States, how long do you think it would be before Great Britain is drawn in? We have a treaty with them, remember?"

"I remember watching American cities turned to ash and rubble on the telly. I don't wish to see Sydney or Melbourne join that list of dead places."

Alexander Cockrell, Minister of the Interior, spoke up. "Neither do I. Sydney is my home."

She could sense she was losing the Ministers. They had been appointed by Governor-General Edward Snow, leader of the opposition party, and owed their allegiance to him. "The Cabinet has no legal authority to make such a move."

Whitehurst smiled. "No, but the Executive Council does, of which we are all members. We do not have time to go through proper parliamentary procedure simply to vote on a proposal we know will pass."

"If we fail to follow the law now when the hour is darkest, of what use are our laws?"

Elizabeth DeGracy, Minister of Industry, Innovation, and Science, and the only other female in the room, cleared her throat. Her voice was strong for a 5'4'' seventy-year-old former schoolteacher as she spoke.

"Gentlemen, Madame Prime Minister, our nation is at a crux. The question seems to be not only how we will survive this alien crisis, but the nature of our nation afterwards. I feel the Americans are brash enough to use their nuclear arsenal if the urge strikes them, regardless of our feelings in the matter. I suggest we broach the subject with the Americans in the form of a query, not a formal request. While our hands might not be spotless in the event of a nuclear strike, they will be fundamentally clean. Under no circumstances will I condone the use of a nuclear bomb on Australian soil. We cannot sacrifice one city or group of people in order to save another. Such a thing is inconceivable. We must stand or fall as a nation."

The room was quiet after DeGracy spoke. Prime Minister Hyde wanted to hug her. They had had their differences over the years, but on this one issue, they stood united.

"We will use all our available forces, land, sea, and air, against this creature. To paraphrase Winston Churchill, we will meet the Kaiju on the beach. We cannot consider any other option until this one succeeds or fails."

"Attack with our entire military might?" Whitehurst asked, his face sour at the Prime Minister's proposal. "We must withhold sufficient forces for a second line of defense."

"Minister Whitehurst, if we fail, no second line of defense, or a third or fourth one, will save our country. A 'maximum effort' I believe it is called."

While the Cabinet members debated loudly, she glanced at her notepad. On it was a message from her secretary. "The Kaiju was sighted moving toward Australia once more. ETA two hours." She looked at

Whitehurst and another Minister standing face to face arguing. She sat down heavily in her chair. She would not inform them yet. She would let them argue a bit longer first.

* * * *

The Kaiju appeared in the waters of Deception Bay northeast of Brisbane just before noon. The alarm sirens sounded throughout the city, echoing across the silent bay. With three entire days warning in which to evacuate the city, the process should have been nearly complete. Instead, massive snarls on the A1 Freeway running north and south from the city and the A2 running west had left lines of automobiles backed up for miles. Out of desperation, many had abandoned their vehicles and fled the vicinity on foot. A twenty-car train derailment on the North Coast Line had cost precious hours, as hundreds of frightened, uncomfortable evacuees waited in hot box cars with one eye glued toward the sea, the direction from which they expected the Kaiju to appear. Prime Minister Hayes had authorized the military and civilian authorities to commandeer barges, tugs, water taxis, and private yachts – anything that could float – to ferry evacuees westward up the Brisbane River to safety.

A constant stream of aircraft, both military and civilian, from the city's two main airports had filled the skies above the city for two days. Still, it was not enough. Of the 2.3 million people in the metro Brisbane area, a third of them remained in the city, many of their own volition. Some, filled with Aussie stubborn determination and self-reliance, refused to leave the homes and businesses they had worked so hard to establish. Others were determined to bear witness to an historical event, even one of such dire consequences – some because of it.

No one knew exactly where the Kaiju would come ashore, but the city of Brisbane in the state of Queensland seemed its most likely destination. Upon this probability, the Australian Defense Forces placed most of its men and materiel along the continent's eastern coastline. The army's First Mechanized Brigade and the Third Light Infantry Brigade, consisting of 3,500 soldiers, formed a defensive arc south of Brisbane. Three *Adelaide*-Class frigates and two *Collins*-Class submarines patrolled the coast from Cairns in the northeast to Sydney on the southeastern tip of the continent. Numerous small patrol craft, helicopters, and F-35A *Lightning II's* maintained a twenty-four-hour vigil of the skies.

The *HMAS Choules*, a landing ship dock twenty miles off the coast of Brisbane, was the first to respond. Immediately upon sighting the Kaiju, it launched four ARH-*Tiger* helicopters armed with AGM114-*Hellfire II* missiles and swivel-mounted GIAT M781 30 mm cannons. They got no closer than ten miles from the Kaiju before an opposing army of Wasps, disgorged by the Kaiju to defend it, presented an impenetrable wall of armored alien flesh. The explosions of *Hellfire* missiles lit up the night sky over the bay. Scores of Wasps died, but more took their place. The creatures quickly overwhelmed the attacking helicopters. The next explosions visible from the shore were those of the choppers crashing into the dark waters of the ocean.

Simultaneously, the Kaiju launched a dozen Squid to attack the *Choules.* The ship's Mk-25 *Typhoon* CIWS, the Close-In Weapons System 25 mm cannon with a 200 rounds per minute rate of fire, kept the creatures at bay for six minutes. Adapting to the ship's defensive threat, the Squid came up from directly below the ship, ripping gaping holes in its keel. Valiant crewmen fought off the creatures with small arms and fire axes long enough to rescue injured comrades, even as the cold seawater rose around their legs. In the end, their heroic effort proved futile. The *Choules* went to the bottom with all one-hundred-fifty-eight crewmen onboard less than seven minutes later, one minute longer than the *USS Arizona* remained afloat after the first Japanese bombs struck it in Pearl Harbor on December 7, 1941.

* * * *

Wednesday, Dec. 20, 1:30 p.m.　　　Deception Bay, Queensland, Australia –

The immediate threat rendered ineffective, the Kaiju came ashore in the city of Deception Bay. Wasps formed an arc along the shoreline from a point five miles north of the city to a point five miles south; then, swept inward through the neighborhoods.

Forty-two-year-old Dalton McKenzie was one of the first people to witness the black behemoth emerge from the sea and begin its orgy of destruction. McKenzie, a former army corporal turned plumber, was one of thousands of army reservists, known as 'cut lunch commandos,' called up for the emergency to keep watch along the coast. He stared in horror as the Kaiju strode ashore, ripping asunder homes, schools, churches, and shops, churning once beautiful neighborhoods into piles of shattered brick and splintered wood.

Sharing McKenzie's vigil was Geoff Lands, a twenty-year-old mechanic and part-time competitive surfer who had come to Australia's eastern coast for the sun and surf.

"It's bitchin' enormous," he said.

McKenzie was too awed to reply. He watched the creature for several minutes before remembering the radio in his hand. He reported to the Redcliff Police Station, the area headquarters for the coast watchers, and then listened to the reply.

"What?" Lands demanded, seeing his companion's stunned expression.

"They want us to keep ahead of the Kaiju and report its movements."

Lands looked back at the Kaiju and the black swarm of Wasps spewing from the orifices in its side to join those already in the air. "Screw that," he replied. "We were told to report when we saw it. We saw it. Let's get the hell out of here."

As much as McKenzie agreed with his younger, visibly frightened companion, being older, he felt duty bound to provide a stable anchor. There would be sufficient time for panic later.

"No, we have to report which directions it's going so the military can set up an effective defensive perimeter."

"Defensive perimeter?" Lands snorted. "They've got Buckley's Chance of stopping that." He waved his hand in the direction of the Kaiju. "Tanks and cannon are like spitballs against that thing. It's going to plow through here like a goddamned bulldozer through a sand castle." He paused for a moment. "We should head for the Blue Mountains."

McKenzie put as much scorn in his reply as he could muster. "And run around naked as a Gundundgurra? I'm no aborigine. My ass burns in the sun."

"Come on, mate. The Blue Mountains are perfect. All those ridges separated by ravines a quarter of a kilometer deep – It's like a giant maze. Those things would never find us."

It was obvious to McKenzie that the young man had put a lot of thought into his fallback destination. Some of what Lands said made sense, but if McKenzie were the type to run, he would never have volunteered for Iraq. "Don't mate me. Deception Bay is my home. I'm not hiding out in the mountains like a bloody bushranger running from the law, talking to the jumbuck and the bloody roos for company."

As they argued, Kaiju Kiribati loomed larger as it approached. Its twelve legs pounded the earth, sending tremors rippling through the streets, and rattling sewer grates. The tarpaper and gravel roof of Deception High School, which served as their observation post, bounced beneath his feet like a trampoline. The massive heating and cooling units rang like struck bells. Houses shattered under the impact of the ebony, lance-tipped appendages. Flames leapt from the rubble of its passage as broken gas lines exploded. Fanned by a brisk breeze from the ocean, a raging inferno soon silhouetted the black behemoth. The Kaiju was a spectacle of abject terror, a shadow devil rising from the flames of hell.

McKenzie observed the destruction for several minutes, noting the creature's movements. His observations were less than analytical. It was his city being destroyed. The pit of his stomach knotted each time a familiar building disappeared from view or burst into flames. He watched the creature trample the sports complex where he attended cricket matches on Sunday afternoons, and then move on to the tavern he usually frequented for a pint or two. The authorities had evacuated Moreton Medical Center two days earlier, where the doctors had set his broken foot a couple of years ago, but he watched its walls crumble with a hollow sinking feeling. Next to go, were the Domino's from which he ordered his pepperoni and Italian sausage pizzas when he was too lazy to cook, and Market Square where he liked to shop. It seemed as if the Kaiju was on a deliberate mission to erase his personal history.

He watched warily as the Wasps dropped from the sky to enter buildings, occasionally emerging with a squirming object grasped in its forelimbs. Whether human or a hapless pet, he didn't want to know. The Wasps seemed as intent on causing as much damage as possible as they were seeking out humans. They ripped apart walls and roofs, and sliced open automobiles, boats, and motor homes, as if finding food for their Kaiju master was secondary to destruction.

Less visible were the Wasps' partners in crime, the creatures someone had named Fleas for the jumping ability. Silhouetted by the flames, they were small dots falling from the Wasps like flakes of dandruff. Facing Wasps would be bad enough. He was not looking forward to seeing the Fleas in action close up.

When his neighborhood along George Street went up in flames, his churning stomach could take no more. He was teetering close to the edge of the limits of his courage despite his braggadocio to Lands. He sat down on the roof with his back against the parapet, facing away from the carnage and ruin, as Lands continued to stare at the Kaiju. The sun shining behind the rising columns of smoke created grotesque dancing shadows. He fought back a tear. His home of sixteen years was among those fueling the flames. Every memento, every photograph, every article of clothing was gone. He battled against the growing despondency threatening to immobilize him.

Gas pumps exploding at a nearby service station brought him back to the grim reality of the present. He glanced around and realized that as exposed as they were, the Wasps would soon find them. It was time to leave. He turned to Lands.

"Look, cobber. Take off if you want to. I wouldn't blame you. I'm going to do my job. I have no family to worry about or anyone who'll miss me but my bartender. This is the best I have to offer my country right now. I might not be the full quid, but I've been called a fool before." He handed Lands the keys to the Land Rover the local authorities had issued them. "Good luck to you, lad."

Lands stared at the keys dangling enticingly in front of him. His hand trembled as it reached out but never quite touched them. After a few moments, he shook his head and pulled his arm back

"Dammit! I can't let an old man show me up. What would the Shelias say? I could never show my face on the beach again."

McKenzie smiled. He thought Lands was more responsible than he protested. It was circumstances such as they now faced that proved a man's mettle. "Good lad. Now, let's try to keep our skins intact and report this thing's progress."

Staying ahead of a creature whose hundred-foot-long legs covered a football field's length with each ponderous stride wasn't easy. Driving south on Deception Bay Road with no headlights and with one eye glued to the rearview mirror, while swerving around abandoned automobiles was no easy task, but McKenzie managed to keep the vehicle, for the most part, on the street. The Kaiju created a wide path of destruction as it made its way to the M1 Expressway. They had to beat the creature to the bridge crossing Hays Inlet or risk being stranded behind the Kaiju and the Wasps acting as rearguard troops sweeping up stray humans.

A twenty-gauge Remington shotgun lay in the seat beside him, a sporting gun he hadn't fired or cleaned in two years. Then, he had shot skeets once or twice a month but couldn't recall having ever shot a living thing in his life, even while serving in Iraq in 2003. The authorities informed him that he could shoot looters, but he had refrained, although he had fired in the air once to frighten away a group of teens attempting to loot a liquor store. What did a stolen telly or a broken store window matter? The entire city would soon be in ruins anyway.

Lands carried an old 7 mm Mauser rifle McKenzie doubted he even knew how to fire. A harried sheriff's deputy had issued the weapon to the young man earlier in the day, along with a handful of cartridges, with no instructions in its use. McKenzie had no qualms about shooting alien creatures, but in a firefight with Wasps or Fleas, he doubted he or Lands would survive long.

Racing down the Gateway Motorway, McKenzie began to understand the Kaiju's methodology. It systematically destroyed the *Ted Smout Memorial Bridge* they had just crossed over Hays Inlet and the M1 Bridge over the Pine River to cut off any escape routes for residents foolish enough to wait until the last minute to evacuate the area, of which there were thousands. The aliens' goal was to separate the weaker or foolish individuals from the herd to dispose of them immediately, while herding the rest into tighter, densely packed human clusters to pick off at leisure.

On the islands, their tactic had not been as obvious. With escape possible only by air or sea and few survivors left to describe their ordeal, the creature's movements had seemed random, chaos designed to create more chaos. Now, it was obvious the Kaiju intended to institute a scorched earth policy, leaving no structure standing and no creature living. They were now waging total war against humankind.

"Look out!" Lands yelled.

McKenzie, absorbed by what was behind them, had allowed his concentration to lapse for a split second, long enough for the Land Rover to drift into the emergency lane where an electrical utility truck sat crosswise half in the emergency lane and half in the ditch. He jerked the wheel to the right, crossed the road, and bounded across the median. The screech of shearing metal as the Land Rover's bottom scraped the concrete curb set his teeth on edge. The vehicle shuddered to a halt with the gnash of grinding metal gears. The motor continued to rev as he pressed the accelerator, but the cracked gearbox was stuck in third gear. He popped the clutch and jerked the gearshift lever back and forth, but to no avail. The Land Rover was dead.

He pounded the steering wheel with his fist, angry with himself. "Shit! That was a dumbass move."

Lands' eyes were now wide with fright. His tanned face appeared as blanched as his white tee shirt in the pale moonlight. "Will it run?"

McKenzie shook his head. "No. The gearbox is cracked. It's gone cactus, useless."

"What do we do?"

Lands was near panic. McKenzie's heart still pounded from the narrow escape, but he knew he had to take charge before Lands lost it completely. "We walk or we find another ride."

Lands pointed a shaky finger to an open garage door. "Like that?"

McKenzie eyed the Suzuki RMZ-450 dirt bike sitting inside the garage with trepidation. It was several years old and looked as though its owner hadn't always managed to land the bike upright on the tires after a jump. One handlebar dipped slightly, and the rear extension of the seat was cracked. He had never liked motorcycles, and he knew nothing about them.

"Can you drive it?" he asked Lands.

Lands smirked. "Dude! Yeah! I can drive anything."

"Okay then, find the keys and let's get out of here."

While Lands checked through the contents of the drawers in a workbench, McKenzie took a moment to glance back at their pursuer. The Kaiju was less than a mile away, wading across Hays Inlet. The water was the equivalent to ankle deep on the creature. The Wasps were even closer, angling across the water toward them. He was sure they weren't zeroing in on them in particular, but their direct approach was enough to shake his confidence.

"You'd better hurry," he yelled at his companion.

He turned at the sound of the dirt bike cranking. It sounded like a cheap chainsaw, but Lands was smiling as if it were the 449 cc Suzuki were a 1000 cc Harley Davidson *Sportster*. "Get on," he said.

McKenzie crawled on behind Lands, careful of the cracked seat, and looked for something to hold on to. Out of desperation he propped his feet atop the rear of the chassis supporting the rear wheel and grabbed the sides of the seat with both hands. Lands' Mauser strapped across his back kept slapping him in the face. Too late, McKenzie realized he had left his shotgun in the Land Rover, but he wasn't about to go back after it. He glanced outside. His eyes traveled upwards to the Kaiju's belly almost overhead. Its long tentacles lashed out at buildings, writhing inside in search of people, and then ripping the buildings apart like kindling. It smashed a house two blocks away.

"Hang on!" Lands yelled, as he gunned the bike, almost laying it on its side as it spun in a half-circle on the garage floor. The sharp tang of burning rubber from the rear tire hit McKenzie's nostrils. He snorted and shook his head to expel the assaulting stench just as Lands straightened the bike and shot through the open garage door. He grabbed the seat tighter to keep the bike's momentum from flinging him off.

Lands didn't bother with the street. He cut through back yards, dodging trampolines, swing sets, and barbecue grills. He sped down alleyways amid a clutter of dumpsters and garbage cans reeking of rotting fruit and vegetables. McKenzie spotted the empty, dilapidated cardboard shelter of a homeless person. Even the indigent had abandoned the city. As Lands gunned the bike across a parking lot, McKenzie hung on and prayed Lands was as good as he claimed.

He glanced over his shoulder. Behind them, the monstrous Kaiju continued its war of destruction on the city, trampling buildings and roadways. The swarms of Wasps accompanying it were expert at ferreting out any hiding humans and ferrying them to the creature's enormous maw. They were close enough to see their orange and black banding and see their four tattered leathery wings. McKenzie tensed his back waiting for one of the creatures' enormous stingers to pierce him back to front, but they continued to stay just ahead of the creatures.

Lands pushed the bike to its limits as they sped through the Boondall Wetlands into Nudgee. To the east lay the runways of the Brisbane Airport. It was the first time McKenzie had ever seen the busy airport so deserted. The last evacuation flight had left hours earlier. An AADF squadron of F-35A Lightning *II* aircraft was using the airport as an advance staging area. As he watched, eight of the jets, ignoring all air-traffic control standards, roared down the runway almost nose-to-tail and launched skyward toward the approaching Kaiju.

"Yeah!" he yelled, pumping his fist in the air at the sight of the sleek stealth aircraft. The whine of the jet turbines drowned out the buzzing of the dirt bike's tiny engine. The bike wobbled as Lands dodged a road hazard. McKenzie lurched forward and grabbed Lands' shoulder, almost spilling the bike. His right foot slipped and brushed the rear tire, showering him with flakes of burned rubber from the tire and from the sole of his boot. He spat out the foul-tasting rubber and watched the jets.

The F-35's stood on their tails as the Pratt and Whitney F135 engines' 43,000 pounds of thrust pushed them skyward at a heart-pounding 10 g rate of climb, over three times that experienced by space shuttle pilots. The high g-forces slowed circulation to the pilots' eyes, creating a tunnel-vision effect, but they were experienced aviators. They would pull out of their steep climbs before G-LOC occurred, loss of consciousness due to excessive g-forces. The eight F-35As split into two groups, attacking the Kaiju from the east and the west. The lead Lightning of both groups swooped in low to the ground, cruising barely above rooftop level, firing their GAU-22A 25 mm cannons and Sidewinder missiles to clear a path for the jets and to draw off as many Wasps as they could.

The west group attacked first. Their external wing pylons carried M299 missile pods, each loaded with four Hellfire missiles. The internal weapons bays carried four more pods for a total of thirty-two missiles. They came within a ten-mile range of the Kaiju and fired their full salvo of missiles. Ninety-six, five-foot-long, one-hundred-pound missiles, propelled by their powerful solid fuel engines, arced gracefully toward the creature. The dense concentration of missiles exploded along the creature's right flank, creating brief bursts of orange flame. McKenzie held his breath, praying the missiles had damaged the Kaiju.

Almost simultaneous with the explosion, a mosaic pattern of iridescent lines of light pulsed along the sides of the Kaiju as the ebony armor absorbed the energy of the blasts and channeled it into the creature's internal power storage organ. A few Wasps caught in the fringes of the blasts died, but the Kaiju, unharmed, continued its forward trek. McKenzie exhaled and muttered a soft curse at the missiles' ineffectiveness. He hadn't expected the attack to kill the creature, but he had hoped for some indication it was stoppable. He knew the Kaiju's were more than simple killing machines or living monsters. They were a bastardized melding of alien technology and living flesh, gigantic cyborgs created from specially grown organs shoved into an impervious ebony armor shell.

The squadron from the east flew a few miles out to sea before looping back toward the Kaiju. The pilots of the second squadron armed with BGU-53B Small Diameter Bombs, a self-guided, fire-and-forget munition, witnessing the failure of the Hellfire missiles, waited until they were less than six miles distant before releasing their volley of bombs. The SDBs weaved a sinuous path through the squadron of Wasps determined to protect the Kaiju. One Wasp threw its body in front of one of the bombs, exploding it in midair. The resulting fireball evaporated five of its fellow creatures pursuing the remaining bombs. The remainder of the SDBs safely reached their targets, the Kaiju's first two appendages on its forward left side. Unable to destroy the Kaiju outright, the pilots sought to cripple it.

Sadly, as in the first attempt, the bombs failed, creating a spectacular light show but inflicting little if any damage to the impervious armor. This time, the Wasps were better prepared. They surged forward, as the eastern squadron of Lightnings banked away from the Kaiju. Swarming each plane like Africanized bees from a disturbed hive, they brought down all four Lightnings within minutes. The first squadron, now armed with only their 25 mm cannons, tried to help, but they were too late. Two of their number promptly joined the other four aircraft in their watery graves.

The two remaining F-135s climbed to 10,000 feet; then dived straight at the Kaiju, releasing wingtip tanks of napalm before pulling out of their dives at 1500 feet. The jellied gasoline landed just in front of the creature, creating a wall of flame that billowed three hundred feet into the night sky. The explosion caught scores of Wasps in the blazing conflagration, cremating them instantly. However, the Kaiju ignored the flames as it had those it had created in its destructive passage. It waded through the wall of fire without blinking the enormous ochre strips it used for eyes.

McKenzie pounded on Lands' back. "Go faster," he urged. If more jets appeared, he didn't want to around when they dropped more bombs or napalm.

At the point where the M1 divided into the Gateway Motorway and the Southern Cross Way, Lands slowed the bike and yelled over his shoulder, "Which way?"

Both roads reunited just north of the winding Brisbane River that cut through the heart of Brisbane. The Gateway Motorway was the more direct route south away from Brisbane and was the logical choice for escape, but Brisbane was his town, or at least he lived in the metro area surrounding it. He knew the Kaiju would storm through the towns of Bald Hills, Bracken Ridge, Aspley, and Chermside without breaking stride, as it had Deception Bay and Redcliff, but Brisbane was one of the Big Smokes, one of Australia's biggest cities. Its destruction would take time. Every minute the creature spent in Brisbane, every minute the military could harry its progress, was precious time for the people farther south. Thousands if not tens of thousands of lives could be saved. He couldn't just run away.

"Take the Southern Cross Way to the M7 into Brisbane. The army has a forward base in Woolloongabba."

Lands was incredulous. He squeezed the hand brake and slid the bike to a halt in the middle of the road, almost tipping them over. He stared at McKenzie. His voice had an edge of panic in it as he asked uncertainly, "Brisbane? You want to go to Brisbane with that thing on our ass?"

McKenzie understood the young mechanic's fear. He was quaking in his boots, but he knew running blindly was no solution. They might save themselves for the inevitable end of mankind, but the prospect of being one of the last men on Earth didn't hold much appeal for him.

"Look. Like it or not, we're assigned to the military. They could shoot us for desertion, you know."

This quieted Lands for the moment. The imminent threat of execution gave him something to ponder beyond his urge to run. "Great, just great," he moaned. "That's some choice: Get shot for desertion or wind up Kaiju chow."

"Sometimes you've got to step up and be a man," McKenzie told him.

Lands cocked his head at McKenzie. "Don't go all John Wayne on me. I know you're scared. I can see it in your eyes."

McKenzie snorted, "Damned right I'm scared. I'm about to take a dump in my pants. I'll admit it: We might not be able to do anything. We may all be doomed. If we're lucky, we'll slow this bastard down long enough for people to get away. If we're really lucky, we might survive and have the chance to try again farther south to stop this monster. Brisbane is bad enough. Do you want to see this Kaiju wading through downtown Sydney or Melbourne like in some cheap Japanese Godzilla movie?"

"And if we're not lucky?" Lands asked.

McKenzie swallowed the lump in his throat. It was a fair question, one he had rather not ponder. "Then we die sooner rather than later," he answered truthfully. He paused to let his answer sink in, staring at Lands to judge his mettle. Finally, he said, "You're driving. I'll leave it up to you. What's your decision?"

Lands shook his head. "You're a real bloody bastard, McKenzie. You know that?"

McKenzie smiled. "I've been told that."

Lands turned around and gripped the handlebars. He cursed under his breath, kicked the bike into first gear, and gunned the engine. McKenzie held on, smiling to himself as Lands aimed the bike into the left lane toward Brisbane.

* * * *

Wednesday, Dec. 20, 3:45 p.m.   Brisbane, Australia –

Lieutenant Colonel Edwin J. Kinder had faith in his men, in God, and in the steadfast belief hammered into him by his Protestant parents that good eventually triumphed over evil, in that order. His suspected his faith was about to be tested. His command, the Fifth and Eighth Brigades of the Second Division, were mostly local reservists based out of Gallipoli Barracks in Brisbane. Morale was high; they were defending their homes. Most had not seen combat in years, since Afghanistan or Iraq. Many had never faced enemy fire. It would not matter. Their training or experience could never have prepared them for the gargantuan creature striding across the countryside toward them. The Kaiju had just entered Eagle Farm, a sleepy industrial suburb on the northwestern outskirts of the city near the Southern Cross Motorway.

Kinder's twenty-five hundred men had assumed a defensive position along a thinly stretched line from Stafford Road and Airport Link north of Brisbane to Kingsford Smith Drive paralleling the north bank of the Brisbane River. Armed with 5.56 mm F88 Austeyr rifles, 5.56 mm EF89 Para light machineguns, and 7.62 mm FN Hersal MAG 58 heavy machineguns, they had little hope of stopping the Kaiju, but the flying Wasps and the hopping Fleas accompanying it were another matter. As difficult as the Wasps were to kill, they could still die. His orders were to bring down as many as possible before falling back across the river to regroup.

Kinder was no fool. He knew most of his men would die in the coming battle. Depending on the Kaiju's line of march, most of them would probably never reach the city or the bridges across the river. They knew as well, but their line held steady. It was a touch of irony that their barracks was named after the infamous WWII battle of Gallipoli where so many Australians had died needlessly due to poor intelligence, inhospitable terrain, and poor command decisions. He hoped the operation about to commence did not repeat that historic blunder.

Backing them were the First Brigade Mechanized, Third Brigade Light Infantry, and the Seventh Brigade Motorized of the First Division. Twenty M1A1 Abrams tanks, fifty L119 Hamel 105 mm cannon, twenty-five M198 155 mm howitzers, and three hundred M113 armored personnel carriers armed with 50 caliber machineguns waited for the Kaiju along the southern bank of the river from Bulimba barracks to Gateway Motorway. The Americans had faced Kaiju Girra outside Chicago with ten times the firepower had not slowed it. Their pathetically small ring of steel stood little chance.

The men on the ground were not alone. The air force had promised squadrons of F-35 Lightning, F/A 18F Super Hornets, S-70A Blackhawks, and ARH Tiger helicopters. Twenty large Seahawk and MRH 90 transport helicopters stood by, assigned to evacuate his men when it became necessary, but due to their limited capacity, it would take ten trips to ferry them all to safety. He was glad he would not have to look into his men's faces as they waited for their turn to fly out.

A roar of thunder erupted behind him from across the river as artillery and tanks began their barrage. The air sang with the whistle of hundreds of shells arcing toward the Kaiju. Before the first shells struck, the cannon were firing again. From his position atop Bartley's Hill in Albion, a few miles west of Eagle Farm, he had a bird's-eye view of the action. The Kaiju's ebony armor pulsed with traces of ultraviolet light as the shells exploded along its sides and wide back. Flame and smoke billowed from around its legs. The light of the explosions barely reflected from the creature's solid shadow shell. The ground shook from the impact of the cannonade, but the creature did not slow. It continued its slow march through the town.

Kinder had watched videos of the Kaiju attack on Chicago; almost everyone had. The image conveyed on the small screen did not do justice to the sheer terror seeing the nine-hundred-foot black monster did in person. He felt a trickle of warm urine flow uncontrollably from his penis and wet his pants, but he didn't think anyone would notice. All eyes were glued to the behemoth moving toward them as inexorably as an approaching typhoon.

"Sir, do you think we should pull back?"

He glanced at his aide, Captain Miles Horath, a short, overweight man whose fear poured from the pores of his face and ran down his cheeks.

"Captain, the Kaiju will be where we need to go before we could get there. We're as safe here as any place in the city."

Horath licked his lips and glanced toward the darkened cityscape of Brisbane to the south, and then at the approaching Kaiju. From his expression, Kinder did not think his aide believed him. It was just as well. He did not believe it himself. They were fully exposed to any Wasps in the area, and if the Kaiju ventured a little farther north in its approach to Brisbane, they would become ground zero for any future artillery barrages.

As he watched, the Kaiju left the ruins of Eagle Farm behind and entered Albion. Against the backdrop of the burning town, he saw the hundreds of specks of flying Wasps.

He turned to Captain Horath. "Captain, order the men to open fire."

The frightened aide spoke into the radio. A few moments later, small arms fire and the sound of heavier machineguns opened up a short distance away. The Wasps took notice of the sounds of gunfire and zeroed in on their locations. He was glad he could not hear the screams of his dying men. After fifteen minutes, it was all over. The guns stopped firing.

He lowered his binoculars. "Order the men to regroup at LZ Green, Orange, and Blue."

They had already lost three of the six secured landing zones. He hoped they could hold them long enough to evacuate as many men as possible.

"Advise the troops too remote from a secured site either to make for the river or head north."

The jets arrived and began unloading their cargo of missiles and bombs on the Kaiju, but it shrugged the explosions off as it had everything else. The pilots were brave; he granted them that. They swooped in at treetop level to avoid the wasps and climbed at the last moment to unleash their salvoes. More than a few of the aircraft received damage from shrapnel. Wasps dove among them in a kamikaze orgy of destruction. More than twenty aircraft crashed in the first five minutes of the attack.

The helicopters fared no better. The Blackhawks and Tigers carried missiles and machineguns, targeting the Wasps in an attempt to clear the way for the F-35s and F/A 18-F jets. Like a five-square mile game of Whack-a-Mole, the helicopters popped up from behind buildings and groves of trees to fire at the Wasps, and then scoot away to repeat their procedure somewhere else. It was a heroic effort, but doomed to failure like all other attacks on the Kaiju.

The creature stepped across Breakfast Creek and within minutes had waded into the spaghetti of asphalt and concrete of the M7 interchange, scattering stacked and looped roadways like a dog leaping into a pile of freshly raked leaves. The artillery continued to pound the creature but caused as much damage as the Kaiju.

"I have reports of men trapped in the Clem Jones Tunnel."

Kinder nodded that he had heard but said nothing. He could nothing for them now. The tunnel crossed beneath the Brisbane River and had been designated as a fallback site, but the weight of the Kaiju had been too much for the structure. Finally, he said, "If the tunnel doesn't flood, they'll be safe enough." He sighed. "Take me to LZ Green. I can't do anything more from here."

Horath, eager to comply, scampered back to the jeep and cranked it. As they drove down Bartley's Hill, Kinder had an excellent view of the giant Kaiju entering the city of Brisbane.

"God help them," he whispered. "God help them all."

24

Wednesday, Dec. 20, 0630 hours   Inside Kaiju Kiribati –

Walker had begun to think all the Wasps and Squid had left the Kaiju. On one hand, he hoped they had not mounted an attack on the *Mississippi,* but he also did not want to face them in his condition. He had seen only a single Wasp in the past hour and strangely, it had not attacked him. It saw him, even acknowledged his presence with a loud hiss, but remained where it was. He was ready to kill it when he noticed its eyes. They were missing. A dark liquid dripped from the two open holes where its eyes had been. At first, he attributed its blindness to battle wounds, but then noticed its shriveled wings and general poor condition. The Wasp stood unsteadily on its wobbly legs for a few minutes longer, but then collapsed. It hissed a few more times before going silent. As he watched, its body began collapsing in on itself, as if being eaten from the inside. As fascinated as he was about how the Kaiju disposed of dead Wasps, he didn't want to be around if the scavengers noticed him. He moved on.

By his reckoning, he was near the control center where on Nusku he, Costas, and Gate had tried to destroy the creature's guidance systems by venting the liquid CO_2 used to cool the electro-magnetic gyros. They had crawled through a narrow tunnel from the creature's mouth. He was somewhere below it. *If,* he reminded himself, *the aliens had not changed the interior design on this Kaiju.*

He stood in a large chamber almost a hundred feet in length and forty-feet wide. The ceiling was low, less than ten feet high. The walls and ceiling were ebony crystal like the creature's exterior. The floor was lighter in color but still composed of a hard substance. A lattice covered a six-foot-wide shaft in the middle of the chamber, reminding him uncomfortably of a shower drain. If the chamber was some kind of liquid storage tank, he hoped it didn't fill before he found an exit.

He was still searching when the first Squid appeared. It had moved silently in the darkness. He had sensed rather than heard it, a prickly feeling crawling up his back. When he whirled and hit it with the beam of his flashlight, it stood somewhat stooped over in the low room, staring at him with its four unblinking eyes. He could not run away. His injured leg was barely supporting his weight, and he was weak from loss of blood. For several tense moments, neither of them moved. Then, it puffed out its gill pouches and began trilling, summoning other Squid to the scene. He raised his SCAR and fired three quick bursts into its head. The ebony crystal-tipped 7.62 mm bullets pierced the thick skin and shattered the fused-bone skeleton protecting its internal organs. Spurts of yellow blood and a second dark liquid sprayed from the bullet wounds. The Squid took a few awkward steps toward him on trembling tentacles, and then collapsed in a tangle of limbs and did not move.

The Squid had entered the chamber from an opening somewhere beyond the one through which he had entered. He chose to travel in the opposite direction. Fearing more Squid were on the way, he tried to pick up the pace, but each step sent excruciating pain racing up his leg to his hip and groin. The weight of the K-2 container added to his misery. He had tried to rewrap the bandage several times, but his boot kept pushing it away from the wound. Finally, he had sliced off the top of his boot, but by then his blood loss had been severe and the damage already done.

As he neared the far end of the chamber, he spotted an opening that led upward at an angle. It was barely wide enough to accommodate him, especially dragging the drum behind him, but he had seen no other exits. Suddenly, as if taunting him, the wall folded in around the opening, sealing it off. Moments later, the ceiling began secreting a liquid. The liquid formed at the surface of the ceiling as if it were a semi-permeable membrane, a type of osmotic filter. The liquid came down in sheets, forming pools on the floor that quickly became puddles. The drain had sealed at the same time as the opening in the wall.

A drop landed on his face. He cautiously tested it with his tongue. It tasted of salt and sea life. The clear liquid was seawater. He had stumbled into one of the Kaiju's ballast tanks. When the water reached the top of his cut off boot and began to spill inside it, he began to worry. With no escape, he either would drown or be flushed out to sea when it vented the chamber. He dragged the drum behind him back toward the opening he had come through. By the time he reached it, the drum was floating free of the floor. It came as no surprise to find the air duct tunnel closed as well. Had the sealing of the chamber been an automatic sequence as the Kaiju submerged or surfaced, or had his killing of the Squid instigated it? His only remaining choice was the opening at the opposite end of the chamber through which the Squid had arrived.

Sloshing through the rising liquid was more exhausting than walking. His injured leg threatened to fold beneath him. He tried moving slower, but the liquid was rising too quickly to dawdle. As if things were not bad enough, he heard trills and hoots coming from ahead of him – Squid. The Squid, amphibious marine creatures, were at home in the water. Though the water was barely waist deep, they raced toward him leaving V-pattern wakes behind them. He raised his SCAR but knew he could not kill them all. Instead, he aimed at the black drum. His last act would be to release the K-2 nanites to do their job, praying the water would not dilute beyond the point of efficacy. Before he could pull the trigger, he heard a voice yell, "Heads up!"

The familiar sound of an M134 minigun and an M107 SASR echoed through the chamber. Muzzle flashes sparkled like fire flies in the dark. Twin beams of light settled on two of the Squid as bullets tore into their bodies. The two squid began thrashing in the water, their tentacles flailing in the air. The water around them darkened with their blood. Walker raised his SCAR and emptied his clip into the third Squid. It stopped ten yards from him, trying to rise from the water on its tentacles. Even dying, it stretched out one of its long tentacles toward the black drum. Walker backed away. The Squid hissed at him, and then died.

Costas and Talent came splashing toward him. Costas wore a big grin on his face. Talent, as usual kept his emotions in check, but Walker thought he detected a slight flicker in his lips.

"You ain't dead," Costas bellowed.

"Not quite. Where are the others?"

Costas cursed and scowled. "Captain McChicken flew the coop after you took your dive. Hightower wanted to stay, but I sent him packing to help with Perez. I didn't trust the captain not to leave her behind. Now there's a woman for you, Major. She's hot, tough as nails, and ain't afraid of nothing. You should ask her out."

Walker smiled at Costas' constant need to fix him up with a woman. He looked at Talent. "Sorry you came yet?"

"I'm a little concerned about the gravity bomb Costas told me about. That item was missing from the travel brochure. Otherwise, here's as good as any other place." He looked down at the water now swirling around his waist. "Well, not here exactly."

"I was headed your direction searching for a way out."

"Don't bother," Costas chimed in. "Nothing but Squid that direction. In fact, they should be joining the party any minute now." He pointed toward the far wall. "Anything that way?"

"I saw a ramp just before the wall closed in around it."

Costas grinned and waved his SASR. "I've got the perfect lock pick right here. Let's go shoot up some shit."

Costas forged ahead through the rising water, lifting the black K-2 drum from the water and tucking it under one arm. "Let's go before this bastard flushes us out."

Walker turned to Talent. "I couldn't tell you about the bomb. It would have been a distraction."

"So Costas said." Talent shook his head. "You don't owe me an explanation. I'm just along for the ride."

"It's been over four hours and the bomb hasn't exploded yet. Maybe the Commander disarmed it. Nothing we can do about it anyway. If the Kaiju resumed its same speed and heading, it should be somewhere off the coast of Australia. That doesn't leave us much time to detonate our bomb. I haven't a clue as to how long it will take for the little nanite buggers to do some damage."

"Yet you haven't detonated it yet," Talent observed. "That doesn't sound like you. If you were waiting to give Costas and me a chance to get out, don't bother. We both know none of us is getting out of this thing alive. We knew it coming in. Hell, I'm surprised we've made it this far."

So was Walker. "We're almost there."

Talent laughed. "Says the man who's about to be breathing sea water in a few minutes."

Costas stopped at the wall, searching it for Walker's opening. It had sealed so smoothly, Walker had trouble spotting it. Only a slight variation in the surface pattern revealed the elusive seam. "Stand back," he warned, and then fired a burst at the wall. The bullets bounced off. "What the fu ...?" He tried again with the same lack of results.

"Maybe this will help," Talent said. He held out one of the grenades from the grenade launcher he had left behind. "I thought it might come in handy." Then he frowned. "I'm not sure how we can use it. There's no pin to pull."

Walker shook his head. "Talent, you amaze me."

He pulled his knife and jammed it into the tiny crack of the seam. It didn't penetrate far, but it held. Using a bootlace, he took the Denel R1M1 anti-tank grenade from Talent and tied it to the handle of his knife. The RDX explosive was powerful enough to penetrate eleven inches of steel. He knew it wouldn't penetrate the creature's ebony armor, but all he needed was a little kick to force the wall open.

"Move down the wall and hug it tight," he told them.

He joined them ten yards away. He would have liked to place more distance between them and the grenade, but the water was rising too fast.

It would soon submerge the grenade. The others pressed their faces to the wall. He took careful aim, fired, and missed. Costas raised his head and glared at him. Angry with himself for missing, he fired again. This time the bullet struck the grenade's tip. The explosion's shock wave hit him and sent him sprawling into the water stunned. He felt Costas' strong arms pulling him to the surface.

"Everyone okay?" he sputtered as he coughed water from his mouth and throat.

"What?" Costas yelled, digging into his left ear with his pinky finger. "My ears are ringing." Then he grinned to show he was kidding.

Walker surveyed the damage. The blast had forced the wall open and water poured into the opening.

"After you," Costas said to Talent. "I'll follow along behind with the refreshments." He held out the drum.

Talent rolled his eyes but went first through the opening, pushing the heavy minigun ahead of him. Walker went next. The slope was gentle, but traveling on his hands and knees was more painful than walking. His leg throbbed and his hip felt as if it were trying to push through his skin. He made better time lying on his belly and dragging himself forward with his elbows, like crawling through a live-fire obstacle course.

He was exhausted by the time they reached an equally narrow tunnel crossing the Kaiju transversely. He checked his wrist comp. To his relief, the tunnel was on his map. It ran adjacent to the Kaiju control center. They were almost there. He crawled along the space feeling the walls. Finally, he found what he was searching for.

"This is the spot."

The spot Walker indicated looked like any other section of the wall "How do you know?" Talent asked.

"The wall is cold from the liquid Carbon Dioxide. The flesh here is not armored. Dig us a way in, Talent. I seem to have lost my knife."

"And hurry, Cowboy," Costas yelled from behind him. "I gotta take a piss."

Talent began hacking into the alien flesh like he was carving a Jack 'o Lantern, venting his fury and frustration with each savage blow. Soon, his hands and arms were slick with the thick fluid that served the creature for blood. Walker sat down to watch as he rested his leg. It was growing numb. He wished his hip were numb. It throbbed in pain with every beat of his heart. The climb up the ramp had taken all his strength. He was not sure if he could continue. Luckily, they had almost reached their destination. It would feel good to sit with his back against the cool wall and let the others finish the job for him. The Kaiju shuddered violently, sending shooting pain through his hip and leg. He noticed the hairs on his arm standing at attention from static electricity in the air.

"Someone's trying to stop the Kaiju. Can you feel the power flowing through it as it channels the kinetic energy into its storage cell?"

"Maybe someone will make a lucky shot," Costas growled. "I'm tired of this shit."

Walker's stomach growled. He realized he was hungry. "Do either of you have anything to eat?"

Costas dug in his pack and pulled out three protein bars. He handed one to each of the others. "I also keep little snack handy in case I get hungry during the night."

Walker practically inhaled his bar, but it eased the growls in his stomach. Talent chewed his while he dug. When Talent slowed down, Costas took over. Three feet into the wall, he made one last thrust with the knife, and he was through to the other side. Once the gash was large enough for them, he pushed through.

"This don't look familiar," he said.

As Talent helped Walker to his feet, Walker, concerned, said, "Let's see if I screwed up."

Walker limped into the creature's control room. As Costas had said, it was different from Nusku. Some things remained the same. The rows of rotating spheres floating in the gravity fields behind a crystal barrier were familiar. They served as the creature's gyrocompass. He had chosen this location for that very reason. Releasing the nanites in the creature's control center would disorient it, slowing its rampage long enough for the nanites to kill it. All similarity ended beyond the gyros.

Also behind the crystal wall sat a pale yellow gelatinous mass the size of a Volkswagen Beetle with a crevassed and convoluted surface, pulsating as fluids coursed through it. The mass took up most of the space of the chamber. Thick bundles of fiber ran from various thick, knobby nodes to various points in the wall. Hollow tubes through which coursed thick, yellow blood emerged from the floor and pierced the object in several places. Other tubes removed waste liquid and carried it away.

"It's a friggin' brain," Costas said, his hands on his hips staring at it. "It really is pea brained. Them Nazir have a sense of humor."

"Nazir?" Walker asked.

"I'll explain later," Talent said.

The Kaiju brain was tiny in comparison to its enormous size, like a dinosaur's, but they, too, could think and make decisions, and they could be deadly dangerous. Not content to control the mindless Kaiju with their vulnerable communications links, the aliens had endowed this

Kaiju with a will and a brain. It had purpose and the ability to think, or at least to react to its changing environment.

Talent raised the minigun. "Why don't we just blow its brains out?"

"No wait," Walker warned, but he was too late. Talent pressed the trigger. The barrels of the minigun spun, and a stream of bullets struck the clear crystal. To their astonishment, the bullets bounced harmlessly off the crystal wall. They ducked as ricochets buzzed passed their heads.

"It's bulletproof glass," Costas growled. "Even the Kaiju shell-tipped bullets don't scratch it. Those Nazir bastards are getting better."

"So what do we do?" Talent asked. "The bomb won't break this stuff. It's as hard as the ebony armor."

Walker sighed heavily, feeling as if fate was determined to beat him at every turn. Had he gambled away their lives for nothing? Had his stubbornness at insisting on doing things his way rather than follow orders blown the mission? The others looked at him, waiting for an answer.

"The walls outside the barrier are flesh. We detonate the bomb here. The nanites will work their way through the bloodstream and enter the brain. It's not ideal," he admitted as he saw their skepticism, "but it will have to do."

"Will it kill the Kaiju?" Talent asked.

"If Allah wills it," Walker answered.

Talent smiled. "Maybe you'd better put in a good word for me next time you talk to him."

"I don't think we'll have time." He pointed to the drum. It reminded him of the baby nuke they had transported inside Nusku. "Fast or slow?" he asked

"Quick," Costas answered at the same time as Talent's, "Fast."

Walker was glad that his companions were of the same mind as him. "I think the Kaiju is walking. The motion feels like it's walking instead of moving through the water. If it's on land, it must have reached Australia by now. Every minute we delay costs countless lives. I'm setting the timer for its minimum setting – five minutes. We're going to die when the nanites reach us anyway. I prefer a quick end rather than a slow, agonizing death from the K-2. However, the decision is easy for me; I can't go anywhere anyway. My leg is useless. You two have time to place as much distance between you and the bomb as you can." He looked at Talent and smiled. "Maybe your luck will hold."

Talent shook his head. "You forgot about the *makai's* prediction that I would die a hero. I wouldn't want to second guess my people."

Costas scratched his head. "I'm too tired to keep running. Blow the damn thing and let's go get them vestal virgins or whatever you keep promising me in paradise."

Walker looked at both of them proud to be among such men. It was good to die with men who had given it their best shot and were willing to sacrifice themselves for the greater good of mankind. Without hesitation, he opened the cover on the arming switch and pressed the button.

Nothing happened.

"What the hell...?" he groaned.

"What's wrong?" Talent asked.

"The timer isn't working. It must have been the fall I took."

Costas face clouded with anger. "God damned sorry way to end a mission because some crack head munitions specialist screwed up. Talent, you got another grenade stashed away somewhere?"

Talent shrugged his shoulders. "Sorry, fresh out."

"Then maybe you'd better punch some holes in the drum and let the little buggers out."

Talent searched Walker's face, but he was out of options. "Do it," Walker said.

Talent aimed the six barrels of the minigun at the drum and pressed the trigger, punching a line of holes through the neoprene drum. Instead of gushing out like water, the thick sludge containing the nanites oozed out of the holes and ran down the side of the drum, forming an expanding pool around its base. The edges of the pool rippled, as if touched by a breeze. Tiny filaments of linked chains of microscopic nanite robots sprouted like fuzz from the liquid, forming and breaking apart as they sampled their new environment. He backed up as the pool spread across the floor toward him. Then, the liquid K-2 soaked into the floor of the chamber and vanished. Within minutes, fine black smudges appeared in the walls, spreading rapidly as the nanites located small blood veins through which they could move more rapidly.

Once released, the nanites quickly utilized the alien flesh as a source of raw material to reproduce exact copies of themselves, each one pumping its microscopic load of K-2 into the Kaiju's bloodstream, and then producing more. Multiplied by millions of nanites, the effects were rapid.

Talent was the first to spot the change beyond the crystal wall. "Look," said, pointing to a darkening in color of the liquid flowing through the tubes into the Kaiju brain.

The walls around them began to darken; then dissolve as layers of alien flesh died and decayed. A glob of Kaiju flesh dropped beside Costas' boot. "Forget what I said earlier. I say we run like hell."

He didn't bother waiting for an answer. To Walker's surprise, Costas scooped him up and threw him over his shoulder like a sack of flour.

"What are you doing, Sergeant?" Walker demanded. "Leave me here and get out."

Costas slapped him on his ass. "Shut up, Walker, and stop squirming. You coming, Talent?"

"Yeah, I guess the party's over here. Uh, unless you can hold your breath a long time, we can't go back the way we came."

"Trust me, I know a short cut."

25

Wednesday, Dec. 20, 1:45 a.m.   Brisbane, Australia –

Dalton McKenzie and Geoff Lands had joined line of men along Kingsford Smith Drive on the north bank of the Brisbane River. Most were reservists like him or volunteers like Lands. McKenzie was beginning to think it had been a mistake. The Kaiju shrugged off the barrage from the artillery massed south of the river near Kangaroo Point and Bulimba Barracks. It strode through Eagle Farm without pausing. A Kaiju could destroy a major city in hours. Small towns and communities did not slow it down.

Wasps attacked from the sky like a rain of death. They swooped down from the sky plucking men from the ground or from rooftops, black and orange demons of death. Around him, machineguns rattled and rifles popped but made little dent in their numbers. Where the Wasps went, the guns stopped firing. Behind the Wasps, the Fleas swarmed down the streets, hopping in and out of buildings searching for humans and finding too many, people who should have evacuated when they had the chance. It was too late now. The Fleas dragged their hacked and dismembered bodies into the streets to await the Kaiju, whose long black tentacles picked them up and deposited them in its mouth.

He had injured one Wasp with the Blaser LRS92 they had given him to replace his lost shotgun. The .338 caliber sniper rifle, used by the police Special Tactics and Rescue Group, was a single-shot bolt-action rifle. He had difficulty with the bolt on the unfamiliar weapon and was lucky to hit it at the base of a wing with his second bullet before it got close enough to kill him. It had flown away with one wing hanging limp from its back. As he had suspected, Lands could not hit the broad side of a barn with the 7 mm Mauser. When the injured Wasp returned with its companions, they would die. He was proud that he had not shirked his duty and ran, as Lands had wanted to do, but he was bitterly disappointed that his death would serve no purpose. The Kaiju and its host of creatures advanced as if the armed might of the Australian

Defense Force were not present. When the order came to fall back, he knew they would never make it to the helicopter LZ assigned to their unit. They had three choices. They could go to the river and find a boat or swim, but that left them exposed to the Wasps. They could cross the river on the Story Bridge, but there too they would be at the mercy of Wasps or Fleas. That left the Clem Jones Tunnel, affectionately known as the Clem7.

The M7 Tunnel toll road ran beneath the Brisbane River from Bowen Hills north of the river to Woolloongabba south. McKenzie had driven down to Brisbane when the tunnel opened in 2010 to be one of the first to walk its length. Touted as a time saving North-South By-Pass, the three-mile-long double tunnel had been a boondoggle from the start. At a cost of $3.2 billion dollars, the tunnel's builders had greatly over estimated the amount of traffic that would use it and had quickly gone bankrupt. Two gigantic Tunnel Boring Machines were used simultaneously to dig the tunnels through the dense metamorphic rock. The tunnel offered the safest way for them across the river. He doubted the concrete tunnel would withstand the weight of the Kaiju, but he expected the creature to head directly to the city to continue its orgy of destruction.

"We'll take the tunnel across the river," he said to Lands.

Lands was so frightened he could not speak. He just nodded his head. Any place would be better than the firehouse to which the four men were assigned. When McKenzie proposed the tunnel to the other two men, they balked at the idea.

"On foot?" one of them said. "You're crazy."

"The helicopter can take us south," the other said. "We'll never walk out of here ahead of that monster."

"The tunnel is safer," he urged. "We'll have something solid over our heads against the Wasps."

"Do what you want," the first replied. "We're taking the helicopter, good luck."

He watched them run away into the darkness knowing they had made a terrible, probably fatal mistake. It wasn't that he felt he was any wiser than they were, but he had seen what Wasps were capable of. They ruled the sky. Helicopters were just noisy flying treats for the creatures. He and Lands took off at fast trot down Breakfast Creek Road. The northern entrance of the tunnel was at the concrete spaghetti M7 interchange north of them, but that meant going a half-mile out of the way. From his tour walk through the tunnel, he remembered the guide pointing out the giant airshafts on both sides of the river to vent automobile exhaust fumes or smoke in case of fire. One was located due west of them.

The cannonade continued behind them, but had little effect on the Kaiju. In fact, it destroyed as many buildings as the monster. The jets, keeping a safe distance to avoid the arcing artillery fire, had better luck hitting the target with their missiles, but the results were just as dismal. The explosions made for a spellbinding light show, especially the ultraviolet tracings racing along the creature's ebony shell as it absorbed the energy and converted it for its own use. The tips of the row of serrations along the edges of the Kaiju's transverse segmented plates glowed purple and arced, bleeding excess energy into the air.

The Wasps formed a moving front half a mile ahead of the Kaiju, dipping to earth to investigate buildings or attack weapons emplacements. The smaller, but deadly Fleas followed close behind as a cleanup brigade, dragging dead bodies into the streets or killing stragglers the Wasps missed. Wasps also flew close escort to their Kaiju master attacking incoming missiles. To say the artillery and missiles were ineffective did not do them proper justice. While they had little effect on the hulking Kaiju, they did kill many Wasps, but their numbers were so large it made little difference.

A point-blank shot from Land's Mauser shattered the lock securing the metal grate over the ventilator shaft. The fans were still operating on emergency power though the power was off throughout the city. McKenzie stared down the shaft at ladder and the spinning blades far below it. A second grill covered the rotating blades, but the openings were wide enough for an arm or leg to pass through. One misstep and he would have to rely on his NDA health card for a prosthesis.

"I'll go first," he said, "Don't fall on me."

"Are you sure about this?" Lands asked, looking at the precarious footing. "The Clem 7 is two-hundred feet beneath the river."

"It's not so deep here. Had you rather try the bridge?"

Lands glanced up at the sky. Wasps were getting closer by the minute. "Get a move on, old man."

McKenzie took a deep breath and exhaled slowly, then placed his foot on the first rung. *So far, so good.* The air blasting up the shaft was warm and smelled of exhaust fumes, motor oil, and river mud, the last from water and mud oozing through the cracks in the joints of the precast concrete panels of the tunnel lining. The STAR LRS 92 dangled awkwardly from his shoulder and caught often in the rungs. As he descended, the force of the updraft became stronger. By the time he reached the niche in the wall by which the ladder bypassed the fan, he felt as if he could fling himself into the middle of the shaft and the cushion of air would support his weight. However, he did not wish to test his theory.

Inside the tunnel, only the emergency lights were working, casting long, pale shadows along the roadway. Their steps echoed loudly in the enclosed space. They were not the tunnel's only occupants. Other members of the scattered units north of them had chosen the tunnel over their iffy promised helicopter evacuation. Five men and a woman wearing SASR patches of the 51FNQR came trotting up to them, almost out of breath from the run. The 51st battalion of the Far North Queensland Regiment was a recon and surveillance battalion. These six were Special Air Service Regiment, some of the elite. McKenzie was pleased to see them looking just as frightened as he was.

"It's getting thick out there," a sergeant said, jerking his thumb behind him.

The sounds of explosions and collapsing buildings grew louder as the Kaiju approached the city. Dust fell from the ceiling with each giant Kaiju stride. The emergency lights flickered and failed. The sergeant switched on the flashlight attached to the barrel of his 5.56 mm Austeyr rifle. In the dim light, their pale faces betrayed their fright. The constant hum of the ventilator fans slowed and then stopped. Without the fans moving air through the tunnel, the air would soon grow stale and hot. With it came the risk of carbon monoxide poisoning from left over exhaust fumes.

"It will soon get thick in here," McKenzie told him.

Spurred by what was behind them, they set out at a fast pace across the river. About a half a mile from the southern end of the tunnel, weapons fire rang out behind them from another group of retreating soldiers.

"Someone's shooting at something," someone said.

"Whatever it is, I don't want to meet it," another answered.

McKenzie silently agreed. Minutes later, he didn't know if he was the first to hear them or simply the first to turn to look, but they all quickly became aware of the presence of Wasps in the tunnel. He stopped running. Lands slowed down and turned to him.

"What are you doing? We're almost there." He pointed to a faint lightening of the darkness ahead of them, the southern entrance.

"We can't outrun them. I'm going to die standing on my own two feet facing these things, not from a stinger in the back."

The sergeant pumped his fist in the air several times. The others stopped running. "He's right. We'll form a defensive line here. Breckinridge, set up the F89 in the center. We'll spread out on both sides across the roadway."

The 5.56 mm Lithgow F89 Para light machinegun was the Australian equivalent of the versatile American M249 SAW or Squad Assist

Weapon. The other SASR carried Austeyr 5.6 mm like the sergeant. Those, Lands' Mauser, and McKenzie's .338 caliber Blaser were the only weapons they had. It was a thin line of defense against however many Wasps were coming.

"I hope those flying bastards paid the toll," the female said. "This tunnel is losing enough money as it is."

This produced a few quiet chuckles, but they died away quickly as the sound of the Wasps grew louder. They appeared out of the darkness, their orange striped bodies reflecting the beam of the sergeant's flashlight. There were four of them, flying just above the surface of the roadway.

"Hold your fire," the sergeant said. "Take out the two in the center first."

McKenzie didn't know if the sergeant was making a joke or being wildly optimistic of their chances against four of the creatures. The sergeant made them hold their fire until McKenzie thought he could smell the Wasps' breath.

"Fire!"

The F89 fired in short bursts. The others fired as quickly as they could pull the trigger. McKenzie tried to remain calm to fire and operate the bolt smoothly. Three of the Wasps veered to either the side of the tunnel. One vanished into one of the numerous cross-passageways connecting each set of tunnels. The fourth dropped lower, but continued straight for them. McKenzie aimed for the spot between its eyes and fired. His shot or one of the others' killed it; however, when it hit the pavement, it retained enough momentum to slide right into them. It missed McKenzie by inches. Two of the SASR went down. The flashlight went out, plunging them into darkness. It rolled against McKenzie's foot. He picked it and shook it. It burst into life. He shined it on the Wasp. It was dead. So was the sergeant, crushed beneath the creature's weight. Breckenridge, who had been lying on his stomach operating the F89, fared better. The machinegun was smashed and useless, but he suffered only a sprained shoulder as collision ripped it from his grip.

To add to the confusion, the two remaining Wasps continued flying past them down the tunnel.

"Are they coming back?" Lands asked. He had frozen and had not fired a shot.

"I don't think so. They'll go through the tunnel and come up on the boys of the 7th from behind. They won't know what hit them."

"But they won't come back?" Lands asked again.

Lands' chronic fear and inability to think about anyone's welfare but his own irritated McKenzie. "No, you're safe," he yelled. "We're all safe."

He had spoken too soon. A loud explosion just outside the tunnel lit up the entrance. He stared dumbfounded as the flaming wreckage of a fully armed *Tiger* helicopter, blades spinning, slid sideways down the roadway toward them. Oddly, Lands saved them, not by words but by his action in trying to escape. He ran toward one of the cross-passages. McKenzie saw that it provided their only hope.

"Follow him," he yelled at the others, just as the missiles the helicopter carried exploded. A gigantic fireball swept down the tunnel. All but one of them made it safely through the cross-passage. A wall of flame engulfed Breckenridge running awkwardly with his dislocated shoulder, and propelled him back down the tunnel. The flames followed McKenzie into the cross-passage. The blast of heat scorched his face and singed his hair, but the flames died before they reached him.

The explosion had been more than the concrete tube lining could withstand. Weakened, the weight of the earth and water above it began widening the cracks. With the sound of a thousand dried twigs snapping simultaneously, the roof collapsed, sealing both lanes of the entrance. Water began pouring through the roof. Faced with drowning like a rat in the dark tunnel or trying to escape through the northern end and facing the Kaiju and its attendant creatures, McKenzie was at a loss. He was tired and what adrenaline he had been operating on was ebbing with the specter of death.

The tunnel they had been using was a sea of flame from burning fuel. Without a word to the others, he shouldered his rifle and began walking north. Silently, they formed a line behind him and followed.

* * * *

By the time they reached the middle of the tunnel, the inrushing water collected in the lowest spot and was now halfway to the roof. They would have to swim. McKenzie discarded his rifle. It was too heavy to swim carrying. The others did the same. The water was almost freezing. The shock of wading in almost forced him back out, but he had no choice. To conserve energy, he lay on his back and used the backstroke. He zoned out, his mind thinking of nothing except the next arm movement. He came out of his trance when his back scraped concrete.

He stood in knee-deep water and counted heads. Somewhere along the way, they had lost one of their numbers, the female SASR. His body was so sapped of strength and numb from the cold he could barely get his legs to move. The skyline outside the tunnel entrance was ablaze. The shells of smashed buildings pumped black smoke into the air. One building had collapsed over the M7 roadway. He didn't bother searching for Wasps or Fleas. If they found him, he had nothing to defend himself. He turned and faced southwest, toward the city.

The enormous black shape of the Kaiju rested against the side of the Aurora Tower. Its three pair of forelegs dug like pickaxes into the sides of the building skewering it with ragged holes most of the building's eight-hundred-foot length. The rubble of other buildings lay around it – Central Plaza One, 111 George Street, one of the downtown hotels, he didn't know which one.

A loud splat behind him drew his attention away from the scene of destruction. A dead Wasp lay on the roadway. *Killed by a missile*, he thought and dismissed it. Then another fell nearby. He looked up and saw dozens of Wasps flying awkwardly, milling about in confusion. Two more slammed into each other, fell from the sky, and did not get up.

"What's happening?" Lands asked.

McKenzie shook his head and turned his attention back to the Kaiju. Its blows against the building had slowed. It lowered its fore section and stood on all twelve legs. Suddenly, it seemed to sit down on its rear end. It emitted a loud, mournful roar. He clamped his hands over his ears to drown out the sound. The tentacles around it mouth stretched straight into the air and whipped around like palm trees in a gale. The Kaiju was in pain. Had a lucky shot or a missile injured it?

It rose on all six pairs of legs, took a few wobbly steps, and collapsed again. Its body shuddered a few times, shaking bricks and chunks of masonry from the buildings still standing around it. It lifted its head and roared one more time, and then laid its head across the roof of a five-story building and ceased to move.

McKenzie would swear later that he had heard its death rattle. In reality, it had been the sound of all the blisters along its sides opening. He had to see the creature close up. He picked his way through the debris of fallen buildings, around gigantic divots of pavement yanked from the roadways by the creature's legs, and the hulks of wrecked and burning automobiles, trucks, and the occasional tank. More Wasps emerged from the open blisters, but they flew erratically and fell from the sky in droves.

McKenzie wondered what had felled the behemoth. Certainly not the missiles, bombs, or artillery shells the ADF had flung at it for hours. It had shrugged them off as one might the irritating bites of mosquitoes. People began to spill from the ruins, miraculously surviving the carnage around them.

Lands hung back, curious but still afraid. He was more afraid to leave McKenzie's presence than to face the Kaiju. "Look," he yelled.

McKenzie followed Lands' gaze to one of the open blisters. It was impossible, but a man stood in the opening, waving his arms, a big man wearing torn and dirty dark camo clothing. McKenzie strained to hear him.

His accent was American as he yelled, "Someone send me up some ketchup. I've had hell killing this thing. Now, I'm chowing down."

26

Tuesday, December 25, 2:00 p.m.   Aboard the *USS Mississippi* –

Talent had mixed feelings about being back aboard the *Mississippi*. On the one hand, he was alive and glad to be anywhere. The nuclear submarine was as close to a home as he had now. On the other hand, its tight confining space reminded him too much of the inside of the Kaiju, an experience he would very much like to forget. He knew he never would. The few hours inside the monster had fulfilled all his daydreams of being in a military action and tested his skills to their limits. It had also been the most horrifying experience he could ever have imagined.

Commander Murdock was dead, but by all accounts, he had successfully disarmed the alien gravity bomb. At the very least, it had not yet exploded. A U.S. Navy vessel had picked up the orca-camouflaged SDV with Captain McGregor, Corporal Hightower, and Specialist Perez aboard only an hour after he and Costas had left them to go search for Walker, and transferred them to the *Mississippi*. Perez had survived and was recovering from her wounds in the ship's infirmary. Hightower was still aboard with her, but McGregor was not.

After filing his report and after a private word from Hightower, Chief Exec Dodd, now skipper of the sub, had him flown McGregor to Hawaii as soon as the sub docked in the Australian Naval Base in Hobart, Tasmania. No official reprimand would ever show on his file, but word had a way of spreading in military circles. If not over, his career was certainly on a fast track to nowhere.

Talent was not sure how he felt about that either. He would have much preferred to corner the captain in a dark corner of the missile room and beat him senseless, but to a soldier like McGregor, the shame that would follow him around like a dark, Kaiju-shaped cloud would probably hurt more than anything he could have done to him. The meticulously fastidious, egotistical captain had rubbed him the wrong way from the beginning. In all honesty, he had not given McGregor much of a chance, but then McGregor had not helped matters with his divisiveness. Talent did not expect he would lose much sleep over McGregor's ultimate fate.

A photo of Costas' triumphant emergence from the dead Kaiju Kiribati's open blister had appeared on the front page of the Melbourne *Sun Herald* with the heading *Mad GI Invades Australia the Hard Way*. Now, wherever he went on the sub, people asked for his autograph. He still limped from his injury, but he still managed to make his way throughout the boat, especially any area where he might bump into the female Yeoman. No reporter had seemed interested in the second or third persons to emerge, as if it were a contest that Costas had won. It was just as well that Walker was content to maintain his anonymity, and that Talent did not much care for reporters.

True to form, Walker had refused a bed in the infirmary, choosing instead to bunk in the missile room with the sad remnants of Fire Team Bravo. He now sat up in bed, propped up by two pillows. His injured leg was in an ankle-to-hip cast. The doctor claimed the cast's purpose was to relieve strain on the groin muscle he had pulled in his fall down the air duct. Walker alleged it was a ploy to keep him in bed.

Talent set a cold bottle of Coke on the table beside Walker's cot. A piece of bright red ribbon and a bow hung around its neck

"Merry Christmas, Major. This is the last bottle of Coke on this sub. I had to trade my Stetson for it. Dodd didn't want to remain in port long enough to resupply."

Walker grinned. "He's eager to take his new command for a spin. I'll buy you one of those white Texas 10-gallon good guy hats to replace your Stetson. You earned it, Cowboy."

Talent wiped his face with the palm of his hand. "Not you, too. Everyone on this boat thinks that's my name now." After a moment of embarrassing silence, he said, "I saw the K-2 leaking from the drum we lost during the fight in the hatchery. You saw it too. Did you know then that it was getting into the Kaiju's bloodstream, was already killing it?"

"If you're asking me if I continued the mission knowing we could have left then, the answer is yes. I came into this mission blind. I had no idea how effective the nanites were or how long it would take them to infect the Kaiju's body. I couldn't take the chance that it wasn't enough. I still had a drum of K-2. I acted as if the first drum didn't matter. Later, when I encountered a dead Wasp, I suspected what was happening, but by then I was too close to the brain to quit."

"When Costas heard your signal over the com set, he went ape shit to go after you. I thought he was going to shoot McGregor."

Walker frowned. "What signal? I lost my comm during Costas' and my fight with the Squid. I couldn't send any signal."

Talent smiled. "Don't ever tell Costas. He thinks he's a hero for going after you."

Walker grinned and crossed his arms behind his head. "Hell, we're all heroes here."

"Not enough of a hero for Dodd to let Costas smoke a cigar on his boat. He's been bitching about it all day."

"If you take a deep whiff, you'll smell wisps of cigar smoke. Costas is smoking a stogie inside one of the missile tubes right now. He said he would get the skipper to fire a missile later to vent the smoke."

"Sounds like him. Will he face any charges for refusing to obey McGregor's order?"

"It's not likely, nor will Hightower. There were extenuating circumstances. After all, he was only trying to complete the mission. Even McGregor didn't press official charges."

"Good. The big lug would probably start a brawl with the court martial panel if they convicted him."

Walker became more serious. "What are your plans now, Talent?"

"The Australian Prime Minister learned I wanted to emigrate and said she would be pleased to fast track the paperwork for citizenship."

"That's great."

Talent glanced away to hide his embarrassment. "Yeah, I guess, but …"

Sensing his pensive mood, Walker pressed him. "But what?"

He was not sure how to phrase what he wanted to say. "I realized running away isn't going to solve anything. I guess I'll go back to Arizona and make a new start."

"With your money you could buy Arizona."

"Well, a nice chunk of it anyway. I'm going to start a volunteer militia, one designed to coordinate closely with the military but able to go it alone if the aliens ever do arrive in force."

Walker nodded. "You'll do well at it."

"I could use your and Costas' input; maybe teach a few classes in the beginning."

"If Uncle Sam will let me, I'll be there as soon as my leg heals, except …" He paused.

"Except what?"

"The *Postmaster* contacted me." Noting Talent's confusion, he explained, "He's sort of my and Costas' handler. He hinted about a special mission related to the Nazir. It piqued my interest."

Talent smiled at Walker's use of Costas' name for the aliens. No one knew what the word he had discovered inside the Kaiju meant, if it was a word. For all he knew, it could be a number. However, the press had turned it into the name of the enemy. Now the aliens were no longer nameless and faceless. No one knew what they looked like, but they had a name. It was easier to hate a label than the unknown.

He tried to hide his disappointment at Walker's news. "Good luck. Don't do anything more stupid than normal. Are you riding this tub all the way back to Hawaii?"

"No, we're rendezvousing with an aircraft carrier tomorrow. I'll fly into Pearl for a stint in the base hospital until I'm back on my feet. From there, who knows?"

"They're sending a seaplane out to pick me up when we get to New Caledonia. Maybe I'll visit you in Pearl, if that's how they route me home. How long do you think we've got?"

Walker knew what Talent meant. "Gate Rutherford tells me they can give us a week's notice now. How long? Only Allah knows. They'll sift through the data and re-evaluate their last sortie, redesign, and redeploy. They're aliens, but they operate a lot like any military. We'll just have to watch the skies."

"I think maybe we made them mad this time. They won't like that."

"Good. It's easier to exploit an angry enemy's weakness. The madder the better."

"Just send them Costas. That ought to piss them off."

The nurse came in and shooed him out of the infirmary. Before he left, he took one last look at Walker, wondering if their paths would ever cross again. He hoped so. Walker had seen something in him and drawn him out of his shell. He was human again. He had Walker to thank for that. As he walked down the corridor to his bunk in the torpedo room, he smelled the air, caught a whiff of Costas' pungent cigar, and smiled.

* * * *

Tuesday, December 24, 7:00 p.m.   Johnson Space Center, Houston, TX –

No longer *persona non grata* at NASA, Doctor Gate Rutherford went over the latest data from the GEMS satellite. The space between Earth and Haumea was clear of gravity distortions, but a more detailed scan of the planetoid had revealed just how extensive the enemy base – He still refrained from calling them the Nazir – was. It was too large to be simply a biological facility for constructing Kaiju. Given their hostility toward humans, he suspected a military base preparing for invasion, but that was up to the military to determine.

The captain of the *USS Mississippi* had prevented the aliens from arming the gravity distortion bomb, at the cost of his life. There were U.S. Navy deep-sea salvage vessels on site already trying to recover it. The nanites had proven effective at killing Kaiju, but they were much too difficult to use to become an offensive weapon. He suspected the military had hopes of building their own gravity weapon. God help the planet when the aliens were eventually defeated. A new Cold War armaments race would begin.

He expected Walker's phone call soon. He had sent him a short, simple message repeating what he had been unable to say before the satellite link failed – Where is Fire Team Alpha? It was merely conjecture, small bits of information here, a strange request there, the quiet relocation of military technicians, but his job as a catastrophist had entailed constructing a model based on scant information. It forced him to see the big picture and sometimes what lay beneath the canvas.

Walker's team had not been the first fire team activated, but all mention of Fire Team Alpha had suddenly ceased. The military's interest in gravity drives, their ability to deconstruct Kaiju armor and create weapons from it, the influx of launch personnel to key military launch sites, and the subtle realigning of telescopes to avoid a certain sector of space all became integral components of the overall mosaic. Most damning of all was the removal of the fleet of the Air Force's new *SR-80 Lance* hybrid jets from Groom's Lake, Nevada. Capable of flying in an atmosphere or in a vacuum, the *SR-80 Lance* was developed as a close orbit military fighter, but it didn't take much stretch of the imagination to see them as the perfect weapon with which to attack the aliens. The only thing lacking was a way to get them there in a realistic timeframe. A gravity drive would solve that problem. He suspected that was what Syracuse University was working on.

Major Walker was the man of the hour. He would have the pull to ferret out what he wanted to know, and he wanted to know how to join Fire Team Alpha. If a fleet was going to attack the aliens on Haumea, he wanted to be at the forefront. He was just obstinate enough to do it.

Rutherford had had enough of the military. His encounter with them had left a bitter taste in his mouth. He would settle for watching the skies and providing Intel on the aliens. Soon, he wasn't sure how soon, Earth would show the aliens, the Nazir, that they had picked on the wrong planet. If the aliens gave them a breathing space. Twice, they had failed. He feared the next assault would be an all out effort to wipe mankind from the face of the planet. It was just a matter of who made the first move.

Personally, he was betting on Walker.

CHECK OUT OTHER GREAT KAIJU NOVELS

KAIJU WINTER
by **Jake Bible**

The Yellowstone super volcano has begun to erupt, sending North America into chaos and the rest of the world into panic. People are dangerous and desperate to escape the oncoming mega-eruption, knowing it will plunge the continent, and the world, into a perpetual ashen winter. But no matter how ready humanity is, nothing can prepare them for what comes out of the ash: Kaiju!

RAIJU
by **K.H. Koehler**

His home destroyed by a rampaging kaiju, Kevin Takahashi and his father relocate to New York City where Kevin hopes the nightmare is over. Soon after his arrival in the Big Apple, a new kaiju emerges. Qilin is so powerful that even the U.S. Military may be unable to contain or destroy the monster. But Kevin is more than a ragged refugee from the now defunct city of San Francisco. He's also a Keeper who can summon ancient, demonic god-beasts to do battle for him, and his creature to call is Raiju, the oldest of the ancient Kami. Kevin has only a short time to save the city of New York. Because Raiju and Qilin are about to clash, and after the dust settles, there may be no home left for any of them!

CHECK OUT OTHER GREAT KAIJU NOVELS

MURDER WORLD I KAIJU DAWN
by Jason Cordova
& Eric S Brown

Captain Vincente Huerta and the crew of the Fancy have been hired to retrieve a valuable item from a downed research vessel at the edge of the enemy's space.
It was going to be an easy payday.
But what Captain Huerta and the men, women and alien under his command didn't know was that they were being sent to the most dangerous planet in the galaxy.
Something large, ancient and most assuredly evil resides on the planet of Gorgon IV. Something so terrifying that man could barely fathom it with his puny mind. Captain Huerta must use every trick in the book, and possibly write an entirely new one, if he wants to escape Murder World.

KAIJU ARMAGEDDON
by Eric S. Brown

The attacks began without warning. Civilian and Military vessels alike simply vanished upon the waves. Crypto-zoologist Jerry Bryson found himself swept up into the chaos as the world discovered that the legendary beasts known as Kaiju are very real. Armies of the great beasts arose from the oceans and burrowed their way free of the Earth to declare war upon mankind. Now Dr. Bryson may be the human race's last hope in stopping the Kaiju from bringing civilization to its knees.
This is not some far distant future. This is not some alien world. This is the Earth, here and now, as we know it today, faced with the greatest threat its ever known. The Kaiju Armageddon has begun.

www.ingramcontent.com/pod-product-compliance
Lightning Source LLC
Chambersburg PA
CBHW020056180626
46812CB00006B/2348